DR FINLAY'S COURAGEOUS BRIDE

MARION LENNOX

A FAMILY MADE IN PARADISE

TINA BECKETT

MILLS & BOON

First published in Great Britain 2022
by Mills & Boon, an imprint of HarperCollins*Publishers* Ltd,
1 London Bridge Street, London, SE1 9GF

www.harpercollins.co.uk

HarperCollins*Publishers*
1st Floor, Watermarque Building,
Ringsend Road, Dublin 4, Ireland

Dr Finlay's Courageous Bride © 2022 Marion Lennox

A Family Made in Paradise © 2022 Tina Beckett

ISBN: 978-0-263-30137-3

09/22

MIX
Paper from
responsible sources
FSC C007454

This book is produced from independently certified FSC™ paper
to ensure responsible forest management.
For more information visit www.harpercollins.co.uk/green.

Printed and Bound in Spain using 100% Renewable Electricity
at CPI Black Print, Barcelona

DR FINLAY'S COURAGEOUS BRIDE

MARION LENNOX

MILLS & BOON

This book is dedicated to all those
who've found the courage to take control again,
and to all those still struggling to find a way.

PROLOGUE

Sydney Central Hospital, twelve years ago

SHE DIDN'T KNOW who he was, but she didn't care.

She'd die without him.

Even in her head that sounded crazy, the sort of wild declaration she might have made as a twelve-year-old, swooning over pictures of rock stars in the magazines her mum brought home after cleaning Harvey's place. Harvey's girlfriends were always leaving magazines behind when they left, and she and her mum loved them. When Dad and Harvey were both away, her mum had sometimes seemed a kid herself, singing along with Maira's favourite songs and grinning at Maira's declarations of undying devotion to the gorgeous guys in the magazines.

That was so long ago now, though. The memory was like a stab of pain to the heart, adding to the pain from… everywhere.

But through the pain came his voice, soft, deep, steady.

"'Weasels—and stoats—and foxes and so on. They're all right in a way—I'm very good friends with them— pass the time of day when we meet, and all that—but they break out sometimes, there's no denying it, and then— well, you can't really trust them, and that's the fact.'"

She wasn't actually sure what a weasel was, or a stoat. She did know foxes—her dad used to shoot them—but that didn't matter. What mattered was that this man, this voice, was here in the small hours, when the hospital was deeply quiet, when apart from her hourly obs, the nurses let her be. She was supposed to be sleeping.

But how could she sleep? She drifted off when the meds kicked in, when the drugs gave her oblivion, but to sleep when she wanted seemed impossible.

But this deep, steady voice said that she might. His voice drifted around the quiet room, an oasis the night-mares couldn't touch.

Would the woman in the next bed feel the same? She must, she thought, for who wouldn't?

She'd figured it out by now—sort of. She was in a two-bed hospital ward. The lady in the next bed was called Hilda. The nurses had introduced them, even though neither of them could speak. 'Maira, this is Hilda who breeds champion Labradors. She was cooking dinner when she tripped over one of her puppies, knocking boiling water over herself as she fell. Her family tell us the puppy's fine, but Hilda's copped all the damage.'

Maira had heard the doctors talking to her—'The swelling will go down, Hilda. You'll be able to speak soon.'

Whereas for Maira…'The oil's burned your throat, Maira. It'll take time.'

She heard the subtle difference—there were no prom-ises.

No future? She couldn't think of a future.

Hilda had visitors—her daughters even smuggled in the offending puppy. But Maira had no visitors, apart from the people from social services and the police.

She had nothing.

Only the sound of his voice.

Mr Toad. Ratty. Mole. Badger. She was starting to know them all.

There'd been other stories. He'd come in first a few nights ago, after a roster change. He'd been with the nurse, checking her chart, talking to her—*at* her?—about pain levels, describing what was happening. Then he'd come back.

'Hi, I'm Rab, here again, but not as a doctor. I'm on meal break, but who can eat at two in the morning? If there's drama outside I'll need to leave, but meanwhile I thought I'd do a bit of reading. How about it?'

Then, as he received no answer from either of them— how could he?—he'd settled on a chair between the beds.

'Okay, here we go. Sorry, guys, I know these are way beneath you, but I've pinched them from the kids' ward. Let's start with this first one—a mouse heading to sea in a stolen boat. It looks like fine literature to me, but stop me if you've read it. A twitch of a bandaged arm and I'll move right on to…ooh, the next is an elephant hatching an egg. Hmm, maybe we should start with this one?'

That had been a week ago. A couple of times he'd been interrupted—the door had opened—'Rab, you're needed in Room Five…'

'Excuse me, ladies, I'll be back.'

He'd kept his promise. He'd come back. She lay still now and let herself sink into the escape of his words.

"'The Mole was bewitched, entranced, fascinated. By the side of the river he trotted as one trots, when very small, by the side of a man who holds one spellbound by exciting stories; and when tired at last, he sat on the bank, while the river still chattered on to him, a babbling procession of the best stories in the world, sent from the heart of the earth to be told at last to the insatiable sea."'

Did Hilda need this as much as she did? she wondered. Maybe so, for the older lady had been stirring and whimpering before he'd come in, but the stories seemed to work their magic on her as well.

Rab. He was Rab. Did he know how much he meant to her?

It wouldn't last. There'd be another roster change. He'd be needed elsewhere, of course he would. But the stories themselves... There'd been few books in her childhood home, but if her eyes started working again, maybe she could read.

Could she ever again?

There it was again, a jab of terror so fierce it cut through the pain. She heard him pause.

'Do you want me to stop?'

She managed to give her head a tiny shake, and there was a momentary pressure on her good arm.

'That's okay, Maira, just twitch this arm if you do. You're in control.'

That was a joke. She'd never been in control.

But the voice disagreed.

'From now on, Maira, the control's all yours,' the voice said, softly but surely. 'When you get through this, the world's your oyster. There are people who can help you, people who will. I promise. Now, where were we?'

He went back to the river with Mole, and while he read she let herself believe.

CHAPTER ONE

Cockatoo Valley Hospital

'I'M SORRY, BUT I believe the hospital will be sold.'

Silence. Twenty people were staring at him in horror, and Dr Rab Finlay was wishing himself anywhere but here.

Rab had asked for this meeting, but that didn't mean he wanted it. It would have been the easiest thing in the world to walk away, to tell himself this was nothing to do with him.

As indeed it wasn't. The consequences of his grandfather's will were dire for this little valley. Now he was facing almost the entire staff of Cockatoo Valley Hospital. They were looking sick with shock, but he couldn't change anything.

'I'm afraid there's nothing I can do,' he told them, trying to keep his voice steady. He'd been dreading this, and he wished now that he'd let the lawyers handle it. 'I haven't inherited my grandfather's land, so it'll pass to six of my relatives in England. I've been in touch with them. It seems they have little to do with each other, but as a group they want the land sold. The lease of the land the hospital sits on doesn't expire until next year, though,' he added. 'That may well give you time to apply for government assistance. The government may well buy it and keep the hospital running. I can help with the paperwork there, but that's all I can do. I'm sorry.'

'The government will never give us a grant big enough to match what the mining companies will pay. We'll lose our hospital.' That was Rhonda, the hospital secretary, sounding devastated.

Cockatoo Valley's elderly doctor, Ewan Baynes, had taken Rab for a brief tour of the hospital before this meeting, introducing him to each of the staff.

'I know you have no obligation to speak,' the shocked doctor had said heavily. Rab had explained the consequences of the will to him, and it had hit him hard. 'But everyone here knows how much we've been indebted to your family. Even though that's over, lives have been saved because of the Finlays—many lives. I believe everyone will want to meet you and pay their respects. Let's do that before we need to break the news.'

So Rab had endured a torturous half hour of meeting the hospital staff, being told how wonderful his forebears had been, how the hospital, the school, the church—the lifeblood of the valley—were all thanks to his family's generosity.

Then Ewan had organised a fast staff meeting so that Rab himself could break the news. At the last minute the elderly doctor had been called to an urgent house call, and Rab had thus faced the staff alone.

To tell them their hospital, their livelihood, even their community was being taken away from them.

'I can't see any way of avoiding it,' he said now. 'My grandfather's will is clear. The buildings on this side of the river are all on my grandfather's land—given to the community on a ninety-nine-year lease. I gather that even though my great-grandfather donated the buildings to the community, he still wanted control. That lease expires next year.'

'But we'll lose everything,' Rhonda said, sounding appalled. 'You know they want this valley for a coal mine. Most of our houses are over the bridge, on freehold land, but if they get this side of the river... They'll pay much more for this land than we ever could. A coal mine... Can't you stop that?'

'I can't.' There was nothing else to say. 'My grandfather didn't leave the land to me.'

'Yeah, he did.' A voice piped up from the back of the room, from a pimply-faced youth who'd been introduced as a hospital orderly. The kid stood up now and crossed his arms, belligerence personified. 'I knew this stuff,' he told them. 'I saw it. Mum works at the local solicitor's, and she says wills aren't private. So she had a look when the old guy died. The will leaves it all to you.'

'Contents of the house only,' Rab told him. 'That's why I'm here, to take what I want and then leave.'

'He left you the whole lot,' the youth threw back at him. 'All you gotta do is to be married. Mum didn't know whether you were or not. Are you?'

Help. He so didn't want to talk about his grandfather's preposterous will—he'd hoped he could simply say the place had not been left to him. But the whole room was looking at him now, waiting for an answer.

The stupid stipulation in the will meant the destruction of this community, this valley. For most of the people in this room—no, for all of them—it meant not only the closure of the hospital, the loss of jobs, it also meant the end of the community of Cockatoo Valley.

'I'm not married.' The three words were said with harsh finality.

'So get married.' The kid sounded angry. 'The will

says you need to be married and settled before you're thirty-five. Mum looked you up on the internet—she says you're a doctor—she found you in some medical list. But Mum says you're only thirty-four. It didn't say if you were married or not, but she reckoned even if you weren't, if you stand to inherit all this then you'd get married pretty damn fast.'

'My birthday's in six weeks,' he told them. 'I'm sorry, people, but even for you I can't work that fast.'

There was another silence while they took the ramifications of that on board. The horror in the room was almost tangible.

'Surely you can find someone. If I wasn't already married with five kids I'd marry you myself.' It was Rhonda again, maybe trying to make light of an impossible situation.

'Thank you,' he said gravely. 'And indeed, if I had a fiancée, if there was the slightest chance of marriage, then I'd do it, but there's no way. I'm sorry but there's nothing more I can say.'

And then came the sound of a car, speeding along the road towards the hospital. They could hear a gunned engine, then tyres screeching as the car spun into the hospital driveway. Brakes hit hard, a voice yelling...

Four of the staff disappeared.

A hospital emergency. Rab knew the adrenalin of hearing such sounds—he'd worked in emergency departments himself, and he knew such an arrival meant total focus of the staff involved.

And for once he felt relieved. He needed the focus to be taken from him. It might sound harsh but there was nothing he could do about this mess. He didn't even know these people, this valley. His father might have been born here, but for Rab there was no connection.

The emergency outside seemed to have marked the end of the meeting. People wanted to be out of here, either to help with the incoming drama, or more likely to talk about the appalling repercussions of what he'd just said.

There was nothing left for him to do.

And then someone re-entered, pushing through the leaving staff. One of the nurses? He'd been introduced to this woman. Ewan had introduced them briefly—'This is our senior nurse, Mia, one of the most valuable members of our team.' He'd met so many but he remembered her—mostly because of the scars that marred one side of her face.

She was a striking woman, tall and slim, with long black hair braided down the back. She had a gorgeous tan—maybe a hint of Mediterranean background? Her wide grey eyes had smiled as she'd been introduced, and it was a lovely smile. But marring that smile were scars, sprawling down the left side of her face, down her neck and disappearing below the neckline of her uniform.

Burns, he'd thought as he'd met her. Old scarring. She must have been lucky to keep her sight, as the scarring started right against her left eye.

It must have been an appalling accident, he'd thought. A house fire? A car accident? The scarring was obvious, but she'd greeted him with a bright, light smile that took the attention from the disfigurement.

But there was no smile now. She was pushing through the departing staff, calling to him in a voice that was both urgent and authoritative. 'Dr Finlay?'

'Yes?'

'Ewan said you're a doctor,' she called. 'A people doctor?'

'I'm a surgeon.'

'Can you help then, please? The car that just arrived.

It's a home birth gone wrong. We have a woman haemorrhaging postpartum, and she's in a bad way. As you know, Dr Baynes is on a house call on the far side of the valley, but we need a doctor. Please, if you will... We need you now.'

Mia had listened to Rab Finlay's announcement and felt sick.

From the time Angus Finlay had died, the community had tried to guess what would happen. The terms of the lease were well known. For years the community leaders, Ewan included, had tried to negotiate with the old man to change the terms of the lease, to somehow make the valley safe, but Angus hadn't been interested. As he'd aged he'd sunk into listless depression, and they couldn't break through it.

'I'll leave the place to my grandson,' he'd told them. 'I can't be bothered with all the legal stuff. He can do it.'

So there'd been uneasiness, but not total worry. Despite his depression, Angus had been in good health— even though he was in his eighties there'd been no sign that his death was imminent. 'I'm good for a few years yet, girl,' he'd told Mia the last time she'd seen him. She'd been assisting Ewan remove a skin cancer from his scalp.

'Well, how about wearing a hat and you might live even longer,' Ewan had told him, and the old man had grunted disdain and headed out to the car park bareheaded.

And died of a massive infarct two weeks later.

But now...

Mia loved this valley, this community. It had taken her in, protected her, given her a life of safety and meaning. The thought of it being torn apart felt as if it was ripping the heart from her chest.

And it would be torn. There was another hospital at Colambool, an hour's drive down river. Colambool was a bigger town, but in this remote rural part of New South Wales even they struggled for government funding. The population of Cockatoo Valley would have to use it, though, she thought, as they'd have to use their school and church.

She thought of the cluster of houses on the other side of the bridge—most of them filled with retired farmers or alternative lifestylers. There was a general store over there, and a café, but without the hospital, church and school…would they stay?

Even if they did, they'd have to watch their beloved town being ripped up. This whole side of the river would be an enormous coal mine. To watch the destruction…

She'd been introduced to Rab Finlay and been impressed. In his mid-thirties, tall, dark, athletic, wearing branded chinos and an open-necked shirt that held the subtle hint of money and power, she'd been interested. When she'd heard what he'd had to say she'd been horrified. When the car had sped up to the Emergency entrance she'd almost been relieved to have to leave the meeting.

And then she'd walked out of the glass doors and any thoughts of the valley, of coal mines, of the loss of her community, were wiped from her mind.

The car pulling up at the entrance was an ancient Ford, pretty much a rust bucket. She recognised the car, and she knew the family spilling out. Tom Cray was in his forties, a helicopter pilot, sort of. He'd left the Air Force after some trauma he never talked of, bought a helicopter with his pay-out, and retired to the valley with his wife and kids. He took tourists on scenic flights, and businessmen to Sydney, but most of the time he devoted to his family. He and his wife, Isabelle, made weird things out of wire and set them up on the roadside, hoping to catch people's interest. Every now and then a passer-by would stop to take a look, but the pieces were big and weird, and the artists' propensity to leave bits of wire sticking out 'artistically' meant you were liable to take an eye out if you stumbled too close. They were also impossible to load into a car, so impromptu passers-by could hardly buy them on a whim.

But still Tom and Isabelle made them, while they scratched a living from their massive garden and occasional chopper flights. They also grew children—six of them, aged between two and twelve.

'I love having 'em, it's dead easy and why not?' Isabelle had told Mia last time she'd seen her. Isabelle had been heavily pregnant, but she hadn't come into Outpatients for an antenatal check—she'd brought eight-year-old Sunny in to have a gashed leg attended to.

Even then she'd come in reluctantly. The family didn't believe in doctors, and Isabelle certainly didn't believe in giving birth in hospital.

'They just pop out like peas out of a pod,' she'd told Mia happily. 'Dunno what all the fuss is about.'

There was fuss now. Tom was out of the car, hauling the back door open. A kid—the oldest... Marigold?— was climbing from the front seat, clutching a wrapped bundle—a baby?

Isabelle was lying on the back seat and the moment Tom opened the car door Mia saw blood.

A lot of blood.

'Baby came fast!' Tom was reaching in to his wife but yelling at Mia at the same time. 'No problems, a great little boy, and Isabelle was okay—and then she wasn't. Blood...she keeps bleeding. Mia, where's Doc?'

Doc Ewan. He was on the far side of the valley, Mia thought. Ray Markham's wife had rung for him to come. 'Ray's not able to get out of bed and he's struggling to breathe. His legs are so swollen. Can you get Doc to come?'

It'd be further heart trouble, they'd guessed, but there was no ambulance in the valley and Ray's wife was older than Ray's eighty. 'I'll contact the ambulance from Colambool and meet it there,' Ewan had decreed, and even though the elderly doctor had wanted to stay to hear Rab speak he'd had to go.

And now… One look at Isabelle told Mia there was no time to wait for Ewan. With this amount of blood, she needed a doctor, now!

Rab Finlay? Did she know him?

It was weird, but memories she'd long tried to put away had surfaced as she'd listened to Rab speak. His news had been shocking, but underlying his words, for her there'd been a sense of…familiarity? Peace? Calm?

It made no sense but, even if she was imagining things, Rab had been introduced as a doctor, and that was what she needed. Now.

'Get her out of the car and into Theatre,' she snapped at the staff behind her. 'IV line, plasma, move.'

She should send someone else to find Rab, but demanding his fast intervention was too important to leave to a junior. One look at Isabelle told her that finding a doctor right now was the only thing that stood between this woman and…

Don't think of it. Just go.

One minute he'd been a man imparting horrific news to an appalled community. The next he was thrust straight back into medical mode.

The woman who'd called him to come was Mia... someone? The nurse with the scarred face. She'd been the first to slip out when they'd heard the car screech to a halt outside.

But now she was standing in front of him. 'Please, if you will... We need you now.'

A woman haemorrhaging, postpartum... It could mean anything. A slight bleed, placental issues...

One look at this woman's face and he knew it wasn't. This was an experienced nurse, and her face said...fear.

No other doctor? Hell.

'Will you come?'

There was no choice. He was already ripping off his jacket.

'I'm with you,' he said and headed for the door.

CHAPTER TWO

THE FIRST SIGHT of Isabelle had left Mia almost sick with dread. This was no minor bleed—nothing that stitching and an IV drip could handle. This was something major—something horrific.

A ruptured uterus? It was an explanation she didn't want to think about, but she must. The diagnosis was only a dread, but it was suddenly front and foremost.

Isabelle was in her early forties—'Tom and I met late, we're making up for lost time,' she'd told Mia once when Mia had talked to her about her kids. This was her seventh birth. If there'd been wear to the uterus, with the strain of the birth, a tiny tear could suddenly turn catastrophic.

Mia had checked the baby—very briefly. He was hugged tight in twelve-year-old Marigold's arms. The baby looked okay. 'Take Marigold into the kids' ward and check the baby,' she'd told Issy, the most junior nurse. Issy was young but smart. She could be trusted to yell if there were any problems, so that meant all their attention could be on Isabelle.

All Rab's attention...

He was here now, supervising as the trolley was being wheeled into Theatre. Steadily but calmly questioning Tom. 'Focus, mate,' he said. He was inserting an IV line as the trolley moved. 'Age? How many previous births? How long's she been bleeding? Are there any medical conditions that could cause bleeding? Do you know her blood group?'

'Forty-three,' Tom managed. 'No...no health conditions. She's been bleeding for half an hour—I thought it was just normal—but all of a sudden it got worse. And I don't know her blood group.'

'Rhonda will make a call to Colambool,' Mia said quietly, matter-of-factly. 'They have a blood bank. They can send a fast car with O neg blood. It'll take a while though.'

He nodded. 'Plasma expander will do for now, then. That's great, Tom.'

Tom was walking behind the trolley, his hand holding Isabelle's, as if he let go she might well drown. He looked panicked, but Rab's steady questioning seemed to have given him direction.

'She's been okay,' he told him. Seventh kid, home birth like always and bub came out just like they all do. All normal but then the blood... Couldn't think... Just picked her up and carried her to the car...'

'You've done well, mate,' Rab told him. He was looking down at Isabelle. Her face was deathly white, her eyes wide with fear. 'Isabelle, we have you safe now,' he told her. 'But you're bleeding a bit too much to be normal. I'm guessing it's probably a tear, a rip that the baby's made coming out.' His voice gentled a little. 'Isabelle, is it okay if we put you to sleep and fix it?'

'Just do it,' Tom broke in, but Rab took Isabelle's spare hand and held.

'You're in control, Isabelle,' he told her. 'What we do is up to you. But I think your uterus might be damaged. If I operate...we may need to remove the whole thing.

That's a hysterectomy. If we need to do that to stop the bleeding, is that okay?'

'I…yeah.' It was a faint whisper. 'Seven kids. Don't need the bloody thing any more.'

'Bloody's right,' Rab said and smiled. 'Great, Isabelle, we'll get this sorted. 'Tom, you need to sign some forms. Can you let one of these people take you to the office? Isabelle, we're putting you to sleep now so we can fix the bleeding and then get you back together with your new baby. Right?'

'R…right,' Isabelle whispered as someone swung open the doors to Theatre and she was wheeled through.

But for a moment Mia stood stunned, motionless.

'You're in control, Isabelle.'

After all these years, the words were still with her, a whisper of the past. A turning point.

'You're in control.'

The faint echoes of recognition she'd already felt co-alesced into certainty. She knew this man.

But there was no time for thinking this through. She gave a faint gasp and then gave herself a mental shake. Her past didn't matter now. Rab would need all the help he could get if he was to save Isabelle's life.

Maybe he'd saved her life, but it shouldn't stop her from helping him save another.

The last thing he'd intended when he'd walked into this hospital this morning was to turn back into a surgeon, but he clearly had no choice.

He wasn't an obstetrician for a good reason—obstetrics had always seemed to him to be a profession of ninety-nine percent boredom, one percent panic.

He had obstetric colleagues and they enjoyed the pro-cess, the emotion, the waiting, as expectant women were transformed into mothers, usually caring, loving, totally committed from the start. For Rab the emotion always left him uncomfortable.

His own mother had been…well, absent. She'd left him with his father when he was a baby, and had rebuffed any attempt to make contact. Rab's father had been a loner who had little time for anyone, and he'd merely shrugged when Rab had asked about her. 'She was a mistake, boy. I don't need her, and neither do you.'

Rab had thus been raised by a succession of nannies. He couldn't miss what he'd never had, but still, the sight of a new mum holding her baby as if it were the most precious thing in the world had always left him with a sense of loss. General surgery had seemed far less fraught, a place where he could help but emotions could usually take a back seat.

Despite that, his training had included obstetric surgery. He guessed what he was facing now, and speed had to be of the essence.

He needed a surgical team. Assistants. An anaesthetist…

Ewan was clearly nowhere nearby. He was on his own.

'I can give the anaesthetic.' Mia was speaking calmly across Isabelle's trolley, as if this was almost routine. 'Ewan's the sole doctor here, and we've had emergencies before. He's trained me. I need orders but if you tell me what to do, I'll do it. Isabelle, you're okay. We have you safe.'

Her words seemed to steady Isabelle. They also steadied him.

'Any history?' She'd know the drill.

'No pre-existing that I know of. Seventh home birth. No antenatal care. But Isabelle's fit and strong, aren't you, Isabelle?'

'I can… I need to live.' The woman's voice was thready.

'Of course you do,' Mia said steadily. 'And we're here to make it a certainty.'

'But this isn't Doc Ewan…' There was still panic.

'No, but this is Dr Rab Finlay, and making sure people live is his specialty. I've known him for ever, and I know you're in safe hands. Promise. We're popping an anaesthetic in now, so lie back and go to sleep. When you wake up, the bleeding will have stopped and you'll have your gorgeous baby to hold and to love. Trust us, Isabelle.'

And Isabelle gripped her hand as if she were drowning and managed to whisper, 'Thank God you're both here. Oh, thank God…'

What followed was surgery that required all the skill he possessed—and more. But his initial sense of panic as he'd thought of the enormity of operating without any backup had been almost instantly dispelled as Mia reassured him, and as the surgery commenced the panic didn't reappear.

A ruptured uterus was the worst kind of obstetric nightmare. With the amount of blood loss, it was amazing that she'd made it to hospital. That she was still alive, that her vital signs were holding…

Her continued survival was down to him, but it was also down to the team around him.

As far as he could see he had two trained nurses, Mia and a younger one, but there were people in the background. The woman who'd been on the desk when he'd arrived—Rhonda—was passing equipment through the door. An elderly man dressed in hospital blues was clearing as they worked, silently taking used bags, equipment, following Mia's soft orders. The junior nurse—Marie?—was handing him whatever he needed, usually instinctively, though sometimes Mia prompted her—always before he had time to throw the order himself.

And Mia herself seemed almost as good as a trained anaesthetist, he thought. He'd outline dosages, give instructions, but thirty seconds into his orders he'd realise that she had a grip on the situation. That she knew not only dosages but what was at stake—that the woman they were working on was in danger of cardiac arrest, that the blood loss had to be arrested fast, that as well as administering anaesthetic and supporting ventilation she had to watch monitors, warn him of any faltering...

The surgery was pushing him to the extent of his skills. He was a general surgeon, not a gynaecologist, and the moment he'd made the first incision he'd realised the tear to the uterus was extending with pressure from the blood loss itself. It must have started small, he thought, or she'd never have made it this far.

But she had plasma on board now, and that and the saline would be holding her blood pressure steady. The O negative blood—the universal group used when fast cross-matching wasn't possible—would arrive soon. They might just manage it.

Thank God she'd made it to hospital, he thought. Thank God for this team.

He was about to close this hospital down.

There was no time to think about that now, but it stayed in his mind, a shadow as he worked. And as he accepted that Isabelle had every chance of surviving, somehow the shadow grew darker.

There was nothing he could do about it. If he could turn back time, speak to his grandfather before he'd died...

Well, maybe that wouldn't have worked either, he decided as he finally managed to get things under control. Rab had met his grandfather for the first time at his father's funeral. The old man had barked questions at him, had obviously disliked his answers and that had been the extent of their relationship.

The will, with its crazy stipulation, had come as a bolt from the blue, but it shouldn't have mattered too much to him. He hadn't expected an inheritance. He was well off himself, he didn't need the money that such an inheritance would bring. The stipulation that he must be married was impossible to fulfil anyway. He'd come to the valley to let them know in person, because it had seemed the honourable thing to do, but now...

Now he had misgivings. Doubts. Consequences he'd never thought of.

He looked down at the woman he'd just operated on. Without a hospital here...

She'd make it, he thought. He was closing now. The uterus was cleared, the final stitches were being inserted, the thing was done.

He gave Mia orders for reversal of anaesthesia and felt his breathing return to normal.

'She should never have had a home birth,' he said, almost to himself. 'With only this hospital in reach... No backup...'

'She would have had a home birth even if this hospital didn't exist,' Mia told him. 'But she'd have died.' She was still watching Isabelle's breathing. She'd removed the endotracheal tube, but it seemed she wasn't taking chances. 'And it's not just incidents like Isabelle being stubborn where we're needed. We service a huge rural area, and accidents happen. Colambool's an hour's drive to the north, but to the south there's nothing. So if there's an accident half an hour south of here, then it's half an hour before we can reach them or they can get to us, and then at least another hour for transfer.' She closed her eyes for a brief moment but then opened them and shook her head, as if she were shaking off a bad dream. 'Still, as you explained, there's nothing you can do.'

'If I'd known I might even have married,' he said, almost to himself, but she shook her head.

'This isn't your call. And maybe… Well, Doc Baynes is over seventy now. He's an awesome doctor but he's slowing and no one wants to take his place. Maybe the hospital would have closed anyway.'

'But not the school and the church as well.'

'As you say.' She sighed. 'I… Can I leave you now? Tom'll be out of his mind with worry. It'd be best if you talk to him—I hope you do—but I wouldn't want both of us to leave yet and…and you have the skills if…'

'There's no *if*. Tell him there's every chance she'll be okay,' he said, a bit too roughly. He was watching the monitors, seeing the steadying of the heartbeat, the blessed rising of blood pressure as plasma intake finally compensated. Yes!

'I'll do that,' she told him. 'And Rab…thank you.'

'You can hardly thank me,' he said roughly. 'Seeing I'm destroying your hospital.'

'It's not your fault,' she told him. 'No one can force anyone else to marry. Ever.'

And she gave a brief decisive nod and headed out to give Tom the good news.

Ewan returned to the hospital an hour later. The elderly doctor was emotional already, and even more so when he heard what had happened in his absence.

'I can't thank you enough,' he told Rab. 'Tom and Isabelle—their lifestyle wouldn't suit most of us but they're great people, great parents. It would have ripped the hearts out of all of us if Isabelle had died.'

'As it will if this hospital closes.' Rab was feeling ill. 'I'm so sorry.'

'Nothing you can do about it, son,' Ewan said roughly and clapped him on the shoulder. 'But thanks for being here today. Not just for Isabelle—thanks for having the courage to come and tell us in person.' And then he hesitated. 'Isabelle… I'm not sure… Maybe I should transfer her to Sydney?'

Rab heard the uncertainty, an elderly general practitioner alone with a patient who'd been near to death. There might well be complications. Ewan suddenly sounded weary beyond his years.

And Rab heard himself say, 'I'll be here for a while. My grandfather left the contents of the house to me, so I'll stay and sort it. There are family papers, things I need to organise, and I'm happy to help out with Isabelle if I can. I think it's safe enough not to transfer. If there are problems I'm a phone call away.'

'For how long?'

'Maybe a week. Isabelle will be fine by the time I leave.'

'And then?' And all of them knew what Ewan's question meant.

But there was only one answer. 'I'm sorry,' Rab said gently. 'I can do no more.'

And that was that. He walked out to the car park feeling a bleakness that was bone deep.

And from the window at the rear of the nurses' station Mia watched him go. And thought…

Control.

Why was that word suddenly front and centre?

She was thinking, weirdly, of her past. Of her childhood in a tiny rural community, almost completely cut off from the world outside. Of her father, who was a coward and a bully. Of her mother, a downtrodden wisp of a woman who never dared raise her voice, who never disagreed with her husband over anything. Of her father's friends, and of the overarching community hierarchy that assumed she, as a woman, had no control over anything.

She was thinking of herself at seventeen, inspired by books from spasmodic visits of a local library van, but more, she was inspired by hope, by the need to fledge her wings, by the desire to escape. *'I want to go to university.'*

She was thinking of her father's derision, and then the slaps. 'You'll marry, and you'll marry Harvey. Be grateful he wants you. Think of the money he makes and that great house he lives in. You're a lucky girl—all you have to do is keep him happy.'

She recalled her disbelief, her determination to leave. But then her mother: 'If you leave, I'll be alone. Maira, I can't live if you leave as well.'

And eventually, in the face of her father's bullying, her mother's sobs, she'd caved in. She'd married. But of course Harvey wasn't a 'good catch'. He'd wanted her as a possession, there to pleasure him.

She was thinking of the threats, the violence, her inability to please, no matter how she tried. Of her mother coming one day and finding her beaten, sobbing, distraught. Her mother trying to take her away.

Harvey's threat: 'She's mine and I keep my own, no matter what it takes. Leave or you'll get what she's already had.'

And then, at nineteen, that last awful night. He'd been drunk. She'd made fish and chips for their dinner but the chips were soggy. The fat hadn't been hot enough.

It hadn't been hot enough for the chips, but it was hot enough for...

Don't go there, she told herself, but she already was. Her hand raised instinctively to the scars etched across her cheek.

Control.

This valley had given it back to her, she thought. Ewan's daughter, Robyn, had been a social worker at the hospital and she'd helped her, organising her safe refuge after she'd left hospital, then—maybe against professional principles—she'd brought her to Cockatoo Valley to recover.

Doc Ewan and his wife had guided her back to health with their gentle care. She'd taken a new name—Maira had become Mia. The whole valley had seemed to surround her, shielding her from the trauma of the trial, Harvey's imprisonment, even lessening the shock of her mother's death.

The community had also scraped enough for a scholarship for her to attend university, to train as a nurse, but the valley had always been her refuge whenever there was a break in her studies. Always there'd been the assurance that Cockatoo Valley was her home.

It'd be lost.

Control.

Rab had reached his car now, but he didn't climb in. He stood and looked back at the hospital building, then seemed to look further, his gaze sweeping over the backdrop of gentle hills, the lush pastures that'd soon be swallowed by a giant coal mine.

Control.

Could she?

This was her valley. Her home. It was her choice, and she knew it.

She looked out at Rab for a long moment and memories came flooding back. The sound of his voice in the night. His words, a mantra that had echoed ever since.

From now on, Maira, the control's all yours.

Enough. She left the room and started to run.

CHAPTER THREE

HE WAS STANDING by the car when he saw her running towards him. Isabelle? he thought, his heart sinking. What had happened? Cardiac arrest? It wasn't unthinkable after such huge blood loss. He started towards her but she stopped, maybe three metres away. Almost skidding to a halt. Seeming breathless.

She was still dressed in her theatre scrubs, blue pants and smock and the plastic clogs that were easy to clean. Her face was devoid of make-up. Her long plait of silky black hair had been under a cap in Theatre. It hung free now and he suddenly thought he'd missed it. Her clear grey eyes were wide and direct. Apart from the faded scars on the left side of her face and neck, her skin was flawless and her...

Oh, for heaven's sake, what was he thinking? Get a grip.

'What is it?' he asked a bit too brusquely. 'Isabelle?'

'No, she's fine. At least...okay. Doc's with her. I just wanted...to talk to you.' She still sounded out of breath, and there was a long pause, as if she were fighting to recover.

The hospital entrance was less than fifty metres away. Why did she sound as if she'd just run a race?

'Sorry,' she said at last. 'But I don't know how to say this.'

'Say what?' Now his concern for Isabelle was allayed he was intrigued. He leaned back against the car and waited for her to collect herself.

Which she did. She almost visibly braced, squared her shoulders and asked, 'How much do you want to save the valley?'

'I can't.'

'No, if you could…how much do you value it?'

What was she getting at?

'I've never thought about it,' he conceded. 'At least, not until I heard the contents of my grandfather's will. I hardly knew him, and I had no expectation of an inheritance. This is the first time I've seen it.'

'It's special.'

'I imagine most people think their home's special.'

What did she want? To plead with him to somehow save it? It wasn't possible.

'It must be possible to save it,' she said, disagreeing with his unvoiced thought. 'There *must* be some way. Look at it. Can you imagine all this as a coal mine?'

He couldn't. That was what he'd been thinking as he'd stood by the car, taking a moment before he left to gaze around him.

Gardens had been developed right down to the river's edge, the river bank denoting the boundary of the hospital grounds. Towering eucalypts grew along the river bank, with sweeping lawns and native flora forming a magnificent garden leading right up to the hospital veranda.

Birds were everywhere. Seats were scattered, some in sun, some in shade. His great-grandfather had been more than generous in allocating hospital land, he thought, and he remembered the lease he'd looked at briefly. It seemed that maintenance had been included in the contract—these gardens must have been funded until now by… his family.

The thought that this place was his family's legacy was disturbing. He had no real concept of the generations of Finlays who'd settled here, who'd made their fortune from this land, who'd called this place home.

He allowed himself now to gaze further, at the cluster of homes and businesses on the far side of the river. They overlooked this place, the magnificent hospital grounds, the river itself and then further, to the gentle hills beyond, the lush grazing land. This was all destined to be ripped up to provide coal.

The thought was almost obscene—and this woman was looking at him as if she expected him to do something about it.

'I am sorry,' he said again, gently, regretfully. 'But there's nothing I can do.'

'You could marry.'

'In six weeks?' He gave a mirthless laugh. 'What do you expect me to do? Advertise?'

'There must be someone. A girlfriend…'

'No,' he said dryly, thinking of Skye, the dippy, funny nurse he'd been spending a bit of time with lately. Their attraction was superficial, though. Skye was about to head to London on the start of an adventure, working her way around the world. They were little more than friends—light-hearted lovers? And even if he asked and she agreed, there was another stipulation to the will: *married and happily settled.*

'You'd need to be together for at least a year,' his grandfather's lawyer had told him, not entirely unsympathetic. 'That would mean living together—at least until the lease expires and everything's settled.'

Skye, settled?

Him, settled?

The idea was laughable.

'So…how much do you want it?' the woman in front of him demanded. And then she corrected herself. 'Sorry, that sounds pushy but…how much do you think you could care?'

'I can't…'

He'd started to say he didn't care at all, but something stopped him. The sun was on his face and the birds were all around him. The hospital, built of mellowed local sandstone, with long verandas, French windows looking out over the river, gracious sun lounges—this was the most perfect place for a hospital.

And the setting. The little school he could see in the distance. The church. The magnificent grazing land.

He thought of it being destroyed, ripped up to become a massive, open cut coal mine. How much did he want to save it?

The woman before him squared her shoulders even more and asked, 'Enough to marry me?'

What followed was a silence that stretched out and out, continuing as if each was afraid to break it.

He was looking at her as if she had two heads.

Well, she was used to being stared at, she conceded. Her scars had faded over time, becoming little more than a series of whitish tracks and a flattening where grafted skin had reduced the capacity of her face to produce life lines. But the memory of those early years was still with her, the failure of people to hide their shock. She occasionally still got it, from people who saw her first from the unmarred side and then were hit by the scarring as she turned.

But Rab's gaze wasn't on the scars. He was searching her eyes. Like a doctor looking for signs of psychosis.

'It's just a thought,' she said at last, a bit too brusquely. 'A possibility. I mean…if you really do want to save the valley… I'm not married and I could agree to whatever conditions you had. Or… I guess…depending on the conditions.' She was talking too fast, and she was trying to sound offhand, as if it was a small thing she was offering. Asking?

'I think it could work, as long as I kept control,' she added quickly. 'As…as long as we both kept control, set boundaries, knew what we were letting ourselves in for.' Because that was the biggie, the stipulation that had hit her the minute the idea had come into her head. This had to be on her terms. She'd had enough of other people's terms to last her a lifetime.

He was staring at her with a mixture of bemusement and shock. 'But…why?' He sounded confounded.

'Because I care about this valley.'

'Is that all? What's in it for you?'

And that brought a flash of anger. And another memory. Of her father standing over her, yelling.

You'll be living in that great house. All you have to do is shut up and submit and you'll get everything you want.

Right.

She closed her eyes, and suddenly Rab's hand was on her arm. And when she opened her eyes again she saw…concern?

'Mia, what is it?' His voice was gentle. 'I'm seeing grief here. What do you stand to lose if this valley's sold?'

The nightmare receded. This was nothing to do with Harvey, with her past. It was…the opposite.

'Everything,' she managed, and fought to find the words to explain. His hand stayed on her arm and she didn't pull away. 'I… Maybe that's not true. If this valley disappears, I'm a trained nurse. I have no roots. I could move away. Start a new life somewhere. But these people…they're my people.'

'Your family?'

'I don't have family.' She said it harshly. 'I have the community that embraced me after my…after I was burned. They cared for me, made my life mean something again, and I'll do whatever it takes to protect them. As long as I can stay…me.'

'As long as you can keep control?' He must have heard the way she'd said the word, as if it was everything.

'Yes.'

'Mia, how could you possibly trust me enough to marry me?'

And there it was, said out loud, the question that was so huge it took her breath away.

And there was only one answer.

'Because once upon a time you read me *The Wind in the Willows*.'

'*The Wind in the Willows*?'

She fought for an explanation, knowing she had to explain because this memory, this slight thing that had seemed so huge for her, was the final reason she'd found enough courage to…propose?

'In the burns unit of Sydney Central, almost ten years ago,' she stammered. 'Late at night. Me and Hilda. A two-bed ward and neither of us could see. I was badly burned and so was Hilda, and the nights were awful. But you came in, night after night—sometimes for a little, sometimes for longer. You were there until I was moved to rehab. It probably meant little to you, but for Hilda and me it was everything. What you did for us—your voice. Rab, I was so close to…to not wanting to go on, but you reminded me there was kindness in the world. You were the first, and then the people of this valley took over. It's a debt, you see, and you're a part of it. So if you could use me…under my terms…'

There was a call from the door of the hospital. She turned and a nurse was beckoning. 'Mia!'

'Sorry, I need to go,' she told him. 'And…and I'm sorry. What I've just said, it's probably ridiculous. You'll probably reject it out of hand, but that's okay. Or it's not okay but it's your right. I just…had to try.'

She pulled a slip of paper from her pocket and handed it over. 'Here's my phone number in case, but otherwise forget I said it. Thank you for *The Wind in the Willows*, if nothing else.'

And she turned and walked quickly back into the hospital without looking back.

He headed out to the homestead, Wiradjuri—it was the indigenous word for kookaburra. That was where he'd been heading. He'd called into the hospital almost as a courtesy, but there was nothing more he could do.

Except think of what Mia had said.

It was a crazy proposition, so crazy he could do nothing but put it out of his mind while he sorted the next thing.

The homestead was set about a kilometre away, around the river bend from the township. Like the hospital, it was built of the local sandstone. Like the hospital, it was gorgeous.

His great-grandparents must have had magnificent taste, he thought, as he drove along the sweeping curve that led to the house. The gardens here were even more fabulous than the hospital's. They were low maintenance, mostly native, but a wonderful blend of nature versus nurture.

An elderly woman, wiry, grey hair caught in a loose bun, dressed in overalls and wellingtons, was on her hands and knees, digging clumps of what looked like weeds from along the garden path. As Rab's car pulled up she rose and he saw bulbs at the ends of the dried stalks.

'Daffodils,' she said briefly. 'Millions of 'em. I'm thinning 'em, cleaning up spares for the school fair.' And then she paused, her brows snapping together. 'Oh, wait. You'll be the new owner, then. Mr Finlay?'

'Rab.'

'Wow, finally.' She grimaced. 'I'm Nora, gardener here for ever, or until the place is sold. Your grandpa told me about you. Married then?'

So she knew the stipulation of the will and was cutting right to the chase.

'No.'

She swore, a loud expletive that seemed to shake the peace of the valley. Then her eyes narrowed. 'You intending to do something about it?'

'There's nothing I can do. My birthday's in six weeks.'

She swore again. 'I told him,' she muttered. 'Your grandpa.' She reached out a filthy hand and shook his, disregarding the dirt. 'Angus mostly kept to himself, but he told me years ago, after your dad died, when he realised you were still single. "He'll be happily married or he won't inherit," he told me, and I kept telling him to check whether you were or not, because I'm sure he decided that in anger. Angus didn't even know those relations he had in England, and he didn't reach out to contact you. But of course he thought there was all the time in the world.'

Her face clouded a little. 'He was just…upset, you

know, thinking you were turning out like your dad. So he put a gun to your head but didn't even let you know. What an idiot.' She hesitated. 'So what happens now?'

'The cousins will inherit and the place will be sold.'

The colour drained from her face. 'The whole valley…'

'Just this side of the river.'

'Makes no difference. The valley'll be stuffed.' She swallowed a few times and then turned and looked out over the river. 'Strewth, isn't there anything you can do? You can't… I dunno…marry fast?'

'Nora…'

'I know, it's none of my business,' she told him, her voice trembling. 'And, to be fair, I guess it's none of yours. Maybe even if you married you'd sell anyway. It's too late for your grandpa to order you into anything. So what…what are you here for?'

'I need to check the contents.'

'Fine,' she said, sniffing. 'Do you have a key?'

'The lawyer gave me one.'

'I'll let you get on with it then,' she said, and she could no longer disguise her tears. She compressed her lips and stared out past the garden, towards a massive clump of briars sprawled over the bank just beyond the river bend. When she spoke again he could see she was struggling to sound matter-of-fact.

'Okay. Moving on. I might poison those blackberries before someone else takes over. Your grandpa loved the berries, and the local kids pick them too. But they're a noxious weed and I struggle to control them. Cutting them back's a filthy job, and if the coal mine ignores them they'll take over the whole damned valley.' She gulped. 'Not that… I guess…maybe it doesn't even matter.' She stared down at her heap of lifted bulbs. 'And I might as well take all of these daffodils. They'd never survive a coal mine.'

And she turned her back, stooped and started digging again. Conversation over.

He felt ill, but what could he say? There was nothing.

The front door key was huge, a great iron key tied with string to a worn wooden...frog? It looked as old as the house itself, but surely his great-grandparents didn't cart around carved frogs.

He knew little about his great-grandparents—or his grandparents either, for that matter. All he knew of his family was that his father, Douglas, had been a twin. His twin, Donald, had drowned in the river when the boys were twelve, and Douglas had been blamed. That blame seemed to have been bone deep. The young Douglas had been packed off to boarding school, to university, to life, with parental money but little else. He'd graduated with honours, become a wealthy financier, moved from woman to woman, been landed with an unwanted son from one of those liaisons—that'd be Rab—but had never seen the need to come home. Neither had he seen the need to introduce his son to his parents.

So Rab walked into the homestead now expecting to feel that this place was nothing to do with him. But as he walked through the faded grandeur of the entrance hall and into the sitting room the first thing that caught his eye was a portrait hanging over the marble fireplace.

Two small boys, obviously twins, arms linked, cheeky grins. Two boys seemingly ripe for adventure.

Douglas and Donald? His father and his uncle?

He stood in the doorway and felt his gut lurch. His grandparents must have spent what was left of their lives looking at this every day. One son lost through tragedy, the other through choice.

His father had hardly talked of it, but once, late at night after an evening's heavy drinking, he'd told Rab about his twin.

'He drowned and I couldn't help him,' he'd said. 'And it almost destroyed me, so let it be a lesson to you. You stand on your own two feet, boy. You don't need anyone.'

He drowned and I couldn't help him.

The phrase drifted through Rab's mind now as he looked at the photograph, and for some reason it seemed to be echoing. Growing louder?

His grandmother had died here twenty years ago, and his grandfather had lived on alone. Rab went from room to room, seeing faded grandeur. It was as if the house had been almost closed up when the boys were gone, maintained but not changed. A couple had lived here, presumably loved, had twins, lost one then rejected the other. And then…nothing?

The library downstairs was the only room that looked lived in, with papers on the fireside table, a coat draped over an overstuffed settee. The kitchen looked cold and unwelcoming. An Aga was set into the fireplace, but a two-ring electric burner, stained with wear, said the Aga had seldom been used.

The place was musty, cold, almost repelling. It was as if the occupant of this house had died fifty years ago, instead of two weeks back.

The sadness… The grief…

He drowned and I couldn't help him.

He headed up the wide staircase to the bedrooms beyond. One room was bright, cheerful, or it would have been if not for the faded wear that came from age. Huge windows looked out over the valley. Boxes of toys were still scattered, the sort of things twelve-year-olds would love.

Two beds were carefully made.

For some reason anger was swelling. What a waste. He got it all—his father's remoteness, his grandfather's appalling will, the stubbornness that had wrecked four lives after the tragedy of one.

Below the window Nora was shoving her spade into the dirt with a fierceness that was surely unnecessary. Her shoulders were shaking. He could almost bet that she was still crying.

This place. This valley. It would go. A whole community destroyed by the bitterness of the past.

He drowned and I couldn't help him.

Enough. He pulled up the window and leaned out. 'Nora?'

She looked up, startled. 'I… Yes?'

'Don't take all of those bulbs away. Not yet.'

There was a moment of stillness. 'You mean…?'

'I have no idea what I mean,' he told her. 'Just leave them be.'

And then he tugged the slip of paper from his pocket and looked at the number.

Mia. A woman he didn't know.

She answered on the first ring, almost as if she'd been waiting.

'Could you come out to the homestead? I… We need to talk.'

There was no hesitation. 'Yes.' Then there was a moment's pause. 'I bet there's no food in the house. You want me to bring fish and chips?'

The note of practicality grounded him. Sort of. One part of him was on shifting sands, the rest knew exactly what he was doing.

'That'd be great,' he told her.

'See you soon then,' she said, and she almost sounded cheerful. As if what was happening was good?

What *was* happening?

He stood at the window of his father's childhood bedroom. He stared over the valley and he had no idea.

CHAPTER FOUR

DRIVING OUT TO the Finlay homestead was probably the hardest thing Mia had ever had to do.

Was she out of her mind? After all these years, to put her head in the noose again…

But this time it'd be on her terms, she told herself, and no, it wasn't putting her head in a noose. It'd be Rab who'd be losing control.

Or both of them taking it?

The road wound along the river. It was early autumn, a gorgeous still night. Cattle—mostly red and white Herefords—were grazing lazily in the paddocks. River redgums shadowed the river, welcome swallows were flitting over the water and herons were wading along the edges.

The valley's beauty was enough to take her breath away. It was enough to risk…everything?

If it hadn't been Rab she could never have considered it, she conceded. This valley had to be saved, but if it hadn't been Rab she'd never have found the courage.

But that thought brought another qualm, and a big one. She was acting as if she knew the guy, and in truth the only knowledge she had of him was a voice in the darkness, dispelling the appalling nightmares.

And now she wanted him to dispel still more. The nightmare of this valley's destruction.

'Am I being a total fool?' She said the words aloud and the dog on the passenger seat beside her turned his head and looked at her as if puzzled. Well, Boris was almost permanently in a state of puzzlement. He was a great lump of a dog, a cross between a boxer and a mastiff. Maybe with a bit of bloodhound in there as well? He had a smooth brown coat, long, long legs, floppy ears, and eyes that looked out on the world as if it was the most exciting thing he'd ever seen—even if he'd seen the same thing two minutes earlier.

Robyn had given him to her as a puppy, when she'd moved back here and decided to rent a little house just for her—the first time she'd lived alone for... Well, since Harvey. Harvey was safely in jail, but protection had still been in her mind. Well, that idea had been a joke. Boris would lick any attacker to death, she thought, but he was frankly adorable and he made her happy.

Harvey was due for release soon. Maybe she needed to get something else for protection.

Another name? She'd changed it once. To do it again could be a double protection.

She could change it via marriage this time, instead of by deed poll.

No. She was not doing this for her own sake, she told herself, but a little voice whispered...it couldn't hurt.

She pulled into the driveway. Rab was sitting on one of the old cane chairs on the veranda and the sight of him had all her qualms rushing back in force.

What was she doing?

But he was rising, walking down the steps to meet her, and it was too late to pull back. He was smiling a greeting. He was...gorgeous. She'd thought he was good-looking when Ewan had introduced him back at the hospital, but now…

Hours ago he'd been dressed in tailored trousers and a business shirt but he'd changed. He was now wearing faded jeans and a T-shirt that looked a bit too tight, revealing a pretty impressive six-pack. He was long, lean and tanned. His dark hair had lost the neatness she'd seen back at the hospital—maybe he'd just had a shower as it looked damp and a bit…rumpled.

He was smiling a greeting and the sight of him…

Post Harvey, she'd sworn off men for life. Independence was everything. More than any nun entering a convent, her vows had been real and meant—but surely the sight of this guy was enough to make even a good nun blink.

Oh, for heaven's sake, was she blushing? Get a grip, she told herself fiercely. She was here with a serious proposition. Emotion—and hormones—had to disappear.

She leaned into the back of the car to grab the parcel of fish and chips, which gave her time to regain her composure. Meanwhile, Boris had launched himself out to greet his new best friend—the world was composed of Boris's new best friends! When she turned, Rab had crouched to greet him, sending Boris into spasms of squirming ecstasy by rubbing behind his ears.

'Have he and I met in a previous life?' he asked, smiling as he rose, and she managed a grin.

'Not as far as I'm aware. Meet Boris.'

'Not into social distancing then, your Boris?'

'You could say that.' Then the big dog swivelled. A rabbit had peeped out from under the hedge at the edge of the driveway and Boris was off, baying as if the hounds of hell were after him.

'He'll never catch it,' she told him.

'Will he come home?'

'Are you kidding? He's been smelling fish and chips since town.'

He smiled again. 'Would you like to come inside?'

'The veranda's good.' Boris might not appreciate the niceties of social distancing, but for Mia social distancing— any sort of distancing—seemed imperative.

'Right.' So they sat on the top step with the parcel between them. Rab had gone inside and come out with two glasses of water.

'I should have wine,' he apologised.

'Water's great. Much safer for what we need to talk about.'

'What do we need to talk about?'

There was an interruption then as Boris tore back— had he heard the rustle of paper opening from the other end of the paddock? Moves had to be made to protect their dinner—which involved Mia carrying a large fish fillet down into the garden, offering it to Boris and then saying, 'That's it!'

And Boris got it. He looked adoringly up at her, wolfed the fish and then headed back to the hunt.

She returned to the steps, and Rab watched her come.

'This is surely one of the strangest dates I've ever had,' he told her, and she shook her head.

'It's not a date. It's a business proposition.'

'Then why aren't we in a lawyer's office?'

Maybe they should be, she thought. Maybe she shouldn't be wearing jeans and a faded sweatshirt, watching her dog hunt rabbits while she ate fish and chips. And the lawyer thing—that seemed deeply scary.

But it had to be faced, she told herself, and made herself say, 'That'll come, if you agree.'

'So what, exactly, would we be agreeing to?'

She met his gaze and held it for a long moment, and then turned her attention back to the fish and chips. She needed to take her time, get her words right. This was too important to mess up.

Right. Say it.

So she did, trying to get it out as quickly as possible.

'So,' she said, trying not to stumble over her words, 'I talked to Eric's mum. Eric's the kid who asked if you were married at the meeting. His mum's read the whole will, and I think… I think it might work. If you were agreeable…if you really wanted it…we could marry. But…just for twelve months. The ceremony would need to be legal, done properly. Because of the "happily settled" clause, I gather I'd have to move in here. We'd need to be seen to be married. But this is a big place and it's not like the olden days, lawyers checking sheets to make sure…to make sure things were consummated. We'd be housemates, that's all. And it would only be for a year, just to keep the valley safe.' She was talking too fast, she knew she was, but she had to get it out.

'And the legal thing. We could each use our own lawyers, people who have nothing to do with your grandfather's legal team. We could draw up agreements that mean we have no hold whatsoever on each other, financially or otherwise. But…' She faltered then but it had to be said. 'But I'd have to trust you not…not to sell the valley for coal mining.'

There was a pause. A long one.

'How could you trust me?' he said at last.

'I hardly know,' she said honestly. 'The marriage thing—that wouldn't mean anything, and I wouldn't want or take anything from it. I could put that in writing for you to use at the end of the twelve months. The valley thing though… When the marriage is over the valley will be yours and I don't think there's any way I could stop you selling it. But I don't think… I can't think that you would?'

She tilted her chin then and managed to meet his look head-on. 'It's trust,' she told him. 'I'm not… I'm not very good at it, but you must be a good man. Surely?'

There was another silence, a long, stretched out pause where they went back to eating their fish and chips while kookaburras chortled for the last time for the night in the massive eucalypts along the river, where bullfrogs started croaking in the reeds alongside the tiny creek bed meandering down through a rock bed to join the main waterway.

And then, into the stillness, he said, 'Mia, this is huge. How could you possibly trust?'

'I don't know. I only know that somehow… I might.'

Another silence and then, 'Mia,' Rab said quietly into the dusk, 'what happened to you?'

'It's nothing to do…' She faltered.

'With me? I think it must be. You're asking me to marry you.' He turned so he could meet her gaze head-on. 'This involves so much trust on both sides that complete honesty has to be the way to go.'

'I can't… I hate…'

'I imagine you do hate talking about it,' he told her. 'But, Mia, what you're suggesting isn't something small. I'd have to move here for twelve months, leave my job, leave everything I know.'

'But you'd win. You've have so much…at the end of it. You'd own this valley. You could sell parts of it, just not for coal mining. Individual sales. There are local farmers renting now who'd love to buy their land. You could make a fortune and leave the valley safe.'

'But you'd walk away with nothing. I need to know why you'd do that.'

'I told you. I love this valley.'

'Yes, and I want to know why. And I also want to know why, when you're talking to me, I can see fear in your eyes. You're making this suggestion, but what I see in your face…it's like you're offering yourself up to the guillotine.'

She struggled with that, but finally she managed a smile. 'It's not quite as bad as that.'

He smiled back, but his eyes didn't leave hers. 'Honesty, Mia. Lay it on the line. Even if this is only for twelve months, I won't marry someone I don't know. I think I have vague memories of you back at Sydney Central, as a burns patient, but I can't remember your history. I was an intern, not responsible for your care, only seeing you at night under bandages. I won't even consider this crazy proposition without openness on both our parts. Spill.'

Spill. Tell him the whole story?

Hardly anyone knew, at least not the whole story. A drunken partner, a fight, burns. That was pretty much what she told everyone now. It was only the social workers all those years ago—Robyn, and then Ewan and his wife, Mary, who knew it all.

This man was asking for everything. It felt like exposing herself to more pain to talk about it. But there was no choice. She'd decided to trust him enough to ask him to marry her. Maybe it was fair that he'd asked her to trust him more.

'It's a horrid story,' she said, determined to get it over fast. 'My father was a small-time drug grower and dealer, and he was damaged by the drugs he used. My mum, well, she was a bit of a doormat. She loved my dad—

or maybe she didn't, it was just that she didn't have the courage or strength to leave. We lived on a sort of farm about ten kilometres north of Corduna. You don't know it? I'm not surprised, hardly anyone does. It's all red sand, rocks, thistles, the remains of opal mining, a community that's pretty much surviving on memories. We had a scraggy piece of land that was useless for growing anything but…but what we grew. But we didn't even own that—it belonged to a guy called Harvey Manton.

'Harvey lived in a huge house at the bottom of the district's only hill, with a succession of gorgeous girlfriends he imported from Sydney. His place was weird but it was his palace, a place where he had total control. He loved it. I made enquiries after…well, a long time after, and I bet it's still his. It was sold when he went to jail but one of his mates bought it, and I'm betting he'll end up back there. It was his own private kingdom. It had dogs, barbed wire, huge gates, floodlights and he was so proud of it. I sometimes think that most of his vitriol towards me in the trial was because what he did to me finally caused the authorities to breach his defences.'

She paused then, staring at nothing. Then shrugged and forced herself to go on.

'Anyway, most of the stuff Dad grew made money for Harvey. He was…he *was* big and mesmerising and violent, and…and Mum and Dad did everything he wanted. Then, when I was sixteen Dad got deeply in debt—or more deeply into debt—and Harvey decided he wanted me.'

He frowned, trying to get a grip on her story. 'Did you have brothers or sisters? Were there people around?'

'No. You need to understand—what Dad was growing was for Harvey, and isolation was everything. So there was just me and Mum. I used to go to school a bit, but it was a fifteen-minute drive into Corduna and then an hour by bus to the nearest town that had a school. There was always a reason why I couldn't go. In the end they enrolled me for home schooling to keep the authorities happy, but that was a joke. I used to read, though, a lot. Corduna had a library van that came most Fridays, and the librarian was kind, letting me borrow heaps in case I couldn't get there the next week. So I suppose I educated myself. As I got older I thought of running away but there was always Mum. Mum had appalling asthma and was always sick. I couldn't leave her. But then, when Harvey wanted me…'

She closed her eyes as the nightmare flooded back, then forced herself to go on. 'Well, Mum didn't have the strength to fight him, and in the end I couldn't either. So I agreed. He even said he'd marry me, and we ended up in a sort of pseudo marriage. When I was seventeen! Totally illegal, but I didn't know it. Harvey used to go away for long periods. I knew there were other women— but I was his.'

'Oh, Mia.'

She shrugged. 'It was just…what was. I've gone over and over it in my mind—and with the psychologists at the hospital before the court case. I accept there was nothing I could have done, not at that age. I was raised to fear him and that's what I did. And then, one day when I was nineteen, I didn't heat the oil enough when I cooked his chips. He was drunk, his chips were soggy, and he threw the oil at me. And that was sort of…that. Somehow I got myself back to Mum and Dad's. Mum was really sick by then, but when she saw me she got me into the car and drove me to the hospital. Even then Dad was yelling at her not to do it. But she did, and then there were police, social workers, you name it. They put Mum in hospital too, and Harvey went to jail.'

He looked as if he felt ill, appalled by the simple story. 'So…did you have support afterwards? Your mum?'

'Mum died before I finished rehab,' she said flatly. 'Emphysema as well as asthma. Dad did a twelve-month jail stint and then disappeared. I don't know where he is, and I don't care. And Harvey's still in jail. He's due to get out soon but I can't worry about that either.' Again a shrug.

'Anyway, the social workers at Sydney Central were wonderful, and one of them was Robyn, Ewan's daughter. She lived here as a kid. She and I… Well, she's supposed to keep her professional life separate, but rehab took ages, and in the end she felt like…my friend. Finally she asked if I'd like to come here for a while after rehab, and her dad and mum—Ewan, that's Doc Ewan, and his wife, Mary—took me under their wing. I still can't believe their kindness. They supported me to train as a nurse. The whole valley did. So the rest is history.'

There was a long silence. Finally Rab lifted his hand and ran a finger down the outline of the graft across her cheek. Like a doctor's examination—only not. She sat without flinching, feeling the touch but not feeling… anything.

'You poor bloody kid.'

And that roused her. The story itself still made her feel ill, recounting it, remembering the awful passivity of being a total victim. But his touch, his sympathy…

She stood so quickly that the paper of remaining chips was knocked and fell between the slats of the veranda steps. She moved to stand before him, at the bottom of the steps so her eyes were level with his.

'I'm not a poor bloody kid,' she said, one syllable at

a time. 'I might have been once upon a time, but I'm not that person any more. I told you my story only because I need you to see how much I owe Robyn and Ewan and Mary, how much I owe this valley. I'll do whatever it takes to keep it safe, but I'll do it on my terms. I'm in control, Rab Finlay. What I'm offering could be good for you—you stand to be very wealthy—but it's my decision, made as an adult. The terms are mine. No one has power over me any more. I'm not being coerced. This is my decision, so take it or leave it. And don't…don't touch me again.'

She was standing before him, her hands on her hips, defiant, angry, challenging. Her dark eyes flashed fire.

What she was proposing was preposterous. To marry someone he didn't know… He shouldn't even consider it, but this woman…her story…

He remembered his stint in the burns unit all those years ago. Three months, done as part of his training. He'd been appalled.

And those weeks on night duty… Unless there were admissions it had been a relatively quiet rotation, but he'd been needed because pain levels had to be constantly monitored. The patients with burns to their lower body had been the easiest to care for in the night because they could tell him, they could call out if their pain became unbearable. But those whose faces had been severely burned… They needed to be watched, their body movements interpreted, rising blood pressure or even a twitching hand or arm maybe denoting there was excruciating pain being borne under the bandages.

He'd hated being helpless in the face of such suffering. His reading during his supposed meal breaks had been a way of watching for those signs, but it had also made him feel as if he was doing at least something.

At least something...

What this woman was offering was far more than something. Marriage...

It could be just as she'd said, he told himself. A simple contract, a house sharing for a year.

Suddenly he was thinking of practicalities. He'd need to give up his job at Sydney Central for a year, maybe work in the hospital here. He'd miss his job, he'd miss his friends, his life. This place was almost the back of beyond. He'd been raised in the city and the thought of living in the country for a year didn't appeal one bit.

He didn't need the money this inheritance brought with it. He was wealthy enough in his own right. But it'd only be for a year.

And this woman—she'd be sharing the house with him for a year but, other than that, her life wouldn't change. She wouldn't be giving up anything.

Except...

Her gaze still met his, the challenge still there, and he thought back suddenly to those nights in the burns unit, of pain, of helplessness. Caused by a guy who had total control over her.

She was offering to marry a man she didn't know for no financial gain at all. To thank the valley that saved her.

He suddenly felt very, very small.

'Your name?' he asked slowly, a sliver of memory surfacing.

'Mia.' And then she hesitated. 'Maira. I was Maira... Maira Somebody. The social workers helped me change it. Harvey...he thought he owned me. I didn't want to be that person any more.'

'Are you still afraid of him?'

'I told you. He's in prison.'

'When's he due for release?'

'Soon,' she said shortly. 'But that's okay. He won't find me. My name's been changed for years and if…if I marry you then I get to change it again.' She tilted her chin. 'Not that that's a reason for me to marry. I told you, Rab, there's nothing in this for me.'

'I'd want there to be something.'

'Free board for a year then,' she said. 'I'm renting a tiny cottage near the hospital. The backyard's tiny. Boris would love to live here.'

Hearing his name, Boris ceased investigating the pellets of poo down by the fence—from kangaroos? Rabbits?—and came dashing up, only to discover chips had fallen between the steps. How had that escaped his notice? His huge head dived straight down, until all that was between them was the dog's massive rear, tail rotating like a chopper blade.

It should have made Rab smile. It didn't. His feelings of inadequacy were deepening by the moment.

He'd had a life of absolute privilege. Sure, he'd lacked parenting, but there'd been nannies to fill in the gaps, often good ones. He'd had an easy path into medical school, and his father's death had left him wealthy. He was in a profession he loved. He had great friends, a great life.

The knowledge that he'd missed out on inheriting Cockatoo Valley hadn't upset him—he'd had no idea he'd stood to inherit anyway. He'd come to give the locals the news that had little to do with him, then visit his grand-father's house to see if there were family mementoes, anything his kids—if he ever had kids—might like. And then walk away.

Being honest, he'd hardly thought of the ramifications

of the sale of this land. He'd hardly thought of the community about to be destroyed.

Yet now... Here was this woman, to whom community seemed to mean everything. She'd been through so much and yet...she was offering to trust again.

He had no doubt that the idea of marriage, accepting that she'd need to live with a stranger for a year, must bring with it an appalling level of fear, subliminal if not overt. Yet here she was, asking for nothing for herself, asking only that he marry her and live with her for a year, to save what she held so dear.

A year. Leaving Sydney. Living in this house.

Suddenly he was taking the idea seriously.

He'd have to work, he thought. He wasn't born to be a country squire. But he'd been in the busy hospital, he'd seen the look of weariness on the elderly Ewan's face. That look surely wasn't solely caused by the thought of losing the valley. Ewan could use help.

So...could he work himself, here in this hospital? His role would be a family doctor instead of a surgeon at the top of his game. He'd have to brush up on a few things. Well, maybe more than a few, he thought ruefully. Diagnosis of minor ailments. What to do with nappy rash.

An overenthusiastic wiggle of Boris's behind pushed him sideways and he looked across the dog's massive backside and saw Mia watching him.

Calmly. Waiting for his verdict.

'I'll... I'll let you think about it,' she said. 'I have no right to ask it of you, so I'll accept whatever you decide. There's no blame on you. This was your grandfather's doing, not yours.' She shoved her hand between the steps and grabbed Boris's collar. 'Come on, mate,' she told him. 'Enough chips, we need to go home. You know where to find me, Rab,' she told him. 'If…if you need me.' And she tugged.

But nothing happened. There were chips down there. Mia was slight and Boris was seriously big. She tugged and tugged again.

And finally Rab grinned and shoved his hand down with hers. A hand each on the collar, a mutual tug and Boris emerged, his mouth full of chips wrapping, his tail still whirling with happiness.

And they stood for what seemed a loaded moment together, hands touching, dog wiggling with delight between them.

The slight contact of hands. It seemed to mean… What? Rab hardly knew. He only knew that he didn't want to pull away.

'I… Thank you,' Mia said at last, and finally their hands parted.

'Think nothing of it,' Rab told her. 'And I have decided. Mia… If you'd do me the honour…' He gave a rueful grin. 'I should go down on one knee, but it seems a mockery in the circumstances. Whatever, Mia, let's get married.'

CHAPTER FIVE

THE WEDDING TOOK place five weeks later. Four weeks was the legal minimum to lodge documentation of intention to marry, but it had taken a week to get that documentation sorted. Even then they were rushed, but a week before Rab's thirty-fifth birthday they stood before Cockatoo's local wedding celebrant and made their vows.

'Because there's no way I'm doing it in a church,' Mia had declared. 'I feel like I can cross my fingers behind my back when it's only Tony Gaylard, who thinks he's the king of everything around here. He's the shire president,' she'd explained to Rab. 'Retired accountant who does weddings and funerals as—he says—a public service. He's a pompous little man with bad taste in three-piece suits, and a huge notion of his own importance.'

Whatever, there was no doubting the delight of the little man who stood before them, taking them through their vows. He beamed as if all his Christmases had come at once.

As did Ewan and Mary, who stood behind them as witnesses. It was only their daughter Robyn, the social worker who'd introduced Mia to this valley, who was looking worried. She'd driven from Sydney because, as she'd told Mia, 'There's no way you're going into this without me being there.' Rab had thought it was an act of friendship, but the night before the wedding she'd driven out to Wiradjuri ready for an inquisition.

'Mum and Dad have told me all about you,' she'd said with no preamble. 'You sound like the answer to the valley's prayers, but I've cared about Mia for almost ten years and I'm not about to stop now. She's doing this for the valley, not for her, but I wish…oh, how I wish she could do something for herself. Anyway, I came here to tell you that if you hurt her…well, I can't tell you how many friends she has, in this valley and beyond. You'll take care of her or else.'

He had no idea of 'what else' implied, but he'd reassured her as best he could. Now she was standing beside her parents and the look of belligerence hadn't faded. Her arms were folded and she was looking straight at him with an air of pure judgement.

But he'd only glanced at her once. His attention was almost solely taken by Mia. His bride.

She'd dressed simply—no full bridal attire for this woman. The marriage was a business arrangement and that was what her clothes implied. A crisp white long-sleeved blouse with a high collar. Plain black trousers. Her hair was braided and coiled into a knot. She wore little make-up, her shoes were sensible—she looked as if she was about to head into a meeting with a bank manager.

Well, maybe that was pretty much what she was doing, he thought. She was making promises, signing documents that would ensure the financial security of this valley.

Her face was set—it hadn't changed from the moment he'd met her outside the council chambers. Oh, she'd given him a tight smile as he'd greeted her but that was all. Now she was staring straight ahead, making her vows mechanically, without expression.

Just how frightened was she? Her vows were sure and steady, but when he lifted her hand to put the ring on her finger he felt it trembling. She looked down at the ring and grimaced, just slightly, but the expression was fleeting. She went straight back to being stoic.

He had an almost overwhelming impulse to stop proceedings, to call a halt, to take her into an anteroom and make sure she hadn't changed her mind. What was he doing, marrying a woman who was terrified?

But the look on her face was transient, gone almost before he saw it. She glanced up at him and gave a decisive nod. *Do it*, her look said, and he slid the ring onto her finger. And then she put a ring on his finger because that was what they'd decided. For the next year they'd be a business partnership, equals. If she was to be married, then so was he.

'I now pronounce you man and wife,' the celebrant said, beaming as if this was the end of a fabled romance. 'You may kiss the bride.'

'You may kiss the bride.'

She remembered those words. She'd heard them years ago when, all of seventeen, she'd been standing before a man she'd been raised to believe was the centre of her family's universe. Harvey had controlled her father absolutely. His word was law, and her father obeyed him without question.

Mia's mother had done her best to efface herself when Harvey entered their house. Mia—Maira then—had also been taught from an early age to disappear when the men were at the kitchen table, drinking. She and her mother had mostly stayed in her bedroom, listening to Harvey's voice booming out displeasure, orders, the way their life should be run.

Then, when she was thirteen, fourteen, Harvey had started watching her. He'd demanded that she stayed during his visits, that she poured his beer, that *she* served him instead of her frightened mother.

And then he'd decreed that she would marry him. And her father had explained how much of a hold the man had over them, that he'd go to jail if she didn't, and her mother too. It seemed they were all implicated.

The marriage had been a mockery. There'd been no documentation and she'd been too naïve to know it had been necessary. Even if it had been legal, she'd learned afterwards that there'd been another marriage that hadn't been dissolved.

But she'd had no choice. Her father was so deep in debt—and so deep into murkier dealings, things he was complicit in—that Harvey had total power. So she'd stood in a strange office, in front of a man the police had told her later was a 'mate', someone Harvey had bribed to say the words.

She'd been wearing her mother's old wedding dress, and they'd both been crying as they'd driven to the ceremony. She'd been a bride but not a bride, and when the pseudo-celebrant had said, 'You may kiss the bride,' Harvey had kissed her with a ruthlessness that held more than a promise of the cruelty to come.

'You're mine now,' he'd said, with an implacability that had made her terrified from that moment.

And now…here was another man standing beside her. They'd made the same vows, and those vows were also a mockery.

'You may kiss the bride.'

What was she doing? Putting herself in this man's power?

No, she told herself sharply. This was very different. It was her choice, her decision. She was the one with the control.

But was she kidding herself? Here she was, once again being asked to submit. *'You may kiss the bride.'* Code for: You may do whatever you want with this woman from now on—she's yours.

Rab was holding her hands, as bride and groom had done for centuries past as vows were made. He was ready to take this next step.

'You may kiss the bride.'

But maybe he saw her panic because, instead of kissing her, he started to speak.

'I think we need to change this,' he said softly, but loudly enough for everyone in the chamber to hear. 'Mia, you've married me, and I honour you for that. I honour the choice you've made, but choices don't stop with this ceremony. Mia, if you wish, and only if you wish... If you wish, you may now kiss the groom.'

There was a shocked hush in the tiny council chamber. Mia looked up into Rab's face and what she saw there...

No pressure, his expression said. *Take all the time you want. Or if you decide not to then it's fine, there'll be no kiss at all.*

She looked around almost wildly, tossed right out of kilter, and she saw Robyn, the social worker who'd been there for her almost from the beginning. Robyn, who had the reputation of being an attack dog where her clients were concerned. And Robyn was grinning. Grinning! Such a thing was almost unheard of.

And suddenly Mia found herself smiling back.

'Mia, if you wish...you may now kiss the groom.'

It was such a simple statement, but with it came an

implicit promise. She might be doing this, but she wasn't losing control.

And she was suddenly thinking of this man's kindness from years ago, and that she'd had to talk him into marrying her. And, what was more, that he was doing so to save the whole valley.

So why not?

'Why not indeed?' she whispered, and she raised herself on tiptoes.

And she kissed him.

It was a feather kiss. A brush of lips, the merest touch. It was part of what was essentially a business deal. It shouldn't have meant anything to Rab at all.

Except when her hold on his hands tightened, when she raised herself a little on her toes, when she turned her face up to his, something twisted inside him.

Something he didn't understand at all.

CHAPTER SIX

THE WEDDING HAD been held in the early afternoon. The service itself was private but what happened afterwards was definitely not.

'Almost all the locals know why we're getting married,' Mia had told him. 'This is…well, it doesn't seem *our* marriage, Rab. It's more a community service.'

'Like the bob-a-job I used to do as a Boy Scout,' he'd joked, and then he'd had to explain the concept of kids doing odd jobs to raise money for charity.

'Exactly,' she'd agreed, and then thought about it. 'Or sort of. How much is a bob, exactly? Possibly a bit less than you'll be giving the valley.'

'But not as much as what you're giving,' he'd said, and she'd smiled but it had been that strained smile he was starting to know. The smile that said fear was still in the background.

'I'm not giving anything,' she'd told him. 'I'm gaining free rent for a year, for me and for Boris, but you're having to change your life.'

He was. He'd gone back to Sydney to quit his job, to pack up his apartment, to figure the minutiae of transferring his life to Cockatoo Valley for a year. He'd had to resign completely, give up the lease on his apartment, tell friends and colleagues he was leaving for good, because the terms of the will stated 'happily settled' and simply taking a year's absence wouldn't cut it.

'What are you doing?' his friends had demanded incredulously, and he'd asked himself pretty much the same question. But, increasingly, he had the answer.

It had cost him more than a pang to leave his hospital job, but there was an inheritance at the end of it. That was what he told himself—and his friends—and it made sense. But, added to that, there was also an element of… well, adventure was the wrong word but the thought of settling in the country, of doing something worthwhile, felt okay. More than okay, he decided as the wedding had approached and the ramifications for the locals became clearer. Often over the past years—maybe since he and Annabel had conceded their relationship wasn't working—he'd endured the unpleasant sensation that he'd been…drifting. Working in the valley for a year, helping out and in the process keeping this land safe for future generation—the prospect felt worthwhile. Even good.

And now, seeing Mia's face the night before the wedding, he'd thought she was giving up so much more. She was supposedly in control. She'd been the instigator, but in the end what was in this for her but another arranged marriage?

She was determined though. She was doing it for the community, she'd see it through, and practically the whole community knew it. So the ceremony itself was private, but the moment they emerged as man and wife they were ushered into the hall next door, where the party to end all parties had been set up. The future of the valley had been secured by this marriage, and the locals were intent on celebrating in full.

But Mia wasn't celebrating. As the afternoon wore on, as Rab received congratulations and thanks, followed by congratulations and thanks, until his face ached from smiling in response, he saw the rigidity behind Mia's smile and wondered again at the personal cost of her decision.

She looked exhausted. How long did they have to stay there? But it was up to Mia, he thought. This was her community, it had to be her call.

In the end it was Robyn who saved them.

Robyn was a big-bosomed, big-hearted woman, and Rab could imagine her years ago, taking the shattered Mia under her wing and bossing her parents to take care of her. Even though she lived and worked in Sydney, she apparently still thought of the valley as home, and when her parents had told her what Mia and Rab had arranged she'd arrived back in the valley within hours. And cornered Rab.

'I hate that Mia's doing this,' she'd said flatly. 'But she's doing it for all of us. It's her decision and I need to accept it. But she's told you her background? In my opinion she's still totally vulnerable, and if you hurt her, I swear, I'll trash your reputation from here to Timbuctoo. You might have a great name as a general surgeon, but I'm pretty high up in the social services network and I can make it happen.'

But then she'd thrown herself into organisation mode. She, with her father, had been witness to their marriage, and now she made her way through the crowd to corner bride and groom.

'Enough,' she told them. 'It's six already, but this party looks like going until midnight. The whole valley's ecstatic but you guys must be bushed. And I bet you haven't eaten. There's more food here than you can shake a stick at, but you've been talked at all the time. So we've packed a hamper and my kids have taken it down to the riverbank at the bottom of your garden. They've set up a picnic for you, everything you need. Dad'll make a speech now, and then you can make a getaway.'

So they listened as Ewan made an emotional speech saying how much this marriage meant to them all. The whole community cheered and Rab took his bride's hand and led her out of the hall. They drove away—with tin cans and old boots trailing from the car behind them.

It had been a typical country wedding. Sort of.

Mia seemed almost mute.

They reached the house—their house—and the silence seemed to intensify.

'Where's Boris?' Rab asked as they climbed from the car. He hadn't thought of the dog, but he thought now that Boris should be here. Mia needed something to take that look from her face. The fiercely independent woman who'd proposed to him was suddenly nowhere. She was afraid?

What should he say? He thought for a moment and then ventured, 'Right, let's start as we mean to go on. Marriage in name only, as we've agreed. We're housemates, Mia, nothing more. So right now we don't need to use Robyn's picnic basket. If you like, you can go to your end of the house and I'll go to mine. Rostered time for kitchen and bathroom use? Do you want to make yourself a meal first? I know Robyn's filled the fridge so we can commence independent living—starting now?'

And, blessedly, the strained look eased from Mia's face. She even managed a smile.

'It does seem a waste,' she conceded. 'Maybe…friends might picnic?'

'So we might. But where's Boris?'

'Robyn's taken him for the night. He needs a decent run and I wouldn't… I didn't think I'd have time. She has four kids who'll oblige.'

'Do you want him back? We could go fetch him if you like.' He hesitated. 'I'm not too tired to walk him—or you could walk him if you're up to it.'

'The kids'll be disappointed if we do that,' she told him, seemingly moving on from discussing independence. 'And so will Boris. Robyn gave him to me as a puppy, and her kids think of him as part theirs.'

'Robyn's been a good friend.'

'She's been my lifesaver,' she said, and he heard the depth of emotion behind her words. 'Between your reading *The Wind in the Willows* and her friendship…' Her voice wobbled but then she smiled again. 'So, moving on… Maybe independent dinner tonight is silly—we can hardly leave Robyn's picnic hamper down at the river. And I'm hungry enough to eat a horse. We can split the picnic hamper down the middle if you like, and maybe turn our backs on each other, but it does seem a bit ridiculous. Between…friends?'

And her voice faltered again as she said the last word. It was a question.

A hope?

He met her eyes. They were wide and strained. He could see dark shadows, and he wondered how much she'd slept the night before. Or any time in the last few weeks.

What a leap of faith this had been. What a measure of trust.

'Definitely friends,' he told her, smiling down into her eyes. Hoping she might smile back. 'Give me five minutes to get out of this damned suit and let's go share.'

It was a good thing to do. In casual clothes, jeans and T-shirt on his part, jeans and an oversized shirt tied at the waist on hers, they headed down to the sandy 'beach' formed by a curve in the river. There they found a picnic rug, two canvas deckchairs, a mountain of cushions and an enormous picnic hamper. A romantic wedding feast.

They opened the hamper and were both astounded.

This hadn't been made by scouring the hall for leftovers, Rab thought. It was almost… Robyn's wedding gift to them. Had she brought it from Sydney, guessing how much they'd need to get away?

Regardless, it was amazing. There was lobster meat and prawns, nestled on a a crisp salad complete with with silver salad servers and slivers of lime and lemon. There were delicate sandwiches with exotic fillings. There were profiteroles stuffed with salmon and a creamy dressing to die for. Olives, pastrami, oozy French Camembert, wafer-thin crackers…

Then tiny meringues, with cream in one bowl, strawberries, raspberries and blackberries in another, plus a jar of homemade lemon curd so they could make their own tiny pavlovas.

And beside the hamper there was champagne in an ice bucket—the best. There was a note tied to the champagne: 'Happy Wedding from the entire valley'.

Mia read the note and her eyes shimmered. Even Rab felt… Well, guys surely didn't do shimmering, but it was a close thing. In the last few weeks he'd realised just how momentous this marriage was for the whole valley. How much Mia had given them.

Now he looked at Mia and he made a silent vow—a vow much more meaningful than any of the fake wedding vows they'd just made. This would not hurt her and he wouldn't let her be hurt. Ever. He'd seen her fear back at the house. For her to suggest this, to make yet another arranged marriage…

'We've done a good thing,' he said, and she managed a wavery smile.

'I…yes. Thank you. I can't tell you…'

'Then don't. There's no need for you to thank me. The privilege is all mine. Yes, you get free rent for a year but I get a year off from a high-pressure job, I get to share a house with an amazing woman, with a great community, and at the end I inherit a fortune.'

'But you won't sell.' He heard the flash of fear and he got it. Even now, she was still frightened for her beloved valley.

'I won't sell,' he told her. And then he grinned. 'You know, when I was talking to my lawyer about this marriage I was reminded that if we live together as man and wife for two years then half of what's mine is yours anyway. That's the law. So you just need to stick with me for an extra twelve months and the valley's yours anyway.'

'Oh, my…' She stared at him in horror. 'But I wouldn't. Rab, I swear I wouldn't. I'll be moving out the day our twelve months is up.'

His smile widened. 'Hey, it's okay, Mia, I'm not sweating on losing anything—and it'll be me who'll be moving. Meanwhile, I can't remember a double shift in our Emergency Department coming even close to today for building an appetite, and here we have a feast fit for royalty. So…'

He popped the champagne cork, filled two glasses and handed one to her. 'Here's to our version of happy ever after,' he told her, clinking their glasses. 'Here's to happy for twelve months, after which all problems will be sorted. And here's to one brave woman, who has the courage to trust.' His gaze met hers and held. 'Here's to you, Mia. Well done.'

* * *

They ate and drank in silence, leaning back on the mass of cushions. They'd have to lug them up to the house afterwards, Mia thought, because otherwise they'd end up covered in possum or kangaroo poo as the wild creatures of the night investigated. But right now it didn't seem to matter. Nothing mattered except the thing was done.

The valley was safe.

She was eating dinner with…her husband.

The word was enough to make her shiver, but the peace of this place, Rab's silence, the magnificence of the food, the luscious champagne—they were almost enough to keep the fears of the last few weeks at bay.

She could trust this man…couldn't she?

She had to. She had no choice.

And that brought a jarring note. No choice? Wasn't this where she'd come in before? Accepting a marriage because she'd had no choice.

The thought broke through the haze brought on by fatigue, good food, great champagne, the comfort of these cushions, the rug, this man's smile… Here it was again, washing back as if it was a part of her, as maybe it was. The eternal fear. It made her shudder and Rab's hand was suddenly touching her arm.

'Hey,' he said. 'It's okay, Mia. Your plan's worked brilliantly. All is good.'

Did he realise? Of course he did, she thought. He'd seen her as she'd been all those years ago. He hadn't remembered her in particular—well, who could? She'd been swathed in bandages, swollen beyond recognition. But even if he didn't recognise her, he'd worked with other burn patients. He'd know the damage.

He'd understand the fear.

'Is this river safe for swimming?' he asked, and she

had to jerk herself out of thoughts that were messing with her head and focus on the here and now. River. Safe?

'It is at the moment,' she managed. 'Wide, sandy bottom, not too deep. I swim a lot, but further downstream. There's the occasional fallen branches so you need to be a bit cautious, and after heavy rains it's treacherous, but we've had no storms recently and the current's slow. It'll be safe enough. Cold though.'

'It's just what I need to wake me up,' he told her, rising. 'You want to come in too?'

'No. Thank you.' Swimming was one of her principal pleasures, but she hadn't swum where anyone could see her since burns had scarred the left side of her body as well as her face. She wouldn't say that, though. 'I'm too tired to swim,' she said, and she said it a bit too brusquely.

But he didn't appear to mind. 'Fair enough,' he said and put his head to one side to look at her. His dark eyes twinkled with mischief. 'But I'm not so tired. Would you be shocked if I stripped to my boxers and dived in? Or could I ask you to close your eyes?'

That smile was impossible to resist. He was looking down at her almost as if he was daring her to laugh as well, and to her astonishment she found her lips twitching, her mood lightening.

'I'm your wife,' she said, making her voice prim. 'I believe there's a legal prerogative for seeing you...'

'Just in boxers. Not the rest.'

'Of course,' she said, still primly. 'As per the conditions of our contract. But I'm a nurse. There's nothing you can show me I haven't seen a thousand times before. Off you go and have fun.'

'You sound like a parent giving her kid permission.'

'Nope,' she told him. 'I have no control over what you do, but I will act as lifesaver.'

'So if a crocodile appears…'

'There aren't a lot of crocodiles in inland New South Wales,' she told him. 'But there may be eels. If any eel wanders by, can you grab it? I hate them—have you ever tried cooking an eel?—but Boris loves them.'

'So I'm heading in looking for dog food.'

'You might as well make yourself useful,' she told him serenely. 'Me, I'm going to make myself another pavlova.'

Except she didn't. She sat and watched Rab.

He strode into the water with confidence and plunged straight in, but he was obviously aware of the dangers of swimming in inland rivers. Instead of swimming, he floated out, presumably using his legs to check for depth, for underwater snags. What he found seemed to reassure him because he then began to swim. Not fast but strongly, his deep, sure strokes taking him from one end of the river's curve to the other.

As promised, he'd stripped to his boxers. He looked superbly fit, lean and muscled, powering through the water with ease. He looked like a man completely at home in his environment.

At home. The phrase seemed to slam into her head. He was at home and so was she. For a year.

Another wave of panic swept over her, but she suppressed it with what was starting now to seem accustomed effort. Every time she thought of this marriage the old feelings of fear surfaced again, and every time she managed to damp them down.

The thing was done. For better or worse…

Rab rolled over and started to do a lazy backstroke. His body glistened, the light from the sinking sun glinting on his wet chest. He glanced over at her and grinned.

'It's magic. You sure you don't want to come in?'

'I'm sure.' There was that flutter of panic again, the thought of stripping—to what, bra and knickers? The thought of being in the water with him. The thought of being close, of not being in charge…

She had to keep control. Whatever happened over the next twelve months, she had to stay apart.

There'd been a moment during those awful months as her parents had bullied and cajoled her into marrying Harvey, when she'd looked at Harvey and thought maybe it wouldn't be so bad. He'd been big, burly, tough, but he had been good-looking. He used to smile at her, and sometimes she'd found herself smiling back. At seventeen she'd even found herself fantasising…

Yeah, well, she wasn't fantasising now.

Except she wanted, quite badly, to swim.

She knew a swimming hole a couple of kilometres to the north, where the river wound its way into bushland, a place no one seemed to use. She'd found it in those first months after Ewan and Mary had taken her in. She'd often swum there, tentatively at first but getting braver as she'd realised how private the place was. It had helped her head as well as her healing body, to swim where no one could see.

But here someone—Rab—would see.

Oh, but to swim… The sun was sinking to the west, its gorgeous tangerine rays shimmering along the river. Rab was doing lazy backstroke, not even watching her.

Dammit, why not? What sort of coward was she? This man was a doctor. He'd seen her maybe at her worst. What was there to fear?

'Just the way he makes me feel,' she muttered to herself, but that was dumb. Why shouldn't she swim?

Do it.

And thirty seconds later she'd ditched her shoes, jeans and shirt and she'd dived straight in.

Fear, after all, was just plain stupid.

He was backstroking steadily along the far side of the riverbank. He saw her dive and he stopped, let his feet fall to the sandy bank, watching as she surfaced.

She found her feet, glanced at him and he saw her chin tilt, almost as in defiance.

'I can swim even if I'm tired.'

'So you can,' he said, grinning. 'Amazing. Wonder Woman Plus!'

'There's no need to sound patronising.'

'I didn't!'

'Yes, you did. And it's unwarranted. I reckon I might even be able to swim faster than you. Four laps, along to the bend and back, repeated. Ready, set, go.'

And she was off, her body slicing through the water like a dolphin.

He watched her go, stunned. This wasn't the Mia he thought he knew. This was a woman of strength, of power. She was sleek, toned…gorgeous.

He could see scars on her upper shoulder, visible when she lifted her left arm. They didn't make her one whit less beautiful.

She reached the bend, did a flip turn, then saw he wasn't following. She found her feet in the breast-deep water and glowered. 'What?'

'What do you mean, what?'

'What are you staring at?'

'You.'

'Then don't,' she said brusquely and almost instinctively hugged her left arm with her right hand so the worst of the scarring was hidden.

'I wasn't staring at the scars. I was watching you. Mia, you're beautiful.

She glowered. 'I'm not beautiful. That's a dumb thing to say. You're just trying to avoid the question as to whether you're faster or me. Aren't you going to race?'

'We are racing,' he said, because he couldn't think what else to say. 'I just missed the gun. Starting now!' And he dived back under and started swimming.

He didn't make the mistake of trying to swim slower than she did. He swam the hardest he could, back and forth, back and forth. He was pushing himself to the limit but, even so, barely keeping up with her.

And the image of her stayed with him as he swam. It wasn't just the image, he decided, it was the consciousness of her. The thought that she was in the water beside him. That she was swimming with him, stroke for stroke.

Her long black hair, coiled for the wedding, had come undone. It was streaming behind her as she swam. He shouldn't even know that, but of course he did. He could see her every time he lifted his head and looked to the side.

She was his wife. It was a dumb thought, an extraordinary make-believe concept, but it stayed with him.

But she wasn't his. She was in control, she belonged to no one. If he didn't accept that then he should never have married her.

Still, he was in one of the most beautiful places in the world, and Mia was swimming beside him. The sense of her presence made him feel... Hell, he didn't know how it made him feel. Magic?

He couldn't examine the feeling. All he could do was keep on swimming.

It was Mia who finished first—of course it was. She did her four laps and she beat him. Then she pulled herself up on the grassy bank, grabbed her gear and headed for the bushes surrounding the clearing.

When she returned, Rab was just emerging from the river, and even though she was dressed again, even though there'd been nothing in the fact that they'd swum together that had altered their relationship, she felt...exposed. It was a dumb sensation, but she couldn't help what she was feeling. What lay between them was too raw, too new, too ridiculous! Confused, she headed across to the picnic hamper, knelt and started packing up.

When she finally looked up, Rab was standing less than a metre away. His wet body was glistening in the last rays of the sun. His hair, naturally wavy, was soaked but still trying to kink. He'd snagged his shirt on one of the bushes and was starting to dry himself with it, but he was smiling right at her.

'That was awesome,' he said gently. 'You're an amazing swimmer, Mia.'

'Nope,' she said, a bit too abruptly. 'I'm not. I never swim in public.'

'Because of your scars?'

'I... No.'

'It'd be a shame if that was the reason,' he told her. 'If you have the courage to marry me, then maybe you could find the courage to swim wherever you want.' His smile changed then, subtly, and suddenly he sounded infinitely kind. Like the doctor he was. 'Mia, you're beautiful,' he told her. 'And you're beautiful from the inside out. Don't let that bastard control you any more.'

She flinched, closed her eyes, felt a wash of grief. But not fear. What was it with this man's voice? Right from that first time, when he'd read to her, it had settled something deep within. Pushed the fear away.

'I might,' she managed. 'Eventually.'

'There's no reason to wait,' he said, his voice still gentle. 'Now's beautiful. Grab the moment.'

She rose. He put a hand out to help her but she didn't take it. She didn't dare.

He was too close. Too wet. Too... Rab.

'I'll take the leftovers up to the house,' she said, a bit too quickly.

'Of course.' The moment was over; he was starting to dress. 'It's time for this day to end. It's been momentous.'

'In a way,' she told him. 'But...you have to remember the marriage means nothing.'

'It saved this valley,' he told her. 'I think it means everything.'

But not personally, she thought as she folded the picnic rug. I might be married but nothing's changed for me.

Was she lying, even to herself?

And then her thoughts were interrupted as a cry rang out from somewhere around the bend in the river. The cry sounded so terrified that her eyes swung to Rab's in instinctive alarm.

'Trouble,' he said.

Trouble—here in paradise?

Whatever, Rab tugged on his shoes, grabbed her hand and they started to run.

CHAPTER SEVEN

IT WAS THE BLACKBERRIES. And kids.

Wiradjuri had been built on a curve of the river. Although the Finlays owned all the land, most of it was leased. The land around the house had been fenced off—a hectare or so kept for gardens—but outside the boundaries was farmland.

But just around the bend, before garden became leased land, a massive clump of blackberry briars grew by the river, clumping out around the trees overhanging the water.

These were the berries Nora had talked of the first time Rab had seen the place. What had she said? A noxious weed, but his grandfather had loved the fruit. He knew them for a problem. The fruit from wild blackberries was delicious, but if left to spread they could envelop the countryside. He'd meant to ask her to get rid of them regardless, but these last weeks had been... Well, there'd been other things on his mind.

And now he and Mia rounded the bend and saw disaster.

A group of three kids, ranging from what looked like around thirteen down to about ten, had obviously been collecting berries. They had buckets set up beside the briars. There was a dog with them, and he recognised him—Boris! Dog and kids were all staring out over the river, and the little girl was screaming.

'Get out! Harry, get out! Harry, you'll hurt yourself...'

What was happening? They were all staring out over the water.

The briars had clumped as they'd grown out, extending almost halfway across the river. The berries above the water looked massive, black, shiny and almost untouchable.

'Help me!' It was another muffled cry, coming from the centre of the briars hanging over the water. It wasn't nearly as loud as the cry from the child on the bank, but it held more terror. And pain. And, even before they reached them, Rab could guess what had happened.

The kids looked like they'd been swimming—wet hair, damp clothes, towels dumped on the riverbank. They must have had a swim and then decided to pick blackberries before going home.

A massive eucalypt grew right near the bank, and one of its branches reached out over the water. Vast, low, the limb hung enticingly above a massive clump of unpicked fruit.

And it seemed one child hadn't been able to resist. He—Harry—must have crawled out along the branch. And then slipped?

The briars were a little more than a metre below the branch, a great clump supported—sort of—by smaller bushes that had grown out over the water. A bucket lay incongruously on its side, resting on the top of the blackberry clump.

They couldn't see the child, but they had the picture. If he'd climbed out on the branch and slipped, his weight would have seen him slip into the centre of the briars. If he'd gone right through he would have ended up in the water, but the briars were thick, twined with age, impenetrable. They were strong enough to hold a child fast.

They were too strong to let a child out of their thorny grasp.

What the…? How on earth to get a child out of this?

'They're Robyn's kids,' Mia breathed, sounding horrified. 'They'll have brought our picnic and stayed.'

'Tell me about Harry,' he snapped. He needed information fast, and she understood.

'Fifteen. Good kid, responsible. Robyn would be trusting him to take care of the younger ones.'

Rab stared out over the water, his brain in overdrive, while Mia headed to the group of kids on the bank. The littlest, the only girl, melted into her arms with a shattering sob. Boris attempted to get in on the cuddle, and the two boys melted into the mix as well. It seemed Mia was known, was trusted. The relief of the group at her arrival was obvious.

'It's okay, we're here now,' Mia said, pulling back. The hugs had been necessary, but they had to move past it. 'That's Harry stuck in the bushes? Yes? Is it only Harry?'

'Yes,' one of the boys answered, turning to stare at the point where Harry had obviously disappeared. 'Mum… Mum and Dad are at the wedding and they said we could swim after bringing the picnic for you guys. Harry's got his lifesaving medallion, and all of us can swim. But we all love blackberries and Mum loves making jam, so we thought we'd bring buckets and surprise her. Will he fall out into the water? It's okay, he can swim really well.'

A child falling into the water was the least of their problems, Rab thought. A child trapped in those thorny briars was far more serious. If he struggled, these thorns were sharp enough to cut him so severely he'd…

Don't go there.

'Harry!' He raised his voice to pretty much sonic boom level. 'This is Dr Finlay. I'm here with Mia, and we're coming to get you out. But for now we need you to stay absolutely still. You're safe as long as you don't move.'

'They're sticking into me,' a terrified voice wailed. 'I'm bleeding. It hurts. I can't… I can't get out.'

'I know that,' Rab called. 'But if you move it'll be worse.'

'Harry, we're here,' Mia called out, adding her voice to Rab's. 'We're going to get you out, but you need to do what Dr Finlay says. It might take a little time to get to you though, so you have to stay still.'

'We need the fire brigade,' Rab snapped. 'Big ladders.'

'We don't have a fire brigade here,' she told him. 'Nearest is Colambool, an hour away.'

'Okay, then.' He moved on. 'Plan. You stay here and watch like a hawk. Talk to him all the time. Keep telling him he mustn't move. Can you contact his parents? Tell them where we are? Then contact anyone else with ladders, domestic ones—we can put 'em together if we must. Ropes too.'

'It'll take too long,' she said faintly. 'And I don't have my phone. Do you…?'

'You can use my phone, but I won't have stored numbers for anyone local.' He hauled it out of his pocket and tossed it to her. 'Security pin's seven-six-nine-six. Got that?'

She caught it easily. 'Seven-six-nine-six. Got it.' She took a deep breath and suddenly he was reminded of colleagues, fellow medics standing in Emergency, waiting for the arrival of trauma victims. From a shocked by-stander, she was suddenly professional. 'I know enough numbers. I'll ring the hospital,' she said briskly.

She was still holding the little girl close but her voice was clipped and sure. 'They need to be put on notice anyway, and they'll contact the hall, get the help we need. Are you going to get a ladder?'

'Even if I find it, one's useless and it'll take too much time to get up to the house and back. Okay, kids… Can you tell me your names?'

'Mack and Wally,' the older boy said. 'And Louise. I'm Mack.'

'Right, Mack and Wally, we have gear we need just around the river bend and I need your help to carry it. Louise, you stay here and keep talking to Harry.' He called out again, 'Harry, we'll be with you in about ten minutes. Can you keep absolutely still for that long? Mia will talk to you all the time, but you must keep still. I know it's hurting but it'll hurt more if you move. Can you do that?'

There was a moment's silence and then, in a quavering voice, 'Yes.'

'Good man,' Rab called. 'What a hero. Okay, Mia, over to you.'

She had no idea what he intended. He was gone and all she could do was trust him.

Trust.

It was being stretched to the limit, she thought, but that was all this day had been about. Trust.

She needed him to save the valley. She needed him to save a kid's life.

And it was as critical as that, she thought. These briars were vicious and if Harry struggled, the cuts he inflicted could well cause enough blood loss to…

Don't go there. Just trust, she told herself, as Rab was asking Harry to trust.

They had no choice.

She crouched and held Louise close—the little girl was sobbing in a mixture of fear and fright—and she talked to Harry.

'Doc Finlay's on his way. He's a big city doctor, he knows exactly what to do, and Mack and Wally are helping. They've gone to get ropes to pull you out.' She had no idea what exactly he was getting, but ropes seemed the most reassuring thing to mention. 'And hey, the bucket you dropped on the briars is still upright. I don't reckon you've dropped a single berry. Your mum and dad will feel so proud.'

But also guilty? They'd only just started to trust Harry to take care of the littlies. Robyn would be beside herself.

Recriminations, though, were for the future. For now she called on, worrying that Harry's replies were getting fainter.

But then, faster than she'd thought possible, Rab and the boys were back. Between them they were carrying the two folded deckchairs, the picnic rug and their towels.

'Hey, Harry,' Rab called the moment he came within earshot. 'We're back with gear to get you out of there. Hang on, mate, we're coming.'

No answer. There'd been no answer for a couple of minutes now. Rab's voice was grim. 'Mia, how are you at climbing?'

'Good as a monkey,' she told him. 'Or maybe better. I do rock climbing in the hills up behind the town.'

'You're kidding me, right?' There was time for a flicker of astonishment. 'Well, hooray for Mia.'

'I could climb out...'

'And pull the kid up? How big is he?'

She thought of Harry, fifteen years old, a skinny adolescent but tall for his age. There was no room for false pride here. 'Too big for me. No.'

'Okay, then.' He looked totally focused on what lay ahead. 'You're backup. I'm heading out to just above where Harry is. I'll take the picnic rug. When I'm in position, Mia, I want you and Mack to climb out after me. Mia, you'll be closest to me. Mack, you'll stay close to the bank, not above the briars. When we're in position, Wally and Louise, I want you to hand the chairs to Mack, he'll hand them to Mia and she'll hand them to me. My plan is to throw the rug down onto the briars, then lower the folded deckchairs side by side onto the rug. It'll make a platform. Then I'll slide down, lie on the platform and pull Harry out.'

You're kidding, Mia thought. The whole thing might slip. And how was he going to pull Harry out? He'd surely have the strength, but his arms… But there was no choice and she knew it. The silence from Harry was an alarm all by itself.

Without thinking, she hauled open her shirt and tugged it off, handing it over. 'Put it on back to front,' she told him brusquely. 'It shouldn't mess with your climbing—even if it catches and rips it doesn't matter. When you're ready to reach into the briars, haul the sleeves down over your hands. It's not much protection but it's better than nothing.'

But suddenly Louise was stepping back, staring at Mia's side in horror. 'What's wrong with your middle?' she gasped. 'Yuk.'

'It's not yuk,' Rab said, before Mia could even think about responding. He was already hauling on her shirt. 'Those marks are like a medal for bravery. Some people get tattoos. Some indigenous Australians use scars to show they're grownup. These are scars that show Mia is a very special person, and here she is, doing something special all over again.' He shoved his hands into her shirtsleeves, tucked the flopping front into his pants and picked up the picnic rug. 'Right, let's get Operation Rescue Harry underway.'

What followed was breathtaking in the worst kind of way. Mia was finding it really, really hard to breathe.

Rab headed out onto the branch, inching his way out over the thick, smooth surface. 'I can see him,' he called and that was a relief in itself. 'I think I can get down to him.'

Then it was her turn to climb, inching out until she was on the branch a couple of metres back from Rab. Then Mack climbed into position.

She watched as Rab lowered the rug—thick, waterproof with a tartan wool top, blessedly sturdy—onto the briars. Then Wally and Louise lifted the first deckchair out to Mack. He managed to manoeuvre it to her and she passed it on to Rab. It sounded easy, but it wasn't. They did it, though, and once it was done, Rab lowered it with care onto one side of the blanket.

Then the other. The platform was formed.

Who needed to breathe? She watched, seemingly not breathing at all, as he lowered himself down. There was a moment of heart-stopping concern as he let go of the branch, but somehow he managed to balance, lowering his weight onto both chairs. Then he was lying face down, his body over the chairs, his face free to look down.

Would his makeshift platform hold? If he pulled the boy up, would their combined weight tip the chairs?

All she could do was keep holding her breath as he pushed his shirt-covered hands down through the briars.

'Grab,' she heard him say, then again, more roughly, 'Come on, Harry, you can do this. One big effort—grab.'

And then that terrifying wait, as slowly he hauled upwards, inching backwards on the platform as he tugged, as the boy emerged from the briars, as Rab gave one final tug. And finally the kid was free, and Rab was back on the platform, holding Harry tight, man and boy a combined heap entwined on the rigid chairs.

There was a long moment of silence, where Rab simply held, cradling the boy tight against him. Where human contact must surely be the most important thing.

Safe, Mia thought dazedly. Safe!

But then Rab was pulling back, just slightly, but far enough for her to see a wash of blood against his chest. He was hauling her shirt from his arms, then using it to form a pad, applying pressure.

'He might have nicked an artery,' he called curtly, speaking up to her, but then focusing again on the boy he was treating. 'It's okay, mate,' he told Harry. 'You're safe now. We've got you. Scratches all over and your arm's cut, but we can fix this. I'll just bandage your arm and then we'll lie still until your mum and dad come with ladders and ropes to get us down.'

'I want… Mum.'

'She's coming,' Mia said, loud enough to reassure Harry. Loud enough to reassure everyone. 'Joanne at the hospital has contacted the hall. I think we'll have everyone in Cockatoo Valley here, any minute now.'

It wasn't quite that soon. It was maybe fifteen minutes before the cavalry arrived, a convoy of cars, stopping at the property gates in the distance, then bumping their way over the paddocks.

And in their midst…a crane.

Mia was still lying on the branch. She couldn't do anything. She'd sent the boys back to the bank, but she couldn't bear to be where she could no longer get a clear view of Rab or Harry. She'd eased herself further out, so she was just above them.

'Joanne's sent the crane,' she told Rab. He was lying very still, holding Harry beside him, supporting his arm, keeping it high above his head. His shirt—*her* shirt—had been fashioned into a tourniquet and the bleeding had slowed but there were so many other scratches. She knew by Rab's face that blood pressure was a problem. Dear heaven, if Rab hadn't managed to get him out…

But he was out, and now good practical help was here. She'd told Joanne, the hospital night nurse, what the problem was and Joanne, from a farm herself, had thought things out and ordered accordingly.

In one of the first cars was Doc Ewan, with Mary and Robyn and her husband. They tumbled out of the car and the kids were enveloped in hugs in seconds.

The second vehicle to arrive was a small, sturdy truck and it was loaded with a stretcher—the good one, the one they kept for hauling rock-climbers down from the steep slopes around here when they came to grief. The one with straps, hand grips, everything they needed.

Then came ladders, ropes and people. The valley's farming community had arrived here in force. And Jeff Burrows had brought his crane, which was small, tough, pretty much a bucket of rust. Its almost sole use was pulling cows out of muddy bogs, which was a neat little side earner for Jeff when the locals didn't fancy spending big on hiring one of the fancier units from Colambool.

These people were mostly farmers, practical, resourceful, eager to help, and in what seemed seconds they had things organised. The crane was in position and the stretcher was being lowered, Mia using her spot on the branch to help stabilise it.

Then Rab, somehow stable enough on his platform to manoeuvre Harry onto the stretcher, was attaching him with straps. Then the stretcher was lifted and slowly swung back across the briars with the crane above holding it steady all the way.

Hands reached out to receive it, hauling it down to the riverbank, Ewan taking charge. 'You're all right, boy, we have you, here's your mum and dad.' Robyn was hugging her son, but sensible enough to keep his arm elevated.

Ladders were being positioned over the briars, many ladders, and the crane was used again, with a harness, so Rab had a handhold while he crawled back.

Meanwhile, people were helping her back, encouraging her until her feet touched solid ground. Rab reached the bank almost as she did, and grabbed one of the towels and wrapped her with it like a shawl. He was hiding the scars she'd hardly thought of, she realised, and she felt almost pathetically grateful. There wasn't time to say so, though—he was heading for Harry.

'I'm right, Rab,' Ewan said gruffly, glancing up from where he was kneeling over Harry's stretcher. Ewan might be elderly but there was no doubting his competence, and he was now the doctor in charge. 'We'll get an IV set up, get Harry into hospital and get these cuts seen to. But, Rab, you're scratched yourself. Mia, can you take care of him?'

'Of course,' she said, and suddenly her voice was shaky. Most of the blood on Rab was Harry's, but his hands... Her shirt hadn't stopped all the damage.

She glanced around at the crowd of people. There was so much help. These kids were in safe hands.

Neither of them was needed any more.

'We'll take Boris,' she told Robyn's husband, who was standing with his arms round as many of his kids that'd fit. They didn't need a spare dog tonight. 'Ewan, are you sure you're okay without us?'

'I'm sure,' Ewan said, glancing up from the stretcher. Apart from the night shift staff, practically every member of the Cockatoo Valley Hospital was right here. 'Go, you two. Thanks for saving my grandson, Rab. I can look after my family now. It's time you took your family home.'

They abandoned the picnic gear—the night creatures could have their way with what was left, they'd collect the rest in the morning. They walked slowly back to the house. Once Mia stumbled on the rough ground between garden and house and Rab took her hand. It was an unconscious action. There was a moment's stiffening but it was getting dark. It was sensible to walk hand in hand and he felt her make the decision to relax.

He was allowed to hold her hand. Why did it feel like a momentous decision?

Family. Why were Ewan's last words resonating?

Boris walked at their heels. He'd obviously had a big day and was content to pad along behind them. Even the rabbit that shot out across their path didn't so much as raise his interest.

'He's a good dog,' Rab said into the stillness, mostly because it was something to say. Something to cut through the strange emotions this day had brought.

'He's a great dog.' Mia's hand was still in his and it felt…okay. No, it felt good. 'I was never allowed to have a dog when I was a kid. How about you?'

'Nope.' And then, because the night was very still,

because the day had been strange, because her hand was in his, he suddenly found himself talking.

'My dad was…damaged,' he said. 'You've seen the pictures of the twins. Dad's brother died when he was twelve and he was blamed. I can't begin to imagine how that felt, but it cut him off from…well, from a lot. He didn't do relationships. I was a mistake, a fleeting liaison with a woman who didn't believe in abortion but who didn't want me. So I was dumped on Dad.'

'Oh, Rab…'

'Yeah.' He shrugged, and tried to block out the sensations caused by the sudden tightening of her hand. Why was he telling her this? He didn't have a clue, but for some reason he went on.

'Anyway, I was looked after—nannies, childcare, boarding school, the best that money could buy. Some of the nannies were great. One—Luisa—took care of me from the time I was about six to when I was ten. And then she told me her mum was ill back in Switzerland and she had to go home. I felt…well, I felt gutted…but for a farewell gift she brought me a puppy.'

'That's lovely,' Mia said, and by her tone he knew she absolutely approved of the absent Luisa. 'What sort?'

'I'm not sure. A Labrador? A golden retriever? No matter, she was a silly, floppy puppy I called Lulu. Lulu had been my pet name for Luisa and it sort of worked. She had a white-tipped tail. I remember holding her at night and her tail seemed to wriggle, even in sleep.'

'But what happened?' And she knew this story had no happy ending—he knew she knew.

'Boarding school,' he said. 'I'd been a day kid—there are very few schools in Australia which take primary-aged boarders but as soon as Luisa left Dad managed it. So three weeks after Luisa left I was packed off. I remember pleading with Dad to look after Lulu and he promised she'd be taken care of. We had staff, gardeners, a housekeeper, live-in people who could look after her, but when I came home at half-term she was gone.'

'Whoa,' Mia said in a small voice. 'Oh, Rab, that sucks.'

'Yeah,' he said, but then he shrugged. They were in the house grounds now and the lawn was manicured smooth, but still he held her hand. 'But I got over it. Kids do.'

'They do,' she said, sounding stronger now. 'But wow, Rab, you've given me an object lesson.'

'How so?'

'Well,' she said as they neared the front door, 'I thought I had a rough deal as a kid, but the one thing I knew was that Mum loved me. You had what? A nanny and three weeks' worth of puppy? That doesn't come close. So guess what, suddenly I feel lucky. Thank you, Rab.'

They'd reached the veranda. He hauled out the frog key, unlocked the door and stood aside to let her pass. But, instead of going straight in, she paused for a moment and then suddenly raised herself on tiptoe and kissed him. It was fleeting, a moment's touch, and then she backed away.

'Rab, thank you,' she said softly. 'Thank you for tonight, for saving Harry. And thank you too, for marrying me. If I had to choose anyone to save the valley with, I'm very glad it was you.'

'Think nothing of it.' He tried to keep his voice light but it didn't come off. 'We need to wash.'

'So we do,' she agreed. 'Bags the bathroom first.'

'There's a shower in the washhouse outside. I can use that. Take your time.'

'Hooray.'

And he was left in the hall, looking after her.

Boris was still by his side. The big dog gave an anxious whine—this place was strange and his mistress had just departed. Rab found himself kneeling, rubbing the dog behind the ears, trying to impart comfort.

Or taking comfort? He wasn't sure. For some reason Ewan's words were still echoing in his mind.

'It's time you took your family home.'

CHAPTER EIGHT

WIRADJURI HAD BEEN built well before the fashion of en suite or even multiple bathrooms. It therefore had only the one bathroom, but the washhouse—the outside laundry— had been built with an outside shower as well. Which was great. She could do as Rab suggested and take her time getting clean.

And get her thoughts in order.

The bathroom was a picture of Colonial splendour, with a vast freestanding tub, an amazing pedestal sink and a shower big enough for two. She stood under the hot water, letting the sticky mess from blackberries and tree sap wash away, and thought she could even have shared.

As if. The emotions of the day needed time to settle— and she didn't need to get one bit closer to Rab Finlay. The outside washhouse might not be as luxurious but it was much more sensible—and sensible had to be their mantra.

When she finally emerged she almost had her head together. She donned pyjamas and a well-worn dress-ing gown—this bride had gone for the modest look in nightwear—and headed to the kitchen, where she found Boris already snoozing under the table, and Rab setting out coffee mugs.

He wasn't looking as modest as she was. He was wearing a clean pair of jeans, but nothing else.

She had a flashback to the sight of him lifting Harry up through the briars—no mean feat, but Rab had pulled him as if he weighed nothing. The sheer strength of the man had astonished her then, and the sight of his body now... Well, it was a body most women would take more than a cursory look at. Gorgeous didn't begin to cut it, and the mass of scratches on his back did nothing to take away the effect of utter...sexiness.

He had his back to her. She stood in the doorway and watched him for a moment, and the realisation suddenly slammed home. *This man is my husband.*

There was still a trickle of fear in the thought, but also...

No! She wasn't going down that road. Not ever.

Sensible, she thought frantically. Sensible!

Thankfully, Ewan's question came back to her, the elderly doctor's request that she check Rab's cuts and scratches. *'Mia, can you take care of him?'* With a certain amount of effort she let herself think, That's why I'm here. Otherwise she could have gone straight to bed, not come in search of him.

But...would she? Liar, liar, pants on fire, she said under her breath, but then she dived back into the safe thought that they'd been through trauma, and after trauma medics needed to debrief. She *should* have come to find him, even if there weren't scratches all down his back which she needed to treat.

But then he turned, and smiled, and all those logical, reasonable excuses disappeared.

'Tea or coffee?' he asked. The prosaic question should have steadied her but it did no such thing.

'I...yes. Tea. Please.' She paused for a moment and

took a long, steadying breath, during which she gave herself a rapid and extremely stern talking-to. Get a grip, woman. 'But I need to clean those scratches'

'That's why I left my shirt off,' he told her. 'I've done my front but I need antiseptic on my back. I could use your help.'

'Let's do it before tea,' she said, thinking the quicker she got this over with the better.

He was already prepared. He had a basin of hot, soapy water, antiseptic, dressings, tweezers. She winced when she saw the tweezers.

'A couple on my arms had a bit of debris in them,' he explained, and she nodded and attempted to flick an internal switch and become a professional.

'Right. Sit and let me see.'

So he sat, and she stood in her faded dressing gown and checked out every inch of him. Or—thankfully— from his waist up. 'I wear heavy denim for a reason,' he told her.

'Are you sure?' The combination of his shirt and hers hadn't protected him enough.

'I'm sure,' he growled, and she even managed a grin as she moved from scratch to scratch. She was carefully swabbing, making sure nothing was left of the vicious thorns, then applying antiseptic, focusing carefully only on the damage. The growl had been one of defence, and she thought of the many men she'd treated in her career and their reluctance to drop their pants for medical reasons.

'I had a farmer come into Emergency once after a run-in with stinging nettles,' she told him. 'Apparently he was caught short out in the paddocks and didn't notice where he was squatting. His hind quarters were a mess—in the end we gave him antihistamine because it was a severe

allergic reaction—but it took us twenty minutes before
he let us see. Doc Ewan was away, there was only me and
Issy. His reaction was so severe we suspected snake bite,
but would he let us look? In the end I had to threaten to
bring in the cavalry to hold him down. Marion and Kate
from the kitchen. They'd have loved it but he caved before we could call them.'

'You don't need the cavalry for me,' he told her hast-
ily. 'I swear the denim did its job.'

'Lucky you,' she told him and went back to swabbing.
'Ouch. Rab, I'm so sorry you had to do this. Digging
your hands through those thorns... You deserve a medal.'

It had been little short of heroic, she thought, shoving
his arms down through the thorns.

'There was no choice. All I can say is thanks be that
we were there,' he told her. 'And hooray, there's another
bonus of our marriage.'

'There are surely bonuses all over the place,' she retorted but her voice must have been strained because he
swivelled in his chair and looked up at her.

'Mia, we have done the right thing,' he said gently.
'You call me brave? What you've done is far, far braver.
I promise you won't regret it. Ever.'

And what was there in that that made her eyes well?
She blinked and blinked again and then applied herself
to the very technical detail of putting a plaster on one of
the deeper scratches on his arm.

'Not so bad,' he told her, looking down at her handi-
work. 'I owe you a new shirt.'

'Yeah, well, we owe you the valley.'

'Maybe we both need to forget that,' he told her. 'Mia,
let's call it quits with the gratitude and get on with...a
year of being friends?'

She took a deep breath. 'I can live with that.'

'Excellent.' She finished his arm, the last of the wounds, and straightened. He rose. 'Right then, what about you?'

'What about me?'

'You crawled on your stomach out along the branch with no shirt on. That bark was rough and there were briars creeping over. I saw blood before you put the towel back over.'

'You put the towel back over—for which I'm grateful—and I'm fine.' She had been scratched—she'd seen grazes while she'd showered but there was no way...

'You winced then as you stood back. You'll have scratched scar tissue. Mia, I'm not letting you go to bed without checking. Fair's fair.'

'I don't need to be checked, and there's no cavalry here to make me submit,' she said, glowering. The thought of him seeing her scars close-up was intimidating. 'Only Boris, though Boris would hardly protect me.'

'He looks like he would though,' he said thoughtfully, glancing to where Boris was sleeping off his Very Big Day. 'Is that why you got such a big dog? To protect you?'

And there it was again, that flash of fear that was always with her. Harvey in court, yelling as he was led away to start years in prison. 'I'll come for you, you b...'

'Boris is great at cuddling,' she told him, but he was looking at her in an odd way. As if he were trying to figure a puzzle.

'So you got him for cuddles?'

'Yep.' She hesitated. 'Like you should have had with Lulu. I'm very sorry you had to lose her. But I'm fine, Rab. Really. I'll forgo the tea, if you don't mind. I need to go to bed.'

'Mia?'

'Yes.'

'I don't need the cavalry. I'll either check those scratches or I'll pick you up and carry you to the hospital and find someone there who can do it. Choose.'

'Rab...'

'I'm your friend,' he told her gently. 'I've seen your face and I've seen the scars on your side. There's no shock and no shame. Let me see the damage you did tonight.'

'But not my butt or my breasts,' she told him. 'I was wearing jeans and bra all the time. There are no scratches under.'

'Promise?'

'I promise.'

'I'll believe you,' he told her. 'But your back, arms and upper and lower chest. Let's see, Mia.'

'Fine,' she said ungratefully and tugged her pyjama top off, hugged it across her breasts and sat where he'd been sitting. 'Do it.'

Apart from the burns specialist she'd had to visit occasionally for checks on the grafts, no one had seen her chest and side for almost ten years. She was appalled that on this first night of her marriage Rab had seen them, once while they'd swum and now at close range.

The oil had hit her shoulder, splashed up to her face then dripped down over her chest. Her shoulder was a mass of scar tissue. It still had the capacity to make her feel ill when she caught sight of it in the mirror.

But Rab made no comment. He was a surgeon, she told herself. He'd have seen worse, and he was surely treating her now as a doctor. The same way she'd treated him in her role as medic.

Yeah, right. As if she could have cleaned those

scratches without that little voice in the back of her head reminding her, *This guy's my husband.*

He wouldn't think anything of it. He had no traumatic marriage in the past, but he must have had lots of girl-friends. She'd known and treated his grandfather and she'd asked about his family. She'd heard the old man's bitterness.

'There's only my grandson and he's a bloody playboy, exactly like his father.'

So Rab had had plenty of women, beautiful women at a guess. He wouldn't be looking at her now as anything but someone he needed to treat.

She sat stock-still while he carefully examined the graze across her chest where she'd dragged herself out along the branch. Rab had done it easily but she'd clung like a limpet and without her shirt her skin—especially the fragile graft skin—had been damaged.

'It's only superficial,' he told her, swabbing with anti-septic. 'But it'll probably weep. I'll put a dressing across the whole graft. It'll protect your sheets if nothing else.'

'Thank you,' she said and sat some more while his skilled surgeon's hands did their thing. And there was no reason why her skin tingled at his touch, why this feel-ing was suddenly overwhelming her, this sensation that she was…being cared for.

And not medically. What she was feeling was not re-motely similar to how she'd felt as doctors in the past had examined, touched, treated.

'I'm your friend,' he'd said, and it was somehow en-veloping her like a warm mist, a fuzzy wrap that made the day's myriad emotions fade to nothing. She needed to think nothing, do nothing, feel nothing… Except that

wasn't quite right. Feeling was everything—the soft touch of his fingers, the sensation that he cared.

Her husband.

And that shook her back into reality. She remembered that first night with Harvey. *'I'm your husband.'*

She couldn't stop the shiver and Rab must have felt it. He finished fastening the dressing and stepped back.

'Done. Now tea.'

'I don't think I want…'

'I'm very sure you do,' he told her, and she watched as he made tea, loaded it with sugar, put it in front of her and then watched her as he drank his. It was late at night, they were drinking tea together, he was her husband…

'He wasn't your husband,' Rab said as she set down her mug, and her eyes flew to his. How could he have guessed her thoughts? 'He was a lying piece of filth, and you were never married. What you and I have—this is a contract between adults, between friends, and you're not to think of it as anything else.'

He rose and picked up her mug and set it in the sink, then came around to help her to her feet. Using her good arm, he gently propelled her up, as if he guessed that her world right now seemed weirdly shaky.

'Go to bed, now, Mia,' he told her. 'Today we've saved your valley and we've also saved one trapped kid. That's a great day in anyone's estimation. Well done, Mia, and well done us. Do you think you can sleep?'

'I… Yes.' The sensation of his hand on her arm was doing her head in. He was too big, too bare, too…male.

'Then sleep, Mia,' he told her softly, and before she guessed what he intended he leaned forward and kissed her.

It was as hers had been, once again the lightest of kisses, lips barely brushing her hair, and then he was stepping away from her, smiling with that oh, so amazing smile.

'You've saved the world today, my brave Mia,' he told her. 'What on earth shall we do tomorrow to follow up?'

CHAPTER NINE

How do you know that you're falling in love? Does it take a moment, a sudden flash of certainty? Or does it take a slow dawning, that here might be a woman to cherish for the rest of your life?

Someone he wished to care for—for ever? Was that what love was? Best guess, he supposed it was.

He was sitting on the bank of a meandering creek, among the rocky crags and magnificent bushland that formed the headwaters of the river that burbled its way down to the valley below.

Mia was maybe twenty metres above his head, abseiling down a cliff face. He had no wish to join her and she, having talked him into trying and then watched the grim-faced ascent he'd attempted a couple of months back, had agreed he wasn't meant to be a climber. It hadn't stopped him joining her, though. This Sunday afternoon was now one of many.

The last six months had passed faster than he'd thought possible. He'd imagined he'd leave his high-powered city medicine, help a bit at the hospital, keep up the pretence of being a married couple, maybe do a spot of study and put his life on hold for a year. Instead, he surely hadn't put his life on hold. For now at least, this was life itself.

Part of that life was Mia, and she certainly hadn't put her life on hold either. She hadn't kept still for a moment.

'If I have free board for a year I might as well make myself useful,' she'd decreed within days of moving into Wiradjuri.

The gardens had been maintained by Nora, but the house itself had suffered decades of neglect. That first morning, after the drama of the blackberries, he'd woken late to find her deep in soot, intent on cleaning out the ancient fire stove.

'It's fantastic,' she'd told him and pointed in disgust at the grimy two-ring burner his grandfather had obviously used. 'He used that when he had an Aga! Wow, Rab, wait till I get it working, these things are awesome.'

'So you're intending to spend the first day of your honeymoon cleaning my stove,' he'd said faintly, and she'd grinned. There'd been a smudge of soot on her nose. She was filthy. She must still be hurting from the grazes she'd suffered the night before, but she'd looked...happy.

'Yep,' she'd told him. 'At the end of the year I'll be leaving you with a legacy. No matter what you do with this place, it'll look fantastic. And I'll love doing it, Rab,' she'd told him, seeing his look of doubt. 'I can't bear standing still.'

She couldn't. She'd thrown herself headlong into the restoration of the old house, and he'd been slowly caught up in her enthusiasm. He found himself painting with her, scrubbing, hauling up old carpets and sanding ancient floorboards. Enjoying himself.

The medicine too... The little hospital was magnificently run but it had taken him only days to realise how much more service it could provide with two doctors instead of one. Mia hadn't been backward in drawing him into that. He'd imagined his surgery skills would be put on the backburner for a year, but she'd had none of it.

'Ewan has anaesthetist skills,' she'd told him. 'The locals hate leaving the valley for health care, so why not do the smaller stuff here?'

He did, and there was enough demand to keep his skills up. As well, he found himself enjoying the normal demands of family medicine. He enjoyed even more the house calls Ewan had tentatively asked him to share, driving across the valley to treat people at home.

He'd never thought of it—the huge advantage of patients being able to stay in their own homes while they either recovered from accidents or illnesses, or faded towards end of life. It hadn't taken him long to realise what a gift it was.

The first few times Mia had accompanied him. 'You know Doc Finlay? He's one of us now. I've come with him just to make sure he doesn't muck up. He's a city doctor, you know, and who can tell what weird new-fangled treatments he might try out on you.'

Mia's infectious cheer, her laughter, her care, had made such visits relaxed and fun. It had taken few such house calls to realise how much she was loved, and when she'd decreed he'd graduated into doing them on his own he'd felt more than a stab of loss.

But then there'd been the weekends. If it rained they stayed at Wiradjuri and worked inside, but if the day was fine Mia would be tossing her climbing gear into the back of her little Mini and heading for the hills.

For the first few weeks he'd assumed she'd want space and he'd watched her go in silence, thinking she probably needed time without him, but every time she'd come back exhausted but with a glow of peace and satisfaction. It had him intrigued.

'It's awesome out there,' she'd said one Saturday evening as she tucked into the casserole he'd prepared—the initial plan had been to eat separately but that had pretty much dissolved the first time she'd tasted his cooking. 'You should come.'

'How on earth did you get into rock climbing?'

'I did all sorts of stuff to get my strength back,' she told him. 'Rehab started it, and then the need to fend for myself. I learned karate first.' She grinned. 'So maybe I should warn you—don't mess with me. I'm a fourth dan karate black belt. You don't know what that means? Just hope you never get to find out.' She chuckled. Maybe the look on his face warranted it—he surely hadn't been able to hide his incredulity. 'And then I got distracted by other things,' she'd told him. 'Climbing's awesome.'

He'd felt...stunned. 'Karate. Rock climbing.' He'd had to know more. 'Would you mind if I join you?'

'Of course not. Why should I?'

So the next day they'd headed out together. Boris was thus relegated to the back seat of the Mini. He was almost glowering with displeasure—it was a tight squeeze—but at least he was happy to be with his two favourite people.

'He's falling for you,' Mia had said comfortably. 'Mind, I've seen you feeding him toast. Give Boris toast and he's anybody's.'

Then she'd introduced him to her world. She climbed like she'd been born to it, but he'd tried and fast decided he was all for keeping his feet safely on the ground.

It didn't worry her. She was an independent woman, he thought, watching her now as she abseiled down the cliff she'd just spider-climbed her way up. She didn't need him watching over her. But at some point in the past few months he'd begun to realise that he wouldn't mind if she did.

They'd been six months married. She talked of the end of their marriage with nonchalance.

'I'm going to miss Wiradjuri when I go back to my place,' she'd said a few weeks ago. She'd hauled a great dust-covered chandelier—a chandelier, for heaven's sake!—down from the ceiling of the drawing room and was lovingly polishing each crystal. 'This is awesome,' she'd said. 'I'm sure you can buy them in plastic, but if I hung something like this in my little cottage I'd have to duck every time I made myself a cup of tea.'

But there'd been no regret in her voice. No envy. Just a statement of fact.

Which was what she was all about, he thought as he watched her. She hardly seemed to look forward or look back. She was smart, loyal and kind. She was also funny, but it seemed to him that she carried her gentle humour almost as armour.

And she still needed that armour, he thought. He saw the ache in her arms at the end of a day's climbing, how she hugged herself when she thought he couldn't see. He thought of what she was doing now, climbing, stretching that inelastic scar tissue to the limit. He thought of the emotional scars inside, and the more he knew her, the more he wanted to protect her...hold her.

But she didn't want to be held. He knew that. That first night, when he'd kissed her, that faint brush of lips on her hair, he'd seen her reaction. She'd kissed him but that had been on her terms. When he'd kissed her...

She didn't want it. This year was working only because they were acting as friends, nothing more.

He was starting to want...more.

'Hey!' She was on the ground again, struggling to rid herself of her harness and bouncing happily back to where he'd set up their picnic rug. 'That was fabulous.

You should see the view from the top. You two lazy-bones are missing out on so much.' She plonked herself down, dived into the picnic basket and retrieved a sandwich. 'Yum.'

'Boris and I walked right up to the top of the falls,' he said, with dignity. 'We probably ended up higher than you, and we didn't risk calling the Angels of Mercy once.'

'You mean you're doing a public service by not risking calling the emergency services?' Her voice was muffled by sandwich.

'Exactly.'

'You're a pair of wusses,' she told him and grinned and then turned back to look out over the valley. 'This is the best. My happy place.'

And there was that thought again… Was he falling in love?

He'd thought he was in love before. He and Annabel had been part of the same set at university—they'd been friends. They'd had fun together, started their medical lives together, worked hard, played hard and finally moved in together. But almost as soon as they had, things had started to seem…distant. He remembered a creeping sense of claustrophobia he couldn't shake.

He remembered that last night. He'd come home late after an appalling shift at the hospital. A car crash. Three children dead, one under his hands on the operating table. He'd been sick with the horror.

Annabel had found him at three in the morning, sitting on the balcony, drinking whisky, staring at nothing.

'Why didn't you wake me?' she'd asked.

'We don't both need to be upset.'

She'd tried to take him into her arms, but he couldn't let his body melt into hers. The horror was too real. The only way he could deal with it was to hold himself tight, internalise the pain, scrunch it into a tight ball and tuck it where it couldn't be seen.

The next day he'd walked and walked, and when he'd finally returned to their apartment something seemed to have died within them both.

Annabel was still his friend, but she was happily married now, to another friend, Max. He'd attended their wedding and Max had come up to him afterwards, enveloped him in a man hug and thanked him—for not marrying her. 'She says you guys broke up because you didn't need her. You must have had rocks in your head, mate, but I'm grateful. I need this woman so much—I'm just so lucky she needs me right back.'

There'd been tears in Max's eyes as he'd gazed at his bride, but Rab hadn't understood how anyone could show emotion like that. He still didn't.

Love?

But now he was watching a woman, grubby with exertion, eating a mammoth ham and pickle sandwich while she absentmindedly rubbed her bad shoulder with her free hand. His heart was twisting with feelings he was struggling to deal with. He'd never expected this, never wanted it, but now…

Mia made it quite clear that she valued her independence above all else. He'd held that as inviolable, but watching her enjoy her sandwich, watching her turn her face to soak in the glint of sunlight through the trees, he was feeling things and he didn't have a clue how to deal with them.

He was thinking of Max's long-ago emotion. And he was starting to feel…the same?

No. Max had talked as if he needed Annabel.

Could Mia need him?

Her hand was still rubbing her shoulder absentmindedly, as if this was a long-term ache, something she barely thought about. Which was exactly what it was, he thought. Her scars, physical and emotional, were just a part of her.

'Let me do it,' he said, and moved to her side, removing her hand and letting his fingers massage what he knew was the scar tissue under her windcheater. He couldn't see it—after that first night when she'd reluctantly agreed to let him clean her grazes she'd stayed firmly covered. Now he felt her whole body stiffen.

'Hey, I'm a crap climber,' he told her. 'But I once did a massage course. Actually, a girlfriend and I both did one. We thought it might improve our relationship.'

'And did it?' She was still stiff.

'Nope,' he said cheerfully. 'Annabel thought the masseur was the sexiest guy she'd ever met. Obviously her heart wasn't in it.'

'Obviously.' She thought about it for a bit. 'So if you'd been a bit sexier you might be married to someone called Annabel.'

'I guess.' Who knew?

She turned and gave him a thoughtful look, seemingly assessing all of him.

'Yeah,' she said and grinned. 'I get that.'

'You don't think I'm sexy?'

'Hey, I'm not allowed to think you're sexy. This is a marriage of convenience.'

'But if it wasn't?'

'How can I tell? I haven't even seen you in pyjamas yet.'

'You've seen me in less than my PJs.'

'Not the same,' she said, definitely.

'You can tell a man's sexy by the pyjamas he wears?'

'Certainly you can,' she told him. 'Let me tell you,

very few men can carry PJs off, and I'm speaking from the position of someone who's checked out thousands. The number of pyjamas-clad guys I've seen in my lifetime...'

He thought of his pyjamas. He usually slept without anything, but he did own one set. Boxers and T-shirt. There'd been a Kris Kringle at the hospital last year and his senior anaesthetist, a woman in her sixties, had drawn his number. He'd opened her gift at the theatre staff's Christmas party and the T-shirt's logo had been received with howls of mirth: *Keep talking. I'm diagnosing you.*

It had been a crack at his distancing. The theatre staff—almost a family they spent so much time together—gave him a hard time. 'We find the juiciest gossip and all you do is listen. We know you listen to everyone. How about sharing?'

That was pretty much the same accusation Annabel had thrown at him, but now... He was looking at Mia in the sunlight, he was feeling the tension in her shoulders and he thought maybe it wouldn't hurt to try and lessen the distance.

'Mia, what would you say if I asked you out on a date?' he asked, tentatively because it seemed like an infringement on the rules they'd carefully set themselves. He didn't want to mess with that. He couldn't.

'A date.' His hands were still on her shoulders, but he felt her stiffen again.

'Yep.' There was a moment's silence and then he added, 'It's what happens when a boy meets a girl and he wants to get to know her better.'

'You don't think living in the same house for six months could do the same thing?'

'I think living in the same house for six months has made me realise I'd like to get to know you better.'

'I don't want...' She'd practically frozen. He had the sense to remove his hands and back away a little.

'You don't want to get to know me better?'

'Rab, I can't.'

'Because?'

'I don't need anyone.'

He thought she did but he wasn't going there. 'I don't need anyone either,' he told her. 'But it doesn't stop me thinking...what we have...it could be good.'

'Or it could be a disaster.'

'Would one date, where we let ourselves be...open to possibilities...necessarily risk disaster? It'd be like web dating. We come with a list of prepared questions and see if there's the faintest possibility we might be compatible.'

'I already know you're afraid of heights. How compatible's that?'

'And you're grumpy before your first coffee in the morning,' he retorted. 'But there'll be other questions, I'm sure.'

'You're thinking of the compatibility of sharing the one toothpaste tube?'

'No!' he said with haste, and she chuckled.

'There you go then. Totally incompatible. Do you know how much waste there is in toothpaste tubes? The one advantage of sharing would be buying those huge ones, but the squeezing has to be done at the bottom.'

'Obviously incompatible,' he agreed, and his gaze caught hers and held. In challenge? 'But we could put it on our list to discuss. One date, Mia. If our lists coincide, then maybe another date in a fortnight or so? Another list. There's no rush, Mia, but maybe...' He hesitated but decided there was no point in not saying it. 'Mia, we have six months. The way I'm feeling...'

'You shouldn't be feeling.' She sounded all at once

terrified. 'I told you. This is a business arrangement. No emotions.'

'There aren't any emotions,' he told her. 'And there won't be in the future if that's what you want, but now we're at the six-month mark…would it be possible to have dinner, check our lists and recalibrate?' And then he smiled, holding her gaze, trying to win a smile in return. 'There's actually a magnificent restaurant in Colambool. Rhonda was telling me she and Gary went there a few weeks back to celebrate their wedding anniversary. She says you'd love it.'

'Have you been talking about me to Rhonda?'

'Hey, not guilty.' Discussing Mia—discussing anyone but patients—well, that pyjama top held some truth. 'But she talks to me about you. She said she's never seen you go out on a date in the almost ten years she's known you, and if I wanted a place to celebrate our six-month anniversary…'

'Oh, for heaven's sake…'

'So how about it?' he asked and discovered he was holding his breath.

She stared at him. He could still see a trace of panic in her gaze but there was something else. An internal war?

She'd had such trauma. How tempting would it be to step, just for a moment, into a place where she could do something she'd never done—go to a fancy restaurant on a date? How simple was that?

But, almost unconsciously, her hand went to her face, to her scarring. No to that, he thought savagely, and he put his own hand up to cover hers.

'Mia,' he said gently, 'you're beautiful. You're a brave, fun woman who climbs cliffs that take my breath away. You should know that you're stunning. How about accepting that about yourself, at least, just for one night, and come out and just have fun? Do you have the courage to do that?'

Their hands stayed where they were, hers on her face, his covering hers. Their gazes stayed locked.

Please.

It was an internal plea and it reverberated over and over in his head. For some reason this seemed one of the most important moments in his life.

Please...

And finally, finally she closed her eyes. She lifted her hand from her cheek and pushed his hand away at the same time, and then she opened her eyes and gave a firm businesslike nod.

'I guess you did try and climb the cliffs with me,' she managed. 'I suppose I can at least try your fancy restaurant.'

He grinned, aware of a surge of pleasure totally out of proportion to the concept of one woman accepting one date.

'And your list?'

'My list's easy,' she told him. 'Independence.'

'Let's start with toothpaste and work up,' he suggested. 'Who knows, Mia? Anything's possible.'

CHAPTER TEN

Wʜᴀᴛ ᴛᴏ ᴡᴇᴀʀ on a date?

Why to think about even going on a date?

Whoa.

She should have pulled out. It was a dumb thing to do, breaking every rule she'd made for herself regarding relationships. Never look at a man that way. Never think about being anything other than totally independent.

On Monday she'd woken resolved to tell him to forget the idea. Unfortunately there'd been an early morning call and Rab had left in a hurry. An appendectomy. Then she'd arrived at work herself, to a frantic call from the principal of the local school. Three kids had arrived with a rash and the principal was panicking. Measles?

Measles was unlikely—as far as Mia knew, almost every kid in the valley was vaccinated—but with Rab and Ewan both caught up with the appendectomy she'd headed to the school herself.

It took time to get the story out of kids who'd been told not to deviate as they'd walked to school, but it finally emerged. It seemed the kids had detoured to roll down grassy slopes in a nearby freshly mown paddock. This looked like some sort of allergic reaction to one of the grasses. As soon as she had the truth she administered antihistamine. The rashes had started fading almost straight away, but it had taken more time to reassure the principal and three lots of worried parents.

By the time she'd got back to the hospital Rab had already made the booking at the restaurant—and worse! Rhonda's sister-in-law was, apparently, a chef there and had taken Rab's call. And had immediately rung Rhonda. 'Hey, guess who we have coming?'

Mia was a loved figure in the valley. As a whole, the valley's population was intrigued and delighted with this marriage of convenience—not only had it saved the valley but it had also brought them another doctor. Now, with the valley realising there was only six months left before Dr Finlay was due to leave again, pretty much every staff member was egging them on to make the arrangement permanent. The news of the restaurant booking had thus spread all over the hospital by lunch time.

By the end of that Monday almost every female member of staff had put in their opinion of what she should wear, and by the time she finally saw Rab she'd realised he was getting the same treatment. He'd even been looking a bit…hunted.

Which had sort of made her laugh. Which had sort of made it impossible to disappoint everyone by saying she was pulling out.

So here she was, the night of the…date, staring into the mirror at a Mia she didn't recognise.

At Maira?

Her old name was suddenly echoing in her head, almost with longing. It was the name she'd discarded along with her identity when she'd moved here. Harvey was a control freak, a possessive, violent bully. She'd received a few messages in those early days, notes appearing from prison, via sources the police couldn't trace. He blamed her for his prison sentence and he still thought he owned her. 'I bought you for your father's debt,' he'd told her. 'And I'll come for you. No matter where you are, no matter how long it takes, you're mine.'

'We'll protect you as much as we can,' the authorities had told her when she'd shown them. 'It's nine years till he's due for parole though. Hopefully he'll have moved on.'

She knew Harvey, though, and she knew he wouldn't move on. She needed to protect herself. A name-change?

So she'd become Mia, a quiet, hard-working nurse in remote New South Wales. Mia, not related to Maira.

Mia, who was standing in front of the mirror now, looking at herself in a dress Rhonda had found when she'd browbeaten her into taking a shopping trip to Colambool.

'Something smart but plain,' Mia had decreed, and Rhonda and the shop assistant had raised their eyebrows and proceeded to ignore her. 'I reckon this'd suit you,' Rhonda had said.

The dress was crimson, elegant—and maybe it was a little bit plain, except what it did for her wasn't plain. Mia had slipped it on and almost gasped.

It had a hint of the oriental, a mandarin collar, with a slit down her throat so she could just see a hint of the swell of her breasts. It had three-quarter sleeves with a line of tiny slits all the way down. She could see a hint of bare arm but not enough to reveal the scarring underneath.

And the rest of the dress—yes, it was plain, but it was *her* dress. It fitted her as if it had been stitched onto her, every curve delineated, clinging close to her knees, with a final slit on the side allowing a glimpse of thigh as she moved.

She'd stared at it in the shop and she'd felt...panicked. But also something else.

A longing to be Maira again?

Or someone else entirely?

Rhonda had also towed her to the hairdresser. 'Let's just see if there's a way you can wear it that's a bit sexier than a braid.'

She'd lost thirty centimetres of her hair, removing enough weight to allow her to play with it. The stylist had shown her how to twist it into a loose knot but tease a few curls down, their twisting enough to distract from the scarring on her face. They were still there, the scars, but as she looked at herself in the mirror now she thought, *This is what I could have been. I could have been Maira.*

Enough introspection. She took a deep breath, slipped on the shoes Rhonda had decreed she bought as well—glossy black stilettos, for heaven's sake!—and she walked back out to the living room.

To Rab.

He turned to face her—and froze.

The sight of him was enough to freeze her as well, she thought. He was wearing the suit he'd worn for the wedding. He looked stunning, absurdly handsome, the kind of man any woman would be proud to be seen with.

And the thought was suddenly front and centre.

He was her husband.

'Mia!' He said her name almost as a sigh. He didn't have to compliment, didn't have to say she looked beautiful. His expression said it all.

And just for a moment she forgot the scars. She was Maira again, a kid leafing through those magazines her mother had brought home, looking at lives she could never have but allowed to dream. Maybe she could dream again. Just for tonight, she told herself. One night…

'Hey, we scrub up okay,' she managed, trying to break

the moment—because it had to be broken. Even if he was looking at her…like that…it was just a dream.

'We do indeed,' he said, and he sounded as if he was feeling pretty much the same. 'Mia, you're always beautiful, but tonight…'

'Dress-ups,' she said, almost roughly. 'I'll be back in scrubs on Monday. This is one night only.'

'Then let's make the most of it,' he told her. 'My car, Mia, because I refuse to take you looking like this in a car that smells like dog.'

'There's an insult,' she said and grinned down at Boris, who was sniffing her legs with faint interest. Her legs obviously smelled…different.

Of course they did, she thought. Everything she wore was different. For this night, everything about her seemed different.

'I've bought you a great bone to make up for our desertion,' she told Boris, speaking a bit too fast, diving for the refrigerator, forcing herself to be prosaic. 'Okay. Let's give the dog a bone and we can go.'

She'd never been on a 'date', and if this was to be the first then hopefully it would be a good one.

Mia's life was divided into two sections, Harvey and post Harvey. Even post Harvey he'd controlled her actions. She was determined to stay independent for the rest of her life. What she was doing tonight was risky, an aberration, but now she'd agreed to it there was no reason why she shouldn't enjoy it, was there?

If there was, it certainly wasn't caused by the restaurant. Mountain Hollow was one of those places written up in trendy magazines as a destination in itself, a foody paradise as well as a location to die for. It was settled in a hollow in the mountains behind Colambool. Built on a platform overlooking the same river that ran down to Cockatoo Valley, it was almost completely disguised by thick bushland. Cars were parked at the top of the slope and a gorgeous path, lit by demure side lights, led the way downward.

The restaurant itself looked welcoming but plain. It was only when you walked inside that you saw the view below, the tumbling waters of the falls, the boulder-strewn river, the whole lit by lights that seemed so natural they looked almost like stars drifting down from the night sky.

She and Rab were ushered to a table right by the window, where the tree tops were so close she felt she could almost touch them. Rab held the chair for her. She sat, feeling like she'd stepped into another world, as outside the window a couple of tiny sugar gliders hung on a branch and peered in.

'They're admiring your dress,' Rab said, and she looked quickly at him and found he was smiling. He must be used to this sort of place, she told herself.

'It's stunning,' he said, and she knew then that he wasn't used to it. That this was taking his breath away too.

'How did you find out about it?' she breathed.

'Rhonda. Remember?'

'Of course.' And the fact that Rhonda's sister-in-law was a chef here—that'd explain why they had what was obviously the best table in the house.

Weirdly, that knowledge made her feel better. That it wasn't completely down to Rab. He wasn't pulling the strings.

Was he?

'I feel a bit like Cinderella,' she confessed. 'Any minute now you'll look across the table and find I've turned into a pumpkin.'

He smiled but shook his head. 'No chance. Not here. Rhonda assured me there's a choice on the menu, and I can't abide pumpkin. One of my nannies thought pumpkin soup was easy to make and good for me. Pumpkin is definitely banned from this table.'

The look on his face made her chuckle, and suddenly it was okay. Not so much a date then, she told herself. Just a special night out with a guy who'd become…a friend.

And then the waiter bore down on them with a menu to make her gasp—there was no pumpkin in sight! Champagne was poured and she decided to forget about Cinderella-like transitions. She was twenty-nine and she'd never been in a place like this before. Rab was a friend, a gorgeous, handsome male, but still just a friend for all that. And there were decisions to be made. Lobster patties as entrée? Why not?

She glanced again at Rab and he was smiling. Just at her.

And—just for this night—she tilted her chin and smiled back, a wide, all-encompassing smile that seemed to almost break something inside her. Leaving her… open?

No. Nothing was changing, this was just a fabulous night.

Cinderella? Bring it on, she told herself. Pumpkins could wait.

She was gorgeous. What was more, she seemed to have decided to make the most of every minute of this night.

She was eating as if she were in a dream, savouring each mouthful, and as he watched her, weirdly, he also found himself thinking of Cinderella. She looked as if she were drifting in a fairy tale from which she expected to emerge, if not at midnight then some time in the future. Soon?

And his own thoughts crystallised. The more he watched her, the more he wanted to make that fairy tale real. To make her safe, happy, secure. To care for her, to cherish her, to look after her for ever. Surely she deserved it.

This feeling had been growing on him for months and tonight, watching her glow with happiness, watching her shrug off the air of defensiveness that she almost always had, he knew for certain.

He wanted her for always.

He couldn't say it now, though. It'd be rushing her, to take this first night when she'd lowered her defences and try to push it further. So he ate and drank and talked and laughed and the night seemed to melt into a pool of perfection. And when coffee was served, along with tiny strawberry and chocolate meringues, barely a taste but just enough to end the perfect dinner, he thought he didn't want this night to end. Ever.

'Walk down to the river with me,' he suggested, and she looked startled.

'Can we?'

'We can.' He'd checked this place out on the website. The pathway they'd used from the car park meandered on, still lit, so they could walk right down to the flood-lit waterfall.

There was a moment's hesitation—and then came that smile again, the relaxed smile that seemed so rare it was a jewel itself.

'Why not?' she whispered, and it was as if she were talking to herself. And he knew she was, and he also knew that he was blessed.

'I'm wearing high heels, in case you hadn't noticed.'

'I had noticed.' Wow, had he noticed. 'But I'm here to help you.'

He rose and held out his hand. That brought another moment's hesitation, and he could almost hear the words echoing in her head.

Why not?

Let's put the risk aside.

They walked silently down the path leading to the falls. Still hand in hand, because the path wasn't exactly flat and her heels *were* high, so surely holding his hand was... sensible?

There was near silence, apart from the sound of water tumbling into the pool below the falls, then splashes as the flow rippled along the rock-strewn stream beside the path. Then there were the whispers of night creatures, possums, sugar gliders, rock wallabies, creatures who could see them but were safe in the undergrowth. Once a tiny echidna waddled across the path in front of them, and behind came its harassed mum, obviously fretting about these human intruders in her domain.

The sight made Mia smile. The night made her smile. The feel of Rab's hand holding hers made her feel... cherished?

Cherished. What would it be like to be cherished by such a man? To let go of her rigid control. To let her hand lie where it was...for ever.

No. The night was a dream. This whole scene was a dream, part of a fantasy that surely had to shatter, but not yet. Please not yet.

And then they reached the foot of the falls. The clever lights were shimmering from above, not so bright that they disturbed the night but enough to shimmer and twin-kle on the foam of falling water.

They stood silently, watching, taking in its beauty. Almost unconsciously, Rab's arm came around her and she let herself sink against him. His warmth. His strength.

It was fine. No, it was better than fine, and she had no need to worry. For now, this was indeed a fairy tale. She'd wake at midnight—or even tomorrow, she thought dreamily, if she let this fairy tale continue. But for tonight…

His arm tightened and he twisted her so he was gazing down at her.

'Mia,' he said softly, 'I really want to kiss you.'

'I guess that's good,' she whispered back. 'Because I surely want to kiss you.'

He smiled but he didn't kiss her straight away. He turned her within his hold, then cupped her face with his hands. She tilted her chin, aching for contact, but instead he searched her face.

'Mia,' he said softly, 'I'll never hurt you, I swear.'

And then, finally, gloriously, magically, he lowered his head—and he kissed her.

What had he expected?

Rab had kissed women before—many women. His grandfather's obvious labelling of him as a playboy wasn't exactly unfounded, and the feel of a woman's mouth on his wasn't new.

Except this was Mia, and this most definitely was new.

For the moment she tilted her chin, raising her mouth to his, waiting to be kissed, he was hit by a realisation so powerful that it shook something inside him that seemed almost…primeval.

This woman trusts me.

This woman is giving herself to me.

Of course it was no such thing. This was only a kiss,

a moment at the end of a glorious night. This was no promise of a future.

Yet the moment his mouth met hers, from the moment when her arms came almost instinctively around his chest, from the moment he tasted her, held her, felt her warmth, her wonder, her…trust?…the night seemed almost to dissolve.

That such a woman could let him kiss her… That he could hold her…

He felt as if the most precious thing in the world, the most fragile jewel, was surrendering herself to him. He kissed her, he held her, and the night seemed to dissolve in a mist of heat and desire.

But more than that. For Rab it seemed almost as if they were merging, as if part of her was becoming…his. He'd hold her safe, he thought. He'd give as much as he could, he'd give and give. Nothing could hurt her again. He swore it almost unconsciously as the kiss went on.

He loved her.

Now all he had to do was convince her that this was not for one night.

This was for ever.

And when finally the cool of the night closed in and it was time to meander back along the path, climb into his gorgeous car and make the trip back to Wiradjuri, the sense of wonder seemed to stay with them. Boris roused himself from his bed beside the kitchen stove and greeted them, but it was time for Rab to head to his end of the house and Mia the other.

But of course they paused and suddenly Rab was kissing her again—or was it the other way around? Then he was holding her at arm's length, his eyes questioning.

'Mia?'

And she knew what he was asking and the answer came, strong and true.

'Yes.'

'Are you sure? Mia, I won't take advantage...'

'You can take all the advantage you like,' she whispered. 'Because yes, I'm very, very sure.'

Except...was she?

CHAPTER ELEVEN

SHE WOKE, CRADLED in his arms, her bare skin against his. Her body felt sated with warmth and sleep and love.

She felt as if she were…home.

All those resolutions, she thought. All that swearing that never again would she be dependent on a man. On anyone. Had it come to nothing?'

Did it really matter if she trusted him? This man was so far from Harvey it was as if they were different species.

At some time during the night Rab had whispered that he loved her. She might even have said the same. Who knew what she'd said? It was all a dream, one she never wanted to wake from.

He'd made love to her. *Love*. It was a strange word.

Once upon a time she'd had romantic dreams of what love could be. She'd even thought the act of making love could be beautiful. That, however, had been an idea gleaned from reading romance novels, the romantic ideal.

Harvey had knocked that out of her, using her body at will, and for years she'd thought she'd never want sex again. But when Rab had touched her his had been a touch that had said the control was still hers. It had been a featherlike kiss as he'd helped her slip off her clothes, a caress of fingers on her cheek, his eyes questioning, as if he knew she was fearful. As if a gesture from her would have made him pull back.

You're in charge, his body language had said, and it had made her feel...powerful. As if she really could pull back. As if this night was all about her pleasure, if she wished it.

Did he understand domestic abuse? Had that been part of his medical training? How had he known what a huge step it had been, to trust?

Whatever, however, suddenly she'd felt as if she could do this. No, she would! She wanted it. Her body had been alight with sensations she'd never felt before. When he'd been naked before her, she'd felt as if she'd never seen a man naked before. Her whole body had blazed with heat and desire, and when they'd fallen onto the sheets she'd taken him and taken him and taken him—and in the end the fierceness of her lovemaking had almost frightened her.

At some time in the night Rab had pulled back, just a little, so she could see the gleam of his smile in the moonlight filtering through the window.

'Hey,' he'd said, laughing, but with a huskiness that told her his passion matched her own, 'we can sleep a little too, love, if we need. We have all the time in the world.'

But did they? That was a concept that almost had her retreating into that bad place in her head. But then he'd kissed the hollow of her throat, and her body had arched all of its own accord. The future—and the past—were forgotten. And when they'd finally slept she'd thought she was...happy.

And now she lay, sated, warm, deeply content, and Rab's words were replaying in her head. Maybe there could be a future.

And then there was a sharp rap on the front door. She heard Boris bark. Rab stirred, still holding her close.

'What the...?' Rab muttered. When a medical call came she knew they'd be wide awake in seconds, but at this time on a Sunday morning, when Ewan was on call and their phones were working... Surely this wasn't medical. She heard Rab's confusion and knew it matched her own. 'What time is it?

She twisted slightly in his arms so she could see the bedside clock. *His* bedside clock. She'd slept the night in his bed and right now she wanted to stay here for ever.

'Just past nine,' she murmured and felt his arms tighten.

'Just past nine on a Sunday,' he said, kissing her bare shoulder. Her scarred shoulder.

It didn't make one scrap of difference. Right now she felt beautiful. Right now she didn't feel scarred at all.

'I think we didn't get enough sleep,' she murmured, and he chuckled and rolled over to kiss her more deeply.

'We had better things to do,' he said, and his kiss was languorous, long, wonderful.

But then the knock came again and Boris's barking reached a crescendo.

'Someone might be stuck in our blackberries again,' she managed, and then heard what she'd said.

Our blackberries. Joint possession?

Where was her heart taking her?

'Catastrophe? It has to be an earthquake at least to warrant this,' he said and sighed and sat up and pulled on his trousers.

She headed for her room and found a dressing gown, then made her way through to where Rab was opening the front door.

There were two men and a woman on the doorstep.

One of the men and the woman were wearing suits, corporate style, a style you didn't see in Cockatoo Valley all that much. The woman had what looked like some sort of camera, a tiny thing attached to her jacket. The younger man was wearing jeans and a shiny leather jacket, with slicked back hair, designer sunglasses, cool trainers. Together they seemed an entirely intimidating presence, and Mia found herself instinctively taking a step back, wishing she had something on under her dressing gown. Wishing she could hide her face.

'Good morning.' The older man spoke first, sounding brisk and efficient. 'We're sorry to disturb you, but we've been asked by Mr Finlay here to do a spot check.'

'Mr Finlay?' Rab said, blankly. He was standing in the doorway, in trousers but nothing else, as confused as Mia.

'This is Mr Noel Finlay. I believe he's a relation of yours,' the older man said calmly, 'from England. I'm George Howard and this is Miss Maria Stein. We're from Howard Stein Legal, based in Sydney. Mr Finlay and two of his cousins have contacted us, asking us to find out if your marriage is all that you say it is.'

'I'm sorry…' Rab sounded stunned but the legal monotone continued.

'Mr Finlay's been informed that you are indeed married,' the man said. 'But he and his siblings believe it's a marriage made to fulfil the requirements of the will, not a true marriage. We've done some research and have found the marriage was only proposed after a meeting here six weeks before your birthday. The accusation is that you hadn't met beforehand, and that this has been organised only to rob our clients of their rightful inheritance. In short, to defraud. We've done our groundwork. This visit is the culmination of that research, and we now need to warn you that this conversation is being recorded and videoed via my colleague's video camera.'

'Is that legal?' Rab asked mildly, and to Mia's astonishment he sounded, if anything, slightly amused. 'Body cameras? Aren't they used for crime scenes?'

'If you're defrauding our client from what's rightfully his, then it is a crime scene.'

'You don't have our permission to film, or to record. And we're within our legal rights to kick you off the property,' Rab said, still mildly. 'You're trespassing.'

'What's wrong with her?'

It was the young guy speaking now, stepping forward, jaw jutted belligerently. He was staring at Mia, who'd tried to retreat to the shadows. She'd tugged her dressing gown around her, but she was acutely aware that it was thin and there was nothing underneath. At some time in the night Rab had unfastened her hair, and unruly curls tangled every which way. She wore none of the light concealer she usually used to conceal the starkness of her scars.

She felt exposed, scarred, completely off balance.

But then Rab turned and smiled at her. It was a quick smile, meant only for her—a message? Courage, that smile said. Let's play these people at their own game.

How could one smile say that? She didn't know, but as Rab reached for her hand and drew her forward she found herself responding with…trust.

Why was that her first reaction? Why was it so deeply, deeply important?

'Are you talking about my wife?' He had her now, his arm around her, turning so they both faced outward. 'There's nothing wrong with Mia.' And his gaze met the young man's and held. There was something in his expression, something implacable, something hard, and Mia wasn't surprised to see the young man take a step back.

But the belligerence was still there. 'I told you,' the young guy muttered to the lawyers. 'I forgot. The people we talked to told us about the scars. Look at her. He's rich already, a city surgeon, he has everything he wants and then he decides to come here and marry *her*.' And he said *her* in such a way that even the lawyers flinched. 'Why would he do that if he didn't want the money?'

'Mr Finlay…' the male lawyer said in a warning voice but the young man wouldn't be stopped.

'It's a con. For him to marry her…'

'Enough.' Rab's controlled amusement had ceased. 'Get off my land,' he said, and there was something in his voice that made everyone there flinch. Recalibrate. Figure Rab was not to be messed with.

The lawyers certainly got it.

'Mr Finlay, stop,' the lawyer said quickly, harshly, and he was watching Rab's face. He knew they'd gone too far—and this was being recorded. 'Dr and Mrs Finlay, on behalf of our client I apologise for those very personal remarks. Could you forget them, please? Mr Finlay, please go back to the car and remain there. I believe we can ask the questions we need to without your presence.'

'But…'

'Go,' the lawyer said, still watching Rab's face. 'Or he *will* get us thrown off for trespass. He's entitled. Leave this to us.'

'Go, Noel,' the woman said. 'We'll handle this.'

There was a loaded silence and then the young man gave an angry huff and turned and stalked back to the car. 'They've obviously just woken up,' he threw over his shoulder. 'Make 'em show you where they've been sleeping. It's a con, I tell you. A bloody con.'

He climbed into the car and slammed the door, and they were left with two lawyers standing on the doorstep, looking apologetic. But also…determined.

'Dr Finlay, we apologise once again for our client's comments,' the male lawyer said, and Mia was aware the female had stepped back a little. So her camera could get a better view? 'But he's jet lagged, and he and his family have put considerable effort into making this happen.'

'A scheduled interview would have been in order,' Rab growled. He'd tugged Mia close against him, making it seem as if they were one. A couple, woken from sleep, bewildered by this intrusion. As they were.

There was no need for Mia to shake. Why was she? It must have been Noel's voice, she thought. The vitriol. The latent threat.

Plus the thought that what was at stake here was the future of the entire valley.

'We could have arranged an interview. We probably still will,' the lawyer said. 'But we thought a visit when you weren't expecting us might answer questions faster than any interview.'

'You can't use the video you're making,' Rab said. His voice was mild again now. 'I reiterate, it's not being made with our permission.'

'It could allay our clients' concerns though,' the lawyer said. 'If you can prove you've been living together as a couple there's no more to be said. It may save both you and our clients a costly law suit.'

Rab sighed. He was still holding her tight, the warmth of his arm a silent message. 'Shall we kick them out or shall we just get this over with? My wife and I are indeed married,' he told the lawyers. 'We have nothing to hide. The entire valley will tell you we've been living together for six months. What else do you need to know?'

'Are you sleeping together?' It was the female lawyer, and in her voice was a trace of the belligerence of the young man.

'Of course we are,' Rab said calmly. 'Why wouldn't we?'

'Except we aren't.'

And Mia had found her voice again. She wasn't a wimp. She'd decided that years ago. Harvey had hurt her, intimidated her, made her a total victim. She'd spent years recovering—had she ever really recovered? But these last months, knowing the valley was safe, increasingly knowing that Rab was her friend, had changed something in her.

And how fortunate was it that these people had come this morning? She'd lain in Rab's arms last night and she'd felt amazing.

Formidable.

She'd relapsed a little in the face of the obnoxious Noel's vitriol, but that strength came back now. Rab was still holding her. The memory of his lovemaking—and the way her body had responded—was still with her.

She could face this threat.

If these people were to be admitted into the house they'd find two used bedrooms and that had to be explained.

'We don't sleep together,' she said now. 'Or at least, not very often. But that's not what you're asking. You're asking if we have sex, and yes, indeed we do. But I've been on my own for many years now, and I like my independence. And that includes being able to retreat when my husband snores.' And then she looked directly into the camera and she smiled. 'Ask any couple how they cope when one of them snores like…'

'Oi!' Rab interrupted, indignation personified, but she peeped a smile at him.

'Well, you do,' she said. 'There's no shame.' And she patted his pecs. 'Most guys who are carrying a bit of extra body weight snore, even if it's mostly muscle…'

'Turn that camera off!' Rab demanded, but his eyes were laughing. Laughing at her?

No. Laughing with her. There was a difference.

'So okay, find any woman whose husband snores.' She chuckled. 'Even if only occasionally. Then ask if they'd like a retreat. In this big house, why not?'

'So you're saying you have separate bedrooms?' The female lawyer looked as if she'd discovered a major piece of evidence. Her tone was suddenly excited.

'Yes, we do,' she said blithely, and she tugged out of Rab's arms and turned and gestured inside. 'Want to see?'

'Mia, we don't have to,' Rab said, sounding worried, but there was still the hint of laughter in his eyes. He'd figured what she was doing, even before Mia turned to him and gave him a reassuring nod.

'I know we don't. This visit is impertinent and probably illegal, but stuff 'em, they want evidence, let's give 'em evidence.' She turned back to the camera. 'You guys agree that you've turned up without warning on a Sunday morning, at a time when most couples could be assumed to be sleeping in?'

'Yes,' the older lawyer said cautiously.

'My husband and I went out last night,' she told them. 'We had a very good time and arrived home late, so we've just woken. Look at us. You agree we haven't had time to stage anything?'

'I imagine that's correct,' the lawyer said grudgingly. 'We made sure you had no warning.'

'So bring your camera inside,' Mia said grandly and gestured inward, and then turned and led the way.

Rab followed, feeling stunned. For the first few minutes he'd played the protector, determined to keep these people out of the house, determined to keep Mia safe. But now it was Mia who was sashaying down the hall as if she owned it.

She reached her bedroom and flung the door open with a flourish, then stepped aside so the two lawyers could enter.

'My domain,' she said grandly. 'My personal retreat.'

The older lawyer stood back, seemingly uncomfortable, but the woman had no such qualms. She walked in and looked around.

Mia had changed little since she'd been here. Indeed, why should she? She'd never intended to stay here past twelve months, and the idea of filling it with her possessions had made her feel uncomfortable. She kept it neat. The bed was starkly made—she was a nurse and she'd been trained in old school discipline—hospital corners, bedcovers without a crease, crisp white pillows plumped every day that now, because no head had dinted them last night, clearly looked as if the bed hadn't been slept in.

There was no mess in the room at all. Not even slippers under the bed—Mia had shoved those on her feet when she'd made a mad rush for her robe. Normally her robe hung behind the door but now there was nothing. There were no photos on the bedside table. No accoutrements except a simple bedside clock and a box of tissues.

It could be anyone's bedroom. It looked as if it was waiting for guests, not a room a woman slept in every night.

Rab was also gazing around for the first time. This

was Mia's domain; he hadn't been in here. Its starkness left him cold.

She was staying here, he thought, and the idea was suddenly bleak. She could take her suitcase from the top of the wardrobe and be gone tomorrow, and the house would close against her as if she'd never been here.

Except…the rest of the house gleamed. The rest of the house looked amazing.

She'd been doing it for him?

For the valley, he reminded himself, but then gazed again at the stark room and thought of the gleaming Aga in the kitchen, the sparkling crystals of the chandelier and he thought, no, definitely for him.

'If I had this for a retreat I might have added a bit of pink,' the female lawyer said suddenly, unexpectedly, and Mia flashed her a grin.

'Depends how much you use it. We're only six months in. I expect by the time we reach our golden wedding anniversary this'll be so stuffed with knick-knacks you wouldn't believe. Maybe even a vibrator under the pillow.'

The older lawyer choked. The woman lawyer stared at Mia—and her face, rigid up until now, suddenly cracked into a reluctant smile.

'He has to keep me happy or I'm back in here,' Mia said serenely and then turned and headed down the hall. 'Right, here's the bathroom…'

The grand bathroom was similarly neat, but here the space was shared. Mia, though, had carefully kept her belongings to one end of the wide shelf that ran along the far wall, and Rab used the other.

'You don't share toothpaste then?' the female lawyer asked, but she was starting to sound as if she was enjoying herself. Mia had her onside, Rab thought, stunned.

'And let him decide how to squeeze it? Look at his tube. Squeezed from the top. I ask you…' She gave a theatrical sigh and the lawyer even giggled.

And then… Rab's room. 'Are you sure you want to see this?' Mia asked as they reached the door. She paused, looking a bit embarrassed, but again Rab had the sensation that she was playing for effect.

'Go on,' Rab said wearily, as if he was done with this whole charade. 'Get it over with.'

'As you wish,' Mia said grandly and threw open the door.

And there was all the evidence they needed—and more.

Last night had been…amazing. It had also been very, very messy. The sexual tension between them had been building from the time they'd walked into the restaurant—or maybe it had been building for the whole six months. Regardless, by the time they'd reached home they both knew exactly what they wanted, and they'd wasted no time. The moment she'd said 'I'm sure' Rab had lifted her off her feet, given a curt nod to the sleepy Boris and said, 'You'll have to excuse us, mate. We have things to attend to.'

Boris had, thankfully, gone straight back to sleep, not even vaguely disturbed by the sounds emanating from Rab's bedroom. By this time he regarded Rab as an extension of his tribe, and saw no need to protect his mistress from him.

And his mistress wanted no such protection. Her need to be with him had been as urgent as his had been to take her, and the evidence lay before them now. A trail of their gorgeous evening clothes led across the floor to the bed. Lacy knickers were on the bedside mat—and how had her bra ended up on the lampshade? The bed itself was a mess—the whole scene pictorial evidence of a very good time.

Rab stopped in the doorway, really seeing the mess for the first time. Evidence indeed. And then he looked down at Mia. She was blushing, but she was also smiling, a faint, cat that got the cream smile.

He had the strongest urge to kick these people out now, sweep her up in his arms again and…

Um…no. They'd come this far, they had to see it to the end.

'Do you have to record this?' he growled, and the female lawyer looked apologetic.

'It's the fastest way to allay the fears of our client,' she told him. 'I promise it will never be shared, and as soon as he's satisfied it'll be wiped. We'll also send you a copy so you can check our filming has been…discreet. George and I can swear to what we've seen if required, but I think we've seen enough. Wouldn't you say, George?'

And the middle-aged lawyer's face was almost beetroot. He was backing out of the door, stammering. 'Indeed. We're so sorry. This has made me feel…tawdry. Indeed, it was only that our client insisted that there was no true marriage that we…'

'He didn't think I could have married Mia because I wanted her?' Rab asked mildly, but he couldn't quite suppress anger. He moved to Mia's side again and hugged her. She'd been fabulous. Brave. Bearing all. Or almost all. He looked again at the sliver of lacy panties on the floor and thought that this was a woman who valued her privacy above everything. That she was so exposed…

'I do want her,' he said, holding her close. 'Mia's my wife, in name and in fact. I love her and I'll protect her for ever. You mess with her, and I'll bring every legal force I can muster down on your heads. She's mine and I'll protect my own, no matter what it takes.'

But his words didn't have the effect he'd intended. Or maybe they had with the lawyers, but not with Mia. He felt Mia stiffen. Not much, not enough for the observers to notice, but it was there. She stayed within the hold of his arms but the warmth, the sinking against him, had suddenly changed.

And when she spoke her voice was suddenly strained. 'That's enough,' she said, and it sounded as if each word was forced from her. 'I hope you've seen what you needed to see. Can you go now, please, and let…and let my husband and me get on with our lives.'

Rab saw them to the door and Mia stayed in the bedroom. It was a warm morning but all of a sudden she found herself shivering. The heat of the night had left her. All that was left were echoes.

Rab's words.

'She's mine and I'll protect my own, no matter what it takes.'

And superimposed were words from years ago. Harvey's voice, imprinted into her brain from so long ago.

'She's mine and I keep my own, no matter what it takes.'

They were completely different, she told herself, but she was staring around the room now and she was feeling as if she was staring into an abyss.

How could she have forgotten?

Rab's phone buzzed into life. It was lying on the bedside table. He was still at the front door, talking to the lawyers, no doubt. Telling them more strongly just how 'married' they were. How much she was 'his'.

It was after nine. Time enough for medical calls to

come through. Neither of them was on duty, but this was a small place and in an emergency...

She lifted the phone, still staring at the knickers. Still feeling sick.

'Dr Finlay's phone.'

'Mia? Is that you? Did you have a great night?' It was Ewan. The whole hospital had been egging them on last night. The whole hospital would have been cheering if they could see those knickers.

'Yes,' she said, and she knew her voice sounded flat. 'Thank you.'

There was a moment's silence. He knew her well, the old doctor. Then, 'Is everything okay?'

'I...' She struggled to pull herself together. 'Yes. Sorry. We've just had a visit from lawyers wanting to prove we're properly married.' She might as well tell him, she thought. The whole valley would have noticed a sleek black car heading for their place at this hour on a Sunday.

'That's why you sound strained,' Ewan said, sounding relieved. 'I imagine you reassured them.'

'We sure did.' And she struggled to put a smile behind her words. 'I guess...they're just leaving now.'

'That's great,' he told her. 'But, Mia...'

Here we go, she thought. Medicine.

'John and Miranda Hutchins celebrated their fortieth wedding anniversary last night,' Ewan told her. 'Half the valley was there, and their daughters catered. Apparently they've been making casseroles for weeks. Put 'em in hired bain-maries, kept them warm all day. We had John come in at four this morning with food poisoning, and a steady stream of locals have been phoning for advice or arriving since. Most are minor but a couple of the oldies have been hit hard. You reckon you and Rab could stop playing married for a bit and come in and help?'

Playing married… The words had been said almost as a joke. Ewan thought of them as truly married.

Playing married…

She stared at the knickers again and thought of how out of control she'd been last night. She thought of every vow she'd ever made since…well, since Harvey.

'She's mine.'

She wasn't. The façade had to continue for another six months, but that was all it was. A façade.

'We'll be there as soon as possible,' she said tersely and disconnected. Then she took a deep breath, gathered her scattered clothes and headed for her room.

By the time Rab returned from seeing the lawyers off she was in the bathroom, in the shower, with the door locked behind her.

'Mia?' he called from outside the door and she heard concern. 'Are you okay?'

'We're wanted at the hospital,' she called back. 'Food poisoning, multiple presentations. Bathroom's yours in two minutes.'

The door was locked. The way she'd been feeling last night, she would have left it open. They could have showered together.

She's mine.

She wasn't. The door was staying locked until she was safely back in her part of the house.

Back in control.

Back being Mia.

Somehow he'd messed it up and there didn't seem a thing he could do about it. He knew from the moment he'd heard her voice from the bathroom that the barriers had been put in place again.

In the car on the way to the hospital he tried to raise it. 'Mia, I'm so sorry they upset you.'

'They didn't upset me,' she said tightly. 'It was lucky that last night happened when it did.'

'It was lucky,' he said. And then, more cautiously, 'It was wonderful.'

'Yep.' But her voice was tight.

'Not for you?'

'Yes.' Then, more tightly still, 'No. I forgot my rules. This is a pretend marriage, Rab. Six more months and we're done.'

'Does it have to be a pretend marriage?' He was driving, needing to focus on the road. Maybe this conversation should have waited until tonight, but she seemed wound so tight, as if she'd...betrayed herself.

'Mia,' he said, gently now, 'you sound horrified. I'm not Harvey, Mia. You know I'd never hurt you. You know I'd protect you with everything I possess and more.'

'I don't want to be protected.'

'You don't want to be loved?'

'I...no.'

'I didn't think I did either,' he said, almost conversationally, although he was struggling to get the words out. 'But, Mia, you've been so battered, you're so vulnerable. I know the façade you wear, how hard it must have been to build that, but I can see past it. Couldn't you learn to let yourself love?'

'You mean, let myself need?'

'Maybe,' he said softly. 'Would it be so hard to lean on me? Would it be so hard to let me in?'

'I can't.' She said it harshly.

'You mean you can't trust me?'

'I do trust you. I just can't let myself need you. I want control, Rab.'

'You have control.'

'I don't. I lost it last night. I've got it back now and I'm not letting it go.'

'So you and me...'

'You might want me,' she said, softly now, staring straight ahead at the winding river as they approached the hospital. 'But you're still as independent as you always were. But me... Rab, if I went further down the road we went last night then I'd lose myself. I would need you and that'd make me so vulnerable I couldn't bear it. You said to those people, "She's mine". I'm not, Rab, I never was and I never will be. You're special and I know you'd care for me, but that's not what I want. I just...'

She bit back her words and closed her eyes. He was slowing to turn into the hospital car park. Medicine was waiting, a way for both of them to switch off personal emotion, to immerse themselves in a world where there was no room for personal reflection. He knew, suddenly, that this was his last chance. She'd climb out of the car, head back into her world and the emotional door would be closed behind him.

'Mia, I think I love you.' He said it a bit too loudly.

'You said that during the night,' she said flatly, her hand on the door. 'It's what people say during...'

'Did Harvey say it to you?'

'Probably. I can't remember. It doesn't mean anything.'

'Mia...'

'Leave it, Rab,' she said wearily. 'Last night was an aberration. It was fortunate it happened at the right time to convince the lawyers, but that's all we should remember it as. A one-night stand with lucky repercussions for the valley, but nothing else. Now...'. She pushed the door wide and climbed out. 'Let's get back to work. Food poisoning, here we come.'

CHAPTER TWELVE

HARVEY WAS OUT of prison.

It was three months on from 'the night of the law-yers'. That was how she'd labelled the restaurant meal and everything that had happened that night, categoris-ing it in her mind as a lucky incident that had cemented the valley's safety for ever. She even somehow tried to rewrite it in her head as a strategic move, something they might have staged.

She couldn't quite get there, but if she blanked out the time from when they'd left the restaurant to the time the lawyers had knocked on the door then she managed to keep it in some sort of perspective. The time in between she left locked away, a memory so vivid she couldn't let it out of the bomb-proof compartment she'd formed in her head.

She had many such compartments. One of them was Harvey, and now, staring at the letter in her hand, she felt it being wedged open.

The parole board had accepted his application, the letter told her. As the victim of his crime, this was a courtesy letter. The letter had been sent via a redirect-ing service she'd set up when she'd changed her name. This letter was two weeks old.

He'd never find her anyway, she thought, fighting a

wash of panic that he'd been out without her knowing. Part of his parole conditions was not to go anywhere near her, but even if he tried, she'd moved to this valley then changed her name again when she'd married Rab. Mia Finlay had nothing to do with the terrified Maira of ten years ago.

She was no longer a victim. Harvey was nothing to do with her. This letter was nothing to do with her.

'Mia? Is something wrong?'

They were eating breakfast, seated on opposite sides of the table, getting ready for work. Reading their respective news feeds and mail. Keeping separate.

She'd headed out early for a walk with Boris and had collected the mail from the post box at the end of the drive on the way back. It was her routine.

Routine was everything now. Since…the night of the lawyers…they'd maintained a formality not usually even seen between housemates. It was as if each of them knew that the chasm was there waiting, one chink and they'd fall.

Into lust?

Cut it out, she told herself savagely, and she made it savage because the concern in Rab's voice was enough to threaten the fragile barriers she fought so hard to defend.

'Nothing,' she said briefly, and laid down the letter. And then, because it wasn't enough to just set it aside, she rose, took it over to the fire stove and set it to burn. 'Just…my ex-husband's out of jail.'

His face stilled. 'Mia…'

'It's okay. He's nothing to do with me now. Nothing at all.' But her voice trembled. Dammit, why? He was no threat. She was not that girl any more. Not that woman.

'Do you think he'll try to find you?'

And for some reason that calmed her, his steady voice

cutting across her panic. It was a reasonable question and it forced her into logic.

'There's no reason why he should. It's ten years ago now.'

'Was the assault on you the only thing that put him in jail?'

Once again, she was steadied by the matter-of-factness in his tone.

'Drug charges as well,' she managed. 'And firearms. When the police came…after the assault…they found a lot of them.'

'So there's no reason he'll have been sitting in jail all this time thinking his sentence is your fault?'

Her eyes flashed to his. There it was—the unspoken fear. He got it, she thought. He understood.

And suddenly Harvey's voice was echoing in her head, as it had echoed for years. They'd set up a screen in the rehab department so she could watch the trial. It was something she should do, the psychologists had told her. 'You need to hear the judge saying what a scumbag he really is. This should help you acknowledge, once and for all, that nothing about this is your fault.'

And maybe they were right, but what she was left with was an image, Harvey screaming up at the camera as if he could see her behind the lens.

'I'll come for you… No matter where you are, no matter how long it takes. You're mine.'

She shuddered and all at once Rab was standing, taking her hands, pulling her up and against his chest. And just for a moment she let herself be pulled. She let herself sink against his sweater, feel the scratch of thick wool, feel the strength of him, the safety…

'You're safe, Mia,' he said firmly, surely. 'I won't let him hurt you.'

And there were the echoes again. He'd protect her?
You're mine.

Whoa. She was being stupid, she knew she was, but she didn't need this man's protection. She couldn't. She'd carefully constructed her life so she depended on no one, and there was no way she'd sink back into that helplessness. She pulled back and took a couple of deep breaths.

'Thanks, but I don't need it,' she told him.

'You don't need me?'

'I can't need you.' She tilted her chin and met his look square-on. 'I can't need anyone. Can't you see that?'

'I guess… I can't.'

'I'm sorry, but I can't explain it any better than that,' she said, and dammit, her voice was bleak. 'And I know you'd protect me, as I know this whole valley'd protect me, and Boris too, for that matter. So I'm safe, but you know what? I'm safe because of my choices, because of my strengths. So thank you for the hug, Rab. It helped and I'll add it to my arsenal, but now…moving on, I have antenatal classes in the school hall in half an hour and I need to move. We both need to move. The letter's burned and forgotten. Let's go.'

She left, driving in her little Mini, leaving him to follow. He watched her go and felt…bad. He couldn't define it any better than that.

Was he afraid for her? Maybe, but her assurance had been firm.

Did he want her to need him? Maybe.

He raked his fingers through his hair and swore and then turned to Boris. 'Come on. I don't have patients until ten and I'm sure you need another walk.'

Boris looked at him as if he was nuts. He'd obviously

done a few kilometres with Mia. He was getting on in dog years. The fire was warm.

'Come on,' Rab told him. 'I need company.'

And then he heard what he'd said.

I need...

Mia didn't need him.

That long-ago line was suddenly playing in his head. *'I need this woman so much—I'm just so lucky she needs me right back.'*

Mia didn't need him, but hell, the way he was feeling...

Was it possible that the tables had turned?

The day turned out busy, more than busy. Some days there was just one thing after another. At five, just as Mia was due to knock off, she heard the dreaded screech of tyres, a car speeding up to the entrance, a car door slamming, a female voice yelling for assistance.

'Help! Help me, please! My husband...'

An accident? Ewan had gone home early. Night staff were about to take over, but both Rab and Mia were there. They headed out together, bracing as they always did.

Donald Myers, a big, beefy farmer from up in the hill country, was sprawled in the passenger seat, gasping for air. His face was puffy, the hand he held to his chest was swollen. He was red-faced, sweating, and his eyes were wide with terror.

'He's just... Half an hour ago... He just started to swell.' Kath Myers was a sensible woman, a stalwart in the Country Women's Association, maker of the best scones in the valley. When fires had threatened the town three years ago she'd been the calmest of them all, but there was nothing calm about her now.

'He can't breathe,' she managed. 'He can't even talk any more. Mia, help...'

'Intubation,' Rab snapped, crouching to the level of the guy in the car. 'Don, hey, this looks like an allergic reaction. Scary, but we have you.' Then back to Mia. 'Epinephrine, methyl prednisolone and prepare to intubate. Don, we're going to get you out of trouble, we'll get the swelling down, but first things first, we need to help you breathe.'

He was tearing Don's shirt. Mia was already moving, grabbing the crash cart from just inside the doorway, motioning Issy to bring the trolley. For the first few moments there was no time for questions, no time to do anything but get him out of the car, get the epinephrine aboard, then get him sedated enough to intubate. This was a procedure so drilled into all of them that there was no need to speak, no need for anything but to use what was almost muscle memory to keep the man alive.

But Mia's mind was racing as she worked. This was no normal allergic reaction. She'd known Don for years now, a no-nonsense farmer who pretty much spent all his time on his land. At this time of the evening, on a weekday, he'd hardly have been out at a restaurant, and Kath was known for good, plain cooking. So what?

He kept bees on his property. 'Has he been near the hives?' she asked over her shoulder. Kath was standing in the background, looking terrified. By rights they should have had a social worker or at least a junior who'd accompany her to the waiting room, who'd sit with her, but right now there were only Mia, Rab and Issy on duty, and they were all needed.

'I'm staying with him,' Kath had declared as they'd wheeled him inside and there'd been no time to argue. In truth, it was probably kinder to let her stay rather than make her sit alone.

'Not since last week,' Kath stammered. 'And he

doesn't react to bee stings. He's been bitten so many times in the past, it doesn't worry him.'

'So today, anything out of the ordinary?'

'The dentist?' The woman took a deep breath. She also had obviously been fighting to make sense of what was happening. 'He's had toothache. We went across to Colambool this morning. The dentist there said he has an abscess. She didn't have time to work on it today, she said come back on Wednesday. She gave him antibiotics.'

'What sort?' Rab snapped, suddenly focused on Kath.

'I don't know,' the woman faltered. 'A green…a green bottle. White pills.'

'Has he had an allergic reaction in the past?'

'No. He never gets sick. He never…'

'It's okay. We'll get through this.' Mia was handing Rab equipment. The anaesthetic he'd administered— mostly tranquilliser to stop the gag reflex—was taking effect and Rab had the intubation tube ready. 'Issy—' she talked over her shoulder '—ring the dental clinic at Colambool. If it's closed, if no one's answering, then ring the police station. They'll be able to track down someone who can access the dentist's records. Tell them it's an emergency. We need to know what was prescribed and we need to know now. Fast!'

The girl turned and fled. She was good, was Issy. She knew the locals—she'd probably be able to track the dentist down herself.

The tube was sliding home, and the moment it did Don's desperate efforts to breathe pretty much eased. The hiss of the air through the tube was a comfort. Standing by the wall, Kath almost visibly slumped.

'Oh, thank God. Oh, my…is it the antibiotic?'

'Most likely,' Mia told her and then glanced at Rab. With the immediate danger past they had a little time.

'Let's make you a cup of tea and ring your daughters to come and join you. You've had a fright and you need company. Oh, and you might ask one of them to stop at your place and pack Don's PJs and toothbrush.'

'Will he need to stay the night?'

Mia's gaze flew to Rab's. Their eyes met and she knew that her guess—that this was no minor reaction, something major was happening—was spot-on.

'Certainly tonight,' she told her. 'It'll take a while for the swelling to go down.'

And then Issy was back in the room. 'There was still someone in the clinic,' she told them. 'Not the dentist—she's a locum there while Marjorie Chambers is on holiday—and she'd gone home for the day. But there was a dental nurse catching up on something. She looked at the records. Penicillin.'

There was a moment's stillness. Anaphylaxis caused by penicillin was as rare as hen's teeth, but the potential consequences were appalling. There was a reason doctors asked for medical history when they prescribed drugs, and this was a major one. Breathing difficulties could be the least of it.

'That's great,' Rab said, but the look he gave Mia said it all. It wasn't great at all, but there was no use terrifying Kath any more. Not now. 'Issy, could you take Kath for her cup of tea? Mia, I need you to keep an eye on this tube for a bit.' He sent an apologetic glance to Kath. 'You've come at a busy time, and I need to make a couple of phone calls.'

The medevac chopper landed in the paddock behind the hospital at eight that night. Two paramedics were aboard. No doctor. 'There wasn't anyone available,' they'd told Rab.

Rab had only seen such an allergic reaction once in his medical career before. It had been a child. He still couldn't bear thinking about it.

He knew he had to go on the chopper.

'There's a real risk of heart failure,' he told Mia and Ewan. Ewan had arrived back at the hospital within half an hour of Don's arrival—this valley had ears.

'Yeah,' Ewan agreed. 'Rhonda's gone to their place with one of the daughters, packing stuff for Kath. Kath'll go with him too, but the kids'll go by car. I told them it might take a few days. Maybe by a miracle he'll come out of it fast but… Anyway, Rab, I agree, you need to go too.'

He didn't need to say any more.

Mia had seen this reaction once before too. An older woman. It had taken her months to recover.

They were busy, trying to stabilise Don, trying to think of every eventuality, every medical crisis Rab could face in the hour-long journey.

And then they were gone and suddenly Mia felt like slumping into the nearest chair and weeping.

It was this valley, she thought. It had protected her, saved her, and its inhabitants felt like part of her. To lose one of them… No.

And now she'd go home tonight without Rab. He was flying back to Sydney—where he belonged. He'd come back, she knew he would, but only for another three months.

Unless…

Dammit, why were these emotions surfacing now?

'Go home.' Ewan was watching her face. He knew her well, this man. He'd seen her almost at her worst and she could hardly hide things from him now. 'Would you like one of us to come and stay the night with you? It's a bit lonely, staying in that big house by yourself.'

He saw too much, did Ewan. He was watching her and she knew darn well he wasn't thinking she was spooked by a big house. But that she'd miss…her husband.

Her pretend husband, she told herself fiercely. Pretend.

'Hey, we've been in and out of that house while we've been on call any time these last nine months,' she said, managing a smile. 'I'm not dependent…'

'On anything or anyone. I get that.' His smile was infinitely gentle. 'And that's a problem I was starting to hope Rab had fixed. But it's okay,' he added as he saw her flinch. 'There's time. And meanwhile you have Boris. Go home and hug your dog, girl. Don'll be okay, Rab will see to that. You can trust him, lass. You really can.'

'I know I can,' she said, and kept her smile determinedly fixed. 'Thanks, Ewan. Goodnight.' And she went out to the car park and headed for home.

Home?

Home is where the heart is. The trite little saying started playing over and over in her head as she drove. So…home?

Maybe home was in a helicopter, somewhere in the night sky. Heading for Sydney.

Why did he hate leaving her tonight?

It was the news she'd told him at breakfast, her expression. She was terrified.

He was totally caught up with Don's care. He and the paramedics were throwing every ounce of their combined skill at preserving vital signs, when the sheer force of the reaction to the antibiotic was doing the exact opposite.

But still there was a tiny part of his brain that was telling him he should have told Ewan about Harvey's release, urged her to stay with him, maybe urged Rhonda or Joanne or Issy to stay with her tonight.

Which was stupid. Firstly, the guy had only just got out of prison. Even if he was intent on revenge, Mia was right, she'd protected herself well. It'd take time and effort to find her.

And, secondly, he knew exactly how she would have reacted if he'd suggested it.

'I'm safe because of my choices, because of my strengths.'

Her voice still echoed in his head, telling him to butt out.

But she did need him. He could see it in her reaction, in the way she'd folded into him for the hug. And he wanted her to need him. He ached for it.

Why couldn't she see that it was no weakness? That it'd be his privilege to take care of her for the rest of her life.

And then Don's body gave a convulsive jerk and he glanced at the monitors. His heart... This was what they most feared.

The thought of Mia disappeared, or almost disappeared, as every fibre of his medical self fought to keep the guy alive. Don needed him, right here, right now. Mia, not so much.

The fact that he wanted her to need him?

Put it away, he told himself. The thought of Mia folded against his chest this morning had to be put aside.

For now. There had to be a future, he told himself.

Please.

She pulled up outside the darkened homestead and let herself sit for a moment. The silence enveloped her. Home.

Home without Rab?

Yeah, well, she was used to it. During the last nine months she and Rab had worked as medics, sometimes together, often apart. They'd both had calls that hadn't involved the other. They were used to coming home alone.

So why was she sitting in the car now, not wanting to go in?

Because the parole board had written her a letter.

Because Rab wouldn't be here.

Both those things were irrelevant. They had nothing to do with her. 'You've spent the last ten years finding independence and control,' she muttered to herself. 'Don't falter at the first hurdle.'

Was Rab a hurdle?

He certainly threatened her independence. She thought of how she'd felt this morning, hugged against his sweater. Safe. Protected.

Stupid.

But he wanted her to need him. She could see that. He'd like nothing better than to protect her for the rest of her life.

Which would make her feel small. She could hardly understand it herself, the sensation of falling she had when she was with him. The desire to be his, and yet the fierce determination to be nobody's.

Maybe she should ring her therapist again. *Hey, Lorna, I have this gorgeous hunk who wants to love and protect me for the rest of my life.*

But she knew what Lorna would say. *Mia, is this another shield against the world?*

Maybe it was, and she didn't need it.

Oh, for heaven's sake, she was emotional and tired and Boris was inside, probably aching for a walk. It'd have to be a quick one tonight, though, she thought. Maybe she could pour herself a glass of wine, sit on the steps and tell him to romp in the front paddock. There were enough rabbits down there to keep him happy.

Do it, she told herself and climbed from the car.

She opened the front door, expecting Boris to come hurtling to greet her.

'Boris?'

Nothing.

And with that the shadows came flooding back, a fear so overwhelming it made her stagger—even before the door closed behind her and hands gripped and held.

Before something jabbed hard into her thigh. Before the hold on her tightened still further.

Before the gasping struggle for breath.

Before blackness.

CHAPTER THIRTEEN

HE FLEW BACK at dawn.

He was exhausted. He'd been awake most of the night and there'd been an offer to stay on and get a decent sleep at Sydney Central. Which would have been sensible.

But Don was in the best of hands. It'd take time for him to recover from such a massive allergic reaction, but he was in the Intensive Care Unit in one of the best hospitals in the world. He had his wife with him. His daughters were driving up from the valley this morning. There was every chance he'd make a full recovery. There was nothing more for Rab to do. When the medevac operator rang and said there was a flight leaving from dawn to pick someone up from Colambool and offering him a lift, there seemed no choice.

He wanted to be home.

The chopper crew—a different team from the one who'd flown the night before—were friendly and accommodating. They checked the paddock in front of Wiradjuri and saw no reason why they shouldn't set him down there, and two minutes after he landed he was opening the front door.

Which wasn't locked.

Mia must have taken Boris for an early walk, he

thought, but then he heard an urgent scratching from further down the passage.

He headed for the kitchen, opened the door and Boris almost knocked him over in his joy to be out. But three quick licks and the dog was gone, hurtling down the passage and out into the yard. He was clearly heading to do what a well-trained dog would never allow himself to do on the kitchen floor.

Rab stared after him, feeling…as if the floor was shaking under him.

'Mia?' His first call was tentative. His next was almost a shout, and he'd turned and was at Mia's bedroom door before he realised it.

The room was empty, the bed was made. The room looked impersonal. Well, what was new? She'd never made it homelike, he thought tangentially.

She didn't feel that she belonged here.

She wasn't here now. If it wasn't for Boris he might have thought…

No. Her suitcase was on top of the wardrobe. He tugged the wardrobe doors open and her clothes were still lined up.

She could have gone to work early, but Boris… Why had Boris been locked in?

He headed back to the hall, kicking open the bathroom door as he went. Just in case.

In case what? That she'd collapsed? Had an accident?

He headed outside. Boris bounded back to greet him, welcoming him like a long-lost friend.

The Mini was still here.

Where…?

He turned and stared inside, and then he saw what he hadn't noticed as he'd gone in the first time. On the sitting room floor, looking as if it had been kicked from across from the hall, lay her purse. Three strides and he was kneeling, hauling it open.

Her phone was inside.

And then he saw the empty syringe.

His heart felt as if it had been clutched by icy fingers. No!

He went to lift it, then had enough forethought to grab an antimacassar from the back of one of his grandfather's chairs. He used it to lift the syringe, holding it to the light. He saw the remains of a clear substance. He squeezed and lifted it to his nose.

Nothing.

Phenobarb? Morphine? That was his surgical training kicking in.

Heroin? Much more likely.

But any of those options made his heart clench. If this syringe had been full, then no matter what it was, it was more than enough to knock out someone a lot larger than Mia.

And side effects were blazing in his head. Irregular heartbeat. Low blood pressure.

Death.

Dear God, if this was Harvey... If he'd administered the drug by force...

It was all he could do not to throw up, but that'd help no one. He forced himself to breathe slowly, staying very still, forcing his mind back from dread.

How long ago had this happened? Where would he have taken her?

Could she be dead?

He couldn't think it. Not for a moment.

Boris came in and sat beside him, looking puzzled, putting his great head forward so he could lick his face.

Strangely, the sensation of the dog's rasping tongue

against his cheek helped. Boris was looking at him as if he was the one to pull them out of this nightmare.

So do something.

Police.

He grabbed his phone and the local cop answered on the second ring. Brian was a friend of Mia's. Everyone was a friend of Mia's.

'I'll be there in two minutes. Don't touch anything,' he growled, and the phone went dead.

What next?

Somehow he forced his dazed mind to think. If he'd meant to kill her, surely he would have done it here. So surely he wanted her alive? He didn't know that for certain, but anything else was unthinkable.

So he wanted her alive, but not here?

Somewhere.

Think!

And then he had it, a sliver of memory from a long-ago conversation.

'Harvey lived in a huge house at the bottom of the district's only hill...'

And... *'I bet it's still his. It was sold when he went to jail but one of his mates bought it, and I'm betting he'll end up back there.'*

Where had she said it was?

Corduna.

He grabbed his phone and did a search. Corduna. Three hours away by road.

There had to be somewhere else. He surely wouldn't take her all that way, drugged, unconscious.

Dead?

He couldn't want her dead, he told himself again, clinging desperately to that hope. If he wanted to kill her, he never would have bothered with drugs. No, he'd want vengeance first, he thought, a way to punish her for ten years of prison.

Boris had sat back on his haunches, head cocked to the side, obviously puzzled that Rab was still on his knees, staring into middle distance. He grabbed the dog and hugged him, and Boris obliged by putting his huge head into his chest and nuzzling. It was pretty much a cuddle of comfort.

It was Mia who needed the cuddle, he thought savagely. It was Mia who needed him.

Where was Brian? There was nothing he could do until the police arrived. He had to sit still and wait.

He held the dog tight against him, using his warmth, the solid trust of him, to catch himself, to regroup, to figure that he could stand up, head out to the veranda, meet Brian, figure a plan.

He had to get to Mia. Mia needed him.

And then, as he held Boris tighter, as the dog's raspy tongue found his cheek again, he thought suddenly, stupidly, that he needed Boris.

And it was as if a chink in his heart was suddenly being crowbarred open. He needed the dog's presence. He needed...

He needed Mia.

This way he was feeling... He had to get to Mia, rescue her, save her, but it wasn't all about Mia's need. He needed her to be where Boris was right now. He needed her against his heart.

He'd told Mia he wanted to marry her to protect her, to love her, to keep her safe. She needed him, of course she did. But now...

He closed his eyes as the wash of self-knowledge grew so great it threatened to overwhelm him.

Somewhere out there was the woman he loved.

Somewhere out there was the woman he needed more than life itself.

It wasn't Mia's need, it was his.

Somewhere out there was…his home.

She woke to blackness. She woke to absolute confusion.

She felt sick, fuzzy, weird. The world seemed to be spinning around her. Nothing made sense. She wanted, badly, to be sick. There were no lights, or maybe there were but they were intermittent. Flash, nothing, nothing, nothing, flash, nothing, flash…

The only thing she could do was to focus quite hard on not throwing up, and it took pretty much every ounce of self-discipline she had. For some reason it felt vitally important not to vomit. To retch alone in the darkness… The indignity as well as the mess… She wouldn't do it. And overriding everything else was the age-old instinct of wounded creatures, to lie still, to stay hidden until they knew the threat.

And the threat was suddenly with her. Slivers of memory were returning.

She lay still, fighting for control of her body and fighting for control of panic as images flooded back.

Harvey. His great body looming over her. Hands holding her down, turning her face to the floor.

A jab… Then nothing.

Drugs. He'd drugged her.

Of course. Once upon a time Harvey had had the means to get any drug he wanted. He'd just come out of prison, but he'd still have contacts on the outside.

He'd used something on her. What?

It didn't make sense. Nothing made sense. She had to get rid of the fog.

There was no choice but to close her eyes and give

herself space, to fight the nausea, to fight the panic. She needed to let the fog envelop her until whatever he'd drugged her with wore off.

Darkness. Nothing, nothing, flash.

They were in a car! The moment she thought it, it made sense. The vinyl feel against her cheek. The sense of movement. The flash of passing cars.

They were travelling fast. Where? And how long had she been unconscious?

There was nothing she could do. She wasn't tied, but they were travelling too fast for her to try and escape, even if the doors weren't locked. She was too fuzzy to move anyway but, even if she wasn't, survival instinct was still screaming at her to not let whoever else was in the car sense that she was coming round.

She didn't feel like coming round. Oh, she felt sick.

She wanted…oh, she wanted…

Rab.

The memory of *The Wind in the Willows* was suddenly with her, the story she'd read over and over in the past years. It was her place of peace and she could use it now.

Her eyes stayed firmly closed and with a conscious effort she let the memory of Rab's voice take over.

"'The Mole was bewitched, entranced, fascinated. By the side of the river he trotted as one trots, when very small…'"

Rab's voice with that long-ago reading was suddenly with her, whispering into her poor foggy head, helping her fight back fear.

Where are you, love? She could almost hear herself say it. The question was nonsensical. She was on her own, she always had been.

But it helped. Somewhere out in the world was Rab and he'd be frightened with her.

And Boris.

And Mole.

She almost smiled, but then another wave of nausea swept over her.

Close your eyes, she told herself. Let yourself sink back into the fog but don't let it frighten you.

Mole. The river.

Rab.

'We're doing all we can.' Brian looked as if he was having trouble staying calm himself. 'We have roadblocks all over the valley. We're contacting the prison, finding associates, trying to find what car he's driving. He's been out of jail for two weeks but he should be reporting in. We'll find out where he's been living. It's just…'

It was seven in the morning and they'd be waking officials and it'd take time. And all that time Mia would be lying in some brute's car, or taken into some motel or refuge they didn't know about or…or…

He was going nuts.

'What about Corduna?'

'Three hours away by car, mate, and we don't even know if he still has a house there. But we're checking. There's no police based there—Corduna's more a hamlet than a town—but they'll send people.'

'How long will that take?'

'An hour maybe, apparently it's bloody rough country.'

'I need to go there.'

'You're best to stay here.'

'Why the hell?'

'In case she comes home.' The big cop stirred uneasily, and Rab had the feeling that, like him, he wanted to be out and doing something. 'Mate, this is a kidnapping.

You're family. You gotta sit it out. We both do. We have people working on it now, guys who know their stuff.'

'But she can't come home. She's drugged and Corduna's our only link. And we have no idea how long she's been gone. Corduna… I need to get there.'

'Doc, we're doing our best and we have no evidence…'

'Okay, you have no evidence,' Rab said explosively. 'But it's our only lead and if he takes her there…can you get the air guys in? Choppers from Sydney?'

'Not yet. They'll need more evidence showing that's where he's taken her. The ground guys will work on that.'

He was losing his mind. He had to do something. 'I'm going.'

'Drive for three hours to a place we don't even know he still owns? Who's to say he hasn't taken her to a motel down the road?'

'He'd want her on his own turf.' The vision of Harvey's retreat, vividly described by Mia, was in his head. Barbed wire, dogs, a compound where he could do what he liked with her. Thoughts were flashing through his head, a kaleidoscope of fear and plans and visions of Mia being… Mia being…

'Tom,' he said suddenly. 'His helicopter. He'll take me.'

'Tom?'

'You know, Tom Cray. He has a chopper. He takes people for a fee. Can you contact him?'

'Hell, mate…'

'Brian, this is Mia. Mia!'

And the cop stood still and stared at him. Mia seemed such an integral part of this community, and Rab could see emotion warring with protocol and sense.

'You gotta stay here,' he said at last. 'Rules. Family stays home. If we find her, you gotta be here.'

'Brian, she's drugged and gone. What are the chances she'll be returned here?'

'If the roadblocks work…'

'How many roads lead in and out of this place? And how long have they been gone? There's a dribble of drug on the carpet and it's dry. I have to go. If it's against rules…arrest me if you must, because that's the only way you can stop me.'

'Not by yourself. And Tom'd be useless…if there was trouble.'

'Then come with me yourself.'

The cop stared at him, indecision warring with protocol.

'This is Mia,' Rab said, softly now. 'You've seen the scars on her face. That's how badly he hurt her last time he had her.'

And he watched as slowly the big cop thought of Mia, thought of the scars. Made a decision.

'Hell,' he said savagely. 'Okay, you ring Tom. I'll get a couple of locals to head out here and look out for this place, just in case she gets back.' He shrugged. 'It's probably needle in a haystack stuff, but if Tom can take us… let's do it.'

All she wanted was Rab.

How dumb was that? She should be thinking all she wanted was freedom, all she wanted was to be free of Harvey, all she wanted was safety.

Instead she lay on the rough cloth of a settee and let herself drift back into the sensations she'd felt in Rab's bed.

That was a good place to be. No, it was amazing. It was the only way she could distract herself—and she needed to be distracted.

From the time she'd surfaced to something akin to consciousness, survival instincts had kicked in. She'd had no way of getting out of the car, no way of escaping Harvey, not unless she could figure out some way she had the advantage—and there was no way she could get that advantage while she was still half drugged.

So she lay and played dead. Even when the car pulled up, when she heard gates creak open, when she heard the dogs and knew for certain where she was and that the gates would close behind her, she didn't make a move. If she got to the door, if she tried to run, the dogs would be on her in moments.

Her stomach was still heaving, and when he picked her up and dumped her unceremoniously on the settee in the living room, then shook her, trying to rouse her, the smell of him, the feel of him, was the last straw. As he tried to haul her upright she retched, but then, as every instinct screamed to fight him, to haul away, she forced herself to slump back, limp, seemingly unconscious.

She heard his grunt of disgust. 'You'll wait,' he growled and she heard him stomp back into the kitchen.

She heard him on the phone. 'Yeah, mate, I got her here. Still out of it—how was I to know how much to give her? Thanks for keeping the place for me. Dogs were no problem, I let 'em out as soon as we arrived. They'll be no problem when we leave—amazing what a bit of steak'll do and you've left us plenty. I coulda done with whisky instead of beer, but you can drop it in later. I won't be in a hurry leaving.' And he gave a mirthless laugh and disconnected.

She lay absolutely still. She had to figure this out and she only had this time to do it.

She had to get control. Now, before this 'mate' arrived.

Strangely, lying on the foul settee, feigning unconsciousness, she felt herself regrouping. She wasn't the woman who'd been so helpless all those years ago. Harvey had caught her unawares and brought her here, but she wasn't *that* woman.

She was in control, she told herself. She just had to figure out how.

The chopper flew through the early morning sky, going two, three times as fast as a car but still not fast enough for Rab.

The local cops would meet them there, but it had taken strings to make that happen.

'The victim's husband's going anyway, whether we like it or not, and I need to go with him.' Brian had stuck to his story, even though the response from the guys on the ground had been less than enthusiastic.

'Harvey's place was sold when he went to prison. We have no idea who the new owner is. Are you suggesting we storm the place?'

'He's going anyway,' Brian told them, stonewalling their objections.

So was it a wild goose chase? He was in a chopper heading for a place that Harvey hadn't owned for years. There were so many other places he could take her. It didn't make sense.

Except his gut said it did.

And Mia's words. *'It was his own private kingdom... I sometimes think that most of his vitriol towards me in the trial was because finally I caused the authorities to breach his defences.'*

So he had to be right. He must. This was Mia. Dear God, if she was hurt... If he lost her.

Something inside him would die, he thought.

He didn't need to save her for her sake. He needed to save her for his.

* * *

She had a plan. There were holes but it was the best she could do. She had one chance, she told herself, and she'd use it. One chance...

She'd trained for this. She had the skills.

So use them.

He was approaching again. She felt herself tense, and had to consciously force herself to limpness again, so that when he walked to where she lay and shook her she reacted as if she were a bunch of rags.

He swore.

Turn away, she pleaded with him under her breath. Turn your back.

How often had she rehearsed this move? 'It's the most effective for total disablement,' her karate instructor had told her. 'But you need to be behind him.' He'd taught her other moves for frontal contact, but she was so much smaller than he was. She knew one false slip and the thing would end in disaster. This was her best chance.

It had to work.

I will be in control, she told herself. It was a mantra. Her mantra. Given to her by Rab all those years ago.

'That's okay, Maira... You're in control.'

Rab. The thought of him somehow settled the panic within. He was out there somewhere. He loved her.

It shouldn't matter. She didn't need him, but it helped.

She had to do this now. Now!

She stayed limp as he shook her again. He swore and let her fall back on the cushions. 'Bloody stuff... If he's given too much...'

She felt rather than saw him turn away, and finally she let her body tense. If he tried to lift her now she'd be rigid. Coiled like a cobra about to strike. Ready.

Now!

And all those years of self-defence classes actually

worked. Robyn, her social worker, had been adamant that she should do them. 'You'll never need them, but they'll help the way you feel. Maira, you've been treated as a doormat all your life. Now it's time to learn your own strength.'

Her karate teacher had seen her scars, learned her background and taught accordingly.

'Here's the nice stuff,' he'd told her. 'It'll teach you all the movements. But here's the dirty stuff, the stuff you only ever use if you're intent on major hurt.'

Which was what she used now. Go!

She flew up from the couch, using her coiled strength, not staggering, covering the tiny distance between them like a well-aimed arrow, giving him no time to turn.

He sensed. He started to twist. He was almost side on…

She raised her knee and she kicked straight out, viciously, using all her strength and more, so the heel of her foot slammed into the back of his knee.

This was a *yoko geri* side kick and it was designed to rip ligaments. It was not to be thought of in any but the most dire situation, but that situation was now.

And it worked. He screamed and dropped, but even before he hit the ground she was on him. She had his arms behind him, pushing them up so hard he kept right on screaming.

In those blessed moments where she'd lain, feigning unconsciousness, she'd figured a plan. She wore clogs at work, plastic things that were easy to wash. They'd dropped off somewhere on the journey, but underneath she wore light socks that reached halfway up her calves. Thin, stretchy socks. She'd surreptitiously pushed them down to her ankles, and it took milliseconds to grasp them now.

She used one for his wrists, using the same method her mother had taught her to tie legs on a roast chicken, trussing hard, tight and fast.

Tackling his ankles was riskier but he hadn't had time to gather himself to kick out. He was rolling in pain, clutching his knee. She shoved his other leg up so his ankles were crossed. By the time he realised what had happened, she was standing in the kitchen doorway and he was lying helpless on the living room rug, ankles and wrists solidly bound. He was swearing, cursing, crying with pain. She couldn't care. She'd done it.

She was in control.

'That'll teach you to mess with me.' She said it out loud and it was a phrase she'd rehearsed over and over, spoken in her head to him, any time these past ten years.

It felt…not good but solid. Powerful. She could cope alone. No man was ever going to mess with her again.

So stop it with the shaking, she told herself—but she couldn't.

Moving on. Call for help. How?

Her phone had been left behind. Harvey's phone? That'd be in his pocket. It'd be locked, even if she was brave enough to try and search him. Which she wasn't.

She could leave, head through the scrub to the town.

The dogs. They were prowling outside—she could hear them. There'd be barbed wire.

Somewhere in this place there'd be guns, she thought, but even if she found them… Dogs…no.

So wait.

For Harvey's mate to arrive? He knew Harvey wanted whisky. Her dad had been one of Harvey's minions. She knew how much the idiots wanted to please him—how much power he had over them. Somehow he must have managed to retain that power through his jail term.

Okay, deep breath. Don't panic. She sank back onto a kitchen chair and tried to clear a bit more of the drug-induced fog. In a couple of moments she'd go see if she could find a gun—but she needed to catch her breath first.

She needed to stop shaking, to keep this sense of control.

She needed to wait for Rab.

What sort of thought was that? Why did she think he'd come? There was no sense in it, but the thought was still there.

Rab. He'd be out in the world and he'd be hunting.

He loved her.

If worst came to worst, she could figure some way to get past the dogs. She didn't need him.

But somehow she knew that he'd come.

The chopper landed five minutes' drive from the place the cops in the nearest decent town knew as Harvey's old haunt. They'd been dubious when Brian had contacted them. 'He's been gone for years. The place was sold when he went to prison. The guy who owns it seldom comes near the place—uses it as some sort of retreat. Harvey wouldn't even have access.'

But this was a kidnapping, it was on their patch and they co-operated.

'Okay, land the chopper on the town oval,' Tom was told via the chopper radio. 'If you fly over the place, if he's there you'll put the wind up him. We'll meet you and take you from there.'

So they landed and Tom stayed—reluctantly—with the chopper. They tried to make Rab stay there too, but Brian took one look at his face and caved.

'He's a doctor, guys,' he told the local cops. 'And we're

guessing she's been drugged. If she's there, who knows what we'll find.'

So two squad cars made their way to the house, with Rab in the second. They parked well back, driving off the track into the undergrowth, hiding the cars in case Harvey was yet to arrive. Was Harvey even thinking of using this place? There were so many unknowns, Rab couldn't bear to think of them. If he was wrong…where was she? He was going out of his mind.

Rab was ordered to stay with the cars, and he did, while the cops silently surrounded the house.

And then there was the sound of a car, being driven fast along the dirt track. Standing well back from the track, with the police cars in the camouflage of the bush, Rab got a glimpse of an ancient red truck.

Harvey?

He had enough sense to know he had to stay hidden. He had to trust.

And then…chaos. The screeching of brakes, tyres skidding on gravel. Frantic barking. Shouts, yelling, then loudspeakers.

'Police. Your mate's under arrest. Come out with your hands up, now.'

And Rab could bear it no longer. He was out on the track, staring at the entrance.

The red truck was slewed against the fence, the driver's door open, a cop standing over someone on the ground. The rest of the team had spread into action that was obviously part of well drilled training. Bolt cutters were slicing through the locks. Lasers stunned the dogs before they had time to attack. For all these were country cops, Rab couldn't fault them.

Another boom from the loudspeakers. 'Come out, now!'

And then, through the now open gates, he saw the

front door open, just enough for someone to see what was happening. And amazingly, stunningly, it was Mia. She was still in her nurse's uniform but her feet were bare and her hair was a tangle of dark curls. Her face was pale, but when she spoke her voice was clear, with only the trace of a quaver behind the words.

'I'm safe. Harvey's here and tied up. Thank you so… so much for coming.'

It might almost be a polite thank you for calling, Rab thought incredulously, and then, even more incredulously, he realised… *She's holding a gun!* But then the police had her away from the door, taking the gun, backing her away into the shadows. There were long minutes of silence—and then, finally, a call.

'We have him. All secure, no one else here. All's well. Let the doc tend the girl.'

And seconds later—or maybe even less than seconds— Rab was in the shadows where Mia stood. Folding her into his arms.

His Mia!

He couldn't speak. All he could do was feel, and in the end it was Mia who took over.

'It's okay, Rab. I'm safe. I tied him up. I rescued me, all by myself.'

'You did.' He could hardly get the words out.

'I didn't need you. I swear I didn't.' It was as if it was a long learned mantra, a vow she couldn't break. But then there was a hiccup that sounded very much like a sob. 'But I'm… I'm so glad you came. I had Harvey but I knew his friend might come. And I found the shotgun but I didn't… I didn't think I could use it.'

'You didn't need to.'

'Because of you. I didn't have to use it because of you. It *was* you, wasn't it, who guessed where I'd be? I didn't need you but I trusted you…' Her voice broke and she buried her face in his chest.

It was so hard to make his voice work, but finally he spoke, one faltering word after another. 'Mia, you saved yourself. You're one strong woman. And, Mia, I know you don't need me, but you're my heart, my soul, and it's me who needs you. You've made me whole again, and no matter what you decide… Mia, no matter where we take this from here, I'll love you for ever.'

CHAPTER FOURTEEN

ASSAULT. KIDNAPPING. FIREARMS OFFENCES. Harvey would be put away for at least another ten years, Mia thought, and after that, she figured, there'd be no way he'd try and mess with her again.

She was free of the ogre that had haunted her all these years. She'd done it and she'd done it herself.

The lightness that followed was almost unbelievable. So many years of being under her father's control, under Harvey's control, under the boundaries of her fear... They were gone for ever—and to have Rab, desperate to find her, acting on a hunch, practically bullying the cops to take notice... It did something to her heart that she hardly recognised.

But in the hours that followed, as officialdom and documentation and blood tests and medical examination took over—as she found herself once more cast as the victim of crime—the feeling grew, becoming a sweet siren song of certainty.

This time was so different. She might have been a victim again, but she'd fought back. She'd taken control and now...now she was free to choose.

She'd been taken to hospital, like it or not. The bruises she'd received as she'd been roughly handled had been photographed, documented. Blood samples had been taken for evidence of the drug she'd been given. A gentle policewoman with a doctor in attendance—not Rab—had asked her questions, and then she'd been left to sleep.

She'd slept off exhaustion, she'd slept off the final effects of the drug, she'd slept off the last vestiges of fear.

And at midday the next day she was discharged and Tom and Brian and Rab were waiting to take her home.

Home. Wiradjuri.

They hardly spoke on the way home. Both Tom and Brian were treating her as if she were a piece of Dresden china. They didn't need to, she thought.

Oh, but she loved them. Brian was sitting beside Tom and he was beaming—what he'd achieved was huge for a country cop. Rab sat beside her in the rear. He was holding her hand as if she might be frightened of flying. Or was it that he was frightened? She sort of got it now. She felt as if she loved the whole world.

She knew she loved Rab.

She knew that fear was shared. That trust was a two-way deal. She knew that control didn't come into the equation when you truly loved.

And then the chopper was landing, and Ewan was meeting them and taking them out to the homestead.

The police had been in, searching for evidence, but once they'd finished the locals had taken over. Rhonda and Joanne and Nora were waiting, three stalwart women who took her into their arms and hugged. Boris was going nuts—as if they'd been away for months. The house was full of flowers and food, the locals welcoming her back to the valley.

Home.

And in Rab's eyes there was a tenderness, a joy—a need?

He didn't push, though. Maybe the words he'd spoken the moments after she was found were not to be repeated.

He *wouldn't* push. She knew that about him now. She'd fought so hard for control and he knew it. It was up to her.

The women left. They stood on the veranda, watching them go. Side by side. Husband and wife?

No, Mia thought. Not yet.

'Welcome home, love,' Rab said, as the last of the cars disappeared from view. There was a moment's hesitation and then his voice became careful, emotion put aside, turning to the practical. 'What do you need to do now? Have lunch? Sleep and eat later? I won't leave.'

'You can leave if you want to.'

'As can you,' he told her, and she knew he got it. He got this whole thing.

Rab. Her love.

'I am hungry,' she confessed, 'but I need to ask you a few things before we do anything else.'

'Ask away.'

And whatever the questions, whatever she asked, it was okay by him, she thought, and suddenly she grinned.

'If I asked you to do a handstand with back flip would you do it?'

There was a moment's pause. 'I might try,' he said cautiously. 'But I might well do myself some major damage.'

She smiled. 'Okay, good answer. What about climbing Mount Aranjalin?'

'You have to be kidding!' Mount Aranjalin was a serious climbing challenge, not for the faint-hearted. Even Mia hadn't tackled it. 'No!'

That brought a chuckle and she tucked her hand into his. This felt so good. This felt awesome.

'Right, then next question. Do you think you could manage to call me Maira?'

The hold on her hand tightened. 'Do you know,' he said slowly, 'that ever since I knew your story, in my head I've called you Maira. You are Maira. You've just been hidden for a while. But now… I'm so glad you're not having to hide any more. Maira, I'm so glad you're free.'

Why did it feel as if her heart might burst?

'Well, that's three out of three, done and dusted,' she said and managed a chuckle. 'One more for a perfect score.'

'And that is?'

There was a long silence while her heart figured out how to say it. She knew what to say, but to get her tongue to say the words…?

It should be up to the guy, she thought. In stories, in movies, it was always the guy. But she'd done it once before. How hard would it be to say it again?

As Maira.

She took a deep breath, then another. Then another, while the world seemed to hold its breath.

And while Rab waited. This was up to her, she thought. And then she thought, no. It had to be…up to them.

Gently she disengaged her hand and she stood back from him, just a little, just enough for her to read his expression. And what she saw there—this was right. It had to be right.

'I think you know what I'm about to ask,' she said softly. 'But maybe it shouldn't be my question and maybe it shouldn't be yours either. Do you think we could do it together?'

And their gazes met—and held.

He knew what she was asking. Dear heaven, he knew.

Rab stood on the sun-drenched veranda and looked into the face of the woman he loved more than anything in the world. Mia. Maira. His beautiful, life-battered, strong, courageous, gorgeous Maira. That she should ask…

That she should ask him to ask…

And it was right. No, more than right, it was the best thing in the world. The only thing. He loved this woman with all his heart. More, he needed her. Not for the practical—he knew she could cope without him, as he could cope without her. But that need was there, and it was growing by the minute.

He needed her to fill his heart. Maira.

So say it.

He took her hands again, both her hands this time, and he looked deep into her eyes. One last question, and it was the most important of all.

'My love,' he said, and his words were more a joyous proclamation. 'Maira, my love, will you marry me?'

And her voice echoed, or maybe it didn't even echo. Maybe it was said in the same breath. 'Rab, my heart, will you marry me?'

The words were spoken almost as if they'd been rehearsed, cued together, said as one.

There was a long, long silence as they stood, hands locked, looking into each other's eyes, and no vow could be made that was more powerful, more binding, than that perfect stillness.

And then the peace was broken. Right by the veranda was an ancient willow myrtle, planted deliberately so its spreading branches gave shade from the afternoon sun. On one of its lower limbs a kookaburra had obviously been watching the comings and goings with interest. Now it decided to offer its opinion. It opened its beak and a raucous chuckle rang out across the valley.

It made Rab smile, and Maira smiled right back. And

then she chuckled, and she moved against his chest and his arms enfolded her and the world was so right it was breathtaking.

But still there was one word to be said, and when he finally said it, somehow she got it, too, because the words were said in unison.

It was a good word. No, it was a great word, and it was said so loudly that for a moment even the sound of the kookaburra, and Boris's most ferocious bark as he tried to see this stupid bird off his patch, were overshadowed. Drowned out by the most important words in the universe.

'Yes.'

'Yes, I will.'

EPILOGUE

Wiradjuri, Cockatoo Valley, two years on

"'THE MOLE WAS BEWITCHED, *entranced, fascinated. By the side of the river he trotted as one trots when very small...*'"

'I know he's bright, but at eleven months maybe we shouldn't assume he knows what a mole is.'

Maira looked up from the easy chair where she'd been sitting, reading to her son. Giles was solidly asleep in his cot. His dad's birthday and the picnic down by the river that had gone with it, had been a big day in the life of a baby, and Giles had enjoyed every minute.

So had his mum and dad.

'And you do know he's asleep?' Rab asked, coming into the room to look down at his sleeping son. 'Wow. How many soft toys does one toddler need?'

'This one's the most important,' Maira said contentedly, standing beside her husband and lifting a blue fuzzy creature with a shiny nose. 'Martin Mole. Of course he knows what a mole is. And even if he is asleep he'll still hear. I read somewhere that knowledge can ooze in while you're snoozing. I think we should start on encyclopaedias next.'

But she knew she wouldn't. Mole had marked the start

of their whole wonderful relationship, and this small blue mole and the book that went with it would always make her smile. She'd fallen in love over this book. Giles might be stuck with Mole for ever.

Like she was stuck with her husband? She smiled as she thought that being stuck with this man must truly be the definition of bliss. Rab's arm came around her and together they gazed at the small, robust ball of energy that was their son.

'He looks so peaceful,' Rab said.

'He's gaining energy for tomorrow,' she warned. Giles had just learned the art of power-crawling. 'Destruction, thy name is Giles.'

He chuckled and kissed her hair. 'He's great. Let's have another.'

That was okay by her. She'd take any comers, she thought. This valley, this house, this baby, this man… Here was her joy. Here was her peace.

Here was her home.

But… 'We might already have another one,' she said now, hearing the sound of a car pulling into the driveway. It was eight o'clock on the night of Rab's thirty-seventh birthday. Robyn had promised and Robyn never broke promises.

'You mean…' Rab turned her within his arms, his eyes gleaming. He was ignoring the sound of the car in the face of much more important issues. 'Are you pregnant?'

'I would have told you if I knew,' she said, but she was metaphorically crossing her fingers. The truth was that she thought she might be, but she hadn't tested. Nor did she intend to for a day or so, because even if another baby was on the way she wanted all the attention to be on tonight's arrival.

The car was stopping at the front door and Rab was pulling away. Reluctantly. 'If this is work…'

'It can't be,' she said serenely. 'They'd have phoned.' It wasn't out of the question for Rab to be called out, though. In the two years since their 'real wedding'—a simple ceremony they'd held down by the river where they'd made vows that would hold them together for life—Rab had quietly gone about helping Cockatoo Valley Bush Nursing Hospital to become a rural medical hub. With the community buildings gifted to the community, with former leased farms sold now to locals, the valley was thriving.

One of Rab's mates from Sydney had now bought a hobby farm and was working as a family doctor-cum-anaesthetist. Two others were working as part-time doctors, and the valley was now in a position to offer internships to trainees.

Ewan could have retired content. Instead, with the injection of so much new life and energy into the valley, with the pressure eased, he'd decided to work on. 'Maybe until I'm eighty,' he'd said happily. 'Or more. I just have to wait and see.'

Ewan was on call tonight, plus one of the interns. It'd have to be a real emergency for Rab to be called out, but as the doorbell pealed and he headed out to find out what was wrong he was looking worried.

But Maira wasn't worried at all. She was smiling and smiling as she headed out to join him.

He reached the door before her. She peered past him, expecting just Robyn, but there seemed to be a crowd.

There certainly was. She flicked on the lights and saw Robyn, but she also saw Ewan. Plus his wife, Mary. Robyn's four kids were there as well, all bouncing with excitement. Robyn's husband was by her side. Joanne.

Rhonda. Nora, Issy. It looked as if half the valley was either on the veranda or just below it.

'Once they knew what was happening I couldn't keep them away,' Robyn said apologetically as Maira came out onto the veranda to join her husband. Who was looking… flabbergasted.

'It seems half the valley wants to say happy birthday. And if you think you're paying for her, Maira, think again. We'd thought this might be a valley gift to both of you, but of course Hilda got in first. Do you remember Hilda, Rab? Maira's roommate in the burns unit? Hilda sends her love and says this little one is free to a good home. To your home.'

And then Robyn's Harry, now almost eighteen, a long, lanky adolescent, just accepted into medical training and with only a small white scar to show for his encounter with the blackberries, was climbing out of the back seat holding…a puppy.

Not just any puppy, Maira thought. The perfect puppy.

A small golden bundle with a white-tipped tail. She was a Labrador, but she hadn't been chosen for her breed. This little girl had been chosen for temperament, for robustness—she'd have to cope with a toddler—for compatibility with an ageing Boris…and more.

For all these years, Maira had kept in touch with Hilda, the lady who'd shared her first appalling weeks in the burns unit. When Maira had contacted her with her request, Hilda had been joyous. Yes, she remembered the gorgeous voice in the night—Dr Rab!—and if Dr Rab wanted a puppy, one of her puppies, it'd be a huge pleasure to find the perfect one. She'd listened to Maira's story with delight, and then she'd said, 'Wait.' She'd find The One.

This, then, was the result. Robyn and her family had

collected the pup in Sydney yesterday and driven her home. They'd already managed a secret rendezvous with Boris—just to ensure they were compatible. As indeed they were.

And now Harry was out of the car, bringing the wriggling pup over to Rab. Handing her over. He was grinning, as was every person present.

'Happy birthday, Rab,' Maira said softly. 'Rab, meet Lulu.'

One minute he was standing on the veranda, his son sleeping in the house behind him, his wife by his side, Boris at his feet, thinking his world could never be any better than it was right at this moment. The next he was holding a soft, squirming bundle, her tongue reaching his chin for a getting-to-know-you lick, her white-tipped tail rotating like a gyrocopter in full flight.

A white-tailed dog, given to him by Hilda, and by people who cared, by people who made this place home— and by the woman at his side.

How could he ever have thought that he didn't need people? He needed every last one of those present—and more. For of course he'd noticed the way Maira had deflected his question about pregnancy. Was another new little person on the way?

But first there was this new arrival. A small dog with a white-tipped tail.

'Boris and Lulu have already met,' Maira said contentedly. 'Lulu thinks Boris is an awesome trampoline.'

'I'll bet.' But he could hardly talk—the emotions were threatening to overwhelm him. This woman... This miracle-worker...

And suddenly he was thinking of all the pain that had gone into making this moment. Maira's appalling background and her scars. The emptiness of his own childhood. The portrait of two little boys, still hanging in the living room, though joined now by the beginnings of a thousand family photographs.

'Thank you,' he said out loud, and Maira and everyone there thought he was talking to them. And maybe he was, but he was also talking to the ghosts of those before.

'Thank you for giving me this,' he said softly, and he tugged Maira into his arms and kissed her, a great, affirming kiss that saw Lulu happily sandwich-squeezed between them. The kiss said everything that needed to be said, but finally, when they pulled apart, he found there were still words to be spoken aloud. To whoever or whatever was listening.

'Thank you for giving us our happy ever after.'

* * * * *

A FAMILY
MADE IN PARADISE

TINA BECKETT

MILLS & BOON

To my children

CHAPTER ONE

CENTRE HOSPITALIER DE TAURATI was no place for children. Especially not this time of year. Not any time of year, really, but especially not when school was out. Sebastien Deslaurier turned the corner to head to a patient's room and almost collided with someone. He swerved, turning his head to mutter an apology, only to tense when he recognized who it was.

Damn.

They both stopped and eyed each other in the same way they had for the last year. With a wariness that said they'd rather be anywhere but face-to-face. Or body to body.

She spoke first. "Sorry." Her voice had an odd tremble.

It wasn't her fault. He hadn't been paying attention, either. But he was now. "What's wrong?"

Her chin went up. "Who said anything was wrong?"

But there was. He'd sat with enough worried parents to know the fear that threaded through mundane phrases.

"Rachel…" His tongue traitorously savored those two syllables, hanging on to them for an instant before releasing them into the air. He swallowed, trying not to remember other times he'd said her name. On a night that had been as hot as their single fiery encounter.

She gave a half shrug, as if she hadn't noticed his

struggle. "It's nothing. My daughter is a bit under the weather this morning, that's all. I'm having her seen."

That brought him back to earth with a bump. He knew all about Rachel Palmer's daughter. It was one of the reasons he tended to steer clear of her. His son had died. While her daughter had lived.

Dammit, not something either of them could help. And it wasn't fair for him to judge her based on that. Hell, his infant son's cancer diagnosis was the whole reason he'd gone into pediatrics years ago.

Speaking of which…why was Rachel standing in front of the exam room door he was about to go in? He glanced down at the patient he'd been called to look at and swallowed. Claire *Palmer*. How could he not have put two and two together?

"Claire is who I'm here to examine, actually."

"You?" Her eyes widened, and she edged closer to the door. "I thought Dr. Rogan was the on-call pediatrician today. If I'd known, I'd have…"

Her voice trailed away.

She would have what? Refused to let him see her? Taken her daughter to another medical facility? He hadn't thought they'd left things on such bad terms that night a year ago. But maybe he was wrong.

And Claire?

How did you ask someone whose child had had cancer if she was afraid it had returned? You didn't. You simply offered an ear. "Why don't you tell me what's going on with her?"

She shook her head. "I would have taken her to an urgent care center. I probably should have, actually. But I figured they would just send me back here." She bit her lip. "I'm hoping I'm being ridiculous and that you'll tell me it's just a virus."

Just a virus. But it wasn't said with a chirp of self-deprecating laughter. Instead there was strange sense of desperation. It was there in her eyes. The way her fingers twisted together again and again. As if she were pleading with the universe to not let it be what she feared it was.

He remembered exactly how that felt.

If that was it, why had she almost taken her daughter to urgent care rather than bringing her here to the hospital? Was she afraid he'd wind up being the attending if she had?

Actually, her comment about thinking that Dr. Rogan was the on-call physician seemed to bear that out.

He could understand why, if so. Their periodic interactions were nothing if not awkward, despite their assurances that their one wild night together meant nothing.

It evidently meant enough to make them steer clear of each other as much as possible.

"Dr. Rogan is taking care of an emergency case, so he asked me to see his next patient." He glanced at the door behind her. "Who is behind that door, I assume."

Rachel nodded. "I just stepped out for a second to give her some privacy while she changed into a hospital gown."

"In that case, why don't you give me a quick rundown on her symptoms before I go in?"

"Fever, lack of appetite, nausea…" There was a long pause. "And a swollen lymph node on the right side of her neck."

And there it was. The real reason why she was so scared.

"This is a new symptom?"

She nodded. "She hasn't had one of those since her…"

Since her cancer diagnosis.

The thought came through loud and clear. His brain worked through some alternatives.

He had to fight back his own sense of déjà vu. "COVID test?"

"That was my first thought. We did a rapid test, and it came back negative."

Of course she had. Rachel was a smart woman. She would rule out what she could on her own before asking for help.

"Let's go in, and I'll examine her."

He gave a quick knock on the door. A voice that was much more cheerful than her mother's said, "Come in."

Letting Rachel enter the room ahead of him, he saw that Claire was already sitting on the exam table. Rachel went to her daughter's side, while Sebastien took the opportunity to study the girl as he casually made his way over. He could see the swollen spot on the right side of her jaw even from this distance. If he remembered right, she'd had Hodgkin's lymphoma. Swollen lymphs were a classic sign of the condition.

"Hi, Claire, I'm Sebastien Deslaurier. You can call me Seb, if that's okay with your mom."

He glanced at her, catching her frown, but she gave a jerky nod of permission.

Continuing, he pulled up a stool and sat next to the bed. "Why don't you tell me what's going on? Starting with your symptoms. What did you notice first?"

"You mean this time? Or since I was born?" Her grin caught Seb by surprise. He couldn't stop the smile that formed on his own face.

"You remember your birth?"

"Well, no. Mom would have to tell you about that. I'm sure it was traumatic."

"Claire!" Rachel's quick admonition came from behind him.

He glanced back at her, the smile still on his face. "Don't worry, we don't need to go back that far." He turned his attention back to Claire. "Just since you started feeling sick this time."

Claire was a carbon copy of her mom, with dark brown hair and eyes that sparkled. Damn. There was so much zest for life here. He hoped to hell it wasn't what Rachel feared. The last thing he wanted was to have to break the news to her that her daughter's cancer was back.

"I got a sore throat a couple of nights ago. I didn't say anything, because I spent the night with friends a week ago and thought I caught something. But then no one else felt sick. Then last night, I felt sick and threw up. And I have this knot." She fingered the spot on her neck. She looked at him with an expression that said it all. "I know that worries my mom the most."

A ball of emotion lodged itself in his gut, and a million memories came skittering along his nerve endings.

So that he wouldn't focus on that, he picked up the electronic chart and glanced at it. "We'll get it sorted out." He glanced at Rachel. "They've already taken vitals?"

"Yes."

He perused what was recorded. Slightly elevated heart rate and blood pressure. And her temperature was still at 101. Low-grade fever. Another sign. "Do we have her records from the States?"

"I can get them transferred. But—"

"Let's start with that." He glanced at Claire. "I want to examine you and then get some blood drawn, okay?"

She shrugged. "I'm not scared of needles. I've seen plenty of them. And my mom's a nurse, so she's talked me through a lot of things."

Like PICC lines and MRIs?

"I'm sure she has." He smiled at the girl, hoping it looked more genuine than it felt.

The idea of being a doctor hadn't even been on his horizon when his boy had been diagnosed. But afterward? Hell, yes.

He made a call to the nurses' station about the blood draw.

Then he examined Claire, listening to her heart and lungs and having her lie back on the table so he could palpate her stomach. Nothing out of the ordinary.

He helped her sit back up. "I'm going to feel your neck. Tell me if anything hurts."

Placing his fingertips just below her ears, he walked them down, feeling for any abnormalities. The node on her right side wasn't huge, but it was large enough to be seen if you knew what you were looking for. He watched if she flinched when he pressed it, but she just sat stoically. "Hurt?"

"No, not really."

Hell, he'd been hoping the thing hurt like crazy. Enlarged nodes from Hodgkin's were rarely painful.

He continued down, checking her thyroid for nodules, but there was nothing. Other than the lymph node. "How's your throat?"

"It's okay. It was sore when I woke up, but…" She glanced at her mom before quickly adding, "It's better now."

Was she minimizing symptoms because she knew how worried her mom was? He checked her throat, but her tonsils looked clear, and there was no sign of strep. But he'd take a throat swab anyway, just in case.

One of the pediatric nurses came in just as he was finishing up. She smiled at Rachel. "I know you're worried, Mom, but I'm sure she'll be fine. Especially with Dr. Sebastien on the case."

How could she be sure, when Sebastien wasn't? Him having anything to do with whether or not Claire would be fine wasn't really up to him.

He moved over to where Rachel was standing as the woman drew the prescribed number of vials. "I'm going to have a spot test for mono done as well. It takes about an hour."

"Yes, I know. I thought of that as well, but I haven't heard of any cases at her school or among her friends. Have there been any here at Hospitalier?"

There hadn't been. "Not that I know of, but that doesn't rule that or the flu out. I want to do a second COVID test as well, just for peace of mind."

"Thank you for being willing to see her."

Did she really think he was that much of a cad? That he'd realize who Claire was and then turn around and walk away because of their night together? He hoped she thought more of his professionalism than that. "Of course. Is Dr. Rogan her normal pediatrician?"

"Yes. But we've only seen him once, to get her health certificate before enrolling her in school. She's been so healthy, we haven't needed to see him…until now." Her voice had dropped almost to a whisper.

The nurse finished up and exited the room.

Claire turned to them. "See? No tears."

"I never doubted you for a minute." The girl's demeanor was engaging and every bit as winsome as her greeting had been. He felt a tug of something akin to affection in his gut.

Hell, he was glad Dr. Rogan was her primary care physician. He'd been involved with her mother. The last thing he needed was to have Claire as one of his patients.

As if reading his thoughts, Rachel went over and kissed her daughter on her head. "I'm going to step outside with Dr. Deslaurier. I'll be back in in a minute."

"Okay." Claire looked at him. "I'm sure I'll see you around, since my mom works here."

He forced yet another smile, his stomach churning. He hoped not. Hoped there'd be no need for the girl to make regular trips to Hospitalier. "I'm sure you will."

He and Rachel went into the hallway. He headed off anything she might have been about to say. "I'll let you know when I get the test results back. Until then, try not to worry."

"Easy for you to say."

No, it wasn't. But there was no way he was going to tell her anything about his son. Not only because it would make an already awkward situation between them even more awkward, but because he didn't talk about Bleu to anyone. He dragged his hand through his hair.

"Listen, I know this isn't easy. And not just because of what happened…before." If he was trying to make her feel better, he was botching things. Time to retreat while he could. "I want you to know, if you need me— for anything—all you have to do is ask."

And that did *not* come out the way he'd expected it to, either. He quickly inserted, "For a second look, I mean."

There was silence for few seconds before one side of her mouth quirked. "Of course. What else could you possibly have meant?"

Oh, she knew exactly the thought that had crossed his mind as soon as the words were out of his mouth. Had it crossed hers as well?

He wasn't going to stand around, though, and let his memories drift back into forbidden places. And if he kept talking, that's exactly what was bound to happen.

But he couldn't quite let her challenge go without a fitting response. He lowered his voice, allowing himself to taste her name one last time. "I think we both know the answer to that... Rachel."

Big mistake. He shouldn't have referred to her by her first name, because the cells at the very center of his brain—where dormant things were sent for storage—woke up. And they woke up with a vengeance.

Her fingers went up to smooth a lock of silky black hair as she reacted to his words, and her tongue flicked out to moisten her lips, making those newly awakened brain cells dance with kinetic energy.

Then she blinked, her hand dropping back to her side. "Well, I need to get back to her."

"And I need to get going, too, and see if Dr. Rogan has any more patients for me." Not that she needed to know anything about that. The need to end their conversation on a more serious note forced its way through him. "I hope the tests all come back clean. I'll give you a call once I know more. And I meant it about calling me if you want me to look at her again."

Her smile was genuine this time. "I appreciate that. Really."

And with that, Sebastien sucked down a quick breath and headed on his way, refusing to give in to the urge to glance back at her as he did.

The second he disappeared around the corner, Rachel slumped against the wall for a second or two, trying to slow her pounding heart. What was it about that man that got her wound up whenever she saw him?

Who was she kidding? It was the way he'd carried her into the resort's overwater cabana a year ago, her legs wrapped around his waist. The way he'd dumped her onto that bed, looking at her as if he couldn't wait to devour her...

Her eyes fluttered shut as memories crashed like ocean waves, drenching her to the skin. She straightened. It was the humidity. It had to be. Besides, what was she doing thinking about him when she needed to get back in the room with Claire?

When her daughter had woken up this morning with a slight fever and a visible swelling on her neck, it had dropped Rachel's heart into her stomach. It bothered her how Claire had acted with him. She'd always been an optimistic child. But when she'd looked for his approval after getting her blood drawn, Rachel had instinctively shifted into protective-mama-bear mode. Claire had never had any contact with her biological father, and even though it made no sense, Rachel feared her being hurt by men. It probably stemmed from her own hurt at being abandoned, but it was hard not to be overprotective. She was sure Sebastien had probably noticed. But she couldn't help it.

Just like she couldn't help that after six years of her daughter's perfect health, Rachel's thoughts immediately ran back toward that first diagnosis of cancer the second Claire felt ill.

She went back into the room. Before she could think of anything to say, Claire took one look at her face and rolled her eyes. "I'm fine, Mom. Really. Did Seb leave already?"

She let herself relax for the first time today. "He did. He had other patients to see."

Which was true, right? He'd said he needed to see if Dr. Rogan had other patients for him to see. "Let's head home. I'll drop you off first, then I'll get us something to eat. Anything special that you want?"

"A mango?"

That made Rachel smile. "A mango. Really?"

"I love them."

They didn't have mangoes where they'd lived in Wisconsin. Or at least nothing like they had in Taurati. Fortunately, she could pick some up at one of the street vendors not far from their apartment. They carried everything from fruits and vegetables to woven baskets. There was a fish market near there as well, so maybe she'd swing by and grab something for dinner. Claire loved the fish on the island.

"Okay, a mango it is. Get dressed so I can get you home."

Claire got up and picked up her clothes, giving her mom a look.

"Oh, okay." She turned her back on her daughter so she could change.

Her daughter was turning into a teenager, and there were days it showed. She pushed back from time to time, which she never had done when she was younger.

Rachel been reluctant to take the job in Taurati at first, because of her daughter's childhood diagnosis, but Claire had talked her into it, saying after being tied to a hospital in the States for the better part of a year doing treatments, followed by periodic scans for years afterward, she wanted to see as many things as the world had to offer. That had made Rachel's decision for her. And it seemed to be the right one, drawing them closer as they struggled to learn a new way of life. But those first days had been hard.

When her mom had come to visit a month after their arrival on the island, saying she wanted to spend time alone with her granddaughter and insisting Rachel take a week for herself and explore the island, she knew exactly why the suggestion had been made. The anniversary of Claire's cancer diagnosis had been nearing, and Rachel always got maudlin, fighting not to smother her daughter with attention and hugs, which only reminded Claire of all she'd been through. Her mom had been right.

They'd compromised on three days rather than a whole week. Rachel ended up not spending that time on the go but opting for a period of quiet reflection at one of the overwater bungalows at a nearby resort. With its thatched roof and dreamy views, it was a tropical paradise.

Never in her wildest dreams had she imagined sitting on a private deck, dangling her feet in the water while colorful fish swam laps around them. It was the perfect place to consider how lucky she was to still have her daughter. To be able to watch her grow up. The magical oasis had probably bewitched her thinking. Because when she was asked if she was okay with being seated at the table of another patron in the resort's packed dining room, she'd said yes.

In more ways than one. Because the occupant of that other table had been none other than the hospital's hunky pediatrician. The outcome of that meeting had been very different than it was today. Because it had been the anniversary of Claire's cancer diagnosis, and she'd been all caught up in her emotions. Her encounter with Seb, and their fun—and very sexy—back-and-forth banter had led to an equally sexy night in her bungalow. The perfect outlet for her churning emotions. At least she'd thought so at the time. The tattoo of a sea turtle on his left shoulder with word *Bleu* scrawled in the middle of it had fascinated her. Was it a reference to the sea life and the gorgeous blue waters of his homeland?

"All done."

Claire's voice pulled her from her thoughts. They went

out to the car and, after arriving at the apartment, Rachel saw her daughter inside before taking off on foot to the market. Once there, she picked up several mangoes, a melon and some veggies, then hurried to the fish market. She arrived back home to find Claire flopped on the couch, back in her pj's. A frisson of alarm went through her. "Are you feeling worse?"

"No, but it's Saturday, and I don't have school. I just changed back, since you won't let me do anything with my friends. Right?"

"Right. Not until we know what we're dealing with."

Claire gave a dramatic sigh that made her smile. Her daughter was definitely an extrovert, unlike her mom, who had to be more intentional in talking to people, due to her job. But she was glad at how easily her girl could make friends.

Except when it came to Sebastien, evidently, since she'd ushered him out of the room as soon as she got a chance. But their conversation in that hallway had shaken her up almost as much as it had in that restaurant a year ago. She'd found herself reading something into almost everything he said.

She smiled to take the sting out of her earlier words. "Well, you're negative for the flu and COVID, so there's that. Sebas—er, Dr. Deslaurier said he'd call as soon as the mono test comes back. It should be anytime now."

Her daughter's head cocked. "I told you you were overreacting. *Seb* doesn't seem worried at all."

Seb. Great. Claire seemed to relish saying the man's name, putting special emphasis on it. She should have objected when the pediatrician had offered it up. But she hadn't. And now it was too late, evidently. Her worry had superseded everything else.

They had both tiptoed around the reason for Rachel's

worry, but they both knew exactly what it was about. Knew exactly what she was afraid of, even six years after Claire had finished with her treatments.

Rachel wondered if her daughter knew just how terrified she was every time she had a little cough or a sore throat. Probably. But tenderness in the lymph nodes in her neck was what had set them on that crazy journey of infusions and tests in the first place.

Claire had been one of the lucky ones. There were so many children who weren't. Rachel had seen it with her own eyes through her job. The offer to work in a smaller hospital on the island of Taurati had been a balm to her soul, since her job in Wisconsin had been at a teaching hospital with a huge oncology department. Each child who came through with cancer was like a knife to her heart.

She decided to shift the subject from cancer…or Seb. "How's your French and Tahitian coming?"

One thing she hadn't thought about was the fact that they would both be learning two other languages simultaneously.

"I would say better than yours, but that doesn't sound very nice, does it?"

Rachel grinned and mimicked her daughter's playful tone. "I would say no, it doesn't, but that it's probably true."

Fortunately Taurati had a vibrant tourist industry, so English was widely spoken. Even her encounters with Sebastien had taken place in her heart language, except for those sexy muttered phrases here and there in that hut.

Which she was not going to think about again. Or about the pediatrician's French accent, which was almost as smoking hot as he was. From what Sebastien had said the few times they'd actually spoken about things other than work, she knew his mom was Tahitian and his dad was French. He'd grown up in the islands and had lived in Taurati for the last five years. There'd been murmurs around the nurses' stations about something bad that had happened in his past, but normally those conversations took place in a language other than English, and Rachel tried not to translate them in her head. Once she heard his name mentioned, she did her best to tune the speaker out. The less she knew about him, the better. Because her reaction to him when she didn't even know him? Well, it was electric. And oh, so dangerous.

Even in hospital hallway, when her sick child had been mere footsteps away, she'd had a hard time not absorbing every syllable he said and letting them linger in her head.

"Let me throw together something to eat and then we can watch a movie." She held up her bag. "And the mangoes look out of this world today."

"Yum, thanks."

Rachel went into the kitchen and cut up some of the fruit and then made a light salad and grilled the fish. It was hot enough outside today that the air-conditioning was having trouble keeping up, so something light seemed like the order of the day. Besides, walking home in the oppressive heat had taken a lot out of her.

Or was it due to the playful banter with Sebastien? *Not going there. Not right now.*

When she had their plates ready, she walked into the other room. "Do you want to eat here? Or at the dining room table?" A table that consisted of an ancient round slab of wood and some whitewashed chairs. Rachel loved the charm of it.

"Sofa, for sure."

"Okay, but just for tonight."

Handing Claire a plate, she settled in and turned the

television on, choosing a romantic comedy that her daughter said she wanted. Romantic comedy. Well, Rachel's love live was certainly a comedy, but the romantic part? Nope. Not in a long while. Claire's father had skipped out while she'd still been a baby, saying he wasn't ready to be a father. And in her daughter's twelve years, Rachel had had exactly two encounters with men, one of which had been with Sebastien, and surely you couldn't even count that.

Oh, it counted. It definitely counted.

But it was up to her to make sure that their time together stayed firmly entrenched in the past. For everyone's sake. But most importantly Claire's. There was no way she was going to let someone into her daughter's life only to have him walk back out of it again. Been there, done that. The only good part was that Claire didn't remember the pain of her biological dad leaving. But she was definitely old enough to be hurt by something like that now. And the way she'd taken to Sebastien had unnerved Rachel.

Her daughter had enough emotional scars. For that matter, so did she. She was not looking to add to that number.

What she was going to do first was make sure her daughter was okay physically. Then she was going to bury her own heart so deep that nothing or no one would be able to find it. With that decided, she threw herself into watching the movie, trying to enjoy every second she got to spend with her daughter, knowing Claire was growing up way too fast. That was evident in her not wanting her mom to see her change clothes.

She put her free arm around Claire and gave her a quick squeeze. "Love you, kiddo."

Claire looked at her. "I know. Love you, too."

And when her phone rang toward the end of the movie,

she glanced down and saw that it was the hospital. Forcing back sentimental tears from the movie they were watching, she took a deep breath and hoped her voice wouldn't shake when she answered.

"Hello?"

"Hi, Rachel, it's Seb."

Seb. Her eyes closed, and she prayed this was the news she wanted to hear.

"The test results?"

"Yes. It's definitely not mono."

Her fingers dug into the arm of the sofa even as she finished up the call, thanking him.

Claire was looking at her with a weird expression. "What is it?"

"It's good news. You don't have mono."

It was strange that good news could also be bad. Very bad.

Because if Claire didn't have mono…what did she have?

CHAPTER TWO

"THERE'S A PROBLEM on the beach."

Rachel looked up at one of the other nurses, who was just putting down a phone. "What is it?"

"Possible drowning victim." Her colleague called out to Seb, who was just exiting a room. "Can you and Rachel run down to the beach out front and help with a kid who's been pulled from the water? Lifeguard is administering CPR but doesn't want to stop to carry the child up the beach to Hospitalier."

There was no time for thought, no time for wondering if she could hand the case over to someone else. She glanced at Sebastien, who was quicker on his feet than she was.

"Let's go."

Grabbing the medical kit that the nurse held out, they headed to the door, Sebastien calling back, "Have them bring a gurney to the edge of the boardwalk so we can use an ambu bag during transport."

"Already on it," said the nurse, phone in her hand.

Rachel raced to the door with Sebastien, a million thoughts and procedures racing through her head.

There was a plank boardwalk at the end of the parking lot that led from the hospital down to the beach. Normally it was used by hospital staff to go out and spend their breaks in one of the colorful beach chairs that the facility placed down there for family and friends. The trained lifeguard was also an employee of the hospital.

Rachel had spent some time down there with Claire, but this was the first time she'd had to rush there to help someone.

As they made the hundred-yard trek over the boards, a stand of thatched buildings on stilts in the water a good distance down the beach caught her eye. They were similar to the ones at the resort where she'd stayed. Rented out as hotel rooms to tourists. Rachel had had visions of paddling a long board out from one of them. Instead, she'd brought Seb back to the one she'd rented, forever changing what she thought about when she looked at the structures.

That was soon forgotten as she caught sight of the desperate life-and-death battle being waged just above the shoreline.

"Oh, God, oh, God, *oh, God*!"

She wasn't sure whether the keening cries coming from a woman who knelt next to the lifeguard were a desperate plea or a horrified epithet, but they were going to haunt her for a while.

Seb reached them first, with Rachel just a second or two behind. He touched the lifeguard's back. "We'll take over and you can fill us in."

The man slid out of the way, his breath coming in heavy gasps as Sebastien handed her the ambu bag while he quickly checked for signs of breathing and a pulse.

"Nothing…yet."

She had a feeling the last part of the sentence was added for the woman who'd cried out a few second earlier. But she couldn't worry about that right now.

Fitting the mouthpiece over the child—a little girl,

who couldn't be more than five or six—she started respirations while Seb did compressions.

Before the lifeguard could say anything, the woman grabbed the child's hand as tears fell freely down her face. "A wave grabbed her from me. I couldn't hold on. I couldn't. I tried!"

The man who'd been doing compressions nodded at her. "I know you did." He then turned to Seb. "The wave knocked the child over, and I lost sight of her for a second. I went in. It took me about three minutes to find her and get her to shore."

Three minutes. Three minutes in which precious oxygen had been cut off from the girl's brain. The waters here were warm—they weren't like the frigid lakes in Wisconsin, where the cold could slow down body functions and provide more time for rescues.

Seb didn't answer, continuing to count compressions, but it was obvious he was listening, his glance coming up and spearing hers for a second. And the flash of pain she saw in his eyes…

Of course Rachel was just as anxious to revive this little girl as he was, but the look on Sebastien's face shocked her. Normally the pediatrician's eyes were cloaked with some kind of secrecy that she couldn't decipher. Not that she tried. Or wanted to. Not since that night he'd whispered into her ear, the hot and sexy syllables needing no translation. From that time on, however, there'd been no break in his steely demeanor. And she was glad of it.

Especially after seeing what she'd just witnessed in his eyes.

What had happened to him?

She remembered the whispers among the staff. Maybe she should have listened a little closer.

About three minutes went by as they worked in silence, then the child moved, her hands opening and closing. As if mentally synced, she and Seb both rolled the girl onto her side, where with a convulsive heave of her chest, a blast of water shot from her mouth. She started coughing.

A shout from the side pulled Rachel's attention to the boardwalk. Two hospital orderlies stood there with a gurney.

The lifeguard had to physically hold the distraught woman back to keep her from crawling over and crowding them.

Maybe the words shouted earlier really had been a prayer, because by some miracle, the child's eyes fluttered open, the blue of them brighter to Rachel than the sun.

Her gaze swung over the people gathered around her. "Mommy?"

The lifeguard let the woman go, and she leaned down and cradled the child's head, raining kisses and tears onto her forehead. "Oh, baby... Thank God."

Seb interrupted. "We still need to get her to the hospital. What's her name?"

"Sharon." The woman's voice caught on a sob before coming back again. "Her name is Sharon."

"Let's get Sharon on the gurney, and we'll get her checked out."

"Thank you. Thank you so much. All of you."

Seb's face visibly tightened. "Don't thank us just yet. We still need to check her over and make sure there's no more water in her lungs."

He climbed to his feet and swung Sharon effortlessly into his arms and strode with her to the gurney waiting a short distance away. The sight of him holding that little girl made Rachel's throat tighten.

The girl twisted, looking back. "Mommy!"

"I'm right here, honey."

Now that the urgency of the situation had faded a bit, Rachel stopped to speak to the lifeguard. "You saved her life. Thank you."

The young man, who was probably not yet thirty, nodded, dragging his fingers through his hair. "Hell, I thought for a few minutes…" His voice took on a rough edge before fading away.

Rachel knew exactly what it was like after that rush of adrenaline leached away, leaving a big hole of nothingness. She reached over and squeezed his hand. "I think we all did. But you didn't give up. That's why she's alive."

Seb's voice came back to her as the gurney moved up the walkway. "Rachel. Could you grab the ambu bag on your way in?"

"Yep. On my way." With an apologetic glance at the lifeguard, she let go of him and smiled. "Well, thanks again."

"Can you let me know how she does?"

"I'll ask her mom if it's okay." With that, she grabbed the lifesaving device, turned and hurried up the pathway, having to jog to catch up with the little group.

Little Sharon was talking to her mom, asking why she was crying.

"Because I'm just so happy, baby."

"Happy I'm okay?"

"Yes, that's exactly it."

The tightness in Rachel's throat moved to her eyes. She knew exactly what it was like to realize your child was going to be okay after fearing they were going to die. The rush of relief that made your legs weak and your words fail.

The day she'd gotten the news that Claire had cancer

had been one of the worst of her life. And she'd had absolutely no one to lean on but her parents. She'd wrestled with whether or not she should try to find Roy, her ex, and let him know, but he'd been pretty adamant that he didn't want to be a father. And he'd never once contacted them, even though Rachel and Claire still lived in the same town in which their daughter was born.

Her daughter. Roy might have been there for her birth, but he'd become distant and moody, seeming totally put out when Claire cried. She should have seen the split coming, but she'd been so wrapped up in the birth and lack of sleep that big swaths of time became a blur.

Claire had asked about her father a couple of times over the years, but so far Rachel had glossed over the fact that her ex hadn't wanted anything to do with her. But at some point, her daughter was going to want to know more. She might even want to try to find her father. And when that happened, Rachel would have to do her best to prepare her for what might not be a rosy reunion.

At the top of the boardwalk, Sebastien gave her a look that made her frown.

"Is she okay?" The ambu bag was still in her left hand, she realized, but there was something about the way his eyes jerked back to their patient that made her frown deepen. As if he were worried more than he was letting on.

"I hope so. We'll need to get her to radiology to check her lungs. Good job, though."

"Thanks." Trying not to let the words cause her heart to jump, she turned her attention back to her patient, getting the child to smile at a story about Claire's first trip to the ocean. And when they reached the door to the hospital, she was glad that her interaction with Sebastien was almost at an end. Because his voice made her want to hang on to his every word. And that was a path that was rife with danger. She knew that from experience.

The doors opened with a whisper of sound as they all went through them. Seb wasn't sure what was wrong with him. As he'd seen the child lying on the beach, her lips taking on a bluish tinge, an image of him standing over Bleu's lifeless body had come back to him. Layla had tried to pull him away, to give him some comfort, but he'd just brushed her off, telling her he was fine when he obviously wasn't.

It reminded him of the lifeguard having to pull the girl's mother away. He thought Rachel had noticed at first, but thankfully she'd seemed oblivious to what was running through his mind.

His and Layla's relationship had started off hot and heavy. But physical attraction and the hormones of youth had rushed them past the important parts of courtship. The parts of getting to know each other. Of learning what caring and commitment truly meant. After their baby died...well, there'd been nothing of substance left between them. He'd been left feeling...empty. It was no wonder she'd walked away from him not long afterward. Just one more person gone from his life.

The emergency room staff was in ready mode, and they went into action as he concentrated on sending out requests for Sharon's blood ox to be monitored and asked them to page whoever the on-call pulmonologist was.

"Are you going to keep her?" The girl's mom, who'd told him her name was Marie, still looked beyond worried. Beyond scared.

"I'd like her to stay overnight, just to keep an eye on her, okay? And I've called for a lung specialist to have a look at her." He didn't want to scare Sharon's mom with possibilities of dry drowning—where lungs became inflamed by the sudden introduction of water into them. Even after the water was gone, the inflammatory process sometimes continued, filling the lungs with fluid produced by the body itself.

"Can I stay with her?"

"I think that can be arranged. Let's get those bloods drawn, and then we'll get her into a room." He forced a smile. "I think she's going to sleep well tonight after all this excitement."

Marie immediately relaxed, and it made Sebastien tense even further. This happened time and time again with the family of his patients, and he'd had to learn to be very careful with his words. Sharon was out of immediate danger, but outcomes rarely came with a guarantee. One of Bleu's doctors had been brusque and cold, as if his son's life—or death—was of no concern to him. Questions were met with irritation and dismissal. Seb had vowed he would not be like that. He would truly invest in his patients' lives—welcome any and all questions. But, at times, it led to a type of emotional exhaustion that was hard to shake.

"That's the kind of excitement I can do without," Sharon's mom said with a smile.

"I agree. Me, too."

Rachel was hanging back a bit, the breathing device clutched to her chest. She looked a little harried. Maybe Claire was worse. He excused himself and then went over to her.

"Are you okay?"

"I think so. It was touch and go there for a while."

"Yes, it was." He paused. "Is the lifeguard okay? I saw you talking to him."

"He's kind of shell-shocked." She crossed her arms

over her chest. "Just like we get after a crisis has passed, when we're trying to find our balance."

Was that even possible? Had he found his balance after Bleu's death? He wasn't quite sure, even after all this time.

A shadow in her expression made him wonder if she was talking about Sharon or if she was thinking about her own daughter. Or was it that emotional exhaustion he'd thought about moments earlier? Before he could work it out, her chin gave a dangerous wiggle, lips thinning as if she was working to hold back her emotions. "Hey, let's take a break and go outside for a few minutes."

She sighed out a huge breath. "Thanks. I don't know what's wrong with me."

"It's okay. I'll be right back." He went over to the staff and let them know he'd be outside in the courtyard area for a few minutes if they needed him. "Let me know when the pulmonologist arrives."

Once outside, he led the way to a concrete bench not far from the boardwalk. Facing the ocean, it was close enough that the spicy breeze from the water reached them, while far enough that they were away from sunbathers or the lifeguard, who looked like he'd resumed his post.

Finding his own balance?

He motioned for Rachel to sit down and joined her, watching as she sucked down a quick breath, her brown eyes not quite landing on any one thing.

"Just take a moment or two to let it run its course."

"To let what run its course?"

She was pretending. It was there in the fingers fidgeting in her lap, the tight set to her shoulders that said she was still making an effort to contain something. How many times had he done that same thing? Pretended not to feel. Not to care. And when his fiancée had left, hadn't he worked even harder at it? He still did—in his private life, anyway. The funny thing was he was more open with his patients than he was with friends and family.

"The energy. Or adrenaline, as you said about the lifeguard. Whether that child lived or died, we did our best by her—you know that, right?"

Was this about Sharon? Or was he lecturing himself about Bleu's death?

"I do know. But I'm very grateful for this outcome instead of what could have happened."

No one knew that better than Sebastien, who'd seen firsthand what the alternative was.

"How is Claire, by the way? Feeling any better?"

Two days had passed since he'd examined Rachel's daughter. He hadn't seen her in that time to ask about her. He'd since asked that all other tests be sent to Dr. Rogan, since he was Claire's primary care physician. Could she have gotten bad news? Maybe that was playing a role in her shakiness today. Hell, he hoped not.

"She is. Dr. Rogan called me. The diagnosis ended up being lymphadenopathy."

"Caused by?" Lymphadenopathy was the technical term for an enlargement of the lymph nodes. It could be caused by anything from tuberculosis to mono—to cancer.

Rachel gave a shrug. "They think from the cold she'd had a few days earlier. Since it's viral, it just has to run its course, which it seems to be doing. The swelling is much less pronounced today."

He hadn't realized he was holding his breath until she said *less pronounced*. He released it in a rush, wincing at how loud it sounded to his own ears. "That's great. I know you were worried."

She tilted her head. "Having kids is hard. Worry kind of comes with the territory."

The inference was *if you had children, you'd understand.*

He wouldn't have corrected her, even if she'd said the words out loud. His private life was his own concern, not hers.

And yet, he'd just sat here and asked about hers.

So he just said, "Yes, it does. I see that every day in the parents of my patients. Anyway, I'm glad she's feeling better."

"Thank you." Her eyes held his for a minute, as if probing for something.

It made him haul himself to his feet. "Well, I probably need to get back and see how Sharon's doing. Why don't you stay here and decompress for a bit?"

"No, I'm fine." She stood as well. "Besides, I want to see how she is, too. And if I had to decompress every time there was an emergency, I wouldn't be a very good nurse, would I? I think it just hit me because Claire was about this age when I got the news that she was sick. Really sick."

Bleu had still been an infant when he and Layla realized his eyes had stopped tracking their movements. It had taken a mere MRI to bring them the news no parent ever wants to hear.

"I can understand that." And he did. Babies who presented with neurological symptoms did the same to him. And the one case of brain cancer he'd diagnosed had caused him to take a few days of personal time. But he'd gotten through it.

Rachel would get through this as well. And in the end, she'd go home to be with her child. Would be able to hug her tight and assure her that all was right with the world.

And it was. With their little piece of it, anyway. But there were never any guarantees in this life.

She nodded toward the hospital. "Shall we?"

"Yep."

With that, they made their way back to the hospital, and he told himself that the next time someone seemed stressed out by a case, he was going to let them handle it in their own way, without any input or interference from him.

It would be easier for that person. And it would certainly be a whole lot easier for him.

CHAPTER THREE

SEBASTIEN WALKED PAST the picture of his son, just as he did every morning. Except normally he gave it a passing glance before moving on with his day. This time, however, he picked it up and looked at it, studying the curly brown hair and tiny lips. Maybe because of his encounter with Rachel yesterday. He wasn't sure why, but he'd had a hard time sleeping last night. And when he had fallen into slumber, he'd had dreams of Bleu being carried away by ocean currents while he'd trudged through the surf, unable to reach him.

The dreams he understood. They were caused by little Sharon's near drowning. Fortunately, she'd been fine the rest of the night at the hospital, and she was set to be released.

Today was a new day. For that he was glad. He looked again at his son's image.

The pregnancy had been unexpected, but he'd been prepared to marry Layla and make a family with her and their child. He'd been young and idealistic and had even managed to convince himself that he loved her. All would be right with the world as long as he believed it was so. But, of course, it hadn't been, and after Bleu died, there'd been a thread of relief when Layla walked out.

Maybe it was because he'd needed to grieve Bleu's

death privately, but he didn't think that was the entire reason. And despite any regret he may have had about Layla's absence, it just drove home the fact that people left. Whether they wanted to or not.

Afraid he might somehow forget his son, he'd impulsively walked into a tattoo parlor a few weeks later and had Bleu's name and favorite toy tattooed on his left shoulder. Of course, he never forgot him, but he did forget about the ink on his body most days. But when he'd done another impulsive thing and slept with Rachel, she'd reminded him of exactly why he avoided relationships. He'd been sitting on the bed reaching down for his clothing when gentle fingers had touched his shoulder and he realized what she'd found. A spear shafted straight to his heart as he relived those terrible days leading to Bleu's death.

He couldn't afford another accidental pregnancy, and despite the protection he'd used, a sense of fear oozed through him right after their encounter. He'd wanted to ask her about it later on when he saw her at the hospital a few weeks after their night together, but he couldn't bring himself to. She'd tell him if it somehow happened, wouldn't she?

And she'd acted so chilly toward him after that night, he didn't think she'd welcome any probing questions about her fertility.

Hell, even thinking about it in those terms made him cringe.

Maybe the tattoo was a good thing. The few times he'd slept with someone, there'd always been *that* question— the one about the meaning of that tat. It would either jerk him out of the moment or remind him of his silent vow not to become a father again. Bleu would keep him on the straight and narrow, even from the grave. Strangely,

Rachel had not asked about it. She'd simply traced gentle fingertips across it and left it at that. But that soft touch had left its mark. He could still feel it in unguarded moments. Or whenever he saw her at work.

He set the picture back down on the end table, swearing he felt a sharp twinge in his shoulder as he did. Maybe there really was an afterlife and that was his son's way of communicating with him.

"Wish you were still here, kid."

Sighing, he went into the bathroom and looked himself in the face. Thirty-five years had not been kind to him. There were gray strands threaded through black hair that was a little too long. He swept it back off his forehead. He always seemed to go too long in between cuts. Maybe because of that huge mirror in most salons and the awkward conversations with strangers who inevitably asked about family relationships. And kids.

How did you answer that question?

He did have a kid. But to speak of Bleu in the present tense seemed like a lie. But to tell the truth? That was even more awkward and usually resulted in shocked silence, followed by swift backtracking and murmurs of sympathy. And it all happened in sight of that mirror.

Yeah. Well, his hair would survive another couple of weeks before he went through that again. Right?

With that, he brushed his teeth and shaved, having taken a shower before going to bed. It was a habit now. Because you never knew when the phone could ring in the middle of the night with an emergency case.

He still got a Christmas card from Bleu's maternal grandparents every year. And almost every year, they updated him on their daughter's life. She still wasn't married. Still didn't have any other kids. It was almost as if they were trying to get him to call her. He wouldn't.

He realized now that their reasons for getting married would have made for a difficult union at best.

Besides, his life wasn't in Tahiti anymore. It was here in Taurati. And if Layla's parents wanted more grandchildren, they needed to look to someone else. Because it wouldn't be him. There were too many might-have-beens juxtaposed with what actually was. Not a good basis for marriage or anything else.

And that held true for friendships as well. His conversation with Rachel yesterday had exposed the same glaring contrasts between their situations. But he could see it a little more clearly now. That while Rachel might feel fortunate to still have her daughter, that clawing fear of loss was never far from the surface. Sebastien had just assumed that it went away with time. But evidently not.

He wasn't sure he could handle going through that every time he faced a difficult case.

Not even if it meant having Bleu still here with him?

Well, that was different. Of course he wished his son had lived. The difference was, Claire wasn't his. And he wasn't going to willingly walk into a situation where he would be reminded day in and day out what the future might hold.

Selfish? Absolutely. But wasn't self-preservation a selfish instinct at its core?

That hadn't stopped him from sleeping with someone who'd had a child, though. But he hadn't known at the time about Claire's cancer. If he had, things might have ended very differently that night. Instead, they had indulged in some sexy give-and-take banter that reminded him how fun it used to be to do that. She'd been new to the island, and he'd offered to show her a few sights. And she'd shown him a few as well—like the interior of her overwater bungalow, where they'd fallen into bed together.

The next morning, she'd traced his shoulder. The memory sent a shudder through him.

Damn. He swung away from the mirror and finished dressing. This was why he didn't connect with people, even in friendship. It was why, despite his years in Taurati, real friends were few and far between. And all the ones he did have were colleagues at work.

He wasn't actually on call today, but most mornings found him in his office doing paperwork. His office was safe. Private. And it was where he liked to pass the time.

To avoid taking part in the world at large? To avoid another incident like the one with Rachel a year ago?

Probably. But it was what it was.

He caught a taxi and headed to the hospital. The second he pushed through the doors, his phone pinged. Weird. Almost everyone knew that Tuesdays were his day off. He glanced down at the screen. It was from the hospital administrator.

Hey, are you here yet?

His lips curved. That was the one downside to being so predictable. Neves was one of those few friends, and the man pretty much knew exactly where he could find Seb. The administrator was sharp and was very good at his job, which was to keep the hospital running well, heading off problems before anyone even knew there was one.

He texted back. Just arriving.

Can you come up?

He sighed before responding. He'd been looking forward to some alone time after his thoughts this morning. But it wasn't like he could just refuse.

On my way.

Neves Bouchet's office was in the same fourth floor wing as his and most of the other permanent physicians' spaces. Waiting for the elevator around the corner, his eye caught sight of the ocean a short way from the hospital. Framed by green palm fronds and white beaches, the calm azure color of the water was as alluring on Taurati as it was on the other islands of French Polynesia. Except he saw it so often that sometimes he had to remind himself of its beauty. His time in medical school in France had given him a new appreciation of the islands where he'd been born.

The elevator doors opened, and he was dumped onto the fourth floor. Rounding the corner, he pushed through the glass door to Neves's waiting area. He frowned when he spied Rachel in one of the chairs. He glanced around. No one else was here.

Hell, he hoped this wasn't about what had happened between them last year. In all honesty, he'd been waiting for that to catch up with him. But after a year?

You're being paranoid, Seb.

They'd both been consenting adults who'd agreed to remain mum about the night they'd shared. Not that the hospital really had any rules against colleagues sleeping together, although the unspoken consensus was that it could be a sticky situation. But it evidently worked for some. There was at least one pair of surgeons at Centre Hospitalier who were married. And his and Rachel's encounter had only been one night long.

Rachel didn't even look at him. Dressed in a gauzy white skirt and a blouse that was as blue as the ocean, she looked almost as inviting as the warm currents a short distance away. And when she crossed her legs—

that slow slide of calf over calf was reminiscent of… He swallowed. *Okay, don't go there.*

But at odds with his thoughts were the tense lines in her face and her refusal to glance his way. It couldn't be a coincidence that she was here. Did she know why they'd been summoned? Was this about the girl at the beach yesterday?

He glanced at Neves's administrative assistant, who must have guessed his thoughts, because she nodded. "He hoped you were in the building so he could meet with you both together."

His eyes went back to Rachel before returning to the desk. "About?"

"Hey, I just work here." Cécile raised her hands, palms out, in a way that said she had no idea why they were here. And he couldn't very well ask Rachel if she knew. Not in front of Neves's assistant.

Cécile picked up her office phone and murmured something into it. Then she looked up. "You can go on in."

When no one moved, she grinned. "Both of you."

Sebastien waited for Rachel to stand and then motioned for her to go ahead of him. It was the polite thing to do, but it would also help him put a halt to his racing thoughts. If Neves wanted to talk about possible rumors or innuendos surrounding their night together, he wasn't sure what he was going to say. And if it was something else entirely?

Well, it would be a relief.

Rachel ducked through the door, and he followed her.

Neves stood to greet them. "Hi, guys. Thanks for taking some time out from your day. I have something I want to discuss, but I'd rather it not go any farther than this room at the moment."

Merde. Maybe there was something floating around the hospital after all.

Rachel beat him to the punch. "I'm not sure I understand, Neves."

Although Neves was technically an internal medicine doctor, once he took over the hospital's administrative duties, he'd stopped practicing medicine. He said it was because of how much time the position took, but he also said it could give the impression of favoritism if one patient got resources that another was denied.

"Sit, please."

There were only two chairs across from the desk, so there was no option but to sit next to her. Seb hoped to hell his afternoon went better than his morning was going so far. Or yesterday, for that matter. Working so closely with Rachel on that case had brought back some memories of its own. And he'd been surprised by the easy rhythm between them as they worked to resuscitate Sharon. He didn't want easy between them. He wanted their interactions to be damned hard. So hard that he kept avoiding her like he had for the past year.

He dropped into his chair and looked at the administrator. "What's this about, Neves?"

The man looked down at some papers on his desk before lifting his head to look from one to the other. "Did either of you catch the news today?"

Seb attempted a smile. "Not today. Is Centre Hospitalier on lockdown or something?" Kind of a stupid question, since he'd just walked right through the front doors.

"Not yet."

What the hell? Was there some communicable disease swirling around? COVID had done a number on them a while back. The last thing they needed was something new on the horizon. "So we might have to go on lock-down? Why?"

"You haven't seen the weather reports?"

Sebastien remembered thinking the good old South Pacific looked pretty calm today. And the sun was a big hot orb in the sky, just like it was most days.

Rachel cocked her head. "No. What about them?"

"There's an area out there that could become worri-some if it develops any further."

"An area, as in a hurricane? I thought those didn't happen here."

Neves nodded. "They don't normally. And cyclones, as they're called in this part of the world, are rare in Poly-nesia. But they're certainly not unheard-of."

The last major cyclone to strike the area was named Wasa-Arthur, if he remembered right. But that had been decades ago. Surely if there was one off the coast, he would have heard about it by now. "What does any of that have to do with us?"

Neves leaned forward. "Again, I don't want any of this leaving this room." His voice lowered. "Rachel guessed correctly. There's a low-pressure system out there."

"A low-pressure system." He frowned. "This is the time for them. Is it threatening the island?" November through April was normally when cyclones formed in this part of the world.

"Right now, I'm choosing to err on the side of pre-paredness."

"What does that mean, exactly?" Rachel's voice slid past him.

"It means I would like you two to go over hospital protocols and make sure everything is up-to-date and in place. I normally have Laurence and Britan do that this time of year, even if there's no system forming out there, but they're expecting and I don't want to put any more on them."

Laurence and Britan were the married surgeons he'd thought about this morning. "I didn't know they were expecting."

"I found out about it last month. But she's had a couple of spikes in her blood pressure. Nothing serious, but Laurence came in after hearing about the depression and asked if they could be replaced as the cyclone committee this year."

Committee. Okay, so that meant multiple people, right?

"Can't other members of the committee pick up the slack?"

Neves laughed. "If there were any other members, then yes. But they worked well together and always got the job done. And since you're here most days, even on your days off, Seb, I thought you could step in." His glance moved to Rachel. "And as one of the newest members of our medical staff, I thought you might like to get an insider's view of how things work at the hospital during emergencies. Unless there's some reason you'd rather not be a part of a working committee."

Several seconds went by with a series of expressions winding across her face. Consternation. Tension. Dismay. And then relief.

Relief?

Maybe, like him, she'd thought the administrator had called her in for a completely different reason. Maybe they could make this quick if they were stuck working together.

Rachel shrugged. "No, it's fine as long as I can help with it during most of my on-duty hours. I have a daughter at home."

"Of course. And if you're swamped with cases, those

come first, obviously. Just in the quieter times of the day. Maybe an hour or two here and there. You two figure out when you can meet."

And hour or two? Here and there? A lot could happen within that set of parameters.

His brain swore at him again. No. Nothing was going to happen. Other than what Neves had asked them to do: review protocol.

"It shouldn't take long, then."

Neves sent his gaze Seb's way. "However long it takes for that system to burn itself out or head in a different direction. I don't want what happened in '91 to catch us unprepared again. Our hospital's power grid was taken out with that one, resulting in the deaths of two patients."

Sebastien remembered hearing about that. "I'm not sure how we can prevent something like that."

"I know you can't make any guarantees. But you can go through the evacuation procedures if it comes to that and oversee their implementation. It's what Laurence and Britan were charged with. I thought if you were both willing..." Neves's voice trailed off.

If Seb said no, his friend would want an explanation—one he was loath to provide. Especially not in front of Rachel.

"I'm fine with it." He looked at Rachel, brows slightly raised in challenge. "How about you?"

"Y-yes, of course. If it will help. My daughter comes first, though. She's just getting over a virus."

"Understood. Bring her to work with you, if it will help."

Oh, hell, no. He and Rachel would have to keep this within the boundaries of work hours. "I'm sure we can get this all done during our scheduled shifts."

He was relieved to see Rachel nod. "Yes, I'm sure we

can. Besides, if it's been that long since your last storm, then I'm sure this one will spin out before it even starts. Nothing will happen."

Even before her confident words ended, a low chill slid through Sebastien's veins. She hadn't been here long enough to know what every islander understood from birth. One thing they were careful never to do. One did not challenge their island and expect to walk away unscathed.

He would do well to listen to his own counsel and realize you did not challenge fire and expect to come away with clear lungs and unsinged hands. So if he and Rachel were going to have to work together in a manner that was unlike what they did on a day-to-day basis at the hospital, then he was going to have to be on guard. Each and every hour that they spent together.

Why her? Why on earth had the hospital administrator chosen her of all people?

He'd already told her. She'd drawn the short straw because she was one of the newer members of Hospitalier's team. Something she wasn't thrilled about at the moment. Especially in light of her shakiness in working with Sebastien yesterday. Her knees had been like rubber. And once they'd handed Sharon off in the hospital, she'd been in danger of falling apart. He'd noticed, inviting her to take a break for a few minutes. Once she realized it would be with him, she should have refused. But to do that would let him know just how uncomfortable she was in his company.

But for the administrator to ask her to help monitor a cyclone?

Which cyclone was she referring to? Sebastien? Or the actual weather pattern?

Right now, it was both. Even sitting beside him for

those few minutes in Neves's office had sent her nerves through the roof. In fact, the second Sebastien had walked in the door of the reception area, her senses had gone on high alert, a feeling of doom hanging over her head.

She hadn't been wrong about the doom part.

They left the office together, and she couldn't help but ask, "How bad was the storm he was referring to? The one where those patients died?"

"I wasn't on Taurati at the time, but it was bad. I was still a kid, living in Tahiti. It was hit pretty hard, too. But Taurati has fewer resources. Less money."

"Fewer options." She hesitated before asking what was first and foremost on her mind. "How can I get Claire off the island if it looks like it's going to come our way? My mom lives in the States, in Wisconsin."

He looked at her for a long minute. "Let's go get some coffee and talk without worrying about being overheard."

That didn't sound good. Did he think she was being totally selfish for voicing that question and wanted to chastise her in private? Maybe he would be right to.

Would they actually be able to evacuate anyone, or would there be widespread panic that would keep people from getting out? She made a mental note to call her mom as soon as they were done here. Maybe Claire could take a week or two vacation from school and leave before it became necessary. Before there was a crush of people trying to get out.

That made her tense and sent her back to her first question—wasn't she giving herself an unfair advantage that others on the island didn't have?

Maybe Neves had been wrong about choosing her. After all, she and Claire could just slip unnoticed off the island and never come back, and she'd never have to face what the rest of the folks here might have to endure.

She already knew she wasn't going to do that.

If she could do something to help on Taurati, she was going to stay and do it. And if it meant sending Claire away so she could focus on her job, she would. Whatever it took. Even if that entailed working with a man who sent her pulse soaring into the heavens. She just hoped that, unlike Icarus, she stayed well out of the danger zone and made sure her feet weren't too far off the ground. And that her heart didn't venture too close to the sun.

CHAPTER FOUR

OF COURSE SHE was worried about her daughter. He couldn't blame her.

Sebastien opened the door to a nearby coffee shop and found a table in a far corner. When one of the waitstaff came over for their order, he nodded for Rachel to go first, his brows going up when she ordered an espresso.

He wasn't sure what he'd been expecting or why, but he found her order matched what he knew about her. She was straightforward without a lot of artifice. Maybe working with her would have been easier if she were totally fake. That would be easy to resist. But he didn't think she had a fake bone in her body. Not with how quick she was to talk about her daughter's illness. Far from telling him to mind his own business, she'd given him an honest appraisal without hesitation.

That was very different from how begrudging he was with information whenever asked his marital status or whether or not he had kids. But he didn't think that was just about his own comfort. It was awkward for everyone involved when he talked about his son.

Neves knew about Bleu, and so did a few other friends. But for the most part, no one at the hospital had any idea that the baby had ever existed. And on some level, that made him incredibly sad.

He realized the waiter still had his pen poised over his pad.

"Sorry. I'll have a café au lait."

Once the man left, he decided to be blunt. "I don't think either of us knew why Neves wanted to see us this morning. If you feel uncomfortable working with me, I can talk to him and see if—"

"Why would I feel uncomfortable working with you?"

He paused before trying again. "Are you saying you're not?"

Rachel leaned forward with a smile he could only classify as sardonic. "If you're talking about that crazy night a year ago, I'd almost forgotten all about it."

Shock made him sit back…until she laughed and continued, "I'm kidding. Of course it's awkward. But if I let a little awkwardness stand between me and my job, I'd have a hard time working anywhere. Not that I sleep with men I barely know wherever I go."

That made him chuckle, his muscles relaxing en masse. "Okay, now that we've addressed the elephant in the room, let's talk about your daughter."

"Excuse me?"

"I'm referring to getting her off the island if it looks like the pressure system is going to turn into an actual storm."

"I realize how that must have sounded, since so many others don't have the luxury of doing that, and I'm sorry if—"

"It's okay. I understand where you're coming from." His hand touched hers just as the waiter arrived with their coffees, making him pull back. They murmured their thanks, and the man slid away on silent feet.

Taking a bracing sip of his coffee, he tried to banish the sensations that brief touch had caused. Her skin was every bit as soft as he remembered. His brain resurrected memories of rolling her beneath him and making love to her far into the night.

Hmm...not making love. It was sex.

Did it really matter what it was called? The experience had left him unsettled, no matter what label he decided to slap on that night.

Forcing himself to return to the matter at hand, he responded to her words. "I would do the same if I were in your shoes. It's not just about keeping Claire safe. It's about eliminating distractions that could interfere with what needs to be done."

Distractions. Like innocent touches that brought not-so-innocent reactions?

"That's what I told myself, too. Then I wondered if I was trying to justify myself for even thinking about evacuating her."

"For what it's worth, I think you're right about wanting her off the island if the system looks like it will threaten Taurati. Part of living here means realizing the islands are not exempt from cyclones. But it's also knowing that they are the exception rather than the rule. There are other places that deal with these types of storms on a yearly basis, including parts of the States. We're fortunate enough that they normally veer off in another direction long before they get close to us."

"So when do you suggest I worry?"

"I'll tell you in enough time to arrange it. Before there's widespread panic."

"Thank you." This time it was her fingers that reached across to squeeze his. And there it was again—that immediate sense of wanting to prolong that contact for as long as possible. Before he could act on that thought, she sat back in her chair. "So what's the first thing we need to do?"

"Do?"

"As far as making sure the hospital is ready?"

He thought for a second. "Maybe we can meet in my office as time allows and run through the stuff that Laurence and Britan have on file."

"Should we meet with them, too?"

"Maybe. If she's having a tough pregnancy, though, I don't want to add to their stress levels. But we also may need some insight that we won't find in the files. I'll feel them out and see what they think."

Sebastien knew the couple, but he wasn't close to either one of them. If Laurence had already asked to be replaced, maybe they would resent being approached. If so, the other man could simply say no. But he had a feeling they would be glad to meet with Seb and Rachel. They just didn't want to be responsible for the whole thing, since they were focused on the health of their child.

"Sounds good. What's your schedule like?"

"I'm actually off today. I just came in because I find it easier to…"

To what? Forget about his son? Forget that there was a social world out there where people still laughed…still loved? He finished his sentence with "I find it easier to catch up on paperwork when I'm not treating patients."

"Or dealing with storms?" She smiled when she said it, her demitasse poised in front of her mouth. And when she took that sip, her lips clung to the white porcelain in a way that made his mouth go dry. Right now there was a storm of a completely different type sending gale-force winds through his insides. Only it wasn't a distant threat, like the low-pressure system far offshore. This storm was right on top of him, threatening to whisk any semblance of caution away and fling it so far he'd have a hell of a time finding it again.

So he gripped it tighter and hoped his damn hands didn't lose hold and make him do something he'd regret.

Like he'd done a year ago? When he and Rachel had been glued together on a bed, unable to get enough of each other? Yes. Exactly like that. And he had a feeling if it happened again, it might not be quite as easy to walk away. So he needed to concentrate on what had to be done. Right here. Right now. Starting with what he was about to say.

"Okay, let's get to work on Neves's project."

Sharon was doing fine. By the time Rachel made it back to the hospital, she was afraid maybe the girl would be released before she'd had a chance to say goodbye. But she was still in her room, sitting up in bed. Marie was perched on the mattress next to her, holding her close.

It had been harder than it should have been to put an end to their coffee meeting. Two hours later, Sebastien had been the one to do it, standing and stretching his back, the bottom of his shirt coming up just enough for her to catch a sliver of tanned abdomen. Lord, she'd been done for. Hadn't been able to get out of there fast enough.

Swallowing, she shifted her attention to the bed. "How is she doing?"

"She seems to be no worse for wear, unlike her mother." Marie laughed, but the sound was brittle, like someone who was barely holding things together.

She understood exactly what that was like.

Rachel moved closer to the pair. "I get it. I had a scare with my own daughter several years ago. I wasn't sure how I was going to get through it."

"Your daughter almost drowned, too?"

"No, but she had cancer, and I was afraid she wasn't going to survive."

The young mother's teeth came down on her lip. "But she's okay now?"

"Yes. She's now twelve years old and doing great. I think Sharon is going to do great as well."

"So do I." A masculine voice came from behind her, and Rachel whirled around.

"I—I didn't know you were coming here." She couldn't stop her eyes from sliding to the bottom of his shirt and the area she'd stared at earlier, only to find it firmly covered.

One side of his mouth quirked. "And I didn't know *you* were coming here."

When Marie looked at them funny, Rachel quickly said, "We just came out of a meeting."

"Well, I'm glad you were both able to see her. I'd like to get a picture of you both with her, if I could."

Both of them? As in together? But what could she say? That she didn't want to be in a picture with him?

Seb seemed anything but worried as he smoothly replied, "Of course. We'd be happy to, wouldn't we, Rachel?"

"Yes."

Marie slid off the bed and pulled her phone from her pocket. "Mommy wants to get a picture of you and the doctors, okay?"

Sharon nodded her head and smiled.

Rachel got on one side of the girl, while Sebastien got on the other, both putting their arm around her at the same time. She shivered when his fingertips brushed against her bare arm. He hadn't done it on purpose, but by her reaction, he might as well have.

Damn. Pull yourself together, Rachel.

"Okay, on the count of three."

Sharon's mom counted down, and Rachel forced her lips to stretch in a wide grin that she was pretty sure looked macabre.

"One more." The phone went still for another shot. "Thank you both. For everything."

Rachel moved away so quickly she almost stumbled and had to put a hand on the bed to catch herself.

Girl, you are in trouble.

To cover her mental discomfort, she turned to the girl. "Take care of your mom, okay? You gave her a pretty big scare." She hoped the child understood. While the islanders spoke a combination of Tahitian and French, most also knew some English. She used her broken French to repeat herself. Four years of college French seemed so inadequate for real-life use.

The girl nodded.

Okay, so she'd understood her. That was good.

It might not hurt for her to brush up on the language and use it more. After all, she was living in their country now. So she was going to do it. At least with their younger patients.

She said her goodbyes and slid from the room so she wouldn't have to stay and make any more small talk. She needed to get back to work—and she needed to get away from Seb. Before she embarrassed herself any further.

But no sooner had she exited than he followed her out. "I called Laurence on my way to the hospital and asked about possibly meeting together. He's agreed to go over what they used to do, but he would rather meet with us by himself so Britan doesn't have to spend any extra time on her feet."

"Okay, sounds like a plan. Do you want me there?"

"Since we're supposed to be in this together, it might help."

They were in this together? He made it sound like they were an actual team.

Well, they were, right?

Yes, but only a professional team. Which was what he'd meant, of course.

"Did he give you a time frame?"

"Tonight after work, since this needs to happen fairly quickly? That system is either going to dissipate or strengthen, so I don't want to wait too long."

Tonight after work. "I have Claire…"

He nodded. "I know. Would it upset her to hear us talk about this?"

"No, I don't think so, since it's still kind of nebulous. We could order takeout and then do it—where? In your office?"

Do it in his office? Why did everything she said seem to have some hidden meaning all of a sudden? She quickly corrected herself. "We could have the *meeting* in your office, I mean."

"I knew what you meant." That corner of his mouth popped up again. "Okay, I'll meet you there with dinner. Anything you don't like?"

"I like everything."

Ugh! Again? Seriously? This time, Seb's glance slid from her eyes to her lips and hung there for a second. She wasn't the only one who was taking things the wrong way, it would seem.

"I'll just take my best guess, then. Seven o'clock? Does

that give you enough time to get Claire and bring her back here?"

"It does. I'll see you at seven, then."

With that, Sebastien finally headed in a direction that was different from her trajectory, and she was glad. Because she didn't know how much longer she could have pretended that everything was just fine.

When it really wasn't.

He hoped she liked fish.

Seb couldn't remember what Rachel had eaten at the restaurant a year ago. Because he'd been too busy trying not to notice how beautiful she was. And when she'd thrown her head back and laughed at something stupid he'd said, the long line of her neck stood out in sharp relief in the muted lighting of the restaurant. He wasn't even sure why he'd wound up at the restaurant that night, other than the fact that it was close to the hospital and he'd been hungry. He hadn't even cared when they'd asked if he would mind sharing his table.

Looking back, that had not been the smartest move.

Adjusting the takeout bags in his hands, he arrived back at his office in time to see Rachel and Claire get off the elevator. He'd tried to get a sampling of several things from the restaurant. Surely there'd be at least something that they would like.

He opened the door enough to motion them inside. Claire was a tall, lanky girl with hair as dark as her mom's.

He followed them in, and Rachel held up a couple of bags. "I brought plates and plastic cutlery."

"Good thinking." Unlike him, since the thought of plates hadn't even crossed his mind.

In fact, these days he didn't seem to think through much at all.

He'd briefly caught sight of Claire a time or two at the hospital but had never actually spoken to her before that day when he'd examined her. His eyes went to her neck, looking for any remaining swelling. If there was, it was no longer visible. A good sign.

He forced a smile. "How are you feeling?" He glanced at Rachel. "And it's Sebastien or Seb, remember?" He glanced over at Rachel to make sure she still didn't object.

"Sebastien is such a cool name."

"You think?"

Claire cocked her head. "Yep. It has a neat pronunciation."

Okay, well, that was the first time he'd ever heard that one. "Well, thank you very much." He held up the bags he had in both hands. "How about we serve this on the desk?"

"That looks like a ton of food."

He shrugged. "I wasn't sure what everyone liked. I'll go ahead and start setting it out."

Taking the containers out of the bag, he opened the largest one first, hearing an exclamation of surprise from behind him.

"*Poisson cru!* I love that."

He turned and found it was Claire who'd said it, not Rachel. His brows went up. "You've had *poisson cru* before?"

"Yes, someone brought it to school for a special birthday lunch one time. You had your choice of that or hot dogs." She made a face when she said that last word.

He couldn't blame her. Faced with that same choice, he was pretty sure which one he'd have elected to eat.

Stuffed inside coconut shells, the mixture of raw tuna,

lime, coconut juice, tomatoes and cucumber was a national dish among the French Polynesian islands. "Do you know what the Tahitian word for it is?"

Claire frowned for a minute as she thought. "*Ota* something?"

"Close. It's *e'ia ota*."

The girl pronounced the words carefully. "We're learning some Tahitian in school—and French—but Tahitian is really hard."

Seb had grown up learning it, since his mom was Tahitian. But he could see that it wasn't an easy language. "I think English is pretty difficult, too."

"But you speak it so well."

"We hear it a lot." He paused. "Tell you what. If you ever have any questions about Tahitian or French, you can ask me, okay?"

Rachel took a step forward, interrupting the exchange. "Well, I'm sure you have better things to do with your time. And with all of this delicious-smelling food sitting here, I'm starting to get hungry. Are we ready to eat?"

He guessed he'd been put in his place. It was pretty obvious that while Rachel might not mind her daughter using his first name, she did not want him involved in her life. And that was fine with him. In fact, it had provided the wake-up call he'd needed. In reality, he'd had no idea why he'd offered to help her learn Tahitian. It had been impulsive.

Like sleeping with her mother?

Exactly like that. The last thing he needed was to get attached to Rachel or her daughter.

She handed them each a plate and put some utensils in each of the food containers to serve it. She moved closer to him and lowered her voice. "I didn't mean what I said in a rude way. I just don't want her imposing on your time. I know you're busy."

He hadn't realized how tense he'd gotten until his muscles went slack. At least she didn't think he was some creep trying to push his way into their lives. That was the last thing he wanted to do.

What he'd vowed after Bleu's death still held. He did not want to be a father. Not now. Not in the future.

He waited for Rachel and her daughter to help themselves to the offerings, glad that they seemed to like everything on the desk. He hadn't been too sure about getting the *e'ia ota*, but as strange as the dish sounded, most people who tried it liked it.

Claire sat on one of the office chairs near the food, while Seb and her mom went over to the small love seat, setting their plates on the coffee table. Rather than sit next to her, he chose one of the two chairs across from her, lowering himself into it. Rachel was looking down at her plate with a weird half smile on her face.

"What?" he asked.

"Nothing, really," she said. "It's kind of weird working together, isn't it?"

Was he that easy to read?

"A little. But it's not something we can't handle."

Claire's voice carried across. "This is really good. And how did you know mango was my favorite fruit?"

He allowed himself to smile. "Isn't it everyone's?"

"It should be."

The rest of the meal was spent in companionable silence, with Claire occasionally asking how to say different Tahitian words.

When they cleaned up the food, stowing the leftovers in his office fridge, Rachel stood. "Claire, can you do your homework while Seb and I get some work done?"

"Are you going to see patients?"

"No, we're just making sure the hospital's rules and regulations are up to date."

She sidestepped the real reason for this meeting. As much as she'd said it wouldn't bother Claire to know there was a low-pressure system hanging out somewhere in the ocean, Rachel evidently didn't want her sitting right next to them while they discussed it.

That was fine with him. The less he had to interact with the girl, the better. And honestly, despite her earlier words, Rachel probably felt the same way. One thing he definitely didn't want was for her to start looking at him as some sort of father figure, because that was a recipe for hurt feelings. He didn't know if Claire's biological dad was out of the picture or if she was the result of a sperm donor, and really, the less he knew about it, the easier it would be to keep himself from doing something stupid.

Like getting attached?

Exactly like that. He'd only been really attached to one child in his life. And that kid's name was inscribed on his shoulder.

Rachel lifted the lid to her laptop and started it up. Once it had, she opened a window that contained weather updates and the projected course for the low-pressure system. Another browser pane displayed hospital protocol. Laurence was supposed to have joined the meeting, but he'd had to cancel at the last minute due to dinner plans his wife had made without his knowledge. And since the other doctor really didn't want her to know he was going to meet with them, he couldn't just stop by.

"Okay, where do we start?"

"Let's start with the evacuation plans."

She scrolled down the different emergency protocols the hospital had in place. When she found cyclones, she stopped, and they both scanned the document that had been updated last year. The bullet points laid things out step by step, moving from the least urgent scenario to the worst.

Not too bad. "Okay, here's how evacuations work." She used her pen to point to an area on the screen.

There were four medical centers on the island, ranging from a community prevention clinic that was only staffed once a week to Taurati's largest facility, which was Centre Hospitalier.

"Oh, my," she murmured.

Since Hospitalier was the biggest, it also had the most responsibility, having to make sure all the medical facilities were locked down and gathering records for patients who were actively being treated. Everything from ingrown toenails to chemo patients would have to be listed and accounted for, both before and after a storm hit.

"Yes, I know." Seb had figured it was going to be a huge task, and he could also see why Laurence had wanted to hand it off this year. "Let's look at storm projections."

They popped open the other screen, and Rachel slowly scrolled so that they could both read. "Oh, no. It's just become more organized."

"I see that."

"What's become more organized?"

Seb and Rachel jerked their heads up to see that Claire was standing there with an open textbook in her hands.

Rachel's eyes widened even as Claire moved closer, trying to read what they were looking at.

"Is that a storm?" Claire's book closed with a snap. Her voice lowered to a whisper. "Is it going to hit Taurati?"

CHAPTER FIVE

"It's the beginnings of a storm, but no one knows where it's going yet or if it will get any stronger. Right now there's nothing to worry about." Rachel had said it was okay if Claire overheard them, but now she wasn't so sure. The *poisson cru* that had been so delicious a half hour earlier now sat in her stomach like a rock.

But her daughter had handled worse. Far worse than a storm that would probably blow itself out in a week.

"Then why are you looking at news articles about it? Is that the reason *you're* here?" The last question was aimed at Sebastien.

Sebastien gave her a smile. "You mean having dinner in my office isn't enough of a reason?"

Claire studied him for a minute. Her daughter was intuitive, maybe because of what she'd been through in her short life. Suddenly she smiled. "Well, it was pretty good."

Going over to give her a hug, Rachel said, "If the storm gets to be a problem, I'll be honest and tell you, okay? Grams has already called me, and she said she'll fly in to get you and take you back to the States if it looks like it's going to be a direct hit."

"But what about you?"

That was a harder question. Flying away before the

hospital was officially under an evacuation order seemed horribly selfish. And the storm had just now been upgraded from a tropical disturbance to a tropical depression. "Honey, I have to stay. If they evacuate the hospital, I'll help with that, and then I'll join you. I just don't want to have to worry about you being at home alone while that's going on. We're all hoping the storm will just dissipate over the next couple of days."

What was the likelihood of that happening, when it seemed it was beginning to get more organized instead?

"And you'll tell me before you ask Grams to come get me?"

"I will. But for now you need to let us work, and you probably have more homework to do, do you not?"

"Yes, but—"

"But nothing. Homework."

Claire gave a dramatic sigh and then headed back to the desk with her schoolbook.

The next two hours were spent reviewing what the hospital already had in place and trying to find any holes in the plans. But it didn't look like there were any. The most critical patients would be airlifted to places outside the storm radius, while those who were less serious would be given the option of going to stay with family on the island or elsewhere. A skeleton crew would remain at the hospital to deal with the aftermath of the storm and to help any injured residents.

"Looks like Laurence and Britan—and those who worked on it before they took it over—have done a great job with things," said Sebastien. "According to this, we'll need to notify staff when the island is officially in the storm's path and is upgraded to a severe tropical storm. Although by then most people on the island will be following the weather reports. I'm sure most residents will remember Tropical Cyclone Wasa-Arthur and will start preparing. We'll want to take care of any...travel arrangements before that time."

She appreciated him speaking in low tones and using ambiguous terms. Although when she glanced up, Rachel seemed to be buried in her studies, her head down, writing furiously on a pad of paper.

"Since Wisconsin isn't actually a hub of hurricanes, you'll have to keep me apprised of the different kinds of classifications."

"They're similar to hurricane classifications as far as wind speed. They just use different terminology."

"How many patients do we have right now?"

"Fortunately, we don't have the numbers that we did a couple of years ago, so I'd say we're not quite at half capacity right now. But if people start doing stupid things while preparing for the storm, we could see an uptick in injuries from power tools and the like."

"Ugh." Power-tool injuries could run the gamut from minor annoyances to life-threatening injuries. She'd seen more than her share of severed fingers from table saws. "Those are never fun."

"No." He glanced down at the paperwork. "Looks like if we get bumped up to a tropical low, then we'll start handing out flyers on storm preparedness, which has a section on tool safety and emergency first aid in case of accidents."

"How much of an uptick in patients could we see?"

He shrugged. "This will be my first major storm here. I'm sure there are statistics somewhere, though."

"Okay. We'll need to ask departments to take stock of their inventory so we can see if we can get in what is needed before we're too far along in the process."

"I was thinking the same thing."

She glanced at Claire again, but she still looked immersed in her studies. Wait. Her books were open, but her pencil was now down, and she had her phone out. "Claire? What are you doing?"

"Texting some of my friends to see if they've heard the news."

Her heart dropped. "Don't do that! Not yet!" She got control of her voice, but it took some doing. "How many have you texted?"

"Just my best friend. She said she hasn't heard anything."

Rachel's eyes closed for a second as frustration pulsed through her. That was all they needed—for her daughter to start a mass panic.

As if guessing her thoughts, Seb slid his hand over hers. "It's okay," he murmured. "People will have already heard about the storm."

The gravel of his voice and warmth of his skin sent a shiver over her, and she realized she'd been holding herself as rigid as a piece of iron pipe.

"I'm sorry, Mom."

"It's my fault. I should have asked you not to text anyone yet. But Sebastien is right. People have undoubtedly already heard. But let's let parents inform their kids in their own timing, okay?"

"Okay. If someone texts me about it, am I allowed to say anything?"

"Not about our work here, because we're dealing with worst-case scenarios, and we don't want to scare anyone unnecessarily. But you can certainly talk with your friends using generalities."

"Generalities. Like if I'm nervous and stuff like that?"

"Yes. Exactly like that."

Sebastien let go of her hand, and she realized how

calming his presence was. If only he'd been there when Claire was going through treatments. She could have used his steady confidence. But he hadn't been. And she'd proved to herself that she really didn't need anyone. Despite that crazy night they'd spent together a year earlier, she didn't need him, either, right? Didn't want him intruding into her space with Claire. Not when they were just getting island living down to a science and figuring out how to do things without having the safety net of her parents or childhood friends nearby.

And the thought of having Sebastien as a safety net? It was terrifying. And impossible. His attempt at deflecting her fear about the storm had worked far too well. Claire had no experience with men other than knowing her father had abandoned her. But unlike Rachel, her daughter wasn't hardened or cynical, so it would be too easy for someone to hurt her without even realizing they'd done it. Not that Rachel believed the pediatrician would purposely try to hurt Claire. But she didn't want to take the chance of her getting attached and then being devastated when Seb slipped off her radar without a word.

So from here on out, she was going to be careful how much contact she allowed them to have with each other. Even if it meant shipping Claire off with her mom earlier than she'd planned. She'd call Wisconsin tonight and ask her mother to check flights to Tahiti for the next couple of days so, if possible, she'd be prepared to pick Claire up and take her home.

Then she could work with Sebastien without worrying that she would be putting her daughter's heart in danger.

Or hers?

No, hers wasn't in danger. If the night they'd spent together hadn't left a mark, then she should be safe.

At least that was her hope. And if she was wrong?

Then she would have to find a way to interact with him as little as possible. Or she'd have to make a choice she didn't want to make.

The pamphlets were printed up a day later, and his plan was to distribute them to each department in the hospital. Seb almost passed them out himself but realized leaving Rachel out of the process wasn't right or fair. Instead, he contacted her to let her know what he'd done and asked her to swing by the office.

Eating with her and Claire in his office had given him an odd warmth in his chest that had set off alarm bells, and when her daughter had been afraid, it had seemed far too natural for Seb to make a quip about dinner to allay her fears. Just as he'd done in the exam room. He'd never hesitated or remained silent to let Rachel deal with it in her own way. No, he'd jumped right in. The way a father might have?

Hell, he hoped not. But deep down, he wondered. He could argue it away by saying he was just doing what any friend of the family might have done, but he wasn't Rachel's friend, despite having been her lover for a night.

A knock sounded at the door of his office as he was reviewing a patient's chart, and he immediately tensed.

"Come in."

The door opened and closed with a quiet click before he looked up from his computer. He knew who it was even before his eyes came up to meet hers.

She came over to his desk, and before he could say anything, she picked up a brochure and looked at it.

"Everything okay?" he asked.

"Not really."

Something spiked through his chest. "Claire?"

"No. You. What are these?" She held up one.

He frowned. "Our pamphlets. They're what I texted you about."

"I thought we were supposed to be working together on these. But it looks like you went on without me." Her voice was very soft. A warning sign if he'd ever heard one.

She studied one of the pamphlets that had the phrase *l'avertissement* printed in bold type across the front. The bulk of it contained all the things they had talked about yesterday.

"I thought we did work on this together."

"Really?" Her brows went up. "I don't remember helping to print these up."

"You're right. I probably shouldn't have. I remember you telling Neves that you needed to limit your time to when you're here at the hospital. I don't have anyone at home who…needs me."

Merde. That had come out sounding pretty pathetic. But it was true.

Her face softened, and her brow cleared. "Sorry, you're right, and they look great. I just don't want you to feel you have to carry this on your own. Just because I have a child and you don't, that doesn't mean I can't carry an equal amount of the work."

Those words cut through his gut like a knife.

Just because I have a child and you don't...

She had no idea that he'd give anything to be in the position she was. Where he had to worry about his *fils* being scared because of an oncoming storm. Or have to distract him with humor or divert him by telling him to do his homework.

If only Rachel knew how very fortunate she was.

Except he was pretty sure she did know.

He opened his mouth to correct her about his not having a child before closing it again. Wasn't this the reason his hair was so long? Why he was avoiding going to get it cut or trying not to talk about having a child who'd passed away?

He didn't need her pity or her sympathy. And that hadn't been what this conversation was about. It was about the division of labor. She was irritated that he'd taken it upon himself to do something without consulting her.

And she was right.

"I'm sorry, Rachel. I should have waited to print them off until you had a chance to review them. Thanks for calling me out on it."

She came in and sat in one of the chairs in front of his desk. "I wasn't trying to call you out on it. Not really. Is this why you wanted to see me?"

"Yes. Why don't you take one and look through it?"

"I trust you. Besides—" One corner of her mouth quirked. "Claire tells me my French needs some work, so I'd be no good at giving you an honest opinion on that."

"I've heard you speak a couple of times. It's not that bad."

Rachel groaned. "That's not much of an endorsement." She drew a deep breath. "I do need to talk to you about something besides the pamphlet, though."

"Oh?"

She hesitated before saying, "I called my mom yesterday evening after I got home and asked her to check on flights. Just in case this thing blows up more quickly than we expect it to."

"That doesn't surprise me. We talked about the possibility of Claire going back to the States."

"Yes…well, my mom called this morning and said

she'd found a flight that was incredibly low and went ahead and booked it. Without asking me first."

"Ah…" He could definitely see why coming to his office and finding the pamphlets already printed up could have *énervé* her, making her feel like everyone was sidestepping her wishes. "And here I am doing something without asking you first. Again, I'm sorry. Truly."

"It's okay. I'm just edgy with everything happening so fast."

"I can understand that." His head tilted. "When is your mom arriving?"

"Tomorrow morning."

"Wow, that *was* fast." He sighed. "But maybe it's for the best. There has been a marginal increase in the storm's intensity."

"I know. I saw it." Her hands twined together in her lap. "And I do want Claire out of the equation, if possible. But Mom hasn't booked their flight home yet, so she's going to stay with Claire for a couple of days and see how things go. If it dissipates, she'll have had a nice visit with her granddaughter."

"That sounds like a good plan."

She then smiled. "And then you won't have to worry about waking me in the middle of the night when you need something."

Like he had in that cabana the night they were together? That whole experience had been surreal and so not like him. But she'd been soft and warm and oh, so sexy with her hair tumbled across those pillows. He'd gotten up to leave in the middle of the night and then found he couldn't. So he'd climbed back in bed and woken her. And when those deep brown eyes opened…

He realized she'd asked him something and blinked back to the present. "Sorry, I missed that."

"I just wanted to know if there was any increase in injuries, since I did see suggestions online for fortifying housing structures in case the storm does hit the island."

"No, not yet. But it won't be long. Is Claire in school today?"

"Yes. I told her teacher that she may be visiting her grandmother in Wisconsin, just so they'd be aware. They're going to get some lessons together, just in case. No one seemed overly alarmed. Yet."

No, that would come later. It was one thing being hit by a hurricane in a big country like the United States, when you could truly evacuate and leave for an unaffected area. On an island like Taurati, however, there were only so many options. If you were lucky enough to have relatives somewhere else, you could leave. If your whole life was on this island, sometimes your only option was to hunker down and pray for the best.

"Let's hope there's not any reason to be alarmed and that Claire simply gets some quality time with her grandmother."

"I truly hope that's how things go."

He glanced at her. "When will you leave?"

"I won't go until we get what we need done at the hospital."

He wasn't sure he liked that idea, and he wasn't sure why. "And if it's too late to evacuate by that time?"

She shrugged. "I can't think that far ahead."

"You may have to. You do have a daughter to think of."

"I know. But I can't just leave my patients or leave the hospital shorthanded. Not yet."

The intercom came on. "Trauma team to the ER. Trauma team to the ER."

Seb winced. "When did you say you saw that internet article?"

"This morning." Her lips twisted. "Surely not."

"You never know. I'm going down there to see if I can lend a hand."

"Me, too. Do you want me to wait for you?"

Seb stood. "I'm ready now. So let's go."

Once they got to the ground floor, a chaotic scene met their eyes. There were several ambulances in the bay and blood pooling on the ground from someone on a nearby stretcher—several layers of bandaging wrapped around his head. Seb found the nearest EMT. "What do we have?"

"Some friends were trying to cut down a tree they said was too close to the house because of the threat of a cyclone. A chain saw, some ropes and large swinging branches did not make for a happy scene. We have some broken bones, and a dropped chain saw hit one man in the head. He's alive, but…"

Merde. His eyes met Rachel's, and he gave a quick nod before jumping into the fray and helping the nearest patient.

It had started.

Rachel found herself helping stabilize an open tibial fracture in one of the surgical suites. A teenaged girl had held her arm up to ward off the huge tree limb that had careened her way. The maneuver had worked, the branch missing her head, but instead it had snapped her arm in two with enough force to drive the bone through the skin.

The girl was a little older than Claire, and it sent a pang of fear through her. Who ever thought that something so terrible could happen to their child? She answered her own question. No one ever expected the worst to happen to them. They expected their lives to run according to a certain plan.

Hadn't she been the same? She'd never dreamed Claire's father would leave them. Or that Claire would get cancer a few years later.

There were no promises. No guarantees in life. It was one reason she didn't date. Hadn't since Claire's diagnosis. In fact, one of the only two sexual encounters she'd had since then had been with Sebastien. And that hadn't gone according to plan, either. She'd expected a quick hour or two that she could dust from her hands afterward.

Instead it had been...

Complicated.

The doctor treating the girl had lavaged the area to clean it before asking Rachel to maintain steady traction on the fracture so they could maneuver the bone back into place. This was the third try. Monica was fortunately sedated, but the process still made Rachel cringe. There was no help for it, though. Rachel closed her eyes for a second to block the out the sight of the streaky tears that were still visible on the child's face. She'd been in agony during the ride over and during the triage process in the ER.

But what Rachel couldn't block out were her thoughts. Monica's dad was still being treated for a head injury, and her brother had a broken clavicle. So much heartache in one family. The mother was stationed in the waiting room, beside herself, as each member of her immediate family had been wheeled in separate directions to be treated.

Rachel was pretty sure Monica's brother would be okay. But her dad? All they could do was their best.

The ortho's voice brought her back. "Okay, I think we got it. Go ahead and gradually release the pressure and see if it stays in place." They would flush the site again as soon as it was stabilized and X-ray it to make sure it was stable before casting her forearm.

They held their breath as Rachel gingerly reduced the traction. Okay. There was no popping sensation of a bone slipping out of place.

"Good. Let's get that X-ray and pray the blood supply to the bone wasn't compromised."

If that happened, that portion of the bone would die and the fracture would not heal. They'd have to go back in and take out the dead section, grafting healthy bone onto the end.

The X-ray showed—just as the orthopedist thought— that the ends of the bone were lined up and so far holding.

"I'm going to flush it out again, and we'll put a temporary cast in place until tomorrow. I want one last X-ray before we do anything permanent. I'm hoping we can get by without pins."

Rachel wasn't a surgical nurse, but because each of the three operating bays was needed for injured patients, she'd had to fill in, which she'd gladly done. She wondered which patient Seb had. The scene had been so chaotic, she'd lost track of him almost as soon as they'd come onto the floor. And then she'd been whisked into surgery along with her current patient.

Fortunately—if there was such a thing for a situation like this—the accident had occurred during daylight hours, when there was more than just a skeleton crew on duty.

The flushing of Monica's arm was quick but thorough, and some medication to manage pain was administered through her IV before the wound was closed and they woke her up.

A tense minute or two went by as the girl lay motionless on the table. Then her head turned from side to side, and her eyes fluttered open.

The surgeon leaned over the table. "Monica, can you hear me?"

She slowly nodded her head, gaze tracking to her doctor's face. Rachel hadn't realized how rock-hard her muscles had gone until that moment. But she relaxed all at once, wiggling her shoulders to throw off the last of the tension.

The cell phone in her pocket buzzed, but she ignored it, hoping it wasn't Claire with an emergency of her own. Their signal for that was for Claire to call back immediately after the first attempt.

She waited with bated breath, but the phone remained still. Once the patient went to recovery, she'd give a quick glance at the readout before heading back to the ER to see if there was anything else she could help with.

And to see if she could spot Seb?

No. Of course not. She was in the ER because she was needed. Not because of him.

"Okay, it looks like your arm is going to be fine," the surgeon was telling Monica. "We'll probably keep you overnight so we can put some antibiotics through your IV line. And then tomorrow we'll get you casted up and on your way."

Monica's pupils were still pretty unfocused, but she seemed to understand what the doctor was saying, because she nodded again.

The surgeon glanced around the space. "Thank you. Good work."

Rachel nodded and started pulling off her mask and gloves to prepare to leave. She needed to get in contact with her mom and get more details on her flight and how this was all going to work. Her mom was scheduled to land in Tahiti, which had an international airport, then finish the trip to Taurati on a smaller plane, which she hadn't booked yet. And once news of the growing storm hit, flights in and out would be harder to come by.

If Rachel wasn't required in the ER, she'd take a break and see if she could find a flight in and out of the smaller island. And she needed to break the news to Claire.

The surgeon smiled at her. "I haven't seen you in surgery before."

She'd never really spoken with Dr. Chauvre before, and even though the hospital wasn't huge by most standards, they still kind of kept to their departments and just saw other hospital staff in passing. "That's because I'm not a surgical nurse. I work in Pediatrics. They just needed some extra hands."

"Well, I was impressed. Any chance we can lure you over to the dark side... I mean Ortho?" His grin revealed straight white teeth and a dimple in his right cheek. "I'm serious. I'm not just saying it."

Well, that was a first. She'd never had a doctor try to talk her into changing departments before. She didn't know quite what to say, but she was flattered. If she did move, she would see Seb about as often as she'd seen Dr. Chauvre—just in passing and not very often. Hadn't she thought about how much easier that would be?

But she loved pediatrics. Had shifted over to it after Claire was diagnosed and treated.

She forced a smile. "How dark could it be, really? Let me think about it. I'm not sure the hospital would even let me transfer over."

"Oh, they would." Another smile.

Okay, that was weird. Did he have some pull with the administration?

"Well, that's good to know. I'll think about it and let you know if it's something I want to pursue."

"That's all I can ask." He glanced at the door. "On to the next patient. If you're interested, come up to the fourth floor and we can talk."

"I will. Thanks again."

She ducked out of the room, her face warm with the flush of pleasure. Good to know that someone wanted her.

Not that Pediatrics didn't. It had just been weird over the last couple of days having to work with Sebastien. It wasn't his fault that the hospital administrator had tossed them into the ring together. He had no idea what had transpired between the two of them.

Although Seb seemed much less bothered about it than she did. Or maybe he was equally good at hiding it.

Maybe he would even be happier if she were no longer in Pediatrics. The thought made her deflate a little. Perhaps that's why Dr. Chauvre's offer was so attractive. Because Sebastien didn't seem to quake each time he looked at her?

Things were such a mess. She'd sworn she wasn't getting involved with another man until Claire was grown-up and gone. She wanted her daughter to be able to enjoy her childhood without the stress of trying to find where he fit in the picture with any relationship Rachel might have. Why did the six years until Claire's eighteenth birthday suddenly seem so far away?

Damn. She needed to just enjoy her daughter while she was still at home. And if she let herself fret over Sebastien Deslaurier each and every day, she was not going to be able to do that. But she wasn't going to think about moving. Not until the current crisis with the storm was over and gone. Then she was really going to have to give some thought to how she wanted to spend the rest of her time on the island. However long that might be.

CHAPTER SIX

"WHAT IS DR. CHAUVRE'S first name?"

"What?" Rachel's reappearance in the ER surprised Seb. He'd assumed she'd gone back to Pediatrics after whatever patient she'd been helping with.

He'd finished treating the boy with the broken leg and had helped stabilize the kid's father, who'd been struck with the chain saw. It had been touch and go since the blade had glanced off the man's head with enough force to breach the skull. It looked like the brain itself had been spared, although there was always the possibility of swelling from trauma. The patient wasn't out of the woods yet.

She wouldn't quite meet his eyes. "I was just in surgery with him and realized I didn't know his full name."

"It's Philippe." That was odd. Although Sebastien had been at the hospital long enough to know most of the staff members by name—first and last—it just seemed an out-of-the-blue question. As was the fact that she was still not quite holding his glance. "How did surgery go?"

"It went well. We were able to get Monica's arm back in place, and she's awake. The arm has a temporary cast that will be replaced tomorrow if everything looks stable."

"Good news."

"How about the other victims? Are they doing okay?"

"Yes," he said. "Even the head injury patient is stable for the moment. All in all, that family was very lucky."

"Yes." This time she did meet his eyes. "It's funny how we classify luck sometimes, isn't it?"

He hadn't thought about it much, but she was probably right. Hadn't he thought about the fact that even though Claire had had cancer that Rachel was lucky enough to still have her?

Rachel probably thought the same thing about someone whose child came through with some minor illness or injury: well, at least they didn't have to deal with cancer.

"Yes, it is." He paused before deciding to change the subject. "Any word on your mom's arrival?"

"Oh, damn. My phone rang while I was in surgery, then Dr. Chauvre wanted to speak with me afterward and I completely forgot."

He'd wanted to speak to her afterward?

Rachel fished her phone out of her pocket and glanced at the readout. "It's Claire."

Without saying anything else, she pressed a button on her phone, mouthing *sorry* at him.

He wasn't sure whether he should just walk away and give her some privacy or if she wanted to touch base about the storm.

"Hi, honey. Are you okay?"

He watched her body language, glad when she drew a deep breath and blew it out. "She did? What time does she arrive on the island?"

Claire must have said something else, because Rachel listened without speaking for a minute or two. "Like told you yesterday, it was Grams's idea. I didn't call her and ask her to pick you up this soon. And no, the storm isn't dangerous at the moment. It might never be. Bu since she's coming, I don't think it's a bad idea to go back to her house for a short vacation if the storm gets worse. She's missed you."

Rachel's eyes suddenly jerked to his. "I—I'm not sure what Sebastien's schedule is, sweetie."

His schedule? Why would she want to know his schedule?

Whatever Claire said next made her mom suck down a quick breath. "I'll ask him. But no promises."

"Ask me what?"

There was a deer-in-the-headlights moment before she put her hand over the bottom of the phone. "She wants to come by the hospital tomorrow with my mom to see you, since she doesn't know when she'll need to leave the island."

She did? He wasn't sure why she wanted to do that, but it made something burn in his chest. "Of course she can. Just let me know what time, and as long as there's not an emergency I need to deal with, I'll be happy to see her."

Rachel gave him a slight smile and mouthed *thank you*. "He said he'll try. We'll work out the time with Grams tonight, okay? I'll bring some food home with me." There was a pause. "I'm sure he has other things to do tonight. See you when I get there. Let Grams know what the plan is for dinner."

She hung up the phone. "Sorry. I thought it was an emergency or I wouldn't have subjected you to that."

Subjected him to what? Her end of the conversation? Or Claire wanting to stop by? So if he hadn't been standing there, he probably never would have known.

It didn't matter. He wasn't sure why he'd been so quick to agree to Claire stopping by to see him, other than the fact that he didn't want to have any regrets if the storm wreaked havoc and Claire and Rachel left the island, and he never saw them again.

The burning in his chest grew at that thought.

It was also obvious that Claire had wanted to invite him over to their apartment for a meal, and Rachel had been quick to put the kibosh on that. As well she should have. Intruding in that space where Rachel, Claire and her mom would try to talk while none of them admitted how scared they were about that situation that hovered a thousand miles offshore put a lump in his throat. How did you leave things when you weren't sure if it was the last time you were ever going to see each other?

Maybe that was part of the reason why Layla's parents kept sending him Christmas cards—there'd never been any true goodbyes said. Layla had left without ever saying she wasn't coming back to the house. And he'd never gotten in contact with her. Instead, their unfinished business hovered out there in the ether, kind of like that storm offshore.

It might be time to pick up a pen and write Layla and her parents a letter, finally cutting the last of those ties and wishing them well. Bleu really was the only thing that connected them now, and that thread was frayed so deeply that one hard tug and it would be over.

"You're fine, Rach. Nothing to apologize for."

She blinked, then stared down at her feet for a second. "I…um, appreciate that. And if you decide you'd rather not meet with Claire, I'll certainly understand. Please don't feel pressured to do anything you don't want to do."

"I do want to. I know what it feels like to not have closure."

Her head cocked to the side for a second before she sighed and nodded. "Yeah. So do I. What time do you work tomorrow, so I can kind of coordinate times?"

"I'm scheduled at eight and will be here the whole day, so whenever they arrive will be fine."

"Perfect."

It wasn't. But he wasn't going to tell her that. He was just going to show up and start doing what he hadn't done for years—close chapters so they weren't left hanging open in his life. Doing that with Claire and Rachel might be a great place to start. Despite the fact that that chapter had barely been opened.

Seb's phone buzzed, and he glanced down at the readout before swearing softly, tapping something on his screen.

"What is it?"

He moved closer, holding his phone so they could both read the warning that was scrolling down his screen, before he realized she wouldn't be able to read the French fast enough to understand.

"The storm has strengthened far ahead of the predictions. So we'll need to get our evacuation plans underway."

"How far away is it?"

"It's still moving in this direction, although its trajectory has changed a bit, canting more to the north. But it's still uncertain where it might make landfall first. Although somewhere in the Leeward Islands is the best guess."

That might be good news for Taurati but would be very bad for some of the islands to their west.

Her hair grazed his chin as she tilted her head to try to look at the small image on his phone, and a mixture of coconut and vanilla hit his senses. He swallowed, forcing his glance to stay on his phone.

"What do we need to do?"

He tried to think past the sense of awareness that was

now swinging through him. "I know you said you were going to take food home to Claire and your mom. But is there any chance they could come here instead? I think we may have to work through the night, just in case. Or if you can't—"

"My mom can watch Claire, so I can. And I will. Let me go call her."

"Tell her she may need to take Claire back to the States sooner rather than later."

She bit her lip and stepped away. "Okay."

Rachel waited for her mom and Claire to arrive at the hospital. She was nervous, and she wasn't sure why. She really didn't want her mom meeting Sebastien, although she couldn't put a finger on why that was. Maybe it was the stress over the storm. Maybe it was because she felt the less Seb knew about her the better, especially since Claire had seemed far too interested in keeping in touch with him. But how could she try to discourage Claire when Sebastien had been the one to calm her daughter's nerves both when she was sick and when she realized there was a storm that would possibly head in Taurati's direction?

Rachel wasn't used to anyone helping with her daughter other than her parents. It had felt good to be able to sit back and let someone else reassure her. Too good, in fact

It would be all too easy to get used to that.

But she had to remember that eventually he wasn't going to be in their lives, so she had to be careful about letting her daughter think that he was anything permanent. He was a work colleague, and that was it. That was all it would ever be.

Sebastien arrived before her mom and Claire did, lugging two bags of food from a local takeout joint.

"Wow, that looks like enough to feed an army."

"It's not. I just decided to get some typical American-style food. Fried chicken."

That made her smile. "Claire will love that. Thank you."

"There was no *salade de pomme de terre*—er...you call it potato salad? They were sold out."

"That's okay. It's not her favorite anyway. And she loves Taurati's food."

He pulled out a mango. "Especially this?"

"Yes. Especially that."

Just then she heard a familiar voice coming from the elevator, which had just arrived on their floor.

Claire appeared first and came careening toward her, arms outstretched. She gave her a big hug. "Grams says we have to leave tomorrow and that you're not coming. Why?"

Her mom, making her way toward them, gave a half shrug. "I didn't think it was my place to tell her without you there."

"It's okay. She knows what's happening for the most part."

Rachel watched as Sebastien smiled at Claire's greeting. Unlike Dr. Chauvre and his perfectly straight teeth, Seb's left canine stood at just a bit of an angle. That slight imperfection made him unique and added to his appeal rather than detracted from it. It was hard not to stare at his mouth every time he smiled. Made her want to do something to make those firm lips curve upward for that very reason.

Oh, girl, you are getting in too deep for your own good.

Realizing she actually had been staring at him, she cleared her throat to say something, but before she could, he nodded at the woman to her left. "This must be your mom?"

Great. Not only had she been staring, she'd evidently forgotten her manners as well. Something about this man made her normally orderly thoughts turn topsy-turvy. "I'm sorry. Yes, this is Marion Palmer. Mom, this is Dr. Deslaurier. I've been working with him on storm preparedness for the hospital."

"So you told me on the phone." Her mom held out her hand, eyes fixed on Seb's face. "Nice to meet you. I trust you'll make her leave the island, if it comes down to it."

"Mom!" Her voice was a little sharper than she'd meant it to be, and she sent her mom a wordless apology before adding, "I will follow the recommendations of the island's officials and hospital administration."

If Sebastien was shocked at her mom's demand, he didn't show it. "Your daughter has a good head on her shoulders. I trust her to do the right thing."

Did he? Did that mean if she decided to move to Orthopedics, he would support her in that decision? Not something she wanted to think about right now.

Claire turned back to face her. "So why are we leaving, anyway?"

"The storm is bigger and moving faster than it was before." She tried to choose her words carefully. "It looks like it might hit one of the smaller islands west of here, and if that happens, there is going to be a lot of panic and maybe even some injuries. Part of my job is to help our patients here at Hospitalier, and I don't want to have to worry about you and whether or not you'll be okay."

"But what about that other island? The one that might be hit." She paused, head tilted as she evidently processed what Rachel had told her. "You're going to help them, too, right?"

"We're not positive yet that it's going to stay on the same path. It's changed a couple of times already."

"So it might not hit any of the islands?"

That was unlikely at this point. The islands of French Polynesia were scattered in a loose pattern, as if someone had skipped them across the ocean and left them where they landed. It would be hard for the tropical cyclone to miss all of them. The question was, would it hit the populated or unpopulated ones before continuing on its way? Their only hope was that the storm would weaken once it made landfall and pose less danger to the rest of the group.

She tried to figure out a way to explain their predicament. "They think it will hit at least some of them. We just don't know enough to say which ones yet. The bad news is, I have to work all night tonight, Claire, to make sure Hospitalier's patients have a place to go in case it does hit here first."

"I understand." Her daughter glanced at Sebastien. "You guys will be together the whole time, right?"

"What?"

"I'm scared you're going to be trapped somewhere by yourself and that…" Claire's eyes watered, and her voice trailed away.

"Hey, I'll make sure your mom is safe." The deep gruff tones from beside her made Rachel swallow, a shiver washing over her.

How long had it been since she'd had someone say something like that? She was normally the one having to make sure others were safe, because her experience was that no one else was going to do it for you. Roy had left her to do everything on her own, and when the going got really tough and he realized having a child would change his life, he'd literally left her to do it on her own. Rachel had sworn to herself that she *could* do it all.

But, man, it felt good to have someone stand there and imply that—if not outright say—she wasn't alone. Just like the other times that Seb had offered reassurance. God. Claire was worried that she might be trapped somewhere alone? Well, she needed to make sure she was ready to rescue herself rather than expect someone else to do it for her. Even if it was just emotionally.

It took another swallow and a few beats before Rachel could say anything at all. To hide her emotions, she enfolded her daughter in a tight hug. "Everyone at Hospitalier will be talking. We'll all be taking care of each other. So try not to worry, okay?"

She wasn't trying to discount Seb's offer to make sure she was okay, but, for Claire's sake, she had to be careful not to buy into that line of thinking, otherwise it would be that much harder when the extra support was withdrawn. And she was under no illusions about its permanence. Her ex had more than taught her that.

When she dared a quick glance beside her, she saw that Sebastien was frowning. But he didn't contradict her. Instead he said, "Well, we'd better eat before we have to get back to work."

"Can we eat on the beach?" Claire pulled her head from her mom's shoulder. "I haven't been able to go in a while."

Seb's frown eased. "I was thinking that exact thing. I even have a blanket in my closet that we can bring to sit on."

That might even be better. The ocean breeze might help to clear her head. Or at least it would prepare her for the reality that was to come.

Rachel took one of the bags of food and Claire the

other while Seb got the blanket. She did her best to not to think about how this was the second time they would be sharing a meal together. Almost like a real...

No. They were not a family.

Leaving the hospital, they walked down the same boardwalk as the one where they'd helped to save Sharon's life. The lifeguard stand was empty, but that made sense, since it was getting to be late afternoon. Looking at the sky, you would still never know that a big storm was threatening to disrupt the idyllic life around them. Her mom glanced at her. "This is absolutely beautiful."

"You've been here before."

"Yes, but it's been a while, and I'd forgotten how lovely it is here."

Yes, it was. And Rachel made an effort not to take it—not to take *life*—for granted. She draped an arm across Claire's shoulder as they stepped onto the sand. "We really love it here, don't we, kiddo?"

"Yes, we do. I wish you and Gramps could come live with us."

Her mom laughed. "You will never get Gramps to leave Wisconsin."

It was the truth. Her dad had been raised on the farm where they currently lived. It wasn't very likely they would talk him into leaving it. And somehow, she couldn't see her dad in swim trunks hanging out on the beach. It just wasn't his style.

She glanced at Seb. "Where do you want to eat?"

"Let's go down a little farther. Maybe between here and the overwater cabanas."

She was glad he hadn't suggested eating inside one of them. Not only would it be warm this time of day, but she didn't want her mind to wander to another—more luxurious—cabana, where some pretty sexy things had happened. Especially not with Claire and her mom here.

They got to the spot, and Sebastien tossed out the blanket. It was larger than she'd expected, with plenty of room for them to spread out to eat.

"Ooh," said Claire as she took her plate. "I haven't had fried chicken since we left Wisconsin."

Rachel smiled at Seb. "Evidently that was a good choice."

While they ate, Seb regaled them with stories about things from his childhood. Claire sat there as if entranced by every word that came out of his mouth.

Rachel felt the same way. She knew he'd grown up in Tahiti, but she didn't realize he'd been a daredevil as a child. He seemed so…calm and unflappable nowadays. Maybe from the result of having a normal, happy childhood.

But then she remembered those whispers she'd overheard about something bad. From his childhood? Or from his later years?

He hadn't actually said anything about his teenaged or young adult years. Was that on purpose? Or was it just an oversight?

A slight movement from the waterline caught her attention, and she tensed. "Something's out there."

"Where?"

"To the right. About twenty or thirty yards." She stared at the spot, thinking maybe someone was swimming in the shallows, although the sun had all but disappeared from the horizon. She hadn't realized it had gotten so late. And then something slowly emerged from the water. And it wasn't a swimmer. Not a human one, anyway.

Seb squinted at the area she indicated and saw it in the shadows. A low shape, pulling itself forward with flippers. It was a sea turtle. He got the group's attention before putting his finger to his lips and making a low sound.

This was nesting season. They sat in silence on the warm sand so they didn't disturb the magnificent creature as she followed the instincts of her ancient ancestors and moved slowly, push by push, over the beach.

It was the first time Seb had actually witnessed this. He made a mental note to mark the spot once she was done so that one of the island's conservation groups could flag it. He wasn't sure what would—or even could—be done if Tropical Cyclone Koji actually made landfall on Taurati. But hopefully with the course being recalculated hourly, this nest would be spared.

Bit by bit, the turtle moved across the sand. There was an intimacy to the scene that was both sacred and profound. And it was hard not to feel a connection with the people he was with as they also watched the creature's progress. Then she passed them, continuing for a few yards before stopping. She looked neither right nor left. The nearby humans might not have even existed, for all the attention she paid them. Which was a good thing.

She stayed where she was for several minutes. Resting?

But then she started moving again, flippers pushing sand with an efficiency that was surprising in a creature that rarely ventured onto land. She was digging. Sebastien didn't dare move for fear of disturbing the turtle.

After what seemed like forever, she stopped again, and although he couldn't see from this distance, he was pretty sure she was busy laying her eggs.

No one said a word, and if he'd never seen this before, he was pretty sure this small group from Wisconsin had also never watched a sea turtle lay her eggs. Claire laid her head on her mom's shoulder, and Rachel grabbed her mom's hand.

A ribbon thread of jealousy went through him. Not for romantic reasons, but more a feeling of missing out on something important. Something he hadn't realized he'd lacked.

Thoughts of storms and loss were nowhere on his radar right now as the turtle showed them that special things only came with much effort.

Like having a family? Something he'd sworn he would never have again?

No, don't think about that right now. Not when you're tired and facing a situation that could prove to be life-threatening.

But the turtle didn't seem to care about any of those things. Didn't care that there might be a storm. Didn't care that her eggs might or might not make it. She could only do the things she had control over, and that was to find the safest environment she could for her eggs. And the stuff she couldn't control?

Well, that she left up to the universe.

Was that same universe trying to tell him something?

He had no idea. What he did know was that he wasn't a turtle. He couldn't just act on sheer instinct and let the chips fall where they may.

But maybe none of that needed deciding right now. He could think about the lessons of this particular turtle later. But right now, couldn't he just live vicariously through Rachel's little family?

As if guessing his thoughts, a voice whispered into his ear, "She's so beautiful."

Rachel was right. And not just about the sea turtle. He found himself leaning closer, having to hold himself back from touching her. "Yes, she is, Rach."

She stared at him for a minute before giving him a smile that went straight to his head, even as a rock settled in his stomach. It would be so easy to give in to the fantasy that he belonged here. That that incredible smile had meant something special, and that this family was actually his.

For twenty minutes, time seemed to stand still. And for once he was okay with not hurrying it along.

Then the turtle's flippers started moving sand again. Only this time, she wasn't digging. Instead, she was pulling it over the top of her eggs. Little by little. Push by push. And when she was finished, she slowly trudged back across the beach, each pull seeming to take a Herculean effort. But it was evidently worth it to her.

Something tickled at the back of his mind before he pushed it away again. He forced his attention back to the turtle.

She reached the surf, and a few more pushes had her buoyed up by the water. She soon disappeared from sight.

Trying not to disturb the group, he pulled his phone from his pocket and took a couple of pictures of the spot, using landmarks of the area to help conservationists find it.

"I can't believe we just witnessed that." Rachel's words were still low, even though the turtle was long gone.

"I can't, either. It's my first time."

Claire glanced around at him. "Really? You've never seen a turtle lay eggs before, even though you're from here?"

"I never have. Even though it's the season, it's still a little early, and it would be almost impossible to plan a time when a sighting would be guaranteed. I'm just glad our presence didn't deter her."

"Me, too."

He realized he was still leaning close to Rachel and immediately sat back. When he glanced at Marion, he noticed she was smiling, and even though she was looking in the direction of the ocean, he got the feeling her expression had nothing to do with the turtle.

Then what was it for?

Maybe the fact that he'd been practically leaning on her daughter?

If so, he needed to be careful. He didn't want to give Rachel's mom any ideas. Or worse, he didn't want Rachel to get any ideas.

So from here on out, he would need to be careful. Not just for his sake. But for everyone's.

Claire still wanted to say goodbye to Sebastien. And today was the day.

Rachel and Seb had worked all night long, securing places for their critical patients. It hadn't been easy. Many of the other islands were also on high alert, and there was an air of uncertainty and tension in all the phone calls she'd made. Hospitalier had agreed to receive patients from Bora Bora and other islands in the event that the storm shifted yet again and hit somewhere other than Taurati.

But they'd done it. And Rachel felt better about where things now stood with the hospital.

She'd barely had time to go home and catch a few hours of sleep before her mom and Claire's flight left today. She felt weepy and out of sorts, and she knew it was due to the prospect of being separated from her daughter. But not just that. There'd been a weird sense of companionship as she and Seb worked together last night. She'd put it down to being tired and having witnessed that magical scene on the beach yesterday. But she needed to banish that feeling—and soon.

They arrived at the hospital, and Rachel dropped her mom and Claire off at the front door and then went to find a parking place. When she rejoined them, she wrapped an arm around her daughter's shoulders and they headed through the entrance. Claire looked a little silly in her thick cardigan and long pants in this heat, but it was still winter in Wisconsin, and she needed to be prepared for it when she got off the plane tomorrow. Hopefully by then the storm would dissipate and things could go back to normal.

Normal? Like Sebastien calling her *Rach* for the first time yesterday? She thought of him as Seb all the time, but it was because everyone seemed to call him that. To hear him shorten *her* name, though, had given it a kind of intimacy she was no longer used to.

And she wasn't sure she wanted to get used to it again. Claire's father had called her that, and so it jolted to hear it roll off the tongue of another man. Although Sebastien's tones had worked some kind of magic over her that Roy's voice never had.

She glanced up to see Seb coming across the large foyer area to meet them. Alarm bells went off in her head. Ugh! She hadn't quite prepared herself for seeing him again. She'd told him what time they were coming but assumed he would just wait in his office until they arrived. He shoved a lock of hair off his forehead, sending a shiver over her. It was a study in impatience and sexiness all rolled into one. And his white shirt accentuated his tanned skin and strong neck. Imagining that fabric sliding across that tattoo of a sea turtle on his shoulder did a number on her.

Not the time, Rachel.

He was here, and she needed to pull herself together. Maybe he didn't want them in his space. Except she'd been there all night long.

Only that had been all work and no play. Not like that night in her cabana. The thought made her stomach tank and edged her nerves back into the danger zone. "Hey, sorry you felt you had to come down to meet us."

"It was no problem. I wanted to." His attention shifted to her daughter. "Claire, how are you holding up?"

"I thought this storm wasn't going to happen. You guys said it might be heading somewhere else." Her voice shook.

She realized then that Claire's eyes were red-rimmed, too. Had she been crying in her room before they left? Oh, God, was she even doing the right thing by sending her away?

Yes. She and Sebastien still had work to do, and she would have a harder time doing that if she knew Claire was here and might be in trouble.

"I know, and it still may. But we can't just sit back and pretend it's not out there."

She was surprised at how good a job Sebastien was doing at being supportive rather than just placating her. The respect she already had for him grew into a seedling.

"I understand that. But I don't really want to leave. Grams and Mom think I should, though. What if that other island gets hit? Who will help them?"

Sebastien seemed to consider his next words. "We will, if we can. And I agree with your mom and grandmother. They want to know you're safe and with the people you love. And we'll be working hard over the next several days."

"I guess." Claire's arms went over her chest in a way

that showed how dubious she was about going. "There are people that I love here, too, though."

Rachel swallowed at the way her daughter had worded that. She knew that Claire liked Sebastien, but her daughter made it sound like he was inside that bubble of people she cared about. *Really* cared about. Claire had always had an open heart that never seemed to run out of compassion and empathy. Rachel liked that most of the time. But someday she was going to let someone in who would hurt her. Roy hadn't been there long enough to do any real harm to Claire when he'd left. But she'd asked about him, and Rachel had tried to answer her questions as honestly as possible, telling her they'd both been very young when they'd been together and Roy hadn't been ready to fully commit to her. She'd left out the part about him not wanting to be a father. But someday her daughter was probably going to want to track him down. What if Roy rejected her? How long could Rachel really protect her from that?

She couldn't. But she could try to protect her from getting too attached to this particular man. "I know you do, honey. But this isn't goodbye forever. It's just until this storm is no longer a threat."

Like the threat that Sebastien posed?

He's not, Rachel. You're comparing apples with oranges.

That cyclone could become an unstoppable force of nature, whereas Sebastien... Well, they could walk away from him at any time.

At least she hoped they could.

Marion gave her granddaughter a hug. "You're acting like this is a kidnapping, honey. This is not just about the storm. I've missed you. Just come home with me for a week, and then I'll bring you back myself, okay? You've always loved staying with us. Gramps would be really sad if I came back without you."

"I've missed you guys, too. It'll just seem strange for Mom and...er...my friends to be so far away."

"You have your cell phone. You can call her every day. This week will go by faster than you can imagine."

Claire's eyes shifted back to Seb. "Will you take care of my mom? Please?"

Horror went through Rachel, and she was quick to take away any notion that she needed anyone to do that. "I'm a big girl, Claire. I can take care of myself. Sebastien has his own family to think about."

She had no idea whether or not Sebastien's parents were even alive. He could have been raised in foster care for all she knew.

The pediatrician's jaw tightened visibly. Probably in response to Claire's outrageous request.

But other than that outward tell, Seb gave no indication that he was irritated.

"She and I will be working together every day, so if I see something I disapprove of, should I call you?"

Rachel's head whipped around, and she fixed him with a gaze that that told him to watch his step.

"Could you?" Claire responded.

"I'm sure your mom will be just fine." Marion glanced down at her phone. "Well, it's that time. We'd better get going, kiddo."

"Okay." Claire came over and gave Rachel a long hug. "I miss you already."

Clenching her jaws together to keep control of her emotions, she squeezed her daughter tight. "I'll miss you more. Be good, okay?"

"I'll try. I'll call you when we get to Tahiti. And when we get to Wisconsin."

"I'll be waiting." Dropping a kiss onto Claire's head, she finally released her.

Unexpectedly, her daughter went over to Seb and hugged him as well. There was a moment's hesitation before Sebastien's arms went around her back. Over Claire's head, his eyes met Rachel's with an odd expression. Almost like…sadness. A lump formed in her throat that no amount of swallowing would dislodge.

Seb took a step back and repeated what Rachel had said. "Be good. See you in a week."

Said like a father. Like the father that Claire had never had. It would be so easy to lean on him for support, just like she had when he'd treated Claire for her swollen lymph node.

This could turn into a disastrous situation for all of them. And yet he'd said nothing wrong. Any friend or neighbor could have said the same thing and she wouldn't have thought a thing of it.

Was it because it came from a man she'd slept with? Probably.

But to overreact would make both Claire and Sebastien wonder about the reason behind it. And in reality, Rachel had no idea why her thoughts and emotions were in such turmoil.

It's because your daughter is about to fly thousands of miles away.

For the first time, she wondered if moving to Taurati had been the best idea. Then she shook that thought aside. It was, actually. Because she was far enough away from home that if things got too weird with Sebastien, or if she developed some kind of crush on the man, she could simply pick up and move house. It had been a lot more complicated when Roy had left, since he'd come from the same Wisconsin town as they had. And although his parents had been killed in a car crash soon after they graduated from college, his romance with Rachel had continued. At least until Claire was born and he decided fatherhood wasn't for him. He'd stayed in town for a couple of months after that before moving to one of the larger cities just north of them.

But there'd always been that specter of fear. What if he decided to move back to the area? What if he decided to lay claim to Claire or said he wanted to forge some kind of relationship with her? What if Claire decided she wanted a relationship with him?

It all seemed unlikely at this point, but she still worried about it. And when Claire turned eighteen, she could decide for herself what to do about that. All Rachel could do now was to protect her daughter as best she could.

And that might not be just from her biological father anymore. More and more she was realizing that Claire craved what she hadn't had as a baby—the fairy-tale notion of two parents who loved each other.

God, she didn't want to be the one who had to smash that fantasy to bits in front of her daughter.

Sebastien broke the silence. "Hey, I have something for you in my office. Do you have a minute to come up?"

Claire looked at her grandmother, eyes wide. "Can we?"

"Yes, just for a minute, though."

"It won't take long."

They took the elevator to the third floor and stepped off. Rachel had no idea what Sebastien was talking about. He'd never mentioned having anything for Claire. But her anxiety levels were starting to climb higher and higher.

Seb opened the door to his office and ushered them in. And then, going behind his desk, he opened a drawer and pulled out a small plastic item. "It's a sea turtle. Something to help you remember Taurati."

His French accent came through thicker than it normally did.

Claire accepted the gift, turning it over in her hands. "Thank you. Just like the one we saw on the beach. I've always loved sea turtles."

"So did…" Sebastien let the words trail away for a minute before finishing it. "So do I. Think you can fit that in your backpack?"

"I'm going to put it in my purse for safekeeping." She looked at Seb. "I'll give it back to you when we come back."

"No, it's yours."

"Are you sure?"

"I am." He gave her a smile.

"Thank you. I love it. I'll put it on a shelf in my room when I come home."

Rachel's misgivings went even higher. But it wasn't as if he'd gifted her something expensive. It was probably just some trinket left by a patient of his, and he'd offered it to Claire to take away some of her anxiety.

Something whispered to her in the deepest recesses of her brain. Something about a turtle. She tried to capture it, but it slid away before she could.

She didn't want to take the chance that Claire would hug him again or form an even closer bond to him, so she interrupted the moment. "Well, you guys better be on your way. I love you. Call me when you land at each of your stops, okay?"

"Don't worry, we will." Marion kissed her cheek, then held her hand out to Seb. "Thank you. For everything. I can see why you treat children. You're very good with them."

"Thank you. It's just the training." Again there was something in his tone that called to her. Like when he'd looked at her while hugging Claire.

"I don't believe that for a second," her mom said.

Rachel didn't believe it, either. She'd seen him with his patients. He was kind and intuitive and seemed to have a gift for helping them calm down.

"I'll walk you out," she said.

Her mom shook her head. "It's probably better if we just go from here. Claire already has her backpack, and I have my things in my whale of a purse. We'll call you when we land, so don't worry. And you be careful."

The admonition was made with love, and Rachel knew it. She gave them each one more hug and then watched as they walked out the door. She stood there staring at it for a long minute before realizing tears were coursing unchecked down her cheeks.

A hand grasped hers and squeezed. "It's going to be okay, Rach. I promise."

Something about those words made a rush of emotion sweep into her head, where it grew and swelled until she felt her skull would split open. She whirled around to face him, not bothering to swipe at the moisture on her cheeks.

What did he know about promises?

"Don't. Just don't. You can't know that. So don't make any promises you can't keep."

He searched her face for a long moment. "You're right, and I'm sorry. I'm the last person who should be telling you that everything will be all right. Since I know first-hand that sometimes it's not, no matter how much you might wish otherwise."

CHAPTER SEVEN

Why had he said that?

He had no idea. But once the words were out of his mouth, he couldn't retract them. And he wouldn't even if he could after seeing the anguish on her face. But at least her separation from her daughter wasn't forever.

When she'd turned suddenly, she hadn't let go of his hand. And her grip was strong and fierce. As if, despite her angry words, she needed to hold on to something—even if it was a fake promise.

"You said you know firsthand. How?"

He had a choice. He could evade the question by acting like he was talking about one of his patients. But he didn't want to do that. And unlike the faceless acquaintances who cut his hair and backed away from the subject almost as soon as they asked that fateful question about children, he had a feeling she wouldn't. And he had no idea why.

"I had a son who died."

There was silence for several seconds, her eyes searching his as if working through what he'd said.

"Oh, God, I should have realized." Her head tilted, fingers tightening further around his. "That sea turtle. It's like the one on your shoulder. That toy didn't belong to a patient, did it?"

"No."

"Oh, Seb. I am so sorry. I had no idea." Her mouth twisted. "I remember implying that only someone with children could understand what it was like to worry about them. Only you did know, didn't you?"

He remembered that moment with shocking clarity. She hadn't used those exact words, but he'd been right about her meaning. "Not your fault. I rarely tell anyone about him."

A couple of beats passed in silence.

"Can I ask what happened? If you don't want to tell me, I'll completely understand."

He shouldn't want to tell her. He'd actually never *wanted* to tell anyone. Until now.

But this was Rachel. Someone who'd feared for her own daughter's life. If he could trust anyone to understand, it was her.

"He died of brain cancer when he was a year old."

A thousand emotions went through her eyes. And he was right. She would understand exactly what it was like to hear the terrible words *Your child has cancer.*

She took a step closer. "Tell me."

And so he did. Told her how his baby's eyes had stopped looking into his. How he regressed on his milestones. How he became more and more difficult to console. And finally the results of that MRI that dropped the last of the puzzle pieces into place.

The process of telling Bleu's story was both terrible and cathartic. He talked until he had no more words.

"I never would have guessed. You've always seemed so…optimistic. Even when talking about this storm."

"It was either that or give in to the grief and go in a direction that helped no one. But believe me, I remember him each and every day of my life."

"Oh, Seb." She grasped his other hand and held it. "What was his name?"

"Bleu Zacharie Deslaurier."

"Bleu. I should have guessed." The words were soft, almost a whisper and said with a reverence that surprised him. "I remember tracing that on your shoulder a year ago."

A ball of emotion gathered in his stomach. "Yes. I remember, too."

He remembered her soft finger as it wound around letter after letter of his son's name. How it had sent a shuddery sense of familiarity through him, as if she'd spoken Bleu's name aloud, rather than just tracing it. It had been hypnotic. And so, so seductive.

Then. And now.

"I'm so glad you told me."

She was. He could see it in her face.

Before he could stop himself, he carried both of her hands to the small of her back and took a step toward her. Her head tipped back to look at him, and he was lost. There was no surprise in her gaze. No hint of rejection.

Instead, there was a warmth that drew him in until his body made contact with hers. And then slowly, slowly, his head lowered until his mouth connected with hers.

It was paradise. The taste. The feel.

Her lips were soft. So very soft.

In an instant, all rational thought fled, and all that existed was feeling. Physical feeling and a sense of being welcomed home, but it was more than that. There was an emotional connection he wasn't sure he'd ever felt before, even with Layla.

Using her hands, he applied slight pressure to ease her even closer, and she made a sound against his mouth.

Some strange melding that was half groan, half purr. It sent raw heat pulsing through him.

Her mouth opened, and just like her gaze had earlier, it drew him in. His tongue filled the space, finding a moist heat that blanked every thought from his head. He wanted her. Wanted her like he'd never wanted anyone before.

Just like last time, when they'd…

Last time.

Merde. He'd promised her it would be all right. But if he went any further, it wouldn't be. This wasn't just about him and Rachel. She had a daughter that he didn't want drawn into the mix.

Letting go of her hands in a rush, he took a step back. Then another. It took a second for their mouths to unfuse, but when they did, he immediately regretted it.

She pressed the back of her hand to her lips, and she suddenly looked lost. More lost than she'd looked when saying goodbye to her mother and daughter. His gut clenched, and he had to press his fists to his sides to keep from reaching for her again.

"Rach…"

"No." She edged toward the door. "Don't say anything. I need to go. Need to get to work. I'm already late. So, so late."

With that, she opened the door and fled his office, leaving him to stare after her. And to wonder if he hadn't just done the most selfish thing of his life by burying his grief in that kiss. There'd been no thoughts of storms or how hard it must have been for Rachel to send her only child away.

Or maybe that's what drove him to kiss her. He knew exactly what it was like to send off a child into the unknown. Knew how heart-wrenching and helpless it felt to say goodbye. But whatever had driven that crazy impulse, he needed to somehow make it right and move forward. The problem was he had no idea how.

Sleep seemed like a foreign concept to Rachel when she went home to an empty house. She lay on her back and stared up at the ceiling. God! She'd been so sure that Seb was going to lay her down on his couch and kiss all her worries away.

Except those worries would have grown exponentially afterward. So no matter how shocked she'd been when he stopped, no matter how quivery her legs were as she'd exited his office, he'd done her a favor by not going any further.

Because he was thinking. Unlike you, Rachel.

She wasn't even entirely sure how that kiss had come about. But something inside her had melted when she grasped the fact that he'd given Claire his dead son's sea turtle to help her feel better. It was probably the same toy that had driven him to get that tattoo on his shoulder. In that moment of realization, she'd have given him anything.

Anything!

Maybe even her heart. And what a disaster that would have been. She needed to somehow get her head back on straight. He'd done an impulsively kind thing by giving away that turtle, but it hadn't really meant anything. Maybe he had all kinds of toys and mementos at home.

But the only one tattooed on his body was a sea turtle.

She hadn't asked him about Bleu's mother. She hadn't even thought about it, really. But she was sure if the mother of his child was still in his life, there was no way he would have been caught dead kissing someone else. She didn't know how she knew it, but she did.

And that gave her a sense of relief. And sadness.

Because in the end, who had held him during those moments of grief? And they still happened, from what she saw in his eyes. The thought of him at home alone, picturing his baby's smile…

God!

She turned onto her other side, punching her pillows a couple of times, and glanced at the clock. Two in the morning. Great.

She would more than likely see the man at work today, and she had no idea how she was going to face him. What she was going to say.

At least Claire would be safe. They'd made it to Tahiti, and their flight to Wisconsin was eleven hours, not including a three-hour layover in Chicago. But since it was an overnight flight, they could at least sleep. Unlike her.

But she'd better make an effort, or she was going to have a hard time keeping her mind on task tomorrow.

She called out to her smart device. "Eureka, find tropical rain forest sounds."

Grimacing, she gave a quick laugh. Well, it was better than asking it to find storm sounds. While she normally loved falling asleep to the sound of rain and thunder, she didn't want to send out any kind of subliminal message to the tropical storm that it was okay to come their way. Because it wasn't. She wanted it to stay as far away as possible.

The predictions were for Tropical Cyclone Koji to intensify even more overnight.

And somehow that seemed like it would solidify things in her mind. While the island could still be in danger. She definitely *was* in danger. From more than just this storm.

Well, she was going to have to push through and do her job. Because there were lives at stake. And she couldn't afford to give in to her heart and throw a massive pity party. That could wait.

With that last thought, she forced her eyes to close and prayed that sleep would finally find her and that she would not dream about that kiss. Or about anything else that involved Seb.

Something startled her awake, and for a second she lay in the dark, trying to figure out if it had been the strange dream she'd been having of Seb and running as fast as her legs would carry her. But she hadn't been running away from him. She'd been running toward him, could just see him in the distance, could almost touch his hand, when...

What?

The sound happened again, and she realized it was her cell phone. Glancing at the clock, she saw that it was five in the morning. Her first thought was Claire.

Sitting straight up, she reached for the phone that was on its charger. It wasn't Claire. She sagged for a moment before she realized it was Seb.

Oh, no! Calling to tell her not to bother coming in to work today? No, he wouldn't do that. No matter what had transpired between them, he wasn't unprofessional.

"'Lo?" The word didn't come out right, and her voice was gravelly and sleep filled. She cleared it and tried again. "Hello?"

"Rachel? Sorry to call so early, but there's news on the cyclone, and it's not good."

"Is it going to hit Taurati after all?"

"It doesn't look that way. It's going to make landfall in the next couple of hours. And Mauhali is set to get the brunt of it."

She blinked trying to get her groggy brain to work. "Is that the island they'd predicted?"

"No. It swung north a few hours ago. Mauhali is one of the poorest of the islands. Its population is on the lower end, and its health care is just the basics. They're not equipped to deal with a disaster like this."

"Got it. Give me a few minutes to get dressed, and I'll be there."

"Thanks. And, Rachel, I…"

"What?"

"Nothing. I'll just see you when you get here."

Seb was running on fumes.

He'd already fielded calls from Mauhali and Neves, asking what the plan was. Not that he had a clue. They'd expected the possibility that patients could need to be evacuated to Taurati in front of the storm. But that the storm would hit Mauhali had not been on anyone's radar. There was no time for evacuations, since the winds were already picking up on the island ahead of the storm. And the storm would basically sit between their island and the other one.

Merde!

He hated calling Rachel in. Not just because of that kiss, but because he knew she was dealing with making her daughter leave, and if she was like him, she hadn't gotten much sleep last night. But it wasn't for much longer. Just until Koji was gone and they'd figured out what resources there were for Mauhali, and then they could go back to their respective corners of Pediatrics.

Was he ready for that?

Maybe not. Maybe the real question was: Was it a better situation?

And the answer to that question was probably yes. Even though, after telling Rachel about Bleu, there'd been a feeling of peace. As if he'd finally been able to lay his son to rest. It made no sense, but it was probably what had led to him kissing her in the first place. The whole rush of relief in finally being able to share what he'd gone through during Bleu's illness and death. He hadn't been able to reveal the depth of his grief with Layla, and they'd been engaged to be married. But that engagement had been more about the pregnancy than it had about love. He could see that now. But if Bleu had lived, he could also see that he would have worked damned hard to make things work.

Seb hunched over his computer monitor, trying to figure out what that next step might be. Whatever it was, it would now take place after the storm had passed.

He got up to stretch for a minute and then decided to grab a coffee before Rachel arrived.

Heading out the door, he rounded the corner to the elevator and stopped. Rachel. She was already here at the hospital. Talking to Philippe Chauvre. Whatever she'd said made him smile, and he reached out to touch her arm.

She smiled back, and Seb tensed.

Was the man asking her out?

And if he was, it was none of his business, although a little spiral of something in his brain called Seb a liar.

When Rachel's head turned and saw him, her smile disappeared, a look of utter guilt appearing in her eyes.

Hell. He wasn't trying to make her feel bad. Or feel anything, really.

He made his way over to them, nodded at Philippe and turned his attention to her. "I'm headed for coffee. Want anything?"

"I—I…ran into Philippe on the way to your office."

He hadn't asked. Maybe she felt guilty for getting sidetracked. But he knew Philippe enough to know there was almost no walking past him without having a conversation.

A part of Seb might not like her getting chummy with the orthopedist, but he wasn't involved with Rachel, and he had no right to feel one way or the other about it.

Rachel was a beautiful woman—why should he be surprised that he wasn't the only one to notice that?

But he wasn't going to stand here and interrupt whatever this was. He needed to go get his coffee so they could finish their conversation in peace.

And if the man was asking her out?

Again, none of his business.

Before Seb could move away from the pair, though, the orthopedic surgeon smiled at him. "I guess I got caught red-handed."

The statement took him by surprise. "Sorry?"

"I came up here to lure Rachel away from you."

Damn! Had she told the man about that kiss? Or worse, implied that Seb was interested in her?

He wasn't, no matter how that kiss had looked. It had been impulsive and stupid, and he was damned sure not going to do anything like that again.

Rachel drew what looked to be an overly careful breath. "He means lure me away from Pediatrics."

Ah, hell. His imagination was going to get the best of him. Of course it hadn't been about anything that had happened yesterday.

"A position just opened up in my department and—"

He didn't need to hear any more. "There's a storm out there, Philippe. Can't this wait?"

The man had the grace to look chagrined. "Of course it can. I just happened to get on the elevator with her and asked if she had a minute."

Rachel stared at Seb like he had two heads. But she was seriously thinking of leaving Pediatrics?

Hell, he'd just been thinking about how much better it would be when they were no longer working together. So wouldn't that kind of move be the perfect solution?

Maybe, but he didn't like it. He and Philippe were both heads of their respective departments. He'd never tried to "lure"—as the other man had put it—anyone away from their position.

He decided to leave it. For now. Because what he'd said was true. There was a storm out there, and this was no time for hospital politics. He forced a smile. "So, about that coffee…"

Philippe shrugged. "I think that's my signal to head back to my own department." He touched Rachel's arm again. "Think about it, though, okay?"

Rachel didn't have a chance to say anything before the other man turned and pressed the button for the elevator.

Wanting to make sure that kiss had nothing to do with the conversation, he said, "Are you unhappy in Pediatrics?"

"No. He mentioned it when that chain saw accident came through the ER and I was helping him during surgery. We really did meet in the elevator. He didn't seek me out for a meeting or anything."

If he'd been worried about that kiss carrying too much meaning, he evidently needn't have. Philippe had a reputation for being competitive, claiming his team was one of the hospital's best. It made sense if Rachel had impressed him in some way that he'd tried to persuade her to join his team.

Would Rachel think about the offer and decide it was what she wanted to do?

Not something he was going to ask. So he decided to

repeat his earlier question. "It's fine. You drink espresso, if I remember right."

She looked surprise. "I do. And that sounds great. I just jumped out of bed and dragged my clothes on, so I didn't even get my morning coffee."

Rachel didn't look like she'd just dragged her clothes on. The morning after they'd slept together a year ago, her hair had been beautifully rumpled and sexy, and he almost hadn't been able to leave.

None of that was evident now. Her hair was neatly pulled up into a clip, whatever messiness there might have been neatly twisted away.

"I'll get you one, and I'll be right back, if you want to wait in my office."

"Sounds good, thanks."

She'd dreamed about him.

Rachel wandered around Seb's office, waiting for him to get back from the coffee shop. His space was neat and organized, just like the other times she'd been in here. On his whiteboard were some facts about the storm.

The name *Mauhali* was at the top and had been underlined several times. Next to it were some facts and statistics about the island. Including the one community health clinic that was housed on the island. There was a helicopter pad, but no real airport.

She hadn't even stopped to listen to the news this morning. And then as she was rushing up to his office, Philippe had waylaid her talking again about the possibility of her moving to Ortho. And like the other doctor had said, they'd gotten caught red-handed.

She'd finally drifted off to sleep but then had had strange fitful dreams. Seb had called her just as her hand was reaching out to grab him in her dream.

Was that her subconscious trying to tell her something? That she was grabbing at something that wasn't in her or Claire's best interest?

Was Philippe's request the universe's way of telling her to get out while she could—before she got entangled in a situation that would only bring her heartache?

No. If she took that job, it wouldn't be because she was running from something. It would be because she thought it was something she'd be good at. Something that would be rewarding in its own right.

Sebastien came back before she had a chance to think through any of it. He was carrying two cups, one of them a disposable paper container and the other a china cup emblazoned with the Centre Hospitalier's name.

Her head tilted. "You could have had mine put in a disposable cup, too."

"I think I remember you saying you didn't care for the taste they gave your coffee."

He remembered that? A shiver of warmth went through her, which reminded her of her dream.

Don't grab at him.

"Well, thank you. But I've drunk plenty of coffee in paper cups and survived the experience." She smiled and took the proffered cup. "Besides, I'm surprised they let you carry this out of the cafeteria."

His lips curved. "Philippe's not the only one who can be persuasive."

Was he saying that the china cup was his way of persuading her to stay in Pediatrics? Or was it just like it sounded—that he'd talked the cafeteria staff into letting him take one of their cups?

The latter, obviously. To read anything else into it was ridiculous.

She decided not to bite, instead saying, "Well, thanks for the coffee."

"Yep. Ready to get to work?"

When she nodded, taking her first sip and savoring the strong brew, he pulled up a map with projections. "This is where things stand right now."

Her eyes scanned the red cone that fanned out from the storm. A storm that was already far too close to shore. Wind speeds were... She swallowed hard. They stood at a hundred miles an hour. "That looks a lot different from what it was last night when I went to bed."

She didn't tell him how long it took her to actually fall asleep.

"Yes, it does. Neves want to meet with us to discuss how Hospitalier can take advantage of the work we've already done. Especially since Taurati is now officially off the critical list. It looks like Mauhali will be the worst hit of the islands, although the outer bands may skate across Bora Bora before it slides back out to open water." He stared at the screen. "Bora Bora has good infrastructure, whereas Mauhali...well, it doesn't. It's known for its mango exports, so there are extra workers there, who I imagine are trying to get everything off the trees they can now before the storm decimates the harvest. So they may not have evacuated even if they were urged to."

"And the population?"

"Right now, we're probably looking at a thousand."

"That's a lot of potential patients."

"It is. And another problem is the helipad's a little distance from the clinic, due to the topography of the island."

"So we're looking at a task that might very well be..."

"Impossible." He finished the sentence for her. "Yes, but if we can coordinate any medevac with other islands and schedule landings, it could work. Neves says they're asking for a team from the hospital to go as soon as the winds die down a bit. So we need get that started, too."

She glanced over at him, noting he had some dark circles going on under his eyes. She wasn't the only one who hadn't gotten a good night's sleep, evidently.

"Have you been up all night?"

"I happened to wake up and looked at the weather. I called you and Neves right after I saw it."

Well, at least he hadn't left her out of the equation.

"When does he want to meet?"

"As soon as we can. Let me see if he's arrived yet." Seb retrieved his phone and dialed the hospital administrator's number. "Hi, are you at the hospital?"

He glanced at Rachel. "Yep, she's here, too. Are you ready for us?" There was a pause. "Okay, we'll be right there."

At Neves's office, they discussed what they could do for Mauhali and who should be on the team that went to the island. They decided on four people, since there was only so much they could do on-site, medically. They'd take basic supplies, but surgeries there would be next to impossible to do. As well as Rachel and Seb, the team would consist of Dr. Monchamp, one of the ER doctors with military training, and a nurse called Kayla Courrier, who would help with triage and identifying the most critical patients. Dr. Monchamp and Kayla would stay on the island and help coordinate who went on which chopper. And she and Seb would ride back and forth on the chopper that would ferry patients to Hospitalier.

"I need you guys to stay in close contact with the hospital, so we know what's coming in."

She nodded. Lord, she hoped she was ready for this. But Neves wouldn't be sending them out if he wasn't confident in their abilities. And although she was a pediatric nurse now, she'd once been involved with search-and-rescue teams right after finishing her nursing degree.

"We'll get the hospitals lined up, since we already know who has choppers and who has space in their facilities."

"Okay. Go. Give me a buzz when you get ready to go. I imagine we still have quite a bit of waiting to do."

Almost twelve hours' worth. Maybe more by the time the last of the bands crossed Mauhali.

The next several hours were spent getting hospitals onboard with their plans, which was easy, since everyone was eager to help out. Only one hospital couldn't, since they'd had an outbreak of norovirus from one of the cruise ships. They were barely keeping their heads above water.

Just as she got off a call, her phone buzzed. She glanced down just as Seb looked over at her. "It's Claire." She pushed a button to answer.

"Hi, honey. Did you guys make it?"

"Yes. Just wanted to let you know that we're at Grams's house."

She sent Sebastien a thumbs-up sign. "I'm glad you made it."

Claire's voice came through. "Did you hear that Taurati isn't going to be hit?"

"We did. But it's going to hit another island, so we're trying to get some plans together."

"You promised you'd help them."

It was so like Claire to remember everything, even things she wished her daughter would forget. "We're going to fly over once the storm has passed. And yes, we'll help however we can."

"Good. And I miss you already."

"I miss you, too, sweetheart."

"Tell Sebastien that I miss him, too."

She swallowed, but what choice did she have but to agree? "Okay, I'll tell him."

"And that his turtle made it through customs without any problem."

Rachel held her hand over the phone when she realized Seb's head had tilted when he realized they were probably talking about him. "She said to tell you that the turtle made it through without being confiscated." She made no mention of what else Claire had said.

He smiled. "Good news."

"Okay, honey, tell Grams we'll call you guys when we get on the chopper for Mauhali." Too late she realized she'd used the word *we*, meaning her and Seb. But there was no way to correct it without it becoming very awkward, so she just let it go.

"Okay. We'll be watching the news."

"Love you, honey. Tell Grams and Gramps, too."

"I will. 'Bye."

With that, she hung up the phone.

"They're doing okay, I take it?"

She smiled. "Better than we are, I think. I'm really glad Claire went back with my mom. And you were right. It would have been too hard to work with her and my mom sitting either at home or here at the hospital worrying about every movement that storm made." She paused. "What happened here during Wasa-Arthur?"

"They rode it out, for the most part. There were surprisingly few fatalities. But they were good about evacuating people from the coastal areas to the interior. That helped a lot."

"Is that what will happen on Mauhali?"

"That island is a lot smaller than Taurati. So the interior of that island is not super far from the coastline. A lot of them will probably shelter in place. But some will move inland. If they can."

She nodded and sat back down. "I need to make some more calls and see if I can make more of those connections we were talking about."

"I'll do the same."

If it came down to it, maybe Rachel would do what the rest of the islanders did, according to Seb. She'd just find a place to hunker down and hope for the best.

CHAPTER EIGHT

"WE NEED TO get some sleep. Is there anything you need from home? I'm afraid it's going to be an early morning." It was after eleven, and they'd been working nonstop all day.

Koji was on the shores of Mauhali, the first of its bands already wreaking havoc on the tiny island.

"I brought a tote bag with me, just in case."

"Okay, good. The couch pulls out into a bed."

She blinked, one side of her mouth going up in amusement. "Well, that takes care of one of us."

He laughed. "Don't worry. I wasn't planning on sharing it with you. I'll be quite comfortable in one of the chairs."

"Even a chair sounds heavenly right now." She stood and stretched.

Locks of hair had fallen free from her clip and scattered around her face in waves. She was beautiful. In more ways than one. And working with her today had been surprisingly easy. Something he hadn't expected, given their past. And given that kiss that now seemed like forever ago.

"Why don't you take the bathroom first, while I get the bed made up?"

She regarded him for a second. "Are you sure you

don't mind me sleeping here? I could probably go to the on-call room and grab some shut-eye."

"You probably would get a whole lot less sleep in there than you would here. You know what those are like."

"Unfortunately, I do." She picked up her bag. "I'll be quick."

He'd just finished throwing the covers over the bed when she came out, hair wet and smelling of that vanilla-and-coconut scent he'd come to associate with her. She was dressed in sweats and a large T-shirt, but hell, he couldn't stop picturing her in his small shower…naked. He knew he was going to have a hell of a time forgetting it from here on out.

"Thanks. I didn't realize you had an actual shower. I hope you don't mind."

"Of course not. Neither of us knows when we'll get our next one."

She tossed her bag on the bed. "It's all yours."

And none too soon. He nodded before turning and making his way in there. And he hoped beyond hope that he was actually going to be able to sleep, knowing she was mere feet away from him.

They both had a job to do. And the sooner he remembered that, the better off he would be.

It was still dark, but the readout on her phone said it was almost five. She could just make out Seb a few yards away. He'd evidently abandoned the chair in favor of the floor, the outline of a blanket beneath his body. He was on his stomach, both arms stretched above his head, the left one curving. He had jogging pants and a T-shirt on, but she could imagine the outline of his tattoo beneath it. In memory of his son. It was heartbreaking. And the sweetest thing she could imagine.

She forced her gaze away from him and surveyed the light that came in through the rectangular sliver of a window on his door. The takeout boxes from last night were all gone. He must have cleaned up after he'd gotten out of the bathroom. She'd been going to do it, but the second she sat on that bed, exhaustion pulled at her. She figured she'd just do it in the morning.

Except he'd already done it.

She tried to pull up the news stories on her phone, but the light must have disturbed Seb, because his voice broke through the silence.

"How long have you been up?"

"About five minutes. I'm just trying to find out what's happening with the storm."

A few minutes later, they sat at his computer. There was no news from Mauhali that they could see, but the storm was almost gone. The last band was just now sweeping through, and wind speeds had been downgraded to a level-one tropical cyclone.

Koji was weakening.

Thank God. But how much damage had it caused?

"I'm going to see if I can rouse our team and get things underway. I'm hoping we can be airborne as soon as the wind speeds are down."

They were in the air an hour later. It had been forever since she'd been in a helicopter, and the closer they got to the island, the worse the winds became, buffeting the small aircraft. Dr. Felix Monchamp and Kayla Courrier were seated behind them. A small medical area at the back of the chopper was ready for up to two patients, or one if the patient was in critical condition. The mayor of Mauhali had declared a state of emergency. There had been no deaths reported yet, but almost every road was blocked by debris.

A particular bit of turbulence dropped the aircraft for a few seconds before they continued on their way. Rachel's fingers scrabbled for a handhold so she didn't end up in Seb's lap.

From behind her, Kayla moaned. "Ooh, my stomach."

She could relate. She would be glad when they were on the ground. By the time they took off again, hopefully the winds would be less of an issue. She could see why they hadn't gotten air clearance until just now.

A hand covered hers. "You okay?"

She nodded, tossing him a smile. "I've been on a couple of rescues before, but never with quite this much wind. How close are we?"

"About another fifteen minutes, and we should be there."

Seb let go of her hand to turn and speak to the two other team members, and she immediately missed the contact.

Stress. It had to be. It had nothing to do with the fact that he'd looked so peaceful and approachable sleeping on the floor this morning. Or the fact that they'd been working so closely together for almost a week. It seemed so much longer than that. Kind of like time had stretched out into a month's worth of encounters. And realistically, it was probably more than the amount of time they would have spend together over a month. And they certainly wouldn't have shared meals or watched that sea turtle together like a...

Like a family.

No. Don't keep thinking of him like that. He is not family, nor will he ever be.

For the next fifteen minutes, she forced herself to

think of the movements of the helicopter and about what they might face when they finally landed. Anything that would keep her from mulling over things that not only seemed impossible but *were* impossible.

The first thing she saw when they set down on the helicopter pad were mangoes. So many mangoes. They were scattered across the clearing like tiny beach balls. And the second the door to the chopper opened, a strange smell assaulted her nostrils, and it was all she could do to keep herself from grimacing. It was a cloyingly sweet mixture of fruit, seaweed and dead fish. She saw why a few feet away, where a huge fish lay unmoving, evidently washed ashore by the force of the storm.

"God," she whispered as she stepped out of the helicopter and peered around her. Downed trees and debris had been flung everywhere. Not too far from them, some kind of building hunched as if in pain, missing its roof, while one side of the structure had collapsed inward. All thoughts of minor discomforts from the trip over or woes about Seb immediately vanished.

This was the look of utter devastation.

A man hurried toward them, his hair blown about by the slowing rotors of the helicopter. Even when the blades stopped, the wind continued. He said something in Tahitian that she didn't understand, until Seb translated it for her. "He's asking us to come to the clinic. They have some injuries that need immediate care. The physician assistant who basically runs the clinic is one of the injured."

The fact that the man was on foot told them that vehicles were not moving freely. They'd probably been lucky to be able to land.

Seb nodded and responded to him. Then he turned to them. "Let's get our gear and two stretchers. The clinic wasn't totally demolished, so we can use whatever supplies are there, although power is out."

It wasn't until they'd picked their way through the streets that the man introduced himself as Ari'i Teriyong, the mayor of Mauhali.

By the time the small community clinic came within sight, Rachel was perspiring, and her hair hung in damp hanks around her head. They'd had to pick their way around trees and debris on almost every road they'd traveled down. With the stretchers being awkward to carry, it slowed their progress. She glanced at Seb to see he still looked a whole lot better than she felt. His hair looked shiny and clean and definitely wasn't sticking to his head like hers was.

She heard the familiar cries of people in pain as they came out of a stand of trees that opened to the clinic. Two of the windows had been blown out by the force of the storm, and there was glass everywhere, but the structure itself was still intact. The scene was one of chaotic order. People sat outside the building, and a couple were lying on blankets nearby.

The team went to work, each person quickly moving from patient to patient to assess. She stuck close to Seb, since her Tahitian wasn't as good as it needed to be. Something she needed to get serious about if she was going to stay on the island.

Was she mentally keeping one foot planted in the States, not fully committing to Taurati? Maybe not consciously. But unconsciously? Claire had been diligent about studying both languages.

Sebastien immediately moved toward a child, who was crying and writhing in her mother's arms.

"Aidez-nous! Aidez-nous!"

The words were in French, and these she understood as a cry for help.

The little girl, who couldn't have been more than five, was wheezing, trying to catch her breath, crying with each exhale. Her face was a picture of pure panic. Seb called to Dr. Monchamp. "We need to treat this one."

"We're still assessing, so go."

They got a quick history from the girl's mom, who said Lara had been hit in the chest by their front door when it was blown off its hinges. She'd carried her all the way to the clinic from over a mile away. They'd arrived an hour ago. The terror in the woman's voice was one she recognized all too well from Claire's health crisis.

Rachel's heart clenched as tears coursed down the mom's cheeks while she whispered over the girl's cries, rocking her back and forth. She put a hand on the woman's shoulder to stop the motion, fearing it would hurt the child even more.

Seb's voice was steady and calm as he explained to the pair that they were going to have to examine her, and that the mom needed to stay as still as possible. Rachel knew exactly why. He didn't want to move the girl until he knew exactly what they were dealing with.

He touched the child's hand. "Where does it hurt?"

Through her cries she pointed at the right side of her chest, over her ribs.

"How about your back? Does that hurt?"

"Non." The second she had to breathe back in, she cried out.

A dark bruise on her cheek testified to the force with which she'd been hit by the door.

"I think her back is clear, so let's get a stretcher and lay her on it. She's going to need to be transported as soon as we can."

She was glad they'd taken the time to drag those things

here. Once retrieved, Rachel laid it close to the mom's side while Sebastien held one of the child's hands. "Lara, we have to move you to the cot, okay?"

The girl shook her head, crying out again. *"Non! Non!"*

"I know it hurts, and we're going to try hard to make it better, but we have to look at your chest."

Again she shook her head, starting to whimper.

That there were broken ribs involved was almost a certainty with this level of pain. But she knew Seb couldn't give the child anything for the pain without knowing what they were dealing with. Narcotics tended to depress the respiratory system and could cause it to arrest.

Seb looked at Lara's mom, who seemed to understand his silent question. She nodded, her chest spasming as if suppressing her own sobs.

"On three. Rach, you support her lower half, and I'll do the upper. Let's keep from twisting her at all."

So he also thought there were ribs involved.

"Un, deux, trois..."

A bloodcurdling scream went up as they gingerly took the little girl from her mom's arms and laid her on the cot. The whole area went silent right afterward.

She glanced at Kayla and Dr. Monchamp and saw they hadn't looked up, leaning over a patient. Their focus and ability to block out what wasn't right in front of them was unlike anything she'd ever seen.

Rachel lifted the girl's top, and right away they saw the ribs on her right side were dark purple, looking worse than even her face. And as she breathed in, a section of her chest sank inward even as the rest of her ribs expanded. When she exhaled, the bruised section moved in the opposite direction. Paradoxical breathing. Not good sign.

She swallowed. "Flail chest."

"I see it. We need to get her in the chopper immediately." He glanced at the mom. "Can you run in the clinic and see if you can find a pillow and a long strip of tape?"

The woman did as asked, coming back a minute later with a pillow and a box of gauze. "These?"

Sebastien nodded. "Yes, those are perfect, thank you."

"You're going to stabilize the flail?" Rachel asked.

"Yes, since we'll be carrying her on the stretcher. I don't want those broken ribs damaging her lungs as she's jostled on the way to the chopper."

Using a long strip of gauze, he slid it between her back and the cot. He glanced at Rachel. "You know what to do?"

"Yes."

She laid the pillow over the right side of Lara's body but didn't press on it yet. Even so, the girl moaned in pain.

Seb touched the girl's head. "I know it hurts. But can you take a deep breath and hold it?"

Through her tears, she did as asked, and then Rachel applied pressure with the pillow to the area that she knew was depressed. The second she did, the girl screamed again, exhaling everything she had just breathed in. But that was what they wanted. The pressure would keep the flail section from pushing up while the ribs were deflating. While Rachel held the pillow in place, Seb tied the gauze around the pillow tight enough to maintain pressure without restricting her breathing even further.

"We're all done," he said.

The girl gingerly took a couple of breaths.

"It should hurt a little less now. We're going to pick up the cot and carry you to a helicopter."

"Maman..."

"Your mom can come." Seb glanced up. "Can you? Or do you have other children you need to care for?"

"She is my only. I will of course come."

Seb nodded. "I'll be right back."

He went over to Dr. Monchamp, saying something to him, to which the other man nodded. When he came back, he had a couple of men with him. "They'll carry the cot in case we need to stop and take care of anything."

He didn't need to say what he was thinking. She already knew. It was in case Lara stopped breathing or arrested on the trip to the chopper.

They started out. The half-mile trip was grueling and tense, since each movement jostled those ribs and caused terrible pain.

But then they were there. While the pilot started the aircraft, she got Lara's oxygen going, and Seb strapped the cot in place.

Then they were off.

They glanced at each other as the chopper flew, and Seb said, "Good work."

She gave him a half smile. "Ditto to you."

Lara's mom was crouched over her daughter, smoothing her hair and telling the girl something.

Rachel's brows went up in question.

Replying in English, he said. "She's talking about the brave doctors who came to help them."

With Lara now stabilized, her own lungs deflated as she released a huge ball of tension. "How were Kayla and Dr. Monchamp doing?"

"They have an emergency case as well, but a chopper is almost there from Bora Bora with a medical team, so they'll load her in and go back to caring for others."

"Do you know how many islands are included in the rescue efforts?"

"Mayor Ari'i said four."

"Thank God. I'm glad it's not just us."

Seb glanced down at the mom and daughter. "Me, too. But I'm glad we were able to be there."

"So am I."

Something unspoken seemed to pass between them, the touch of softness in Seb's glance making Rachel's chest clog. Then the moment passed, and they got back to work, calling the hospital and asking them to have a team ready to receive them.

They arrived at the hospital an hour later, and four medical staff members rushed toward them with a gurney. Within minutes, they got Lara off the chopper and were headed toward the door.

Seb ducked his head into the aircraft. "Do you have enough fuel for another trip?"

The pilot nodded. "I do. Then I'll need to refuel the next time we get back."

Seb glanced at Rachel. "Are you up for heading back to Mauhali?"

"Absolutely."

He smiled. "I was hoping you'd say that."

CHAPTER NINE

TWO MORE CHOPPER trips and the clinic's clearing was finally empty, other islands having also transported the worst of the patients. Dr. Monchamp and Kayla both volunteered to stay on-site for a couple of days to help with the more minor injuries and to oversee the clinic getting the power restored via the generator.

The second they'd set down at the hospital for the last time and their patient had been transferred, he sighed before thanking the pilot. It had been a long day. But a very good one. To his knowledge not one of their patients had died, and there'd been no casualties on Mauhali. And the other islands that had gotten some of the stronger winds had come through pretty well.

He turned to Rachel.

Her hair was mussed in the best kind of way, although it looked like she'd dragged her fingers through it to try to get some semblance of order back into it. The clip she'd stuffed it into partway through the day was long gone and her tresses hung long and free. She was beautiful and working with her on the island had been…

Like nothing he'd ever experienced. She was strong and capable and had balked at nothing, including putting pressure on a flail chest and helping him stabilize it

No wonder Philippe Chauvre wanted her on his team. Seb knew he didn't want to lose her.

In more ways than one?

That had to be the exhaustion talking. He realized he was just standing there and forced himself to speak.

"Thank you, Rach. For everything. Coffee?" Somehow, he didn't want her to go her separate way just yet.

"Yes, that sounds heavenly."

"The cafeteria is closed, but they let you do self-serve after hours."

Leaving the chopper pad and going into the building, she said, "Can you go on ahead so I can call Claire? I'll catch up with you."

"Okay, see you in a few minutes."

He went into the elevator just as he heard Rachel say, "Hello, sweetheart, how was your day?"

He swallowed past a lump in his throat. How would it feel to have someone say those words to him?

His and Layla's relationship had been passionate, but looking back, he could see that their young love had been largely driven by hormones and a sense of infatuation. It was no wonder their relationship had disintegrated once Bleu was gone. He'd been their glue.

He got to the cafeteria and found one of the carafes still had coffee in it. He then glanced at the espresso machine next to it, perusing the knobs and settings with a frown. He knew that's what Rachel liked. But he also had no idea how to use the thing.

"Something I can help you with?" The voice from behind him was the one he'd heard repeatedly over the last week. And right now it was filled with amusement.

He turned to face her. "That was fast."

"I wanted to make sure she knew I was okay and that we had done what she asked us to do. I told her I'd call her tomorrow with details. Once I've had a chance to decompress. Starting with coffee."

He motioned at the espresso machine. "I was going to try to tackle that, but…"

"Here, you get your coffee, and I'll get mine."

He watched as she expertly packed coffee into some kind of large spoon-looking device and then twisted it onto the underside of the machine, setting a paper cup underneath. Then she pressed a button, and the machine made a bubbling sound, then hissed out a thin, dark stream of fragrant brew.

"See? Not so hard."

He chuckled. "Easy for you to say. Sorry they don't have any real cups out."

"It's okay. I'll survive."

For his, he picked up a carafe and poured. "Mine's a little easier to figure out," he joked.

"Yes, but is it as good? Sometimes the best things take a little effort. But the results are well worth it."

Sometimes it didn't matter how much effort went into something. The results weren't always perfect, like that dark, rich coffee. His son and his relationship with Layla were two examples of that.

But how much effort had he really put into anything after Bleu had died? He was realistic enough to know that he'd been pretty emotionally unreachable for a long time after that. Looking back, he couldn't blame Layla for making the choice she had. She'd probably needed him, and he hadn't been there. Or maybe she hadn't. What he did know was that he hadn't been willing to become that vulnerable with anyone for a long time. And he wasn't sure he was capable of it anymore. But working with Rachel like he had… It made him wonder. It was almost as if they'd anticipated each other's thoughts on treatment and had worked together seamlessly. It had come as a surprise. Maybe it had been the setting and the need for quick action. But what she'd said was true. The effort they'd put into those patients on Mauhali had been worth it in the end. But relationships? That was another story.

"I'm good with my no-effort choice." But was he really? Or had he just settled for what he was comfortable with? Like he'd done most of his life. Since his son's death, he'd very rarely stepped outside his comfort zone.

Why? Mauhali had been outside his comfort zone. And yet he was very glad he'd gone. Had been very glad to see his and Rachel's work on preparedness put to good use.

"Are you sure you don't want to at least try this? I'll even walk you through how to use the machine."

Her words weren't a challenge, necessarily, but maybe it was time he took that first step and tried something completely different. Like today had been.

Without a word he set his coffee down. "You're on. Teach me. But I can't promise I'll like it."

"No promise expected." She took a sip of her brew, then took the cup filter thing off the machine and pounded it on the side of a metal can labeled Used Grounds. Then she handed it to him while she took another sip.

She walked him through the process, correcting him when he didn't tamp the coffee into the reservoir hard enough. "It uses pressure to push water through the grounds, so they have to be tightly packed."

A minute later, the water hissed through the machine like it had done with Rachel's.

"There's sugar here. How sweet do you like it?"

There was something about the way she said that last phrase that caught him off guard, and he found himself saying, "I like a good balance between sweet…and not so sweet." He smiled. "So how much should I add for that?"

She grinned at him. "Maybe half a packet of sugar, since these are bigger than what we have in the States."

He dumped half of the sugar in and gave the concoction a quick stir. Then he sipped.

Okay. He'd expected it to taste like something akin to used motor oil, since it was as dark as that. But it didn't. It was strong, yes, but it had a body to it that his own coffee didn't have. A bite that slid across his tongue in just the right way.

"How is it?"

"Not as bad as I thought it might be."

Her brows went up. "Hmm…but is it *good*?"

He thought for a second as he gave it another try. "Yes. It is."

"And worth the effort?"

"The jury is still out on that." And it was. Not just about the coffee, either. But about a lot of things.

"I'll take it." She took one last drink, then crumpled her cup and tossed it.

He did the same. Then he picked up his regular-size cup of coffee. "Mine lasts a whole lot longer, though. So maybe that's where my coffee beats yours. Maybe the enjoyment of savoring the experience, down to the final drop, is what makes it so great."

She pursed her lips as if thinking. "But maybe leaving your mouth wanting more makes you look forward to the next time that much more."

He went very still. Were they still talking about coffee or about something else entirely?

She'd left him wanting more a year ago.

But that didn't mean they should pick up where they'd left off. Right?

But he could use some downtime after their frenetic time on Mauhali. And he found he didn't want to be alone with his thoughts right now. "Let's go sit out on the beach for a bit and clear our heads. Unless you want to go home and get some real rest."

"I'm too keyed up to sleep right now. And listening to the ocean while it's still quiet sounds like an amazing option."

Seb chugged the rest of his coffee down, and they headed for the exit. Warm air hit him as soon as they made it through the doors, the heat both familiar and foreign. You wouldn't know it from how still the air was that a powerful storm had just blown through an island similar to theirs. Leaving destruction in its wake.

"The stars are incredibly bright tonight."

He glanced up and saw she was right. The moon, along with thousands of pinpoints of light, were on clear display, the quiet flickering making for an ever-changing show. They were there, just as they always were. A reminder that no matter what, there were some things you could count on. "Yes, they are."

Picking their way across the boardwalk, they finally came out onto the sand, which was still warm from the day's sun. Rachel kicked off her shoes, burying her toes in the soft surface. Pink polish shone up from her tanned feet. It was a good combination.

The moon cast its light across the space, making some of the individual grains of sand sparkle, adding to the mystical feel of the night. It was almost eerie how different it was from the day they'd had.

Still. Quiet. Peaceful.

They walked toward the water, and Rachel stepped into the low surf, fisting the fabric of her loose skirt up to her knees. "You know, I never considered myself a beach person before I came to Taurati. It just seemed like too much work with the sand and salt."

"Didn't you say a little while ago that some of the best things take a little effort?"

She laughed and kicked a bit of water his way. "Touché. But then again, it looks like I was right, because the ocean is definitely worth it." She glanced down the beach. "I can't imagine those cabanas being washed away, can you?"

"No. These are used for fishing and sightseeing spots rather than overnight guests. The hospital pays for their upkeep. They're rustic, but the charm is definitely there."

"Yes, it is. I didn't realize the hospital owned them, though. I just assumed that they were part of a resort like the one I stayed in when…"

She didn't finish her sentence, but he could pretty much guess what she'd been about to say.

"No. The hospital had these four put in for the use of patients' families and staff. There have even been several small weddings held in them. You've never been inside one?"

"No. Like I said, I didn't know the hospital owned them." She smiled. "My French and Tahitian language skills could use some work."

"It just takes time." He tilted his head in that direction. "Come on. I'll show you one of the cabanas."

The last thing he wanted to do was go home. Despite the crazy day, he'd enjoyed spending it with her. He hadn't been in one of these cabanas in four years. It had been part of the tour the hospital had given him when he'd signed on at the center. He was surprised they hadn't done the same for Rachel.

While she continued to walk in the water, he stayed

on the shore, making his way toward the first of the cabanas about a hundred yards down the coast.

There was something about the moonlight playing across the water and her dark hair that made his fingers itch to slide through it. He remembered exactly what it felt like. And the cabanas weren't helping, because they were bringing back memories that were quickly crowding his brain.

The thought of going into another one of them with her...

Maybe this was a mistake.

Hell, but even that thought wasn't enough to make him stop and call the tour off.

Just then she called out, "Hey." She came out of the water and grabbed his hand, pointing. "What's that?"

He turned and looked in the direction she'd indicated, her fingers warm and soft, just like they'd been as they skated over his body that night a year ago. He almost groaned aloud. He needed to cut it out.

She spoke again. "Is that where we saw the turtle?"

There was a flag stuck into the sand with a caution symbol and the words *Ne Pas Déranger* printed in bold letters.

He had sent his pictures to a conservation site. Since there were no other flags nearby, it had to be the same one.

"I think it is."

She leaned against him. "I'm so glad that wasn't destroyed." She whispered the words into the night, the feeling behind them very clear.

She was amazing. After the day they'd had, the fact that she could be grateful for something so small...yet so important...

Dieu.

He turned her toward him and stared into her eyes, an overpowering urge coursing through him. Without stopping to think, he murmured, "I think I want to kiss you right now, Rach."

Her mouth turned up in a slight smile. "I think I'd like that, too."

Maybe the moonlit night was affecting his ability to make rational decisions, or maybe it was the lingering urgency from the day's events, but that was all it took. His head came down, and he took her lips with a fierceness that surprised him.

Maybe it had nothing at all to do with the moon or the day. Maybe it was the woman herself and the fact that he'd had a hard time working with her without thinking about that night a year ago. Had wanted to recreate it so many times. Was this the universe giving him permission?

Probably not. But how would this be any different from that night? It hadn't wrecked either of them, had it? They'd both moved forward with their lives, right?

His heart seemed to agree with his head for once as he deepened the kiss, using her body language as a guide for how much pressure to use and where she wanted it. His lips trailed down the side of her jaw, relishing the way she tilted her head to give him access to the areas he knew she liked.

The shoes she'd been carrying dropped to the ground as she wrapped her arms around his neck.

Hell, if they were going to stop, they needed to do it now. His eyes caught sight of the nearest cabana, and it seemed to beckon to him, whispering for him to come inside. They had a choice to make. "Rachel."

"Mmm?" Her eyes looked up at him with a heat that matched what was running through his veins.

He nodded toward the nearest bungalow.

"Yes," she whispered.

That was all he needed. He swept her into his arms.

Rachel giggled. "My shoes…"

"Leave them for later."

She made no protest as he carried her to the dock and strode down it with her. The sign on the door read, Staff and Patients of Centre Hospitalier Only.

Well, they fit that description, right? He reached down and pulled the knob on the door, and it swung open without a sound. There was no one on the beach at this hour, and he could barely even see the hospital from here. Moving inside, he set her down, closing the door and leaning it against it. Then he hauled her against him.

The kiss changed from something hurried and frantic to more leisurely. He wanted to slow things down. To do what Rachel had said and be willing to take the time needed—to pack those grounds tightly enough to make the end product good. So very good.

So he used tiny touches to kiss her mouth, her eyelids, the crook of her neck, his hands sliding beneath her shirt and pressing against the warm, bare skin of her back.

So silky. So soft. Just like she'd been the last time.

There was no bed in the hospital cabanas. Just a couple of hard wooden chairs. But they didn't need a bed this time. Didn't need anything except what was happening right now, here in the dark, quiet confines of this space. There were no stars to guide their path, since the front shutters that opened toward the ocean were shut tight. But he didn't need stars. Didn't need anything to guide him but instinct. Whether that was a good thing or bad, he didn't know. And he didn't really care right now.

Sweeping her shirt up and over her head, he held it in one hand for a few seconds, unsure what to do with it. Then she took it from him and threw it against the wall.

"It'll survive." She stood on tiptoe to reach his mouth.

It might survive, but would he?

She followed suit, unbuttoning his shirt and pushing it down his arms until it too fell away. Her fingers skated down his chest and reached the waistband of his jeans. He shuddered and grabbed her hand.

"Rach. Are you absolutely sure?"

She gave a low laugh. "Does it feel like I'm sure?"

It did. Oh, hell, it did.

He bent and swooped his arm under her ass and picked her up off her feet, walking to one of the chairs and lowering himself into it while her feet planted on the ground. His hands went to her hips, and with a grin, he inched her forward until her knees bumped against his, wordlessly asking her to make a decision.

She bent down and kissed him, hands on either side of his face, and then, just as he'd hoped she'd do, she straddled him, coming to rest tightly against him.

He groaned. "You're right about packing those grounds. It makes it. So. Much. Better." He punctuated each of those words with a kiss.

"I told you." She nipped his bottom lip hard enough to make part of him jerk against her.

Yes, she had. And right now, he believed her. Very much so.

He took her skirt, bunching it up in his hands, finding it had a stretchy waist. "Will this slide over your head?"

"Why don't you try it and find out?"

Her tone said she already knew the answer to that question. So he slid it upward, taking his time, knuckles purposely lingering over the swell of her breasts. He paused there for a long minute before continuing on his way until her skirt was no more. Instead, this hot, fierce woman who sat astride him was dressed only in her bra and silky underwear. And when she did a little wiggle in his lap, he almost lost it.

"Not so fast," he muttered against her mouth.

His hands went to her waist, and he leaned forward to breathe in her scent, starting at her neck and moving to her collarbone, which he licked across. Then, using pressure from his palms, he tilted her back, farther and farther, until she was arched in just the perfect position.

Dieu, she looked wanton and so, so sexy with her hair tumbling behind her and her breasts jutting out for the taking.

And take he did, leaning forward to take one hard nipple into his mouth, sucking in a steady stream that made her gasp, her hands coming up and holding his mouth to her.

There was no need. He had no intention of leaving, using his teeth to hold her in place as his tongue swept over her again and again until he could stand it no longer.

With a growl, he reached behind her and undid her bra while she squirmed against him. The tiny garment fell away, and he buried his face in her breasts, sucking and kissing until he thought he was going to burst.

His breathing unsteady, he leaned back so he could get at his pocket to pull his wallet out. He took out the condom he'd carried ever since their first encounter and ripped it open.

Rachel seemed to sense his impatience, or maybe she

was as impatient as he was, because she slid backward on his legs, fumbling with the button and zipper to his jeans, and then freed him, the warm air flowing around him in a tantalizing hint of what was to come. She wrapped her hand around him and held him there, her eyes finding his as her teeth bit into her lower lip. And then she pumped.

"*Mon Dieu, femme*, you're killing me."

"No. Not killing you. Just hoping to drive you to the brink."

If her hand wasn't already doing that, her words certainly did. He grabbed her to hold her still while he counted to ten in his head.

When he finally opened his eyes, there was this seductive, cunning smile on her face, as if she knew exactly how close he'd been. He leaned her closer so that his mouth was against her ear. "You are going to pay for that."

With that, he sheathed himself and tugged the elastic of her panties to one side, then he lifted her hips and set her down on top of him, thrusting up as he seated her fully onto him.

Tight—crazy tight—were the only words that came to mind as her heat and wetness squeezed at him. He had to hold her still yet again as he strained to control the urges that were telling him to lose himself in her. But *Dieu*, he wanted this to last. *Needed* it to last.

As soon as he could breathe again, he balled up a handful of hair, the silky locks trailing over his wrist, and leaned over her until she was lying back across his thighs. He shifted his hips forward and slid off the edge of the chair until his knees hit the ground, still buried inside her. He needed to be fully against her, to feel the scrape of his body against hers, so he laid them both down on the polished wooden planks.

"Okay?" he asked, looking at her face.

"*Oui. C'est fantastique.*"

He smiled at her attempt at French, then responded in kind, a steady stream of words and phrases telling her how long he'd wanted to do this. What he wanted to do, how many times. And those times were as numerous as the stars they'd looked at when they stepped onto the beach. Her hand slid up his back and toyed with the hair at the back of his neck. And it felt so good. So damned good.

He began moving. Slow. Deep. Steady.

Rachel braced her feet on the ground, moving just ahead of him, forcing him to quicken his pace. As if she couldn't get enough. Her hips edged higher and higher with each thrust, taking him impossibly deep. She was tugging him toward a place he didn't want to go. Where the rising tide of desire became harder and harder to push back against. Harder to override. Harder to say no to.

"Seb… Seb…"

Her fingers dug into his back, and she arched into him, a sound coming from her throat. Then she suddenly pumped hard and fast against him, eyes closing as she went rigid.

Spasms rocked his world as he tried to somehow remain anchored to reality. But it was useless. Her orgasm shot him over the edge to his own climax as he thrust into her again and again.

Then it was over. His pace slowed, a sense of well-being and languorous satisfaction washing over him. He pulled in a breath and released all the stress from the last couple of days.

Rolling to his side, he drew her to him and settled her against his chest, not willing to think about anything right now. Not the ramifications. Not the reality of what they'd just done. Not how it would affect their future dealings. All he wanted to do was sleep for a little while. Next to her. Inside her. And then he could deal with all the other stuff later.

Much later.

CHAPTER TEN

"BLEU..."

The sound of his voice woke her up. It was pitch-black, and she was disoriented for several minutes before realizing she was lying against something.

No. Against some*one*.

It was Seb. His head turned to one side, and he muttered again in his sleep, the words unintelligible, but the grief behind them caught at her heart. He was dreaming about his son.

Horror washed over her at catching him in such an intimate moment. Was that what had been behind him pulling her into his arms—missing his son? She didn't know, but she suddenly didn't want to be here anymore. Didn't want to know what his reasons were, because she was afraid his answer wouldn't be the one she wanted to hear.

Oh, God! She loved him!

She quickly but quietly scrambled to her feet, her gaze going to him time and time again, and she wondered how she could have let this happen as she found her clothes and slipped them on. Fortunately, he didn't move, even when her toe accidentally slid her phone a few inches across the wooden floor and the screen lit up. Three o'clock. She could make it home and shower and then be at work again the next day looking completely normal. Unfazed by what had happened.

Except it would all be a lie. Inside she was a mess. A scared, crazy mess of conflicting emotions. What if he thought she expected something from him? Wanted them to be a family.

And she did. Dear God, she did. But she couldn't be a substitute for what he'd had with his own family. Couldn't risk getting involved with someone again so quickly. Just like she'd done with Roy. Look how that had turned out.

She and Seb had only really gotten to know each other over this last week. A week wasn't long enough. Hell, she doubted two years would be long enough to feel secure in a relationship. And then there was Claire…

Her daughter… Her eyes shut. She just couldn't risk it. Not yet.

Slipping from the cabana, she started to pad down the beach on silent feet before stopping. Could she really leave him in there naked? What if he didn't wake up until morning and some unsuspecting fisherman came up on him?

She would call his phone as soon as she got to the boardwalk, when she was far enough away that he wouldn't see her. When he couldn't catch up with her. With that decided, and using the moon and stars to guide her way, she hurried down the beach. Just to the left was the sea turtle's nest, and she gave it a wide berth so it could remain undisturbed.

Please, please stay asleep, Seb. Just until I get farther away.

She had to get home. Home, where she could dissect everything that had happened and figure out where to go from there. One thing she did know was she could not sleep with him again. Not and maintain any semblance of professionalism. She loved him. And she didn't want him to know. Not yet. Maybe not ever.

The last time they were together like this, he'd recoiled from her after they'd woken up. She couldn't go through that again. Not with him. Not with anyone. It's why she couldn't wake him up before she left the cabana. Couldn't bear to see the look in his eyes if she stretched her hand out toward him.

For some men, it really was all about the sex. At least, that's what she'd heard. And God. *God!* She wished it could be that way for her, too. And it had been the time she'd been with a completely different man when Claire was younger. But from the first time she'd slept with Seb, there had been a weird sense of finality about it. As if he was going to be it for her.

And she didn't want him to be it. Not with all the baggage they both carried around with them.

By the time her feet hit the boardwalk, she was running. Running as fast as she could to her car, only then realizing her shoes were still somewhere on the beach where they'd left them.

But there was no way she was going back for them now. She'd do it tomorrow, in the daylight. When he was no longer in that cabana, waiting to look at her with eyes that told her to get the hell away from him.

Because she was so afraid that, just like Roy, he would run. As fast as he could.

Like she was doing right now?

No, that was different. She was running to keep from being hurt all over again. To keep Claire from being hurt. And no matter what it took, that's what she was going to do. Keep her daughter from paying the price for her stupidity. Even if doing that caused a pain she thought she'd never feel again.

Once seated in her car, she took a deep breath and tried to calm her nerves before dialing his number. She waited and waited until he finally answered. His voice was low. Sleepy. And so so sexy. How she wanted to go back. But she didn't. Instead, she quietly said she'd had to leave. And then she hung up the phone and put the vehicle into Reverse and drove away.

All he'd found were her shoes. Just like Cinderella. Only this was no fairy tale. This was reality.

Sebastien had woken up to his phone ringing and Rachel's voice saying she'd had to leave. No explanation. Just that. He came fully awake in a flash, realizing he wasn't in his bed. And he was completely alone.

He glanced at his phone. It was three thirty in the damn morning.

Things came back to him in a rush.

He and Rachel had spent the night at the cabana. At least, he had. How long ago had she left? Right afterward? She couldn't face him, so she just walked out?

By the time he'd dragged his clothes on and left the structure, he was angry, and he had no idea why. He trudged up the beach, spotting a pair of white shoes on the sand and realizing they were Rachel's. So she hadn't erased every sign of her presence.

He understood that it might be embarrassing to face him before leaving, but the least she could have done was say goodbye.

Like he'd done the last time they were together?

He'd been hell-bent on escape when she'd woken up and caught him and, probably not realizing that he was looking for a quick exit, had reached out to trace his tattoo. She hadn't gotten the chance to touch it this time.

He'd made sure they were front to front the whole time they were together. Even as they fell asleep.

Had it been a move of self-preservation?

Maybe. Or maybe a way to control the intimacy level. To keep things from getting too personal. That was a more likely scenario. And looking at it now, it came across as selfish and cold. That woman had given everything she had, both at Mauhali and during their lovemaking. At the time, he thought he was, too. But looking back, he could see a sense of calculation behind keeping the focus on the physical and completely off the emotional.

Had she guessed?

He slid through the door at the hospital and into the elevator without attracting any attention. Things were normally pretty quiet this time of night. He made it to his office. Plunked her shoes onto his desk and then sank onto his couch for a few minutes to try to pull himself together.

The anger was gone, dissipated during that walk of shame down the beach. None of this was her fault.

Rachel was probably already home, fast asleep in her bed. Hopefully they could both put this behind them and go about their professional lives without any problems. Without any complications.

Without any...

That tiny flicker of fear came out of nowhere, just like it had the last time they'd been together. He'd forgotten about it until this very second, when it hit him full force again.

He and Layla had used a condom, too.

And something had gone wrong. She'd wound up pregnant. At the time, he'd been over the moon. He'd always wanted to be a father. He'd leaped at the chance to propose to her. Layla had wanted to put the wedding off until after she'd had the baby and lost the baby weight. He'd been fine with all of it.

Until something worse than a condom failure had gone wrong after Bleu's birth and his baby had been diagnosed with cancer.

What if it happened again?

What if there was something in his DNA that was defective…that had caused Bleu's cancer? That could cause it again if he ever made someone pregnant? The oncologist at the time had brushed off his concerns, saying it wasn't possible. But how much did they really know about genetic code?

This wasn't just about Sebastien and his fears, though. There was a lot more at stake than that.

There was Rachel. She'd already gone through cancer with one child—was he willing to risk it happening again, all because he couldn't control his impulses?

What if it was already too late?

The likelihood of two condom failures for the same man was probably pretty remote. But once the thought had taken hold, it was becoming impossible to shake.

He got up from the couch and grabbed a set of clothes, going into his tiny office bathroom and stepping under a blast of brutally cold water. Flagellating himself for what he couldn't take back?

He stood there for as long as he could stand it and then soaped himself up and rinsed before turning off the tap.

Drying himself, he slicked back his hair and dressed in his fresh set of clothes, stuffing the ones from last night into a plastic bag. He could do those when he got home.

He went back into his office and then clicked open the screen of his laptop to see a set of headlines in bold letters across the top of his screen: Tropical Cyclone Koji Is No More.

Except it was. Because in its aftermath, it had caused some changes that no one could have predicted. Not even him. Because somewhere amid those strewn mangoes and fallen trees, something else had fallen.

His heart.

Was that why he'd been so focused on the physical part of lovemaking—because he hadn't wanted to recognize the truth?

Merde. He repeated the epithet over and over in his head until the word came out in an audible growl.

How could this have happened?

How could he have *let* this happen?

He lay down on his couch to get a couple of hours of sleep. And he must have, because the sudden sound of knocking dragged him to his feet. He scrambled to find his senses. Hell, that was probably her, and he had no idea what he was going to say to her this morning. Or any other morning, for that matter.

He strode to the desk and picked her shoes off the desk, dropping them to the floor behind it before he moved to the chair and sat down. He pushed the shoes under his desk with one foot.

Just in case it isn't her.

He was a liar. He just didn't want to have to hand them to her and acknowledge what had happened last night. Although maybe her leaving the way she had meant that she had no more desire to start a relationship than he did.

He might love her. But that didn't mean he should be with her. Or with anyone.

"Come in."

He schooled his features to look as impassive as possible.

The door opened, and a woman stood there. Except it

wasn't Rachel. It was someone who looked vaguely familiar, but...

Then a little girl stepped out from behind her, and it hit him. It was Sharon, the drowning victim, and her mom. Man, it seemed like eons ago that he and Rachel had spent time on the beach under completely different circumstances.

He stood in a rush and ushered them into his office.

Marie smiled at him. "Sharon wanted to come by today. She couldn't wait." She nudged the girl deeper into the office. "Go ahead. Give it to him."

The child stepped forward, holding two envelopes in her hand. "This is for you." She held one out to him.

He smiled and knelt in front of her. "For me? Thank you." He glanced at the manila envelope. "Can I open it?"

She nodded.

Seb stuck a finger under the glued flap and coaxed it free. Then he slid the single item from inside and turned it over to face him.

His smile was still firmly affixed, but a lump formed in his throat. He vaguely remembered Marie wanting to take a picture of him, Sharon and Rachel right before she was discharged from the hospital. In the photo they were all smiling. All totally happy with the miraculous outcome. And Sebastien had been totally unaware of what was to come less than a week later.

Right now there was no miraculous outcome in sight.

"Thank you for this. I like it a lot," he said to Sharon.

Sharon gave him the biggest smile ever, one front tooth missing. "Can you give this one to the lady doctor?"

Seb glanced up at the child's mother who nodded. "We asked for her at the nurses' desk in the emergency room, but they sent up us here, and the people here said she hadn't arrived yet this morning."

"And I have to go to school."

The last thing he wanted to do was hand Rachel a picture of the two of them, even if there was a child separating them. Maybe having a child in the shot was even worse…it teased at something he felt he could never have again.

But he wasn't going to tell Sharon any of that. All she wanted to know was if he would see that Rachel got it. "I'll make sure she gets it." Even if that meant having it put in her staff mailbox.

He climbed to his feet and gave Marie another smile. "Thanks for coming in, and I'm really glad Sharon is doing so well."

"Yes, and we're glad the storm has gone."

"I think we all are." He held out his hand to Sharon and gave hers a gentle shake. "Enjoy your day at school."

With a last goodbye, they left his office.

He put Rachel's envelope on one of his end tables after he'd scrabbled under his desk to retrieve her shoes and made a mental note to do something about them. As for his own picture, he stuffed it back in the envelope before fishing it out again. He glanced over at his wall of kids, where he posted all the pictures sent to him by families of patients. If they ever came back again, they might question why their picture wasn't on his wall with all the others. So he retrieved a thumbtack from his desk drawer and stuck the picture on the wall, tempted to put another picture in front of Rachel to keep him from staring at her, before deciding that was immature and cowardly.

Like he was being about giving her the other snapshot?

He was going to see her in the flesh, day in and day out, unless she decided to take Philippe up on his offer. The last thing he wanted, though, was to be the reason she felt she needed to transfer out of the department.

Whether he wanted to or not, he needed to talk to her face-to-face and decide how to avoid something like last night happening again.

He would do it as soon as she came in.

Right on cue, Rachel popped her head around the door. "Can you come out and see a patient?"

She looked totally calm, totally relaxed. There was no sign that she was upset about anything. But he still needed to do the right thing.

"Sure. Is it an emergency?"

"Not exactly, but he's not happy. He has a fishhook stuck in his hand. He wouldn't let the ER doctors near him."

Even as she said it, he heard the sound of wailing coming from down the hall.

So much for hoping he could have a quick word with her before he went down to see the patient. It would have to wait until afterward.

"Let's go."

"Um…actually, Stella is down there with him. They're waiting on you. Hope that's okay."

In other words, she wasn't going to work with him on this case. Instead it would be a different nurse. "Yep. It's fine."

It was a lie, but what else was he going to say?

He got up from behind his desk, the shoes and envelope on the end table catching his eye. Now was not the time.

Making his way toward to the sounds of distress, he gave a quick knock before entering the room.

Inside, he found a patient he knew well, sitting on the exam table holding one hand in his lap. And, yep, there was a large fishing hook embedded in the flesh of his palm. The wailing stopped when he saw Seb. Maybe seeing a familiar face helped. "Looks like you caught your-self, Jacque, instead of a fish."

The boy's dad was sitting in one of the chairs. "Well, um, part of it might have been my fault."

Stella gave them both a smile. "This isn't the first fish-ing accident we've had up here."

"I didn't realize he was behind me getting a drink out of the cooler. And I went to cast my line..."

And he'd hooked his son.

"We'll get you all fixed up and on your way. You might even have time enough to do a little more fishing."

By the time Sebastien had taken the hook out of Jacque's hand and checked the date of his last tetanus vaccine, an hour had gone by.

The rest of the day went just like that case, with other nurses doing the workups and being there for the exams. He didn't work with Rachel once.

There was no way that was just coincidence. Which meant no matter how she'd looked when she came to get him this morning, she was upset about what had hap-pened. She couldn't even stand being in the same room with him, evidently.

He didn't want to leave things this way. Didn't want her to feel so uncomfortable in his presence that she felt avoiding him was her only way out. Not only did he not want to cause anyone that kind of discomfort, he didn't want the other nurses to notice and wonder what was going on.

Because they *would* figure it out.

Picking up his phone, he dialed her number. Four rings went by, and just when he thought it was going to go to voice mail, she picked up. "Hello?"

"Hey, Rach. Can we meet somewhere to talk?"

"About?"

Despite himself, he couldn't help but smile.

His communication skills obviously left something to be desired. At least with this particular woman.

"I think you might have some idea."

"I'm off in an hour. Can we meet in the courtyard area?"

"I'll see you there."

An hour later, he made his way to the courtyard, her shoes in a bag. She was already there, sitting on a bench in a more secluded corner away from those who were eating at the tables that were scattered throughout the space.

She sat straighter when she spotted him coming toward her, hands clasped tightly in her lap.

He set the bag beside her, wishing he'd brought her coffee as well. She tilted her head before peering inside. Her eyes widened. "Oh! My shoes. Thanks for bringing them back. I didn't realize they were missing until I got back to the parking lot."

"Not a problem." He hesitated and then motioned her to a seat. "You could have woken me, you know, instead of sneaking away and calling me on the phone."

"I didn't sneak away…" She gave him a sheepish look. "Okay, I might have, but I just wasn't sure what to say. I don't think either of us meant for that to happen. And I have Claire to think about. It's been just her and me for a very long time."

"Her dad?"

"He's been out of the picture since she was an infant. He just one day decided he wasn't cut out to be a father. And that was that."

His jaw tightened. Wasn't that the exact thing he'd decided? That he didn't want to be a father? But hell, he would have never walked out on Bleu. Not ever. "I'm sorry, Rachel. I didn't know."

"So you see why I don't want to be involved with any-one right now. Not even to…" She gave a shrug.

He assumed she was talking about sex.

He'd come here, expecting to be the bad guy and tell her that what happened couldn't happen again, but it looked like she was beating him to the punch. Letting him off the hook, the same way he'd plucked that fish-hook from young Jacque's hand.

He decided to be up-front with her, even though it was one of the hardest things he'd ever done. "I'm sorry you had to go through that. Bleu was the result of a failed condom, but I loved him more than anything. When he died, I decided I couldn't face being a father again. And even though I know the odds of another condom failing are astronomical… I still think about it. So you don't have to worry about anything happening again."

"Is it going to be too awkward working together? There's that position in Orthopedics, and after going to Mauhali, I've been thinking it might be a good fit for me."

Was it going to be too awkward? They'd survived the awkwardness last time, so something didn't ring quite true. Was there more to it than that?

"With Dr. Chauvre. Yes, I remember. Pediatrics would hate to lose you. You're good with your patients, and I'd hoped you like being here as well."

Okay, so now he was sounding like a boss, which hadn't been his intent. But he didn't want her leaving because of him.

"Yes. I do like it here. I just have a lot to think about. And Claire—"

Her phone buzzed, and they both froze for a second before she looked down at the instrument in her hand. She stared at it as it rang a second time, then she closed her eyes for a second and stood. "I need to go answer this."

She gave a visible swallow. "And just so you know. You don't have to worry about last night ever happening again. I've taken care of that."

With that, she walked away, answering her phone. The last thing he heard her say was, "Hi, honey," before she was out of earshot, leaving him sitting alone. Alone with his thoughts. Alone with her shoes. Alone with his future.

A future that suddenly stretched before him like a vast wasteland.

CHAPTER ELEVEN

HER FLIGHT HOME was a whole lot harder than she'd thought it would be. Claire had called as she was talking to Seb, and all of a sudden she knew she needed to go be with her daughter. He'd said *Pediatrics* would hate to lose her and listed some reasons, but none of them had to do with him. He'd never said *he'd* hate to lose her. That had been a blow, even though her reasons for thinking about Orthopedics had been true, that she thought it might be a good fit for her.

And with his confession that he never wanted to be a father again, she'd heard a second nail hitting the coffin of hope. With his fear about being caught in the circumstances surrounding his son's birth, she realized she didn't have the stomach to work with him day in and day out. Not anymore. Not after that last night together and knowing there was no hope that he might return her feelings. Not that she wanted him to. She'd told him the truth. Claire had to be her first priority. Especially knowing how he felt about fatherhood.

So she'd booked a flight, leaving a few hours after her talk with Seb. Because every time she thought about what they'd done on that beach, it left her shaky and out of sorts. The last thing she wanted was for him to guess. And if she saw him before she could sort out her thoughts, he would see it written across her face. That she loved him. That she wanted to be with him again. Far too much. Having him tuck her against him had felt more right than anything had in years. And the way Claire had hit it off with him would make it harder.

So much harder.

She'd already gotten matchmaker vibes from her daughter. As if she might like to see the two of them together.

Sorry, baby, he doesn't want it. And I don't want you hurt.

She stared out the window of the plane as it started its descent into Wisconsin. Taurati was already a long way behind her, and so was Sebastien. The hospital administrator had been great when she'd said she needed some personal time. He'd acted like it was a simple case of burnout after putting in so much overtime. But it was so much more than that.

And somehow she had to face Claire and her mom and act like everything was fine. She somehow had to pretend that a lightning bolt hadn't hit her on her walk back from that cabana, when she'd realized she loved him.

She'd stupidly done what she warned herself not to do for years. In fact she'd shrugged off men, telling herself she'd have plenty of time for that once Claire was grown and gone.

But for it to happen now? *Now?*

How had she let this happen?

And what was she going to do about it? The easiest thing would be to stay in the States. But Claire would not believe that her mom had simply decided she missed her home country enough to quit her job and fly home. And it wasn't fair to her daughter not to let her have a say in the decision. Claire loved Taurati. It was as if she'd finally been able to put her diagnosis behind her and start living.

They both had.

And to backtrack on all that?

She didn't know. So she was going to take a week. Maybe two. And she was going to do some soul searching and try to make some sense out of all that had happened.

The wheels hit the runway, and the sensation of air brakes engaging was unmistakable. It was as if the whole plane gave a collective sigh of relief. Not that it had been a rough flight in the sense of turbulence or anything. Nothing like that helicopter ride to Mauhali. In fact, if anything, the weather had been silky smooth on each leg of her journey. Except for in the pit of her stomach, where a mini cyclone was busy whirling her insides into a mess of self-doubt and fear.

Just enjoy Claire. That is all you have to do right now.

Sebastien and Taurati could wait for a couple of days. In fact, if they had to, they could wait forever.

The plane finished docking at the gate, and the doors opened. Rachel gathered her belongings and started wheeling her carry-on down the narrow aisle. She hadn't checked any baggage. She'd fled with just a few possessions. If it came down to it, and she decided to leave the hospital, she could have a moving company pack up her apartment and ship her stuff to her.

She would never have to face Seb again if she didn't want to. One thing she knew, though. She was never going to forget him. Not for as long as she lived. It would take her heart a long, long time to get over him.

Entering the airport terminal, her eyes sought out and found her loved ones within seconds. Claire raced toward her and caught her in a fierce hug. "I'm so glad you're here. Grams said the storm died out and that no one died on that other island."

"It did." Her next words were chosen with care. "Taurati was very lucky."

It may have been. But she didn't think she'd come out quite as unscathed as they had.

Her mom reached her and put her hands on her shoulders, studying her. "Welcome home, honey."

"Thanks, Mom." Rachel's smile felt brittle and so very fake. Because this didn't seem like home. Not anymore. She wasn't sure there was any place on earth that felt like that right now.

Except for Taurati. And she didn't know if she could face going back there.

"How is Sebastien?" asked Claire. "Does he miss me?"

The question slashed her heart in two. She'd tried to prevent her daughter from becoming attached to the man. To any man. But in the end, could you really choose whom you loved?

"He's fine. I'm sure he's really tired from all the work he put in on the cyclone and the rescue efforts on the other island. Everyone's relieved that they didn't have to evacuate the hospital."

Ugh! She'd left her shoes beside Seb on the bench. She'd been so intent on getting out of there that she'd totally forgotten about them until now. If she didn't go back, she assumed he'd toss them in the trash.

Actually he'd probably toss a lot more than just her shoes. In the end, she'd saved him from having to let her down easy. The last time he'd run. This time it was her.

And damn, she'd thought it would feel a whole lot more empowering than it did. As it was, it just seemed... cowardly.

She should have stayed. Should have been truthful

about how she felt and then made her decision based on his reaction. And she might have, if he hadn't talked about not wanting to be a father. To her, that was his decision.

Maybe if she'd been more careful with her heart...

But she hadn't been.

She dropped a kiss on her daughter's head, realizing she wouldn't be able to do that much longer. Her daughter had grown over the last year. And not just physically. She'd grown in confidence and knowledge. How could she tell her they might not be going back to Taurati?

She wouldn't. Not yet. Not until she decided what to do about the island and about Sebastien.

"Can we call him? He promised to help me with my French and Tahitian."

"Let's hold off on that for a while. I'm sure Seb needs some time to unwind after the crazy week we've had."

Had it only been a week? It had.

A week to fall in love. The words sounded like they belonged on the cover of a romance novel. But this novel's ending? Uncertain at best.

She decided to distract Claire as they headed for the parking garage. "Guess what I saw a couple of days ago?"

"What?"

"I was walking on the beach and saw a flag where that sea turtle laid her eggs."

"Oh, wow. You're sure it was the same spot?"

"Yes. It was nighttime, so it was dark, but the moon was shining and we... I mean, *I* know it was the right spot."

"I wish I could have seen it. I miss Taurati."

"I know you do."

Rachel's heart ached as she reached for her daughter's

hand and held it tight as her mom motioned toward one of the rows of cars.

"Speaking of sea turtles, I put the one Sebastien gave me on a shelf in Grams's house. I can't wait to get it back to our apartment on Taurati and put it in my room."

She swallowed past a lump in her throat. "I can't wait for that, either. But for right now, let's just enjoy Grams and Gramps and being all together, okay?"

"Okay."

And with that, they reached the car and the conversation turned to what had happened in Wisconsin since Claire had arrived. Rachel settled in the front seat and leaned her head against the headrest and listened to her daughter, all the while trying not to break down in front of them. That could come later. When she was all alone, and no one could see her cry.

Neves Bouchet paid Sebastien a visit two days after his conversation with Rachel.

"To what do I owe this sudden appearance?" he asked the man as he settled onto the couch in his office.

"I just wanted to thank you for all your and Rachel's hard work on the hospital's behalf. And for going to Mauhali to help with the rescue attempts. I'll admit, it's the first time I've ever been glad for hospital plans to have been abandoned midstream. But at least Mauhali benefited from them. I hear that your flail chest patient is doing well after surgery to stabilize her ribs."

"Yes, I heard that as well." Out of the corner of his eye, he caught sight of his end table. Hell! The shoes Rachel had left behind again were there in plain sight. He'd taken them out of the bag and then totally forgotten about them. But to get up and move them now would just draw attention to them.

Hopefully Neves hadn't noticed.

"I wanted to thank Rachel in person, but she decided to take some personal days, saying she wanted to go see her mom and daughter. I assume she'll be bringing her daughter back with her?"

The question slid past him as he processed what the man had just said. Rachel was in Wisconsin? He'd been so relieved not to run into her yesterday that it had never dawned on him that it might be because she wasn't here at the hospital. Or on Taurati. He'd assumed that it was her day off.

"I'm not sure. I didn't realize she was gone."

"She didn't tell you she was leaving?"

Merde. No, she hadn't. Was it because of their conversation?

He swallowed as another thought hit him. Was it permanent?

"Actually, she didn't. When did she ask for the time off?"

"Day before yesterday."

The day of their talk. There was no way that could be a coincidence. His mind ran through everything he'd said, trying to figure out what could have made her suddenly decide to leave. He thought they'd been in agreement on everything.

"Did she say when she'd be back?"

"She said she needed at least a week. Maybe two."

Or maybe she needed forever. Maybe she'd never be back.

His chest tightened as a thousand emotions went through him. If he'd known, would that conversation have ended differently?

"I didn't know."

"Yes, you said that." Neves fixed him with a look. "Is there anything *I* should know?"

The man's head turned toward the end table, and he caught sight of the shoes before his gaze swiveled back to Seb.

So much for hoping Neves wouldn't notice. Truthfully, not much got past his friend. It was what made him such a good hospital administrator. And such a great judge of character.

And he'd pegged exactly what might have happened.

"I think you've already guessed. I'm just not sure what to do about it."

"I take it it's complicated. Not like Laurence and Britan?"

"Nothing like that."

The other couple had followed the normal trajectory of romance—One: Noticing each other. Two: Going on the usual number of dates. Three: A proposal followed by marriage.

"Okay, I'm taking off my hospital administrator hat and putting on my friend cap. Do you care about her, Seb?"

This time he looked the man in the eye. "I do." The answer was simple. So simple that it seemed ludicrous when he said it aloud. It was that simple. And that complicated.

Because he wasn't sure he could do the whole family thing again. Sometimes love just wasn't enough. And after hearing about Rachel's ex taking off because he couldn't handle being a father? Well, he wasn't going to pursue Rachel unless he knew beyond a shadow of a doubt that he could handle the fears and ramifications of what a decision like that might entail.

"Then you've got a decision to make, haven't you? And I suggest you figure it out, Seb. If you don't even try…" His friend stood and glanced again at the shoes. " Well, you'll regret it more than you know." With a smile to soften the words, he headed for the door.

Figure it out. Easy words to say. Not so easy to do.

But Neves was right. If he just continued to coast through life, he could very well miss out on something good. Something beautiful.

Like having a family?

The door clicked behind his friend, and Sebastien shook his head and then tried to bury himself in his work.

CHAPTER TWELVE

IT HAD BEEN a week.

And there was still no sign of Rachel. Neves said he hadn't heard from her, either.

The hospital administrator had told him, "Figure it out, Seb. Or I think you'll regret it more than you know."

Would he? Hell, yes, he would.

He'd been so sure he couldn't be a father again after Bleu. Had been steadfast in that commitment. Then along came Rachel and her daughter, making him doubt everything in his life.

Hell, he loved her. Loved her for her fierce determination to do the right thing for herself and for Claire. To do the right thing for her patients.

But could he let his heart rule and forge a life with someone whose daughter could relapse in the future? After six years, it was unlikely but not impossible. Just like cyclones on Taurati.

But even if she felt the same way, what if Rachel wanted more children? The neurosurgeon years ago had told him that neuro cancers were rarely caused by genes that were passed down. The key word being *rarely*.

Could he take the chance that the doctor he'd despised all those years ago was actually right?

It was either that or let life go on the way it was now.

Let Rachel make her decision to stay in Wisconsin or come back with no interference from him. He'd done that for a week. Had sat back and let nature take its course.

And he'd been the most miserable *enfoiré* the hospital had ever seen. He didn't see that changing anytime soon, if he didn't take Neves's advice.

He'd told her he hadn't wanted children, right after she'd talked about her ex walking out on her. He could well imagine what had gone through her head. That if she opened her heart to him, it could very well happen all over again.

What she didn't know was that if he made the decision to be in her life, he wouldn't go back on it, which was one of the reasons that decision was so damned hard to make.

Make it. Just make it. And then tell her.

She might not believe him…might tell him to shove off, but all he was responsible for were his own actions.

And his own inactions.

A cyclone of a different type hit his heart. Neves was right. He didn't have to sit back and passively watch something wither away, the way he'd been forced to do with his son. This time he actually had the power to do something about it. If he was willing to try.

If Rachel was willing to let him try.

He went over and picked up one of her shoes, turning it over in his hands before setting it down with a sense of fierce resolution. Yes. He was willing.

It was a terrifying prospect, but then again, falling in love with her had been just as terrifying. But it could also be something beautiful. He'd seen that during their time in Mauhali. During the night in that cabana.

If he was willing to get off his ass and go after it. He had no idea what kind of reception he'd be met with. But that didn't matter. What did matter was that he made the effort. That he was willing to be honest with her. And with himself.

To find out if she was willing to risk everything— just as he was—in order to become a family. And yes, he wanted it. Like he'd never wanted anything.

He called Neves. The man picked up on the first ring, as if he'd been waiting for the call, barking into the phone, "Did you figure it out yet?"

Seb laughed. "How did you know?"

"I couldn't imagine any other reason you'd be calling me. Or at least, I'd hoped not. So what's the plan?"

"Hell, I have no idea." Sebastien realized it was true. But he was done sitting at his desk mooning after what he'd let slip through his fingers. "But I need some time off."

"You've got it."

"Don't you want to know how much?"

"Nope." His friend paused. "All I care about is that you both find what you are looking for. For all our sakes."

"Why can't I call him?"

Claire's requests had gotten more and more insistent, and Rachel was running out of plausible excuses. She hadn't heard from Sebastien since she'd left.

But had she really expected to?

No. But it hurt that he could just let her leave without doing anything to stop her.

Had she tried to stop Roy when he left? No. She'd just kind of given him a mental good-riddance boot, and then she'd had to work through so many layers of anger and despair afterward.

She bit her lip. Hadn't she done the exact same thing Roy had done—run from a situation that she didn't think she could deal with?

Why would she expect Sebastien to react any differently than she had when faced with someone wanting out of her life?

Except she didn't really want him out of her life. Much to the contrary. But she was scared. Scared it wouldn't work out. Scared that she and Claire were both going to be hurt if he rejected them. Scared that Sebastien's fear of becoming father again was something he couldn't get past. And she knew that's what it was. A fear of loss. It was the same thing that had led her to reject him.

So she'd left Taurati before he got the chance to hurt her and Claire.

But she'd also left before either of them had had time to fully process what had happened in the beach cabana. Things between them had changed so fast that she hadn't thought straight that day in the courtyard. He hadn't rejected her, though. She'd been the one to initially say that what had happened would never happen again.

Claire had been the only thing on her mind. But her daughter liked him. Even if things didn't work out romantically between them, she trusted Seb enough to know he wouldn't reject her daughter.

His offer of help with her French and Tahitian? It wouldn't be withdrawn. If she'd learned anything about Sebastien over the last year of working with him, it was that he kept his word whenever possible.

He'd lost his son in a horrible, devastating way. From what he'd said, he was just as scared as she was. Maybe even more so. He'd as much as said that loss weighed on his mind when he was with someone.

Didn't Roy's behavior weigh on hers when she thought about falling in love? Yes, it did.

She looked at her daughter, who was waiting expectantly for her answer. Then she sucked down a deep breath and decided to risk it all. For love.

And for Claire.

"There's no reason why you can't. Go ahead."

Swallowing hard, she watched her daughter punch the number in.

Please, Seb, don't hurt her. God...don't hurt her.

"Sebastien? It's Claire! How are you?"

Her daughter's face was animated, her smile wide as she listened to whatever he was saying. "I miss Taurati a lot, but I'm keeping up with my French studies. I still need help with Tahitian, though."

Her eyes widened. "You're where?"

Rachel's heart tightened. Had he left Taurati, like she had?

Her daughter pulled the phone down from her ear. "Mom, he's here! Sebastien is here."

"What? Where?" Her heart began pounding out of her chest.

"He's in Wisconsin. He wants to talk to you." Claire held the phone out to her.

Seb was in Wisconsin? Was there some kind of symposium?

No, that was ridiculous. He wouldn't come all the way here for that.

Then for what?

A ripple of hope went through her, starting at the outer reaches of her limbs and moving with ever-increasing speed toward her heart. Nails that had been pounded in during their last meeting started losing their hold.

She took the phone with a hand that shook. "Seb?"

"Hi."

That one simple word filled her with a warmth tha

made her relax into the couch. "Hi yourself. Claire said you're in Wisconsin? What in the world?"

"I am here. I was getting ready to call you, but Claire beat me to it."

He really was in her home state. But she still had no idea why. "What part of Wisconsin?"

"Your part. Black River Falls."

Her lips parted. She'd been imagining Madison or Milwaukee. So no symposium. Which meant he was here for...

"A-are you staying in a hotel?"

"Not yet, but that's not what I want to talk about. Can we meet?"

Very aware that Claire was watching her with an expectancy that made her heart burn, she tried to think this through. She didn't want to talk here at her mom's house, just in case this wasn't the kind of meeting she was envisioning. The kind she was hoping for. Maybe he'd been sent to tell her her services were no longer required at the center.

That was ridiculous. They wouldn't have sent Seb here for that.

Which brought her back to that other reason that was tickling at the edges of her mind.

"Can you get to the library?"

"I can. I've rented a car, so I can meet you there."

"I'll see you in thirty minutes?" In truth, it would only take her about ten minutes to get to that particular place, but she needed a few minutes to gather her wits and figure out what she was going to say to him.

Tell him you love him.

"See you then."

The second she disconnected the call, Claire was all over it. "I want to come! Please, Mom, *please*!"

This was the hard part. There was no way she could tell Claire what had happened between them, or what she hoped might happen now, just in case she was wrong. "Not this time, honey. Seb and I need to talk. But if he's here for longer than just today, maybe we can work something out."

Claire's eyes went wide again. "What the… Do you love Seb or something?"

One thing she'd promised she would never do was lie to her daughter, if she could help it, so she simply nodded before adding, "But I'm not sure we can work it out. We're just going to talk, so don't get your hopes up."

As if she hadn't heard a thing Rachel had said, Claire flung her arms around her and clung to her for a minute. "You're going to tell him, aren't you?"

"It depends on why he's here." She stood, dislodging Claire, before kissing her on the cheek. "But now I need to go get ready."

She stopped and looked at her daughter. "No matter what happens, I want you to know that Sebastien is a good person. He and I have to do what's right for us. And what's right for you."

"I already know he's a good person. And I promise not to be mad at him—or you—if you don't get together."

"Good to know, kiddo. Good to know." She dropped one last kiss on her cheek before sprinting to the bathroom to brush her hair.

She arrived at the library just on time and exited the car, pulling the hood of her down parka up around her face as she headed toward the entrance. She saw him before she was even halfway there. Rather than waiting inside the warm building, he was standing outside, in a simple gray sweat jacket. His hair was shorter than it had been when she was in Taurati.

"Why aren't you inside?" she said when she reached him.

"It's a little colder here than where I'm from." His nose was red, hands dug deep into the pockets of his jeans.

"Yes, it is. Come on. There's a coffee shop a few doors down. Let's go in there."

She still had no idea why he was here, but he looked so out of place in her environment. She smiled. Probably about as out of place as she looked in Taurati at times. But she loved it there. Missed the heat and the beach... and him.

They made it to the nearly empty coffee shop, and she pointed to table tucked away in the back, but first they had to order. "Have you eaten? They have some sandwiches, if you want something."

"I don't. Just some coffee."

Rachel glanced up at the menu, where the choices were mind-boggling for such a small town. "Do you have a preference?"

"I've taken a liking for your espressos. With sugar."

"Why don't you go get that table in the back, and I'll bring the coffees?"

When he nodded, she went up to the counter and ordered for them, waiting while their drinks were being prepared. She glanced toward the back, where Seb sat. He was blowing into his hands in a way that made her smile. He really was an island boy.

And she was a small-town girl. But somehow, together, they'd made a kind of magic that she doubted she'd ever experience with anyone else.

She was going to tell him. She couldn't let him leave

without knowing. But first she needed to tell him why she'd left.

She got the cups and then headed for the table, setting his espresso in front of him. "One sweet espresso."

"Thanks." He took a sip.

God, she loved looking at him. Loved that he was here, in her world. But she needed to know. "Why are you here, Seb?"

He set his coffee down and shrugged out of his jacket. "Isn't it obvious?"

"Maybe. I don't know." She bit her lip.

He sighed. "What happened— I've gone over and over the whys of that cabana, but I'm still not sure why you left Taurati so suddenly. Without any explanation. Did I do something?"

She needed to tell him. But she had no idea how. Maybe she could go back in time and help him understand.

"Remember when I told you about Claire's biological father?"

"Yes." He frowned. "Is he here? Is that why you came back?"

She blinked. "No. No, of course not. As far as I know, he'll never be back. But when you said you'd decided you didn't want to be a father again..."

Seb seemed to pale in front of her, and a few seconds went by before he replied. "You were afraid I might do the same thing? Leave?"

Something squirmed inside her. Did he feel the same way? "Are you saying you wouldn't?"

If that was the case, she wasn't sure why he'd made the trek halfway across the globe to find her.

"What I said was true. For a long time, I didn't want to be a father, because of Bleu. I didn't think I had it in me to lose another child." He swallowed. "And I knew Claire had had cancer. It brought back so many memories. So many fears. And then I got to know her. And you."

"And now?"

"Over the last couple of days, I've come to realize that life can't be shoved into a neat package and be expected to stay there."

She smiled. She'd thought much the same thing. "I've been protective of Claire for a long time because of what she went through. And because of what her father did. I haven't wanted to see her get hurt. Especially by my dating anyone. I told myself my love life could wait until Claire was all grown-up." Time to lay it on the line. "And then you came along. But I also watched you fall all over yourself to get away from me that first time we were together. And so when we were together at the beach that last time, I left before you were awake because I was so afraid…"

His eyes closed, a muscle working in his cheek. "You were afraid I would run again. Like Claire's father. And hurt her. Hurt you."

All she could do was nod.

"I was afraid, too, Rach. Afraid I couldn't commit. Afraid I wasn't cut out to be a father."

He said all that as if it was in the past. Did that mean…?

"You're not afraid anymore?"

"I am *pétrifié*. You can't imagine how much. But I've decided the risk is worth it. You're worth it. And if I say I'll stay, you can believe it." He reached for her hand. "I love you. I think I have since that very first time we were together. I just couldn't admit it, even to myself. But I don't know how you feel about me. Or whether or not Claire could accept having me in your life."

A sudden rush of joy filled her heart. "So you mean—?"

"I want you in my life, Rachel. If you trust me. I promise I won't run. No matter how hard things get."

"This time I was the one who ran. And I'm sorry. I promise it's the last time. Because I love you, too."

"Dieu miséricordieux." His fingers tightened around her hand. "And Claire?"

"Claire has done nothing but talk about you ever since I got back. I had no idea how I was going to break it to her if we couldn't go back to Taurati. But she says she trusts us both."

"So this means you'll come back to the island with me? I'd be willing to stay here, but I'm not so sure I can survive the winters."

She laughed. "I'm not so sure you could, either."

"But I'd be willing to try, if that's what you wanted." Seb's palm slid behind her nape, and he met her halfway across the table, kissing her softly. *"Je t'aime,* Rachel Palmer."

As it always did, hearing her name murmured in those husky French tones made her shiver. "I love you, too."

There was another kiss, and when they parted, he murmured. "By the way, I brought your shoes."

The words were so unexpected, they made her laugh all over again. "To hell with my shoes. I'm just glad you brought you."

"You are, are you?"

She smiled and touched his hand. "I am. So, *so* glad."

They came together again, this kiss holding the promise of an enduring love and the happiness of a lifetime.

EPILOGUE

Two months later

SEB SAID HE wanted to take his time, using her own words against her, saying that the effort they put into their relationship now would make things even better. Any worry that he might back out and break Claire's heart, he kissed away whenever they could manage to find time together.

This time it was she who was impatient. But they'd worked through so much of their pasts. Together. Going step by step, telling each other their fears.

She'd told him hers—that she was afraid he might walk away from them like Roy had. He'd promised her he was here to stay. And she believed him.

And he'd told her how afraid he was of losing another child, how gutted and lost he'd been after Bleu had died. But despite that, he was willing to open his heart and love again. And Claire already loved him to pieces. They hadn't yet officially told her that they were together, but she knew. She just let them go on pretending she didn't. And Rachel loved her for that.

The doorbell to her apartment rang. Frowning, she went to answer it, thinking it might be one of Claire's friends, until she opened the door.

Seb stood there in shorts and flip-flops.

"Hi. I wasn't expecting you—or did I forget something?"

"No, but I have a surprise for you. Can you come?"

"Claire isn't home right now. Is this something she needs to be in on?"

He grinned. "Yes, but not right this second. I want you to see something. It'll take a couple of hours."

"So if you're in casual clothes, I'm assuming I can come as I am?" She glanced down at her gauzy skirt and T-shirt.

"You're perfect. We'll be in the sand, so bring shoes you can easily kick off."

Okay, she had no idea what he needed her to see at the beach, but she did as he said, sliding her feet into the easy-off sandals she'd worn the time they'd made love, and then grabbed her purse. "I'll text Claire on the way and let her know where I am."

Once in the car, he headed in the direction of the hospital, which was strange. He'd said they were going to be on the beach. So maybe it was the one out there.

He parked the car, and she noted there were a few people trekking up and down the boardwalk carrying cameras and binoculars. Was there a whale or a school of dolphins out there or something?

"What is it?"

"I want you to see it for yourself." He got out of the car and came around to unlatch her door. He held his hand out for her.

Seb seemed almost…giddy. And he was never giddy. He could be amused, bemused, sardonic and happy. But giddy?

She climbed out, and he opened the back door to the

car and pulled out a pair of his own binoculars and a large towel.

Okay, it definitely had to be a whale or something she wouldn't normally see, which could be any number of things.

They walked down the boardwalk, and she noticed no one was in the water, which was strange. In fact, there were several people in uniforms directing the few folks that were arriving where to go.

When they got to the end of the boardwalk, one of the uniformed men asked Seb for his name, which he told them. He checked a clipboard and nodded. "Okay, go ahead, but stay behind the yellow tape and keep voices low."

It was then that she saw stakes with yellow tape snaking down the beach as far as the eye could see. What in the world?

Sebastien took her hand and led her down the line of tape, moving a long way from the boardwalk until they'd almost reached the cabana where they'd made love. That seemed so long ago.

"Did something happen?" she whispered, hoping there wasn't some kind of tragedy.

"It's in the process of happening." He stopped to look through his binoculars for a second before moving forward again. "We're almost there."

There were about fifteen people along the tape—at least as far as she could see—a much smaller number than was normal at this time of day.

Sebastien went about fifty more feet, then stopped and spread the towel out. "Let's sit here."

She had no idea what was going on, but everyone was looking at something.

Handing her the binoculars, he whispered, "Look toward the cabana about halfway from here to there."

Putting the binoculars to her eyes, she scanned the water before realizing he hadn't said to look at the ocean. She felt him behind her, reaching forward to cover her hands with his and helping to guide her line of sight to look at…sand.

Lots and lots of sand.

"I don't—"

"Just look for a minute."

He settled himself against her hip as she stared at the white grains, straining to catch sight of whatever it was that he—and everyone else—was looking at.

Something caught her peripheral vision, near one of the flags marking a nesting site. Her gaze shifted slightly to the right as she realized something was moving. And the way it moved was familiar. It was just like…

Oh, God!

It was a baby sea turtle. The tiniest, most precious sight she'd ever seen. She followed its waddling course down the beach as it seemed to move with an unfailing confidence that defied logic.

Or did it?

Hadn't she and Seb been moving toward each other in the same way? Not knowing why or how, but only knowing it was in their nature to find the other…as surely as a sea turtle sought and found the sea.

A thought struck her, and she pulled down her binoculars to look at him. "Is that…? Is this the same…?"

"The same place we saw that sea turtle lay her eggs?" He nodded. "Yes. That is the exact nest."

Rachel's eyes filled with tears. Who knew between the time that that mama turtle had laid her eggs and the time they hatched that so much would have changed between her and Sebastien? And she loved him. So very much.

He reached forward and used his thumb to wipe a stray tear, just as something was being pressed into her other hand.

Her heart stopped, eyes widening.

Sebastien gave her a slow smile. "I wanted to wait for the perfect moment. And that moment is now."

She set the binoculars on the towel and looked down at her hand. In it was a small jeweler's box. She swallowed, her gaze swiveling from it to Seb.

He took her chin in his hand and tilted her head, placing a gentle kiss on her mouth. "I didn't have your dad's number to call and ask him. But I did talk to Claire before doing this. We talked about quite a few things."

"Her sudden trip to a friend's house?"

"Yes. That was me. I didn't know exactly when the hatch would start, so when I heard, I had to act fast."

She gulped. "A-and Claire—what did she say?"

"She said yes. To both things. As long as you did, too."

"Both things?" She had no idea what the second thing was, but cupping the tiny box in both palms, she looked at him. "Seb…are you sure? You said you wanted to take it slow."

"I realized a couple of weeks ago that this has been a long time coming. Maybe even since that first night we spent together. I don't think I could have gone any slower, do you? I love you, Rach. I always will."

Unable to speak, she looked at the box and snapped open the lid, revealing a beautiful blue gemstone surrounded by tiny diamonds. The color was the same clear hue as the ocean, and she had no doubt that Sebastien had chosen it with that in mind.

And he was right. This was the perfect time. Like

those turtle eggs, which had gone from being tiny embryos to fully formed beings that were ready to start their lives, Seb and Rachel's love had gone through the same cycle. They were ready to move forward to the next stage. *She* was ready. And it was all because of Seb's love.

"So what do you say? I promised Claire I would text her as soon as I had your answer." He grinned, that one crooked tooth filling her heart with love. She didn't need a perfect smile. Or a perfect man. Because she had her own little imperfections. And despite them, Sebastien Deslaurier loved her. And she loved him.

"I say yes."

The second the words left her mouth, Seb grabbed her to him, kissing her for a long, long time. When he finally let her go, he leaned forward and whispered, "Thank you. Because my yes to Claire would have been a little harder without your yes."

She blinked, having no idea what he was talking about. "What did you say yes to?"

Seb took the ring from the box and slid it onto the fourth finger of her left hand.

"She asked me if I could be her father and to make it official. I said yes. I want to adopt her. If it's okay with you."

Her throat worked, but no sound came out. Instead, she threw her arms around him, burying her face in his neck.

He seemed to understand what she was trying to get across, because he squeezed her to him and said, "Thank you."

His words opened the door to a gift more precious than anything she could have imagined—the love of a man who would be there for her. And for Claire. Always. No matter what the cost. No matter what came their way. Like those tightly packed grounds of coffee that only revealed their true flavor when the waters of life rushed through them, her love for Seb was the same. It was strong and enduring and incredibly rich.

And it always would be.

* * * * *

COMING SOON!

We really hope you enjoyed reading this book. If you're looking for more romance, be sure to head to the shops when new books are available on

Thursday 27th October

To see which titles are coming soon, please visit

millsandboon.co.uk/nextmonth

MILLS & BOON®

Coming next month

CHRISTMAS WITH THE SINGLE DAD DOC
Annie O'Neil

Harry was still on the ground, and although he'd definitely grazed his knee, he somehow seemed entirely unfazed by it. Normally there would be howling by now. But the woman crouching down, face hidden by a sheet of glossy black hair, was somehow engaged in a greeting ritual with his son.

'How do you do, Harry?' She shook his hand in a warm, but formal style. 'It's such a pleasure to meet someone who loves Christmas as much as I do.'

If she was expecting Lucas to join in the I Love Christmas Every Day of the Year Club she was obviously recruiting for, she had another think coming. It was only November. He had enough trouble mustering up excitement for the day of December the twenty-fifth.

Clearly unperturbed by his lack of response, she smiled at Harry and pointed at his grazed knee. 'Now... Important decision to make. Do you think you'd like a plaster with Santa on it? Or elves?'

'Elves!' Harry clapped his hands in delight.

The woman laughed and said she would run into the house and get some, as well as a cloth to clear away the small grass stains Lucas could see were colouring his son's little-boy knees.

Her voice had a mischievous twist to it, and underneath

the bright, child-friendly exchange was a gentle kindness that softened his heart.

'I'm ever so sorry. Harry is just mad for—' Lucas began, but when she looked up and met his gaze anything else he'd planned on saying faded into nothing.

Though he knew beyond a shadow of a doubt that they'd never met, his body felt as if it had been jolted into a reality he'd always been waiting to step into. Every cell in his body was supercharged with a deep, visceral connection as their eyes caught and held. Hers were a warm brown…edging on a jewel-like amber. Her skin was beautiful, with an almost pearlescent hue. Glowing… Cheeks pink. Lips a deep red, as if they'd just received a rush of emotion.

Perhaps it was the unexpected excitement of a three-year-old boy careering into her front garden. Perhaps it was the fresh autumnal weather. Or maybe…just maybe…she was feeling the same thing he was. A strange but electric feeling, surging through him in a way he'd never experienced before.

She blinked once. Then twice. Then, as if the moment had been entirely a fiction of his own creating, realigned her focus so that it was only on Harry.

Continue reading
CHRISTMAS WITH THE SINGLE DAD DOC
Annie O'Neil

Available next month
www.millsandboon.co.uk

MILLS & BOON

THE HEART OF ROMANCE

A ROMANCE FOR EVERY READER

ODERN — Prepare to be swept off your feet by sophisticated, sexy and seductive heroes, in some of the world's most glamorous and romantic locations, where power and passion collide.

STORICAL — Escape with historical heroes from time gone by. Whether your passion is for wicked Regency Rakes, muscled Vikings or rugged Highlanders, awaken the romance of the past.

EDICAL — Set your pulse racing with dedicated, delectable doctors in the high-pressure world of medicine, where emotions run high and passion, comfort and love are the best medicine.

ue Love — Celebrate true love with tender stories of heartfelt romance, from the rush of falling in love to the joy a new baby can bring, and a focus on the emotional heart of a relationship.

Desire — Indulge in secrets and scandal, intense drama and plenty of sizzling hot action with powerful and passionate heroes who have it all: wealth, status, good looks…everything but the right woman.

ROES — Experience all the excitement of a gripping thriller, with an intense romance at its heart. Resourceful, true-to-life women and strong, fearless men face danger and desire - a killer combination!

To see which titles are coming soon, please visit

millsandboon.co.uk/nextmonth

JOIN US ON SOCIAL MEDIA!

Stay up to date with our latest releases, author news and gossip, special offers and discounts, and all the behind-the-scenes action from Mills & Boon...

 @millsandboon

 @millsandboonuk

 facebook.com/millsandboon

 @millsandboonuk

It might just be true love...